RESTORING
TIME
JENN LEES

COMMUNITY CHRONICLES BOOK 4

Copyright © 2020 by Jenn Lees

All rights reserved.

No portion of this book may be reproduced in any form without written permission from the author. This book is a work of fiction. The names, characters, , places, and incidents are products of the author's imagination or have been used fictitiously and are not to be construed as real. Any resemblance to persons, living or dead, actual events, locale or organisations is entirely coincidental.

This novel is written in British English.

Cover by Fiona Jayde Media

www.fionajaydemedia.com

To my mother, who gave me a love of reading; an appreciation of story through her love of novels, theatre, and cinema; and encouraged me to write something every day. Thanks, Mum.

Elizabeth Margaret Thompson
(nee Fancourt)

Contents

PART ONE ... 1

1. Invercharing Community Compound. Two and a Half Months after Summer Solstice, 2061 ... 3
2. Scottish Government Bunker, Edinburgh ... 8
3. Invercharing Community ... 14
4. On the Road ... 21
5. Scottish Government Bunker. Autumn Equinox 2061 ... 28
6. The Kingdom of Fife ... 33
7. Invercharing Community, 2067 ... 37
8. Invercharing Community, 2067 ... 41
9. Invercharing Community, 2067 ... 46
10. Invercharing Community 2067, Autumn Equinox ... 51
11. Edinburgh 2061, Autumn Equinox ... 54
12. Scottish Government Bunker, 2061 ... 61
13. Scottish Government Bunker, 2061 ... 66
14. Scottish Government Bunker, 2061 ... 71
15. Scottish Government Bunker, 2061 ... 75
16. Scottish Government Bunker, 2061 ... 80
17. The Kingdom of Fife ... 85
18. Derrick Lloyd's Office ... 89
19. The Road Home ... 95

20.	Tummel House Community, Perthshire	101
21.	Tummel House Community	105
22.	Tummel House Community	110
23.	Culloden Moor	118
24.	Culloden Moor	123
25.	Invercharing Community, 2061	127
26.	Invercharing Community, 2061	132
27.	Invercharing Community, 2061	139 |//
PART TWO		142
28.	Invercharing Community, 2063	143
29.	Invercharing Community, 2063	149
30.	Invercharing Community, 2063	154
31.	Invercharing Community, 2063	158
32.	The Gorse Covered Mountainside	163
33.	The Gorse Covered Mountainside	167
34.	Invercharing Community, 2063	173
35.	Invercharing Community, 2063	178
36.	Scottish Government Bunker	185
37.	Scottish Government Bunker. Winter Solstice, 2063	191
38.	Scottish Government Bunker. Spring Equinox, 2064	195
39.	Tummel House Community, Perthshire	199
40.	Fife	206
41.	Scottish Government Bunker	213
42.	Scottish Government Bunker	218
43.	Perth	221
44.	Perth to Fife	224
45.	Lloyd's Mansion Kingdom of Fife	227
46.	Lloyd's Mansion Kingdom of Fife	230

47. Lloyd's Mansion Kingdom of Fife	234
48. Scottish Government Bunker	238
49. Lloyd's Mansion Kingdom of Fife	241
50. Edinburgh	244
51. Scottish Government Bunker	248
Acknowledgements	254
About the Author	256
Also By	258

PART ONE

S trange what a lack of sunlight can do.

The high mountains surrounding their secluded glen are a darker brown, a duskier green.

Little heather blooms its purple this year.

The cloud-kissed mountains maintain their usual cloak of grey; now deeper; now darker.

Clouds swirl under the weaker sun; its insipid light struggles to break through the cloak the Earth now wears.

He walks through the field of oats; palms forward beside his thighs with fingers splayed.

His habit at harvest time—to stroke the plants and guess the yield.

Like sailing in a wee boat, trailing his fingers in the silky water of a still loch.

The stalks are thigh-high but sparse. The glossy heads hanging from each thin stalk are less than last year, and the oat grass grows yet thinner.

Rory lifts his head to the ash-filled sky, and sighs.

It is the time of shadows.

Chapter One

Invercharing Community Compound. Two and a Half Months after Summer Solstice, 2061

Rory stomped through the internal walkways and halls of the Invercharing Community Compound. His shoulders were tense, and his neck had an ache that went right up into his head. Almost three months of being cooped up was teeth-gritting.

He'd ordered the use of the last of the silver duct-tape to patch the wind-shredded plastic that shielded the eastern window. He walked past sheets of old plastic and tarps that covered doorways and larger windows. Hay bales lined the walls, providing extra insulation against the dispersing nuclear fallout cloud that had made its slow way up to the northern hemisphere and, hopefully, was now dissipating to nothing.

Rory peered through cracks in the plastic sheeting. Outside, the autumnal sun shone on the hills lining either side of their glen. Green, windswept mountains and high Munros—those elevations over three thousand feet—surrounded the guarded Invercharing Community Compound, its grazing lands and fields of crops. Grey granite outcroppings peeked past the last purple flowering of heather.

Beckoning him.

Rory growled and strode to the stables, grabbing the grooming supplies as he entered the stall. His horse tossed his head, stomped a hoof then let out an annoyed whinny.

"I ken how you feel, Boy." Rory brushed down his stallion. "Surely the nuclear fallout cloud—what there was of it—should have passed by now?" He brushed more vigorously. "That's if it even spread up this far."

Siobhan was adamant they had to remain inside in case the Scottish Government's intelligence wasn't accurate. He heaved a sigh. Whatever the source, the Government had more links to the outside world than his isolated Community in the North Western Highlands, that was for certain.

Every day confined to the compound meant one less day with Siobhan. The heart-wrenching, gut-churning sensations clenched Rory's insides again. If that Bethany Watts wouldn't let Siobhan go as soon as it was safe to travel—he didn't care whose First Minister she was—

"Rory," Kendra said right behind him.

"Och!" He spun. "Will ye desist from sneaking up on a man!"

Kendra flinched and her eyes widened, then she took a step back. "Sorry, boss. It's just that the natives are restless again." She flicked her long, dark plait over her shoulder, regaining her warrior-like composure. "You needn't be so jumpy."

Rory relaxed his clench on the curry comb. When Siobhan had advised him a nuclear fallout cloud was heading in their direction, Rory had sent a message out to the local bandits. There were bandits, and there were *bandits*. Four of the local groups had arrived at the Invercharing Community's compound and pledged their best behaviour then settled into the outer buildings. Under guard, of course.

Rory had tracked down Webster and his clan of nomads, offering them the same safe shelter and hospitality. He'd intended it to be in exchange for all Webster's group had stolen from his crew on their journey from Loch Ewe—including his father's rifle.

Wester had refused. With a strong company of militia behind him, Rory had forced the recovery of their goods, leaving the group of wanderers and their well-educated leader to hunker down in the caves of the mountains and hope for the best.

That was two and a half months ago.

Almost a lifetime.

"So? Boss?" Kendra asked, bringing Rory's attention back to the present.

"Oh, aye. Let them go." Rory pressed his thumb to his forehead. "I dinnae blame them. We are nae sure the air's clear but if they want tae take the risk, I'll no' prevent them."

Kendra raised her dark brows. "Right, boss. I'll tell them to pack up."

"No, it's okay, Kendra." Rory put the curry comb aside then pointed toward the main barn. "I'll do it."

The makeshift enclosed walkway from the main buildings to the Community's largest barn was barely holding together. Rory walked past the iron sheeting and bales of hay that comprised the tunnel-like structure, the breeze blowing through gaps brushed his cheek. Angry voices came from the barn ahead of him. In between comments holding annoyance and discontent, Callum's deep tones rumbled down the tunnel. Rory stepped through the door-within-a-door to the barn.

"Och, here he is," Callum said.

Rory's twin's expression, in an identical fair-skinned face dusted with ginger freckles, was one of relief; his hunched shoulders eased as Rory approached.

Rory turned on the packed-earth floor of the large barn where they usually sheltered stock for the winter. Bales of hay lined the walls with tarpaulins covering any gaps. Now the goats, sheep, cows and horses were crammed into another of the large sheds to make room for the human guests. Rory faced the crowd of bandits.

This group was a mix of previously independent bands of men and women who lived and roamed the local countryside. Although they did thieve and poach anything they could to survive and sell to each other or on the black market, they weren't violent, brutal murderers and thieves. Rory snorted. Why they still called it the *black market,* he'd never know. Nothing was official. Most things were black market now, apart from what people could honestly grow and glean from the land or make for themselves, as did members of the Community System.

"I believe ye are all wantin' to leave," Rory said to the weary faces before him to a rise of angry and defensive comments. He raised his hand. "Can ye decide on one representative to come and speak with me, please?"

The shouting settled down and Micah McNair, the leader of the largest group to stay with them, stepped forward. Micah wore his hair in dreadlocks, not from a sense of fashion, more from the lack of personal grooming. He was a tall man in his late thirties who looked like he belonged on a beach. His dreads were sun-bleached, and his face tanned—although that might just have been dirt. The bandit groups lived an outdoor life for most of the year, and it had been a good summer. Out of all of them, Micah would be the one Rory would trust the most—if trust could come into a relationship with a bandit.

"Micah, I'll give each person two day's rations," Rory said. "And you may leave when you're ready."

"Two days?" Micah double blinked. "But you guys have stores full o' stuff."

"And how would you ken that, then?" Rory squinted at him.

"We assume," Micah said, standing taller.

Micah flicked his leather jacket aside and placed a hand on his belt, an action that usually exposed a weapon. Now it revealed a well-worn, handmade leather accessory bereft of its holster and gun.

"Two days' worth o' rations for each person when you go," Rory reiterated. "I'll no' have my people short for the sake o' yours."

Micah's brow drew in, forming a line above the bridge of his nose.

"It was out o' the goodness of our hearts you got to be safe from the nuclear fallout cloud," Rory said, his voice low and stern. "Be grateful for that, and two days of food."

"But what if the water's contaminated?" Micah asked. "And everything else?"

"Then we're all in the same boat." Rory glared at Micah, whose blue eyes were as pale as the winter sky.

Micah turned wordlessly from Rory and stalked back to his people.

Xian stepped beside Rory, his arm lightly brushing Rory's. Xian could be so quiet at times, but his presence was always reassuring.

"What if," Xian asked, "due to the kind hospitality we have given them in our crowded barn for over two months, some wish to stay?"

"As in permanently?" Rory couldn't hide the edge of doubt in his voice. "Och, we'll immediately issue them with orders, give them chores, set a timetable for—"

"I thought as much." Xian chuckled. "One sure way to put them off."

Xian lifted his chin in the direction of the bandit groups' leaders, who stood with their heads bent together in discussion.

"They seem to have got along surprisingly well," Xian said. "The two and-a-bit months in each other's company has forged relationships that you and your wife might do well to pay attention to."

"It may have done more good than harm," Rory said. "And could come in handy when the meaningful dialogue is to happen." Rory didn't remove his stare from the surprised and dismayed conversations of the bandits. "There are the makings of a leader in McNair," he said. "He may have the skills to pull these reprobates into line, to our benefit."

"Some would say they're hard-core and it's too late to change them," Xian said in his usual soft tones. "Too many years of doing what they know how to do well. Some would advise not to let this short period of co-operation fool you. That it's pure survival under the current circumstances."

"Aye?" Rory raised an eyebrow. "And what do you say, my Chinese philosopher?"

"I'd give them a chance," Xian said.

Rory returned his attention to Micah, who was gesturing to the men and women surrounding him, an earnest expression on his face.

Hmm. It would be nice, for once, to see the potential for good in people. *Or am I getting soft?* Rory shrugged. The safety of the Invercharing Community must always come first. Dad had drummed that into him. It was no different now. The bandits had a lot to prove, and this time of collaboration could be a start—or a fleeting aberration.

Micah strode forward, the group of bandits parting around him as he headed for Rory.

"We wanna go," he said.

"Right now?" Rory stood straighter.

Micah nodded.

"Give me a wee bit o' time to get your weapons out of storage and prepare some provisions," Rory said. "Then you can all leave at once."

***

Rory stood between the table set with various small firearms, containers of shells and shotgun cartridges, and another table covered in blades of all shapes and sizes. At the door through which the departing guests would exit, Callum and Xian stood beside barrels containing more weapons, ready to return them to their owners. Rifle butts, sword handles and archer's bows clanked against each other as the departing guests rummaged in the barrels for their own weapons.

Kendra and Cèilidh portioned out non-perishable foodstuffs into sacks and handed them to the members of the bandit groups who'd lined up. Micah was last in line and stood chatting to Cèilidh. Her cheeks were rosy as she looked up at him from beneath her eyelashes. She tugged at her long ginger-blonde hair, which sat over her shoulder in a thick plait. Her cheeky comments were causing laughter to surround her as always. She'd grown into attractive young woman.

When had that happened?

Micah lingered by her.

Och, no you don't.

"You'll be wantin' to leave before it gets dark, McNair." Rory stepped closer to Cèilidh. "Better get your people out of here now."

"Okay then," Micah said, dragging his eyes away from Cèilidh. "But next time we meet, Rory, I trust we'll be civil to each other."

"Depends on if you behave yoursel' or no', McNair," Rory said.

Micah followed the last of his band out of the barn, trailing behind the other bandit groups making their way through the section of the tunnel now open to the outside world.

Rory spun on his heel and headed to the CB radio room. He would check with Siobhan if all this nuclear weather had reached them for certain.

And if it was clear, it would be time for her to come home.

Chapter Two

Scottish Government Bunker, Edinburgh

Siobhan stood in her bedroom in the single-female quarters of the accommodation sector of the underground Scottish Government Bunker. LED downlighting glowed over her and a lamp spilled soft light on her serviceable dressing table. The narrow dresser was now bare except for her toiletries and make-up paraphernalia. Packed bags and boxes crowded the floor at her feet.

Apart from her single bed and functional wardrobe, the only other unpacked items were a turntable and speakers. She'd borrowed the record player on permanent loan from the archives. The rock bands of the 1970s had intrigued her. Some of their names were odd, with no hint of the fantastic electric guitar riffs in the tracks she'd played, like the one she listened to now.

Beats thrummed through her body. Music filled her cramped room, as though the lead guitarist was strumming the strings in her presence. Vibrations bounced from the speakers and drove into her soul. The lyrics expressed exactly what she felt: she and Rory had waited so long to be *together*.

Her time apart from Rory had been a hard couple of months' anticipation of life with him. Soon they'd be together every day and she'd enjoy exploring who he was, which was far more than the talented, resourceful, and very masculine man who'd attracted her attention. She recalled his reaction to the possibility of a nuclear fallout cloud moving toward Scotland and how he'd shown compassion to those even his community would regard as enemies by offering the bandit groups shelter. His sense of fairness was admirable. He had the makings of a great man, and she relished the thought of witnessing that potential bloom.

And beginning their intimate relationship. She couldn't deny the promise of their sex life had its own pull.

Somebody banged on her door. Louise opened it, entered and switched on the main light. She mouthed something.

"Pardon?" Siobhan lifted the stylus off the record.

"Siobhan," Louise said. "It's *so* loud!"

"Oh, sorry." Siobhan removed the record from the turntable and replaced it in its cover. She wiped her wet cheeks dry with her palm before turning to face Louise.

"You okay, Siobhan?" Louise asked.

"I'm fine," she sniffed.

"No, you're not." Louise stepped forward and hugged her. "But I've some good news for you."

"Yes, what?" Siobhan dried her eyes with the back of her hand.

"The drone returned," Louise said. "The Geiger Counter strapped to it was clear. Well, just the usual background radiation readings. Our contacts in the French Government were right. It never reached us but blew to the east. So, we can safely say it's over."

"I can go?" Siobhan gasped. But that would only happen if she got permission from the First Minister. Siobhan's shoulders sank a little.

"Oh, I doubt you'll be able to leave." Angela poked her head into Siobhan's room, her long, red hair hanging loosely about her face.

Siobhan sighed at her sister-in-law. Rory had warned her of Angela's ambitious nature, and he hadn't exaggerated either. Louise released their hug.

"The First Minister wouldn't want a valuable person such as yourself out of her sight," Angela said, pushing strands of straight hair behind her ear. She moved to stand fully in the doorway. "What are you going to do?" Angela asked. "Rory will never leave. He loves it in his middle-of-the-bloody-nowhere-highlands. And he's too busy being king of the compound."

Siobhan had to admit Angela was right. Rory loved his mountains and clear blue sky, even though it was often grey and the mountains shrouded in mist. It was his home, and he belonged to the outdoors. Rory wouldn't survive underground. Siobhan had to find a way of getting to him. Recollections of fresh mountain breezes and Rory's warm, strong hands flitted through her thoughts, then tears welled in the corners of her eyes and her throat tightened.

Angela remained in the doorway while Siobhan groped for a hankie on her dresser.

"For someone interested in politics," Louise said, "diplomacy isn't your strong point, is it, Angela?" Louise shut the door in Angela's face.

"It's okay, Louise. But thanks." Siobhan dabbed her eyes and inspected her face in the mirror. "I'm going to see Bethany." She wiped her face and began to reapply her make-up.

"Ah, I don't think she's in her office," Louise said.

"Where is she?" Siobhan paused with her make-up brush still poised and looked at Louise's reflection.

Louise glanced at the floor.

"What?" Siobhan turned.

Louise raised her head. "She's visiting Major McLellan in his cell."

"Antony? What's wrong with that?" Siobhan asked. A cell was where that man belonged after the crimes he'd committed while dealing with the submarine leaking radioactivity *up top*.

"Nothing," Louise finally answered.

"Why are you so cagey about it?" Siobhan narrowed her eyes.

Louise didn't speak.

"Tell me," she demanded.

"Oh, okay. She sees him a lot." Louise's cheeks were rosy.

"What do they have to talk about?" Siobhan replaced the foundation on the dresser, she was only half done but Louise's reaction was troubling.

Louise shrugged, her cheeks now bright red.

"So, Antony still has the ear of the First Minister," Siobhan said, "even though he's incarcerated in the depths of the Bunker."

Louise didn't reply, only studied the floor.

Oh, it was making sense now. This past year, it had been the aim of the Bunker's occupants to restore the Government's rule over all of Scotland. The nuclear submarine issue had become the impetus for accelerating the reinstallation of the Government's leadership. And an opportunity to meet the different groups of citizens who lived *up top*.

Antony's opinions on Community life wouldn't change, that was for certain. According to him, Community people were anti-government anarchists who would incite revolt at any sign of the Government's return.

If Siobhan knew Antony at all—and she did—he was probably still spilling his negativism and inaccurate beliefs about Community life and Community people to Bethany.

And Rory would be the main topic of conversation. She dug her nails into her palms.

No, Antony having the First Minister's ear was *not* a good thing.

Turning back to her reflection, Siobhan quickly finished her make-up and checked her French roll was still in place. She slipped into her high heels then *click-clacked* down the smooth concrete corridor to the office sector of the Bunker, leaving Louise behind in the single-female quarters.

LED lights flicked on at her approach, flicking off again when she'd passed, leaving a dark passage in her wake. Paintings and prints of old Scotland, pre-Crash, lined the passageway. She arrived at the government offices and the First Minister's secretary pointed her to the chair beneath a painting of the previous parliament house opposite Holyrood Palace. Siobhan sat, the muffled hum of the air conditioners and dehumidifiers continued the usual background noise. Government staff, whom her father had labelled *public servants*, attended diligently to their duties in the surrounding offices while she waited twenty minutes outside the First Minister's office before Bethany walked along the corridor.

"Bethany." Siobhan rose from the chair. The First Minster of Scotland strode past without a glance and opened the door to her office. "May I speak with you?" Siobhan asked.

"Come in," Bethany said, her tone lacked its usual warmth.

Bethany stepped into the room, avoiding eye contact with Siobhan.

Siobhan followed, swallowing down the slight sense of dread that Bethany's tone had evoked. Bethany walked around her desk and sat in her high-backed office chair. Her dark, tailored skirt suit sat well on her shapely figure, though her blouse was misbuttoned at the top.

Odd. Bethany was always fastidious about her attire.

Bethany straightened the neat pile of paperwork on her desk then finally looked up at Siobhan.

"What can I do for you?" she asked.

"You've heard the radiation-alert has cleared," Siobhan asked. "And the cloud hasn't reached this far north?"

Bethany nodded.

"I wish to be with my husband," Siobhan said. "At the Invercharing Community. I'd like to leave as soon as possible."

For some moments, Bethany stared at Siobhan without speaking. Her mouth tightened and she absently fiddled with a pen beside the stack of papers she'd neatened.

Siobhan raised an eyebrow. "Bethany?"

"Siobhan," Bethany began. "I need to tell you that the Government doesn't recognise your marriage to Rory Campbell."

"Pardon?" Siobhan couldn't hold the incredulity from her voice.

So, Bethany is heading down that path, is she?

"Whether or not you acknowledge it," Siobhan said, "is of no consequence, Bethany—"

"First Minister," Bethany spoke low.

"First Minister," Siobhan said, crossing her arms and endeavouring to enunciate every syllable. "In that case, I request permission to resume diplomatic talks with the diverse groups of Scottish citizens who live outside of the Scottish Government Bunker. I believe consultation and information gathering will be constructive to our steps toward the reinstatement of a fully functioning government that has the true needs of its people at heart. I shall commence with the communities out there, those who adhere to the Community Model developed and encouraged by the late Caitlin Murray-Campbell. I will begin with the Invercharing Community, where my *husband* resides."

"No," Bethany said.

"Pardon?" Siobhan's mouth remained open, and she leaned closer to Bethany's desk.

Bethany held her stare. Siobhan closed her mouth and stood straighter, determined to be ready for whatever objections Bethany was about to proffer.

"No," Bethany repeated. "I do not give permission."

"Why?" Siobhan asked. A sense of disbelief whirled in the back of her thoughts. "Why *not* liaise and communicate with our people out there? Our Scottish people whom we desire to be on our side?"

Bethany's lips were a thin line. "Not yet, Siobhan," she said. "We need to know those groups *will be* on our side."

"How can you be certain of that if you don't interact with them?" Siobhan asked.

Bethany picked up the pen on her desk and began clicking its top—over and over.

Siobhan scratched her neck.

"First Minister, they are real men and women with intelligence and skills," she said. "They're not the wild, ignorant barbarians into which the inhabitants of the world *up top* were meant to have devolved." Siobhan planted her palms on Bethany's desk. "They're nothing like our teachers said they would be, Beth—First Minister."

Bethany screwed her mouth to the side and continued clicking the pen but didn't answer.

"First Minister, I'm ideally positioned to be an ambassador for the Government, if you wish to see it that way. I can be there among them, get the feel for where they're at. What they're really thinking, not just what we assume they think."

Or what Antony tells you they think.

Siobhan stood tall.

Bethany stayed silent.

"You owe it to the people of the Invercharing Community," Siobhan said. "They have done Scotland a great service and rescued us from annihilation." Siobhan slapped Bethany's desk. "Why are you being so resistant?"

"With *our* assistance, Siobhan," Bethany growled, fixing her glare on Siobhan's hand where it pressed onto her desk. "They successfully neutralised a nuclear radiation issue with our invaluable equipment and trained personnel—two of whom we lost."

Siobhan removed her hand from Bethany's desk. "I will be an advocate for the Government—"

"If you have married someone in the Community System," Bethany interrupted, "then your opinions and sentiments are biased."

"But if I'm one of them, surely they'll feel more accepted and akin to us," Siobhan said. "So, no more of this *us and them*. Just *us*."

The pen clicking continued—gaining in rapidity. Siobhan's pulse beat in time with it.

"Bethany, I'm asking you as a friend. Please, may I go and be with my husband?"

"I have already informed you, Siobhan, the Scottish Government does not recognise your marital union with Rory Campbell and, therefore, is under no obligation to support it by facilitating access to your so-called spouse."

"But—" Siobhan began.

"This meeting is over." Bethany bent her head, engrossed in the file under her nose.

"What has Antony said to you?" Siobhan's question rang out in the quiet office.

Bethany's nostrils flared though she didn't look up. Her shoulders rose and fell with a deep breath.

"Do you wish me to call security?" Bethany said.

Siobhan blinked, her skin cooling. She stepped back from the invisible wall now before her.

"Very well. Good evening, First Minister." Siobhan turned and strode to the communication centre.

Chapter Three

Invercharing Community

It was another seven days before Rory was able to hail the Government Bunker on the CB radio, the severe static only clearing after a week of trying.

"May I speak with Siobhan Campbell, please? Over," Rory said into the handset, then took a breath and made himself sit down while he waited.

Who was that you wished to speak to, sir? Over, the radio handler at the Government Bunker asked.

"Siobhan Campbell. Over," Rory repeated.

There's no one here by that name sir. Over.

Rory let out an expletive. "Och, may I speak with Siobhan Kensington-Wallace? You have one of those, do ye not? Over."

Yes, sir. I will get her for you. Over.

Moments of silence, punctuated by static, filled the communication area of the smaller hall where they kept the CB radios. Callum came into the hall and ran up to Rory.

"Mandy's in labour," he said. Concern mixed with the smile stretching Callum's face.

"Och, good luck." Rory stood, pulled his twin into himself, and held tight. "You're officially relieved of any duty." He released Callum and winked as the radio jumped to life.

Rory! Siobhan voice came through the handset.

"Siobhan! I'm sorry I have nae been able to reach you for a while. The interference has been bad lately. Must be that wee cloud. Over."

No, it wouldn't be. We've tested the atmosphere and there are normal readings. It's all clear, and if our friends in France are correct, it didn't get this far north. You can move about now and let your guests go. Over.

"Och. They went a week ago. Cabin fever," Rory said. "Could nae wait a minute longer to be away. I miss you. When are you coming home now it's safe to travel? Over."

Static crackled for half a minute.

"Siobhan?"

That's the thing, Rory. Siobhan had lowered her voice. *The First Minister won't let me leave. Over.*

Rory closed his eyes and rested his forehead on his arm leaning on the radio.

"So, Bethany-stuck-up-Watts will nae let you go. I'm comin' to get you! Over."

Static once more.

"Siobhan," he said, "do you no' want me to? Over."

Oh, Rory I want you to more than anything. Over.

"I'm coming. Och!" Rory dragged a hand across his face. "I have a couple o' things to organise but I'll be there as soon as I can. In a week maybe, if I push the horses. That's too long as far as I'm concerned. But you be packed. Over."

Bethany won't be happy. Over.

"Her happiness is none of my concern," Rory almost yelled. "You be ready to leave. Over."

Okay. Siobhan's voice was softer.

"What did you say? Over," he asked.

This isn't a private conversation, Rory. I love you. Over.

"I love you, too," he said. "See you in a week. Out."

What was going on that the people around her hearing her husband was coming to the Bunker bothered her? Bethany Watts was as much trouble as he'd anticipated. Maybe more. The sooner he got there the better.

***

Rory handed over the militia business to George Stobbart, then took his saddlebag of clothes and provisions to the stables and prepared Boy for the journey. Xian entered the stables and threw his gear on the bale of hay next to the stall where Rory was checking Boy's tack. Fine motes of hay floating past tickled Rory's nose.

"You know I'm coming with you now Callum's almost a father?" Xian said.

"Oh aye, Xian, I was countin' on it," Rory said. "I asked Kendra to stay here now that Callum will be busy being a new father. Need a level-headed soldier to assist George with the militia."

"The recent sojourn in our company should have left the bandits with a favourable view of us. Our local ones, at least," Xian observed. "This trip should be an eventless one."

"Hmm. I hope they've passed the good word about us to those further south. Have nae been Edinburgh way for a while." *Like, my last journey through time.* "Probably nothing like I've ever seen it."

"My parents were there when they blew the bridges. They said it was devastating." Xian busied himself with a saddle. "That's when they left the city. I've been to Edinburgh once since then. I know how to get to Arthur's Seat."

"Oh, excellent, my friend," Rory said. "Still not a safe place, though. I intend to be well armed."

"Which horse will you choose for your lady-wife?" Xian pressed his lips together, attempting to hide his amusement.

"A placid one." Rory grimaced. "Siobhan will need a few more lessons before she masters riding."

***

Rory rode out of the Invercharing Community Compound with Xian, trailing a packhorse and another gelding for Siobhan. Sunrise tinged the horizon a soft magenta to his left. The guard on early watch opened the large iron gate. The renovated farmhouse and extensive buildings surrounded by high fencing fell behind, and a wee way along, they passed the Community's meadows filled with stock now free to graze.

Most of the fields of crops had gone to seed after three months of neglect with community members forced to abandon outside work. Now groups of workers who strolled behind Rory and Xian, turned off the road into these fields ready for a hard day's work. Yesterday Rory had ordered the harvesting of crops that hadn't run to seed or weren't ruined by rain. Now it was certain the radiation hadn't reached them, they would gather all the crops they could. Food was food.

"I estimate one week's travel," Rory said. "We could push the horses to a fast walk, but any more and we risk them going lame, which would ruin our chances of a decent ride home." Rory glanced at Xian. "I don't plan on staying in the Government Bunker for long."

"Road trip," Xian said.

"What?"

"In the good old days, guys used to go on road trips to bond." Xian raised his eyebrows and cocked his head. "What do you say?"

"We're already bonded, Xian. What you and I have been through together is more than bonding."

"Yes," Xian replied. "Did I ever thank you for saving the world?"

"It was nae me. It was Angus. And not the world, just Scotland." Rory sucked the cool crisp mountain air deep into his lungs, fogging it around his face with his outward breath. "Well, maybe the only part of the world that I'm concerned with," he added.

They rode through their long, narrow valley. Steep, green-sided mountains funnelled a river into a loch whose glassy sheen reflected the silvery sky above. Clouds swirled up high, and an eagle cried as it scoured the glen. They passed forest to their right. Leafy cool emanated from it along with the earthy scent of leaf litter. Rustling followed by the beat of many hooves told Rory deer were nearby.

The clouds moved closer as they travelled the morning. Misty rain hit Rory's face and covered their surroundings in a white haze. To their left, moss-covered grey drystone walls edged the trail. These boundaries had remained intact for centuries, in contrast to the deteriorated roads and bridges of more recent history. The leaves were turning; oaks browning, birches becoming yellow-gold, and maples flames of red. Droplets gathered on the leaf tips as fine rain soaked Rory's gloves and Boy's mane.

"The men and women of the Chief Council are ageing." Xian broke Rory's observations with one of his own.

Rory scanned the sides of the road then glanced at Xian.

"They all look to you as their natural leader," Xian said. "You know that, don't you, Rory?"

A heaviness settled on Rory's shoulders, and he didn't answer Xian.

"And not because you're a child of Scott Campbell and Caitlin Murray-Campbell," Xian said. "For there are plenty of those."

"What're you sayin', Xian?"

"You practically run the militia—"

"No, I don't," Rory interrupted. "That's George's role."

"You know he's let you have free rein of it. He's stepped back," Xian said.

"Aye." Rory sighed.

"You need to take your place on the Chief Council," Xian said. "Rory, you were born to it."

"No, Angela was born to it and mentored for it." Rory tightened his grip on the reins as he viewed the road ahead.

"Yes but…" Xian appeared to gather his thoughts. "She is not humble enough. Angela would ultimately and always put her needs above the Community's. Our Community needs someone who knows what sacrificial leadership is. And that person is you, Rory Campbell."

"You know, you're beginning to sound like Angus." Rory slid his gaze from the tree line back to his companion on the horse beside him.

Xian raised an eyebrow. "A man I respected, and now you reveal he had great wisdom."

Rory shifted in his saddle as they travelled on in silence and their valley widened. Ahead of them were mountain peak upon mountain peak and the crumbled road through the valley would go on for the next day or two.

"I'm not as capable as everyone in the Community thinks I am." The pressure on Rory's shoulders matched the tightness in his chest. "I'll never be as good as Mum or Dad. Never." He stared at Boy's damp mane. "I wish they were both still here."

"No one's the perfect leader." Xian's voice was gentle. "I didn't know your parents, but I'm sure they didn't slip into their roles. From what everyone says, your mother was an exceptionally capable woman, but someone must have mentored her gifts and talents. Just as your parents and George mentored and encouraged your strengths and aptitudes. You *are* able, Rory Campbell."

The warmth of Xian's confidence in Rory was the yang to the yin of the ice in Rory's gut.

"But what if I'm not?" Rory hitched his shoulders and adjusted his rifle strap. "What if I'm just the most obvious one to do the job? The only person who *will* do it?"

"Apart from Angela," Xian said.

"Aye, apart from Angela," Rory agreed.

"Oh, please don't let her do it," Xian pleaded.

"See? That's just what I mean." Rory's words came out with more force than he intended. "Nobody wants her to lead, so it has tae be me."

"No, it's not like that, Xian said. "You're a better leader than Angela. You'll do a superior job, and everyone knows it. It was a good thing she went to the Government Bunker. It gave the community a chance to breathe and rethink." Xian gave a short nod. "And it is appropriate you have married. Being a parent is beneficial for a leader."

"I haven't... we haven't..." Rory's cheeks warmed.

"You didn't?" Xian's eyebrows reached his hairline. "Not even when you were on the Isle of Ewe—?"

"No. So I don't know why you're speaking of fatherhood, friend." Rory recalled the vision he had on waking on the Isle of Ewe, of a toddler holding tight to his trouser leg, and a pregnant Siobhan.

I'll never be able to explain that one to Xian.

Hoofbeats came from the forest beside them, the cadence making it clear it wasn't the hooves of deer, but of horses.

Many horses.

"Bandits!" Xian kicked his horse to a gallop.

"We may need to fight," Rory yelled. "We'll no' outrun them with the packhorse."

Rory spun Boy to face the oncoming horses. The riders had reached the road behind them. They were bandits though he recognised none of them. Their dirty clothes were rags and their horses in poor condition.

Rory pulled out his Glock from where he'd tucked into the back of his belt and fired in the air.

The bandits didn't stop. They continued to head straight for them—yelling.

Roaring at them.

Rory hesitated. His recent long-term encounter with Micah McNair had changed his opinion of bandits. But these weren't like McNair's crew. Their eyes blazed with malevolence and their charge didn't falter.

Rory stuffed his Glock into his jacket pocket, then slid his rifle from his back and chocked the firearm's butt tight into his shoulder. It would waste a round, but he aimed wide. A bullet flying close could still halt them. Rory squeezed the trigger. His weapon discharged, kicking his shoulder.

The bandits still bore down on him and Xian.

Rory fired his rifle again.

One down.

A riderless horse sped past. The man riding behind it held a rifle outstretched. Rory kicked, pressing with his knees to move Boy. Twisting in the saddle, he took aim and fired again. That bullet went wide.

Thwack.

The barrel of the bandit's rifle whipped Rory in the side. Kidneys stinging, he lost his seat and crashed to the ground, his rifle flying out of his grip. Boy snorted.

In Rory's peripheral vision, Xian was air-born, but of his own doing. His extended leg collided with a bandit riding past him. The man slumped forward in the saddle.

Rory stood; his side throbbing. A woman with short cropped-hair and wide solid shoulders charged at him. She held a shotgun in her massive hands, not ready to fire, but to whip him as her companion had.

The only shots fired so far had been his own.

That could mean only one thing.

The bandits were out of ammo.

The woman rode near. Rory grabbed the stock of her shotgun and pulled her from her mount. His Glock flew out of his coat pocket and hurtled to the ground.

The female bandit rolled to stand and delivered a powerful punch to his jaw.

Rory blocked the next one, which she aimed at his throat, and caught her arm in a lock. She stepped in close and kicked his leg from under him. Hard ground hit his back with a shudder. He slipped his hand into his boot and slid out his Buck knife. She landed a forearm onto his throat, her upper body weight behind it.

An effective choke.

The rest of her body weight pressed through her knee on his upper arm of the hand holding his knife, where it pinched and burned.

With his hand numbing, he pushed the knife up to her thigh.

No reach.

Her continued choke on his throat dotted spots over his fading vision. He blinked to clear it and keep his sight on her.

Yelling came from the woods and guns fired, all sounding distant compared to the thundering in his ears. She turned to the gunshots and the pressure on his throat eased. Rory drew in air and the spots faded. Focussing, he stabbed again at the female bandit and struck flesh in her meaty thigh. She screamed at him; raw and angry. He blocked her punch to his face with his free hand, caught her hand and twisted it out.

"Go!" a stern male voice shouted above them and the pressure on Rory's throat lifted.

Rory dragged the misty air into his lungs.

The woman grabbed the saddle of the horse trotting past and flew up into it. She leaned over and grasped the packhorse's reins. Siobhan's horse followed.

"Boy!" Rory's husky shout rang out, tearing his throat. Hooves clattered on the road by his head as the rest of the bandits retreated. Boy's soft muzzle nudged the side of his face.

"Why'd they go?" Xian stepped beside him, his breath coming hard.

"Don't know why but glad—" Sitting up, Rory coughed through bile.

"You okay, man?" Xian squatted beside him; his brow creased.

Rory took another deep breath in and nodded.

"She made Kendra look like a kitten." Xian's lip curled for a second, then pursed. "The packhorse and Siobhan's gelding are gone."

Rory nodded again.

"We going back?" Xian asked.

Rory shook his head till it hurt. Xian stepped to his horse and returned with a water bottle then handed it to him. Rory sipped, the cool liquid soothing his grazed throat.

"They got what they wanted, I expect." Xian held tight to the remaining horses' reins and moist dirt clung to his buckskins.

"Aye, and you wished for bonding time." Rory's gravelly voice sounded worse than it felt. "Looks like we'll be hunting and fishing for our supper all the way to Edinburgh."

Chapter Four

On the Road

Rory woke with a start.

"You dozed off—again," Xian said, suppressing a smirk.

"It is nae funny, Xian." Four long days of riding had left Rory with the ability to snooze in the saddle, but his muscles were heavy and spasming. Boy snorted beneath him as Rory adjusted his position, creaking the leather saddle. Xian remained quiet beside him.

An uneasy sensation lingered in Rory, as though he'd had another vision. In a previous vision of a dim sky and sparsely growing crops, a murky feeling had accompanied his waking. His visions were like a vague *second sight* as the old Highlanders would have named it. But this vision was like those dreams you can't quite recall. Rory's mind clawed for it. Each time he reached out the images eluded him, only to leave a prescience of foreboding.

It was something to do with Siobhan—and it was nae good.

In the distance, the old Kincardine Bridge lay across the narrow segment of the River Forth. A rusted handrail ran its entire length to the other bank. Rory peered past the crowd that had gathered ahead waiting to cross the bridge. People on horseback, driving carts or on foot, moved in small groups. Dust rose from the action of the travellers who crossed on the road that sat in the belly of the bridge.

Rory and Xian rode closer, slowing their pace once they reached the end of the line waiting to cross. Rory imagined the stone-littered road surface had originally been smooth bitumen. Now years of neglect and non-existent road maintenance had made it a dirt track over a structure with questionable stability.

Ahead at the entrance to the bridge, a group of men stood in front of a ramshackle hut; a semi-permanent construction that sat beside the road. The men wore dark clothing of a sturdy material—maybe denim—and almost uniform-like. Two of them holding submachine guns stood at the head of the queue. Rory looked around. His rifle and Xian's Katana were the only overt weapons, apart from the HKs held by the guys uniformly dressed.

"I don't like the look of this," Rory said, feeling for his Glock still tucked in his belt at his back, then touching his rifle hanging over his shoulder.

"Looks like a tollbooth," Xian commented. "People are handing stuff to the men at the shack."

"Och, these guys look like someone's army." Rory grimaced. "There's some extortion going on."

They rode closer, moving with the queue. The people ahead handed over money, goods or livestock before the armed men permitted them to cross. A chicken clucked wildly, feathers flying as a traveller passed the hen to a man sitting at a folding table. Rory and Xian inched their way forward with the crowd and reached one of the armed men.

"Halt!" The man raised his firearm.

Rory pulled Boy up and stared from the saddle.

"Your names," the man demanded. "Move slowly if ye are going to."

"Rory Campbell."

"Xian Law."

"Why are you armed?" he asked.

"We're always armed." Rory kept his gaze steady. "Did nae think it was a problem."

"Where do ye come frae?" The guard had tilted his head a fraction while he listened to Rory. "Ye sound like ye are a lang way from hame, like."

"Aye." Rory stirred in his saddle. "Up north."

"Way up north, lad." The man squinted his left eye, studying Rory. "Why are yoo down this far?"

"Why are you askin' me these questions?" Rory leaned forward.

"Rory," Xian spoke softly. "Settle down."

"Right! Git off ya horses." The guard waved the HK, indicating Rory to dismount.

Rory flung his right leg over Boy's neck and slid off in one fluid motion, landing lightly on the ground. Xian dismounted as well. The guard's hand tensed around his weapon and another man with an MP5 stepped closer.

A short, stocky man with neat greying hair, and wearing trousers and a shirt, strode out from the shack and elbowed past the guards.

"What's going on?" he asked.

"These men are armed." The guard stepped back but kept his HK trained on Rory. "This one's got a mouth."

"What's your name?" The man spoke with authority.

"Och, I need to know who's askin' before I give my name out again," Rory said in a low voice. Xian tensed beside him.

The man gave a slow shake of his head. "Now, I did ask nicely," he said, changing his head motion to a barely discernible nod.

The guard holding the submachine gun stepped forward and Rory focused on the muzzle.

"No," Xian whispered.

The guard snapped out a short leap-kick and his heavy-duty boot connected with Rory's midriff. Burning pain accompanied the wind driven out of Rory's lungs. He staggered, forcing himself to remain upright. The guard's hand clamped around Rory's upper arm as he seized him and yanked his rifle strap over his face, then ripped his Glock from its home in his belt. Rory glanced at Xian. The other guard removed the Katana from Xian's back. He raised his hands in submission and Rory did the same.

"That's more like it," the man said in a polite voice.

"His name is Rory Campbell, sir," the guard said while examining Rory's Glock.

"Let's do that again. My name is Maxwell Lloyd. How do you do?" The man in the shirt and tie looked pointedly at Rory. "And where are you from?"

"Northern Highlands, Mr Lloyd," Rory replied.

Maxwell's eyes narrowed. "Campbell. Hmm. Wouldn't be related to Caitlin Murray-Campbell, would you?"

"She was ma mother," Rory said.

"And she was a great lady." Maxwell nodded his approval. "You must be proud."

Rory didn't answer but stifled the heat burning through his veins.

Maxwell cast his gaze over Rory, scanning him from crown to toe, then did the same with Xian.

"Pat 'em down," he ordered his guards. "They're coming with us." To Rory he said, "I'd like you to meet a great man—my father. You shall accompany us and be our guests in the Kingdom of Fife."

"But I'm on ma way—" Rory began.

"I don't care where you think you're going," Maxwell snapped. "You'll see my father first and get his permission to travel through."

Rory's brow tightened. "We are no' in medieval times, ken? I'm free to travel Scotland without anyone's permission."

"Oh, is that what you think? How wrong one can be." Maxwell turned and walked back to the hut.

Maxwell Lloyd's guards searched them for concealed weapons, removed the knives tucked down their boots, and the handgun at Xian's belt, then made them climb into a covered wagon. The horse-drawn vehicle, which sat beside the road near the hut, was one of many loaded with the goods taken for road tax.

"What about our horses?" Rory asked the guard who jumped in beside them, training his HK on their every move.

The guard yelled out the back of the wagon, "Mac! Tie the horses here."

The guy called Mac, who had been holding the reins of the two mounts, led the horses to the back of the wagon and secured their reins to the tailgate. The wagon jerked to a start, and the horses trailed behind. The wagon vibrated along the track while they travelled for half an hour past low undulating hills skirted by fields patch worked with different crops. Rory gave a pensive snort. It always amused him that this part of Scotland had retained its title of *kingdom* over the centuries and even up to this *post-Crash* era. White sheep dotted green meadows here and there. Organised planting and food production seemed abundant in these parts. There were few drystone walls, and neatly trimmed hedgerows bordered fields. Large crops of rapeseed flowered in bright yellow. Rory's nose itched, and so did his eyes.

"They don't seem to have bothered about the fallout cloud warning. Even though it didn't get up here." Rory rubbed his nose and stifled a sneeze.

"Maybe they didn't know," Xian said looking out of the wagon and watching the passing countryside.

They rumbled past a well-worn sign indicating a holiday park further on. Then another sign had a barely visible painted arrow pointing down a lane. The wagon turned in that direction and soon cabin-like huts came into view; a small village worth.

"Holiday park. Or it was, years ago," the guard explained. His submachine gun had remained pointed at Rory the entire journey. "It's now one of Derrick Lloyd's places."

"Derrick Lloyd? The father of the Mr Maxwell Lloyd we just met?" Xian asked.

The guard grunted.

The wagon drew up next to a line of about twenty similar wagons where the guard jumped out the back and indicated with his weapon for them to follow.

Rory and Xian trod behind Maxwell, while a guard walked in front and another behind them. They passed small cabins made of a tough substance, not wood; a faded and weather-worn plastic of some sort. Most of the glass windows had curtains that were half disintegrated and sat torn on their rails. The cabins stood crammed together on the wide, grassed area. Rory recalled his mother speaking of a time when people used to go on *holiday*.

Women lounged on the narrow front porches of these huts. Some were very young, just girls, and wouldn't make eye contact with Rory. Others were older and sent propositioning looks in their direction. All of them were in various states of undress. One leaned on the railing and eyed him while running her tongue across her lips.

The scene brought back memories to Rory of a way-house near Fort William, where slavers involved in the sex-trade had taken his mother and sister. Back in the past, with Dad and Alistair, he had rescued Mum and Kelly. That was his first time-journey and, sometimes, he wished it had never happened.

A scene flashed before his eyes for a fleeting moment. Dad's blood-drenched body. Helping Alistair wrap Dad's body in a canvas tarpaulin and place him in their 4WD vehicle.

Rory sighed and followed the guard, passing more huts. No women stood on the decking of these, and Rory glanced in an open door. Stacked boxes came right to the doorway. They were old, the writing on them faded and the cardboard and plastic weather-worn.

They approached the main building of the former holiday complex. The guard grunted, implying Rory and Xian should wait outside while Maxwell continued in. He soon returned and wriggled his fingers in a beckoning gesture. Rory slid a glance at Xian who was looking straight ahead. Rory complied, following Maxwell. Xian was close behind.

Rory and Xian entered a small front room with a counter, and Maxwell led them along a passage behind it, to a larger room where pictures covered the walls. These posters were much bigger versions of the photos on the calendars Mum had refused to throw out. Photographs of places in Scotland, faded by the sun and time, were posted near the large windows. He recognised Loch Maree and Ben Nevis. There were stunning pictures of iced lochs and snow-covered mountains. He could just read the faint writing on one. It was Glencoe, where his parents had lived when Dad went back in time to be with Mum.

Other photos and paintings were of castles. Edinburgh Castle was one. He'd seen the base of it on his most recent journey to the past. There were posters of Carlton Hill and Arthur's Seat. Rory grunted. The Scottish Government Bunker was hidden away from the rest of Scotland beneath Arthur's Seat. His destination. One he hoped to reach soon. That's if this Derrick Lloyd—even the name sounded over-inflated—didn't hold him up for too long. Rory held his hands by his side, clenching and unclenching his fists.

The door behind Rory opened, and he turned to face a small, elderly man. His hair was white and his face quite wrinkled, but he stood straight and walked with a spring in his step as he crossed the room and sat on a high-backed chesterfield. Maxwell followed him in.

"Father, these are the men of whom I spoke," Maxwell said.

"Hmm." Mr Derrick Lloyd pushed up his sleeves with rheumatic-knuckled hands, revealing faded tattoos on his forearms. "I'm told you are the son of Caitlin Murray-Campbell." Lloyd was not as well-spoken as his son. There was a hint of rough to it.

"I am," Rory replied. "But I dinnae ken who you are, and I object to you forcing me here against my will."

Maxwell strode forward and landed a hard slap on Rory's face.

Rory suppressed a flinch and held his head high, endeavouring to settle the ringing in his ears and the sting on his cheek. He straightened his shoulders, hoping to cover his shock at the speed with which the man had moved. The Lloyds appeared to be gentlemanly, but they were far from it.

"Well, now you've seen me, may I be on my way?" Rory asked. "I have important matters to attend."

Mr Lloyd senior shook his head. "You have no idea, do you?"

Rory clenched his jaw.

I have a theory, but I won't risk another stinging slap expressing it.

"I own this part of Scotland. Some would say that I am the king of the Kingdom of Fife." Lloyd smirked. "Over the years since the Crash, people have come to me for their needs, material or otherwise. I monitor those who pass through, and particularly, as you now know, who gets to cross the Kincardine Bridge. So, if you wish to go about your business, you'll need my permission." The man folded his gnarled hands, placed his chin on them, and positioned his elbows on his knees.

His rheumy eyes rested an unruffled gaze on Rory.

Rory's jaw-clench tightened, sending a sharp pain into his scalp. He needed to get to Siobhan, but this guy bugged him. This man who *owned* people and had stores and stores of goods hoarded to sell for a mega-profit, or however much he could bleed from those who desperately needed it.

Some would say.

Didn't matter what *some would say*, this guy *was* a megalomaniac and Rory was having trouble stopping himself from flying forward and punchin' the tiny man's wee piggy nose up into his cold, grey eyes.

A warm hand touched his forearm. He turned to see Xian shaking his head a fraction.

"Aye, a wise friend you have there, Mr Campbell," Lloyd said.

Lloyd snapped his fingers and the guard standing behind Rory thrust the butt of the submachine gun between his shoulder blades. Burning sharpness radiated from the centre of his back, out and down his arms, forcing him to his knees. Xian knelt of his own accord and raised his hands. The guard behind him halted the HK mid-descent.

Great! My martial arts teacher has gone all pacifist on me.

"I think a little time in a cell is required for you, young man." The leather chair creaked as Lloyd leaned forward. "It may enable you to come to your senses."

A guard grabbed Rory from behind, lifting him to a stand with a handful of Rory's jacket scrunched in his massive fist. A guard grabbed Xian and marched them along the corridor to a room, threw them in and bolted the door. Rory rolled to a sitting position and leaned against the far wall, his back aching.

"What now, oh non-violent one?" Rory glared at Xian.

"Man, if we did what you wanted to, we'd be dead," Xian said. "And you know Siobhan would kill you if that happened. No, worse than that—she'd kill me."

Rory leaned his head back against the wall, closed his eyes and breathed hard.

Siobhan.

He had to get to her.

Chapter Five

Scottish Government Bunker. Autumn Equinox 2061

Siobhan tossed onto her right side. The wall alongside her bed was just as blank as the last time she'd turned to it. Wow, this night was long!

And this week.

Rory will be here soon.

Siobhan rolled onto her back and stared at the ceiling.

"That will be an interesting conversation," she announced to her room at the prospect of Rory's impending confrontation with Bethany.

She got out of bed, stepped over to the dresser and pulled open the bottom drawer where the clothes she hadn't yet packed waited for their turn. Her fingers spread over a soft home-spun, handloom-woven shirt.

Rory's shirt. Had he noticed she'd taken it? She lifted it to her face and breathed him in.

Horse and heather.

It still smelled of him even after three months.

"I give up." Siobhan put on Rory's shirt, slipped into some cargo pants, and padded out her bedroom door then along the down-lit concrete corridor, which reflected the softer night-time lighting.

She paused, listening. The only sound was the hum of the fans that circulated air through the Bunker.

All were asleep. No fellow night owls suffering from insomnia.

Damn.

Siobhan walked to the empty kitchenette.

"So, I'm awake," she whispered, throwing open the cupboard door. "What harm is a little caffeine going to do?"

She got out a mug, scooped a teaspoon of instant coffee into it and poured water from the hot urn, mixing it before taking a sip then making her way to the stairwell. She wouldn't use the lifts; the guards didn't need to know she was awake when everyone else was having sweet dreams.

Siobhan walked up a flight, holding her mug tight to avoid scalding herself with the hot coffee.

She went to the next floor up. Of the many floors in the bunker built deep underground, this one always drew her. The main garage was situated on this floor, and the access road led out of it. The road travelled up a long ramp that eventually came to the small, above-ground compound, which was the only outdoor area available to the occupants of the Scottish Government Bunker. The exit to the rest of Scotland was through the high, solid steel doors of this continually guarded compound.

Chill from the concrete garage floor seeped into her bare feet, so she clambered onto the bench seat by the wall. Cars, jeeps and tanks were parked in silent rows and when in use were powered by the Bunker's finite fuel supply. The light blue of a saltire flag among the grey-green camouflage caught her vision. It hung from the thick aerial of the tank they'd taken to the Invercharing Community at Antony's insistence.

That'd put Rory's hackles up.

Rory had expected them, and he, with his crew and the rest of the Community's militia, had been waiting at their gates. They must've had an early warning system to be that ready. Siobhan recalled her first sight of him. Rory stood tall in jeans and a body-armour vest. His solid stature and rusty hair stood out among the other militia personnel. He was menacing, with a submachine gun at the ready. He was the only one to come through the gate to make the initial contact. What had he thought? A tank and the possibility of *all guns blazing.*

Bloody Antony.

Siobhan jumped off the bench seat, leaving her coffee mug behind, and stomped to the stairwell, then raced down. She ran until the burn of anger that had begun in her chest had travelled along her arms; letting breathlessness push it out. She found herself on the floor of the laboratories and wandered along the corridor to the lab at the end that housed the Time Machine. It was open.

The lights were on, and someone was singing to themselves.

"Hello?" she called.

"Oh!" a young voice said.

The singing ceased, filling the lab with an abrupt silence.

Siobhan walked the short distance to where the Time Machine stood. A metal object clattered on the concrete floor.

"Murray?"

A dark-blond head popped up from behind the army-green console of the Time Machine off to one side. Siobhan's mouth tugged at the edges at such an unimaginative name for a complex instrument. And at her younger brother-in-law.

"What are you doing?" she asked.

"Ah, I couldn't sleep," Murray said. "So, I thought I'd have a look at… it." He pointed a dirty rag in the machine's direction.

"MacIntosh still at you to get it going?" she asked.

Murray raised his brows. "You could put it that way."

"He doesn't give up," Siobhan said, rubbing her chin and recalling how the head IT tech hadn't stopped pushing Murray to get the machine working since he'd arrived in the Bunker three months ago.

Siobhan had grown fond of Murray. Her heart warmed at his untidy enthusiasm. His hair was unbrushed and, if she recalled correctly, he'd been wearing the same T-shirt for the past three days. She'd felt some pride at his brilliance, and at how surprised the scientific team had been to discover this genius had come from among those who lived *up top*.

The Time Machine was an odd thing. Murray was part of the Invercharing Community's team who had built it. Its action end, as Murray had named it, was an old fibreglass shower cubicle, such as they had in the 1970s. Siobhan had seen photos of one in the old house and style magazines in the archives. This one looked like it had spent many years at a dump. Murray had explained they only needed it to focus energy into an area. It did nothing scientific, only gave them a visual guide.

Murray retrieved a spanner from the floor. "It's the equinox, you know?"

"Yes, but it's the *longest* night." Siobhan sighed. "I've hardly slept."

"No, the equinox is equal day and equal night." Murray quirked a brow. "Surely you know—"

"I know what it is, Murray, I was just saying…" Siobhan squinted an eye. "Why work on this so early in the morning?"

"Brendan disappeared as he stood right where the Time Machine had been positioned in the barn at the Community." Murray stepped away from the console, absorbed in his thoughts and not answering Siobhan… or perhaps avoiding her question. He walked toward the cubicle, looking very much like the absent-minded professor… only younger.

Siobhan rested her hand at her throat. This was the first time Murray had mentioned Brendan to her since Rory had informed him of his twin's disappearance at the sunset of the Summer Solstice. She'd endeavoured to have a conversation with him, but MacIntosh had him holed up down here almost all day, every day.

"Murray?" Siobhan stepped behind him. "You miss your brother?"

"Murdo," he whispered, staring into the cubicle.

"Murdo MacDonald?" Siobhan said. "Yes, that's right. He was Brendan. You know that don't you, Murray?"

"Yeah. I do." Murray fiddled with the spanner in his hands. "Brendan lived through the past and made it to this future. He'd waited for the day when the submarine would arrive in Loch Ewe." Murray's throat worked with a swallow. "He'd positioned himself where he could act immediately the submarine docked on Drumchork pier. Rory said his crofter's cottage on the Isle of Ewe was right opposite the pier." He raised his head, staring straight ahead. "They couldn't have done it without him and everything he did."

"Yes, your twin was a brave man," Siobhan said. "You should be proud of him,"

Murray ran his right hand over the cubicle without looking at it. His fingers trembled, then his shoulders. Siobhan placed a tentative hand on his shoulder and stepped around to face him. Tears ran tracks down his cheeks.

"Oh, Murray." Siobhan wrapped her arms around him, and he rested his head on her.

Murray's tears were silent, only a small sob escaped before he pulled away and wiped his face with the bottom of his T-shirt.

"Rory mentioned Ley lines too." Murray sniffed and turned away, walking back to the console.

Siobhan stayed by the cubicle, giving Murray room to collect himself and his emotions. On the cubicle's floor lay a crumpled resin pod. It was of a size in which an adult could squat comfortably, and it looked like a dark, clear balloon, but with an opening and clasps. Siobhan stepped into the cubicle and examined the inside: three smooth walls with enough room for a person to stand and shower.

It *was* only a shower recess.

"The archives here are brilliant," Murray said, his speech rapid and his tears replaced with enthusiasm. "The ancient Celts had little written history. It's mostly from their oral tradition or recorded from research conducted at the end of the twentieth century." He tinkered with something on the console.

"What is?"

"The information about the Ley lines throughout Scotland." He spoke like she should know what he was talking about.

"Are you speaking of superstition?" Siobhan asked from the cubicle. "Because it doesn't sound like science."

"Ah." Murray looked up from the console and his tinkering. There was a grease stain next to the newly added damp tear patches on his T-shirt. Or was it brown sauce? "Siobhan," he said. "I've tried everything scientific to make this thing work again. But it won't. So, I'm looking beyond science."

"And?"

If he was going to go *all mystical* like Rory had once before, she may as well hear it.

"Our Invercharing Community sits on a Ley line," Murray said. "So does Edinburgh, Arthur's Seat actually. Well, anyway, that might be what really powers this thing." His shoulders slumped a little. "Which means all my calcs were pointless."

Siobhan picked up the crumpled pod abandoned on the cubicle's floor.

What must Rory have felt when he travelled?

He'd been there. *Through* time.

Was he a different man for having done so? Is that what made him so unique? So attractive.

"Brendan time travelled without any power—" Murray interrupted himself and then spun in her direction, eyes wide. "He travelled at sunset on the Summer Solstice." Murray ran toward her. "Get out Siobhan—"

Murray's voice and presence blotted to nothing, and Siobhan's world went white.

Siobhan disappeared before Murray reached the cubicle.

She was there; then she wasn't.

Murray's temples thudded. He looked at his watch—the one William MacIntosh had given him.

6:03 a.m.

Sunrise on the Autumn Equinox.

"Oh, shit," he yelled. "Rory's gonna kill me."

Chapter Six

The Kingdom of Fife

Dawn sunlight shone through the only window high in the closet-like room, illuminating the wooden floor between Rory's legs. He sat leaning against the hard wall, hands resting on his bent knees. This bright patch of floor had sixteen nails, ingrained dirt in between the planks, and a stain in the shape of the Isle of Skye.

He'd behaved badly. He should've introduced himself as a representative of the Invercharing Community's militia. But no, instead he let his eagerness to be with Siobhan, and his intense dislike for people who lord it over others and own some, to get in the way of—what did they call it? —*public relations*. Now this Derrick Lloyd would think all Highlanders were bad-tempered idiots.

Because that's what he'd been.

A heat smouldered within him. He flicked the balled-up piece of ancient sticky-tape he'd picked from a poster on the wall. It hit the door with a *ping*.

"You're in a stressful place," Xian said beside him. "Calm yourself or you'll get us killed."

"You could wipe all those guys out," Rory said.

"They've all got high-powered firearms," Xian replied. "As elegant and deadly as a Katana is, it's no match for a room full of bullets."

"What sort of leader am I if I cannae handle a guy like that?" Rory pursed his lips. "I suppose you never know who you may have to align yourself with. Keep your enemies closer, and all that."

Xian nodded.

Rory sighed. "I might need to make an alliance with this entrepreneur-scum who owns people and trades in hoarded goods."

Lloyd had the potential to be part of the conversations between the Government and concerned parties, something for which Siobhan was keen. She was a nuclear physicist but also had a natural bent for diplomacy and politics.

If only he did too.

"Yes, Rory, keep all your options open," Xian said.

"I dislike people who hold their power over others—like the Government does. Galls me they have Murray under duress," Rory said.

Footsteps echoed down the passage to the door, the lock clicked, then it opened.

"Mr Lloyd wishes to see you." The guard, whose sole weapon was a holstered handgun, flicked his head, indicating they were to follow him.

What? They are treating us with civility this morning.

Well, maybe he could do the same.

They followed the guard to the same room as the previous day. Lloyd sat in the high-backed chesterfield. A china teapot with a cup and saucer in blue floral pattern rested on a small antique tripod table beside him.

"Good morning, gentlemen," Lloyd said. "I hope your overnight accommodations weren't too uncomfortable for you."

Rory's brow tightened in a frown, and he didn't answer.

"Yes, thank you," Xian said.

"Very well. You'll wish to continue your journey and attend to your business in the Government Bunker." Lloyd picked up the steaming cup of tea and took a sip.

Rory blinked.

Does this scumbag know about Siobhan? He stopped himself from shouting it out loud.

"We would definitely be wishin' to go on our way." Rory stepped forward, ignoring the fist squeezing his insides. The guard beside Lloyd tensed. "Sir," Rory said. "I wish to apologise for my rudeness yesterday. I am anxious to get to Edinburgh. May we have our weapons and horses returned? We would like to go immediately."

"Hmm. It's a humble man who can apologise. I see it very little these days." Lloyd replaced his cup and saucer on the table then scrutinised Rory from head to foot once more.

Rory stood straighter; a niggle of unease running down his spine.

"We fed and watered your horses last night," Lloyd continued. "And my son is readying them for you as we speak."

"Thank you, Mr Lloyd," Rory said.

Lloyd waved his hand in a dismissive manner then the guard ushered them out of the room. Maxwell passed them in the corridor.

"Goodbye, and thank you for tending to our horses," Rory said.

Maxwell snorted and peered down his nose. "I don't work in the stables. Goodbye, Mr Campbell."

Rory turned to Xian, who shrugged.

"Come this way, Mr Campbell." The guard led them outside and along in front of the old holiday cabins. Guttering hung from some and peeling paint and boarded windows belonged to others. They reached the cabins that housed the women, and the guard turned.

"Mr Lloyd said you could partake of the ladies' or the boys' services if ye wished, before you go."

"Och, no thank you," Rory replied and glanced at Xian.

Xian shook his head. "That's a no from me, as well."

The stables housed many animals for their numerous wagons, and there wasn't a fuel-powered vehicle in sight. Xian nudged him and pointed. Near the stables, Boy and Xian's horse were ready saddled, and Micah McNair was loading their packhorse, and the gelding for Siobhan stood beside it.

"What're you doin' here?" Rory strode to Micah. "How did you get our horses?"

"That's a fine way to speak to your rescuer." Micah's dreads flew around his shoulders as he spun to face them; smugness filled his expression.

"What do you mean?" Rory asked.

"My men and I saw ya were in trouble no less than a day's ride from your home. Why d'you think those bandits didn't finish you off?" Micah rested his fist on his belt. This time the gesture revealed his weapon. "You are most welcome." Micah flicked a look at Rory's horses.

"Och, aye, thanks," Rory said.

"I put in a good word for you with Lloyd, too," Micah said.

"Why would that make any difference to Mr Lloyd?" Rory asked.

"Because he's my dad, and sometimes he listens to me."

"You look nothing like him." Rory eyed Micah's tall, muscular frame.

"Bastard son," Micah said. "My mother was one of his women, but he actually liked her. And me." Micah smiled. "I take after my mum."

"No kidding," Xian said.

"Just as well." Rory ran his hand over his stubbled beard. "You were followin' us?"

"Yep," Micah replied.

"How d'you know we're going to the Bunker?" Rory asked.

"Didn't. Just guessed. Impressed ma dad enough to let you go. He's curious." Micah rubbed the back of his neck and chewed his lip. "Ah, a word of warning. You'd better be alert when my dad's curious. Sorry, but it was the only way he'd free you."

Rory rolled his eyes as he stepped to Boy to stroke his nose. His stallion nickered softly in greeting. A guard came toward them with their weapons and Rory took his and mounted Boy. Xian mounted his horse and grabbed the lead reins of their other horses.

"So, I can see your sister now, yeah?" Micah asked.

"No." Rory stared at Micah while he turned Boy around.

"But I've just saved your life." Micah's voice trailed to a squeak. "Twice."

Boy pranced, ready to go. Rory held the reins firm as his stallion skittered sideways.

"Still no." Rory nudged Boy to a walk.

"But *you're* co-operating with the enemy," Micah shouted behind him.

Rory pulled his stallion up and spun him back to the bandit. "What?" Boy jiggled his head and whinnied at the change of direction.

"You're married to that Government chick, aye?" Micah said.

Rory tilted his head. The rogue had his attention now.

"Think of it like that," Micah continued. "I see your sister and things are cool between us, yeah?"

Alliances again. Rory wrinkled his nose, grateful for Boy's unease giving him time to think.

"Only if Cèilidh wishes it," Rory replied.

"Oh, she wishes it," Micah said.

"What have you been up to?" Rory frowned.

"Nothin', man." Micah placed a hand on his belt. "There's not much you can do in a crowded barn."

Chapter Seven

Invercharing Community, 2067

White light filled Siobhan's vision and white noise deafened her with the buzz of tinnitus.

Then the cubicle encased Siobhan once more and the room tilted.

No, it wasn't a room. It wasn't even the lab at the Bunker. She felt gravity's pull and a hard-packed earthen floor rose to meet her. Someone grabbed her, their arms digging into her waist, then the floor stopped short of slamming into her face.

"Woah. Got to you just in time." Murray's grip jolted her, then he helped her regain her footing.

She stood, the shaking in her legs travelling up to her ribs.

"Murray?"

"Yeah, it's me, Siobhan. How did you—?" Murray's eyes widened. "Wow!"

"But you look almost the same," Siobhan said, peering into his face. "Don't the travellers of this particular machine always go back in time? Usually forty years? That means you, Murray, wouldn't actually *be* yet. Because, that's what's happened." She blinked into his expression dawning with comprehension. "I've time travelled, haven't I?"

Murray nodded and he let her go, a tight smile appeared on his face as he scratched his head but said nothing.

"When am I?" Siobhan looked around, her inner jitters settling. The draughty building was a barn of some sort with a high roof. "Where am I?" she asked.

"You're here at the Invercharing Community, and it's…ah." Murray squeezed his mouth to the side. "The future."

"But it's not far into the future," she said, "as you don't look that much older."

"It's 2067," Murray said. "We got the Time Machine back off the Government a couple of years ago. When did you come from?" Murray chewed his lip. "I need to get you out of here."

"Where's Rory?" she asked.

"That's why I must get you out of here," Murray mumbled and placed his hand on her shoulder.

Siobhan stood straighter and resisted Murray's push toward the barn door.

"Tell me what's going on," she ordered. "Why can't I see Rory?"

"Rory isn't here—" Murray began.

"He's not dead, is he?" Siobhan's mouth went dry.

"No, no, no. Rory's okay." Murray continued not-so-gently trying to move her to the door. "He's just not here... at the moment."

"Then why are you pushing me out of here?" she asked. They'd reached the barn's exit.

"I need to hide you"—Murray's gaze darted around, like he was thinking—"from you. Remember? Space-time continuum. Imploding universe and all that?" He bustled her along the corridor then into a room with a tattered poster of Andy Warhol's Einstein above an immaculately arranged desk.

"Stay here till I come back for you, okay?" Murray asked. "I gotta make sure the coast is clear."

The door slammed shut, so Siobhan sat on the end of the bed. It squeaked. She picked at her cargo pants and pulled the long sleeves of Rory's shirt over her hands, then buried her face in the soft, Rory-scented material. She'd see him soon.

But no. She couldn't. *Damn. That* was annoying.

She'd have to hide from herself until Murray could return her to the past. Back to the Bunker in 2061, waiting for Rory to arrive.

Siobhan sat bolt upright.

Murray *could* get her back, couldn't he? Her arms cooled. She must have returned to tell him she'd gone to the future that time she stepped into the Time Machine and disappeared.

As one does.

She slumped again.

Outside, a clamour erupted. The thud of horses' hooves and the shouts of men and women came from the main building. Their cries, tinged with alarm, floated along the corridor inside. She couldn't remember much of the layout of the compound, but she vaguely recalled the medical centre was nearby.

Siobhan opened the door a crack. At the far end of the corridor, men in grubby, bloodied clothes stormed toward the medical centre. Two men carried a stretcher bearing a man, his bloodied arm hanging over the edge, then ran into the room. Another man, his stride stiff and almost ambling, blocked Siobhan's view, his back to her. He wore a sturdy hat and a thick jacket, and his hand pressed to his left shoulder while he peered into the medical bay.

It was Rory!

"You okay, boss?" A woman—Kendra, but a little older—approached Rory, eyes full of concern.

"I can wait. George requires more attention than I do." Rory's deep voice and Highland accent sent shivers of longing into Siobhan.

She couldn't go to him in case *she* was out there too. Siobhan pushed the door a fraction more, heart slamming into her ribs. Kendra looked her way and her eyes widened. From the angle of Rory's head, he was intent on the commotion in the medical bay and probably missed her expression.

"Just need to do something, boss. Be right back. You sit over here." Kendra pointed to a chair and made Rory sit, then ran off.

Moments later, Murray marched down the short corridor to Siobhan. He stepped into the room, pushing her back, and slammed the door behind him.

"What're you doing?" His eyes were wide, frantic.

"He didn't see me," she said.

"No, but Kendra did."

"Rory's hurt. What happened?" Siobhan asked. "Why am I not there beside him now he's returned and injured? If it were up to me, I'd be there!" Her breath came out ragged, and she stopped herself because any more, and she'd sound distraught.

"Sit down, Siobhan." Murray gestured for her to sit by the desk. "I need to explain some things to you."

She sat and clasped tight to her hands in her lap. The tone in Murray's voice was disconcerting.

"There's been another battle," he said.

"Another?" She leaned forward.

Murray held his hand up, gesturing for her to be silent. "The Government Forces are gathering near here. And Rory's Alliance is trying to push them back."

"Government Forces? Alliance?" Siobhan shivered. "What are you saying? There's a war?"

Murray nodded; his mouth grim.

"What happened?" she asked.

Murray shrugged. "A lot. Most of it stupid. Most of it because some people were greedy, and others were, well, grieving."

Siobhan sank onto the bed. She was starting to not like the future.

"Tell me something positive about this time," she asked.

"You and Rory have two children—"

"Oh, can I see them?" she asked. "What are they? Girls, or boys? Or one of each?"

"No." Murray's voice strangled the word.

"We can arrange for me to meet them when I'm not around," she said. "They won't notice I'm younger."

"Siobhan," Murray sounded exasperated. "No, you can't see them. Please, listen." He frowned like he was in agony then dragged his hand across his face then said, "Siobhan, I'm sorry to tell you this, but you're dead."

Chapter Eight

Invercharing Community, 2067

Siobhan sat silent for a few moments, barely noting the rough material of her cargo pants she'd scrunched in a tight grip.

It was the future. And when you're in the past, looking forward, there are many possible futures. Aren't there?

And she didn't like *this* one.

"Siobhan, did you hear me?" Murray squatted in front of her, his blue eyes boring into hers. "It's okay, I've seen this before. More than I've wanted to, actually. This is the shock stage of grief—"

"No, it's not," she interrupted. "It's the *Siobhan planning stage*. Tell me everything that happened for us to get to this ludicrous state of affairs." She released her grip on her cargo pants. "First, how did I die?"

Murray sat back on his haunches. "You died just over three years ago having your baby, Connald," he said in a small voice.

"How? Did I bleed to death?"

Murray grimaced and studied the floor.

"Oh." Siobhan tried to blink away the lead in her gut. "What caused it? Was it preventable? Apart from not becoming pregnant in the first place, is there anything we could... I could have done?"

Murray's gaze roved around the room, his eyes not seeming to focus on its contents, his mind elsewhere.

"Placenta premia? No," he said. "Placenta previa."

His index finger trembled in triumph at his memory as he pointed at her. Then he sat at the desk, satisfaction leaving his eyes. His Adam's apple bobbed. Twice.

"Aunty Bec died the year before," he said, "and, well, we just don't have the facilities for a complicated thing like that. And Christine couldn't handle it. Nothing had prepared her for it. When it was all over, and people were working out why it happened, Christine said you should've gone to the Government Bunker months before when she'd first figured it out. She said they would have had the equipment and expertise to cope with it."

Placenta previa. Siobhan had no idea what that was, but she'd research it when she returned. If she returned. Her mind reeled with the information, competing with a cold numbness raising its ugly head.

No, Siobhan. Get a hold of yourself.

"What else?" she asked.

"What do you mean?" Murray asked. "Isn't that enough?"

"No, how did all the stupidity begin?" she demanded. "What about the sensible talks we were to have? The meaningful dialogue the Scottish Government planned with the diverse groups living in Scotland?"

"You know I'm not politically minded. You'll have to ask Rory." Murray stood from his desk and strode back and forth.

"You'll let me speak to him?" She watched Murray pace the room.

"Yeah, I must. He... he really misses you. Your death hit him hard."

"I shouldn't see him, then." Siobhan's heart ached at the thought.

"No, you must. Then you'll know what to do." Murray stopped his pacing. "Maybe you've travelled so you can experience *now*, this future, and do something about it." He spoke in earnest.

"What did I say to you when I returned to the past?"

"What d'you mean?" he asked.

"When I travelled back from this *now* to our past?"

"Ah," Murray said, "in the past I've lived in, you didn't."

"I didn't disappear at the Autumn Equinox when we were in the Bunker?" Siobhan's forehead tightened in a frown while icicles tousled her intestines.

Murray shook his head. "Not in *my* past," he repeated.

"Well... what does that mean? Have I changed things just by being here?" she asked.

Murray shrugged.

Oh, no. If Murray couldn't figure it—

"Can I get back to *my* past?" she asked.

"I can try to send you. It's the equinox here today—"

"I think that's how I got here," she interrupted, "at sunrise."

"Well, you have till sunset to find out what you need to know."

***

Siobhan followed close to Murray while he sneaked her along the corridor. People still milled around the medical centre and focused on the activity there. He led her into the old farmhouse where she'd stayed when she was here last, six years ago. Or, actually, only three months ago. She had to focus. This had the potential to become confusing.

The farmhouse was Rory's quarters.

And their home.

The walls were clean, not with the grubby stains she'd noticed the night she'd stayed over before their journey to Loch Ewe. Pale blue cushions sat on the couch. Dirty dishes soaked in the sink and wooden toys—a boat and a wagon—lay in the middle of the floor.

"I'll stand guard, so I can speak to Rory before he comes in," Murray said. "To make sure the children don't see you."

"But—" Siobhan began.

Murray shook his head vigorously. "They mustn't, Siobhan. It will traumatise them. Jake took forever to stop crying himself to sleep when you died. Sorry, but you just can't."

Siobhan stood by the doorway to the bedroom, biting her lip. Murray left, closing the door behind him. Crumpled sheets and blankets disturbed one side of the double bed. She stepped to the bed and lay on her stomach, her face buried in Rory's pillow, letting his scent surround her. Her throat tightened.

Muffled voices came through the front door. She sprang off the bed and stepped closer.

"Why?" Rory's deep tones rumbled.

Warmth flashed through her, and the muffled conversation continued.

"Daddy, I want tae go with Uncle Murray," a young child declared.

The centre of Siobhan's heart melted like wax. The child's voice must belong to her oldest son.

"Och, okay, Jake. Just behave yoursel', aye?"

"Aye, Daddy."

"Give me a kiss," Rory said.

The resonances of domesticity and a father's love for his children—their children—reverberated through the door and brought a sob to her throat. She clasped her hand over her mouth.

"Who's in ma place?" Rory's tone was sharp.

"Someone you'll want to see, Rory," Murray said. "Here, let me take Connald." A shuffling sound of what must have been Rory handing Connald over to Murray, came through the thin door.

The door opened and Siobhan stepped back.

Rory stood still. "What!" His hand remained on the doorknob.

"The machine worked," Murray's heavy whisper came down the hallway behind Rory. Rory stepped in.

His chest rose and fell rapidly, despite one shoulder wrapped in a heavy bandage. He was dirty, covered in grime and blood sprays. The acrid scent of propellant and male sweat hung around him. He had bags under his eyes and lines beside them, and he appeared much older than the six years from when she last saw him.

"Siobhan." His voice came out in a whisper.

"Yes, I travelled from the past when I was waiting—"

Rory strode forward and slid his arms around her, holding tight. He slid his hand into her hair at the same time he covered her mouth with his own. His eyes closed as he held her lips with his. His body was still firm, masculine, muscled. And lean and warm.

He broke off, tears welling in his lower lids.

"Why are you here?" His voice faltered.

"I accidentally travelled at the equinox," she said. "Murray was fiddling with the machine, and—"

Rory kissed her again and his warmth surrounded her. His strong arms criss-crossed her back and pulled her closer. So close there was no space, nor time, between them.

He lifted his face from hers. "I love you. I've missed you!" He sobbed then.

Rory's body-wracking heaves of emotion washed over Siobhan as his shaking arms held her, his tears soaking her neck. It overpowered her and she held her breath to stop herself from doing the same.

"Rory, come sit down. You've been injured." She led him to the couch, and they sat down against the soft cushions.

Her eyes raked every inch of him and her pulse spiked. She fought to stay calm, determined to make the most of this time with Rory, her man whom she'd waited so long to be with.

Rory pulled her close, then flinched.

"What happened?" She pointed to his bandaged shoulder.

"Through and through. Just muscle. I'll be fine." He looked her in the eye then. "You are as beautiful as the last moment I saw you."

"For me, the last time we were together we were being hastily married, and I left the compound." She caressed his damp face and he blinked. Rough beard stubble flicked under her fingers. "The Time Machine brought me forward, Rory. It doesn't usually go that way, does it?'

Rory shook his head. "The last time... I saw you was the day you died, and I held you in my arms." His voice broke.

Rory's raw grief and pain stirred a hurt of its own within her. He had a heaviness about him, and he seemed broken. She turned away and stood, unable to bear seeing it.

He clasped her hand from behind. "I'll go wash," he said. He pecked her on the cheek as he walked past to the bathroom.

"You must be hungry after fighting," she said down the hall.

Water ran in the bathroom but there was no answer from Rory. Siobhan went to the kitchen and opened the cupboard where there was a rustic loaf of multi-grain sourdough bread, a chunk of cheese and a tub of freshly churned butter. A dirty whisky glass sat on the bench next to a half-empty bottle of scotch. Her bare feet knocked into the empty bottles on the floor, their *clank* ringing in her ears while she sliced the loaf with shaking hands.

The noises in the bathroom ceased as she cut the cheese sandwiches she'd made and placed them on a plate. She walked to the living area and put the plate onto the coffee table. Rory stepped behind her.

"I thought you'd be hungry." Siobhan turned.

Rory wore a towel wrapped around his waist. His long hair was loose, dripping wet across his shoulders. A thick streak of grey grew from one side—the place where a Katana scraped his scalp on their way to Loch Ewe. His chest was bare, his shoulder bandage now damp, and his sleeve of tattoos was as deep blue as ever. His defined abdominal muscles had fine tufts of russet body hair, which grew in the mid-line from his navel to the top of the towel. She returned her gaze to his face. His eyes were soft, and he wore a smile that reached them.

"The only thing I'm hungry for is you." He scooped her up in his arms and carried her to the bedroom.

Chapter Nine

Invercharing Community, 2067

Making love with Rory was everything Siobhan had imagined it to be. No—it was better. He was... *so* much a man—raw and real and loving.

Rory had touched her with gentleness, tracing his fingers over her body like she was someone to be worshipped. He knew every inch of her and now she'd memorised every inch of him.

She lay in the crook of his arm, her head resting on his chest, moving with the rise and fall, and hearing his heart slow to a resting rate. Her own waves of pure physical delight were now fading to a contented glow as a sleepy state of relaxation washed over her.

Siobhan knew him—he'd known her for longer, but now she'd seen Rory with his guard down and had looked into his soul.

She played with the hair on his chest. Rory picked up her hand and entwined her fingers in his own, splaying hers, stretching them wide in his hand's span.

"Why were you wearing ma shirt?" he asked.

"I missed you," she said. "It smells like horse and heather."

He frowned.

"That's you, Rory Campbell." Her voice was soft. "My man of the wilds."

"Where were you that you ended up here?" he asked.

"In the Bunker waiting for you, three months after we married."

Rory chuckled. "I remember the first time I went there." He tried to squash his grin, his dimples deepening. "I dinnae think I made a good first-impression on your boss." He raised his eyebrows.

"What did you do?" she asked.

"Oh, not much." He gave a flick of his head. "Let's just say the First Minister would nae dare say no to me takin' ma wife back home with me."

Siobhan let her mouth curl at the corners and rested her head back on him, wrapping her arm tightly around him.

"What are you up to now, Rory Campbell?"

"You really want to know? This is nae your time. You've gone." His voice was husky. "Ye'll go back to the past. You're nae here anymore."

She leaned up on him to look him in the eye. "What do you intend to do? Why have you been fighting the Government? Why a civil war, for heaven's sake?"

He looked away at the small window; hazy daylight spilled onto the bare floorboards. She poked him in the ribs, and he flinched.

"We tried it your way, Siobhan, but it did nae work," he said, then faced her. "Negotiations with the New Scottish Government broke down about six months after ye died. We had parleys and debates that seemed to go nowhere. McLellan had nae changed. I warned them, but they would nae listen."

"Antony?" she asked. "What's he got to do with anything? He's behind bars."

Rory grunted. "If only that were so. They released him on good behaviour. They reinterpreted his crimes as patriotism. Faithfulness to the New Scottish Government in trying to expose us *usurpers* for what we are. That's what the First Minister of Scotland says of us." His expression was one of disgust.

"He is First Minister?" Siobhan covered her mouth with her hand.

"Aye." Rory nodded.

Roils of nausea replaced the last echoes of the pleasure Rory had given her.

She had known that man intimately too—Antony McLellan. He hated Rory completely. She shuddered at the recollection. Antony's distrust for Community people, and anyone other than Government, could only grow.

And so, it had.

"Murray implied you command an alliance," Siobhan said, her post-sex tranquillity dissipating fast. "Who are our allies?"

"The other nearby Communities in Scotland, Micah McNair and his group, whom we no longer call bandits. Webster and his people, of a sorts. More recently"—Rory took a deep breath, as if to brace himself for the announcement— "Derrick Lloyd."

"Out of those, I only recall Webster," she said. "How did you get them all to co-operate? You've done a wonderful job of unifying the masses, Rory. What an achievement." Her mouth stretched wide. "You should be proud."

"Well, dinnae look so happy. It's led to civil war, as ye put it, but I dinnae see any way out."

"Why not?"

"Lloyd is why not. How that old bastard is still alive I dinnae ken, but he's way better than his son. We've committed our militia to his side in exchange for our freedoms."

Siobhan bore her stare into his. "Freedoms?"

Rory slipped from beside her and got out of bed. She stared at his back, at the way the rippling muscles played and danced across his shoulder blades while he dressed. For a moment she forgot her question.

"You remember, after the volcano erupted and covered the northern hemisphere in ash, we had a time of poor harvests?" Rory halted. "Och, no, you would nae. That has nae happened for you yet."

"Volcano?" Siobhan blinked her eyes wide.

"Aye. Vesuvius." Rory put on his buckskins.

Siobhan recalled that for years the experts had predicted another eruption of Vesuvius in Italy, on the scale of Pompeii. So, it had occurred. What poor timing for Europe, and for the rest of the world, it seemed.

"Och, well, Lloyd has storehouses full o' stuff." Rory pulled on a home-spun top and grimaced as he put the arm of the injured shoulder down the sleeve. "Hoarded it for years, since the start of the Crash. Because we had been friendlier with Micah and his mob, on account of him marrying Cèilidh—"

"What!" Siobhan sat up. "Wait, your sister Cèilidh married a bandit leader?"

This was information overload.

"Aye, they joined us when pickings became lean, ken?" Rory said. "At your suggestion, I might add. They were family now, you said. Well, anyways, our store of food was nae enough, and I was aware of Lloyd's stockpile. I'd run into him, shall we say, on ma way to get you." His stern expression, which had persisted throughout his explanation, mellowed for a moment at the mention of her. But the severity soon returned. "He sold us supplies. More and more, as the sky was still dark, the winters longer and more severe. And the summers shorter, so less time to grow crops and the harvest yields were poorer. It was a famine, Siobhan. My people were hungry. We bought Lloyd's provisions until we got to the point where we could nae pay him."

Rory shoved his shirt into his trousers with the hand of his uninjured arm. "We got into debt. We were nae the only Community that did. The man said he would withhold his demands for repayments, which are considerable, if our militias joined with his private army to give the New Scottish Government a lesson."

"That's appalling." Siobhan scrunched a pillow in her hand.

"Och, it does nae stop there, lass. Lloyd says our youngsters will be in his employ if we dinnae. By *employ*, he means his sex-workers, who are virtually slaves, who he trades far and wide."

"The beast!" Siobhan exclaimed.

"That he is. I'd like to see him try and get them." Rory gritted his teeth. "We'd fight him tooth and nail. For if he took them, we'd never see our own again. He'd surely send them far away. The man's reach is astonishing. He's spent the last forty years building his network." Rory's shoulders slumped like he carried a heavy sack and the lines on his face deepened. "I've made mistakes, Siobhan. Stuffed up big-time and ma people will pay for it."

"Rory, you haven't. You're not responsible for volcanic eruptions and poor harvests!"

"Och, no." He flicked a shake of his head. "Getting involved with Lloyd was my greatest mistake. I wish I'd never met the man."

"You don't have to send your people to fight in his army for his ambitious cause," she said. "You can demand he wait for payment until the harvests improve. Band together with the others and fight him."

"The man's bigger than us, Siobhan." Rory shook his head. "You have nae lived through it. You don't know. We have nae choice."

"Everyone has a choice, except the powerless. You, Rory Campbell, were never powerless!" She stepped out of bed, the sheet slipping to the floor. During their lovemaking he had loosened her hair from the French roll and its soft caress now extended down her neck and onto her breasts.

"Och, is that true now?" Rory stepped forward and placed his warm hands on her upper arms. He pushed strands of hair away from her face, his fingers moving down, tracing the line of her jaw.

"I became powerless when I lost my anchor, my rock, my best friend, my love—my you, Siobhan." He crushed her to himself and his whole body heaved with a sob.

Siobhan wrapped her arms around him and smoothed her hands along his firm, back. She sought to soothe the churn of fear swirling like a cyclone among her own emotions.

"Any barrier that kept me from you," Rory whispered holding her close, "you ken I'd climb it. Kick it down if I had to. Find a way around it... till I reached you. But you went to a place where I could nae get to you... nor could I bring ye back."

Siobhan's breath hitched and she held him tighter, pressing her head against his chest, which vibrated with his words swollen with emotion.

"All I kenned was how to fight," he continued. "But even then, I was powerless over it... over death. *Your* death, Siobhan. I held you in my arms and felt the last beat of your heart; your final breath brush ma' face." His ribs heaved as she hugged him, trying to hold her own emotions tight.

But death will be Rory's end if this civil war continues.

Rory couldn't do it. Mustn't go head-to-head with the Government. They had access to more firepower than Rory could imagine, and if Antony had anything to do with it, they'd use it. Antony would love to wipe out Rory, she was certain of that. She prayed Antony wouldn't even think of the nuclear warheads the Government had hidden away.

What sort of world was this now?

It'd had the potential to be a new start once people recovered from the disaster after the Stock Market Crash of 2018. Everyone could've been on a level plane. Shared resources. Rebuilt Scotland together.

But, no. Selfish, stupid people!

The afternoon sun angled through the window, illuminating the bed. She'd have to get back to Murray and the Time Machine before sunset. She had to stop Rory—had to convince him. Her man's warm body held her close, shooing away all the horribleness of this time.

Siobhan eased her embrace and kissed him. Rory responded, mouth and moist cheeks brushing against her face. She undid his buckskins and loosened his shirt from them. Rory groaned.

He moved her back to the bed then dragged his still buttoned shirt off one-handed and kissed her. He held her close, the beating of his heart coming through his ribcage pressed against her. She slid his buckskins down and he stepped out of them then eased her onto the bed. Sheets crinkled against her back while his warm skin covered her belly, and his chest hair tickled her breasts.

For now, the future didn't matter. Neither did her death.

It was all Rory, and she with him here, where their love and passion met.

Her longing rose to almost excruciating as Rory held her close, his yearning for her reflected in his face. Her body reached for his, their breath mingling as their lives entwined once more and pleasures joined, consuming them both.

And for that moment, time slipped into eternity.

Chapter Ten

Invercharing Community 2067, Autumn Equinox

Thuds echoed through the room, the farmhouse, and Siobhan's body, shaking her serenity as she lay in Rory's arms. Rory sprung from the bed at the same moment someone banged on the door.

"Get dressed quickly," Rory said, throwing his buckskins on and rushing to answer the door.

Siobhan slid out of bed and dressed.

"Rory." It was Murray at the door and his voice trembled. "George died."

"Och, no." Rory's husky tone travelled back to Siobhan.

"That's not all. Government tanks are coming up the glen." Behind Murray's voice were the alarmed shouts of men and women. "A missile hit the wind farm. We've got to get Siobhan out of here before we can't."

"Where are the boys?" Rory yelled at Murray while he rushed back to the bedroom.

"They're with Cèilidh," Murray said from the door.

"Come, Siobhan." Rory waved her to him then grabbed her hand. "Follow us. Keep your head down so no one recognises you, okay?"

She hurried into the hallway with Rory and Murray.

A roar followed by a thud came from the front of the compound. Walls rattled, and the ceiling showered Siobhan with dust.

"Shit," Murray yelled.

Rory's hand tightened around hers. "That was close," Rory said. "Come on."

He pulled her away from the panic. An alarm bell clanged, followed by pounding boots and people shouting. Rory moved faster as they exited the main building and faced the large outbuildings. Siobhan stumbled to keep up with Rory's long strides; her bare feet scraping over the rough ground. In the barns, animals stomped and snorted, and men and women carrying guns mounted whinnying horses. Another thud hit the mountain behind the compound. The ground vibrated beneath her, and dirt sprayed on the green hill now left with a gouge of dark brown.

"At least their aim's bad," Murray said.

"Och, no. They're warning shots." Rory urged Siobhan to the old barn where they kept the Time Machine.

Behind them, the report of rapid gunfire was a popping clamour at the compound's front gates. Rory dragged Siobhan through armed men and women, dodging those mounted on horses, all hurrying to the combat. People shouted orders and loaded weapons.

"I'll be there soon," Rory shouted to one of the militia.

"Okay." The voice belonged to Xian.

They reached the barn and Murray fumbled with the lock on the old door. Bullets pinged off the path beside them while a missile whooshed overhead. The door opened, and Rory pulled Siobhan in after Murray, his large hand clamping tight around hers. They ran to the far end of the barn where the Time Machine sat.

"I'll get Siobhan in the cubicle, Murray," Rory yelled over the whoosh of another missile.

"Yeah, it's almost sunset," Murray said.

The side of the barn rocked with a thunderous crash. Rory pushed Siobhan down onto the hard-packed earthen floor. Cold and pain struck her cheek and her side. Rory's warm body flinched above hers. Splinters of wood and shards of metal flew around. Dust billowed toward them. Rory shielded her further while broken fragments of timber whooshed over them.

"The machine's all right," Murray spoke through a choking cough. "Thankfully."

Rory lifted himself off Siobhan and pulled her to a standing position. They were both covered with fine dust; Rory's hair, now a grimy russet, poured dirt like a river.

"Will you be okay?" Siobhan searched Rory's face; the creases of his brow were deeper and a look of knowing emerged.

"This is just the start, Siobhan."

"Are you going to be all right?" she asked more firmly.

"I don't know." More powdered debris poured from Rory's hair.

"Rory, you can't... You know the Government has nuclear warheads?"

"What!" Murray shouted from the console.

Rory's nostrils flared but there was no expression of surprise on his face, only concern. His grip on her upper arms grew tighter.

"Will our boys be safe?" Siobhan's throat tightened.

Their children caught in this... this... battlefield.

Rory swallowed and opened his mouth to speak.

"Rory!" Murray shouted from the control panel. "Siobhan needs to be in the Time Machine now!"

Rory ran her to the cubicle and shoved her in. Dim sunlight from the gaping hole in the barn wall landed on the machine. Through the haze of fine particles remaining from the shower of debris, the sun's beams angled to horizontal, the setting sun lowering to a hair's breadth from the horizon.

Rory leaned in and kissed her soundly on the mouth.

"I love you, Rory," she said, when he released her.

"Aye, like we say. Yours for all time—whatever time may bring us." A look of pain filled his face. He leaned in and kissed her again then held her close. "It goes against all I believe," he whispered into her ear, "concerning the ethics of time travel—" A crash rang through the barn, showering them with more dust. They both flinched. "But," he continued, "I'll say it anyway. Change the past to make a better future."

At Rory's words, the tension in Siobhan that had built throughout her day in *this* future, now released. But his charge wasn't only personal, it was about the lives of their children and a whole Community.

Hell, it was about a whole way of life and communities of people.

"Everyone has a price, they say." Rory grimaced. "I'm willing to go against my convictions to prevent ma people being enslaved to Lloyd and prevent this war with the New Scottish Government." His look was grim. "And every other bad thing there is in this time."

"What do *you* want me to do, Rory?" she asked.

"Don't die, Siobhan."

Chapter Eleven

Edinburgh 2061, Autumn Equinox

Rory and Xian travelled along the old Queensferry Road and headed toward Leith then cut across to Arthur's Seat. Xian had advised it would be best to avoid the old central business district of Edinburgh proper, Edinburgh Old Town, and the Royal Mile. They passed soot-stained stone dwellings with boarded-up windows and overgrown hedges. Rubbish lined the wet streets. The stench of stale milk, rotten meat, and human excrement seared Rory's nostrils. He covered his nose with his neckerchief.

Groups of men stood at crossroads and glowered at them as they passed. Some younger men eyed the pack horse's load. Xian unsheathed his sword, which glinted in the grey daylight, and the youngsters stepped back and waved them on. Rory and Xian trotted the horses around the wide green at the bottom of Arthur's Seat and arrived at the base of the hill.

"Where's the entrance?" Rory asked.

Xian shrugged.

They followed the old road that curved behind the steep hill. Here, a tall, concrete wall covered in rusted barbed wire protruded out from the base, making a three-sided enclosure, the back abutting the mount. A double gate of thick steel had a guard tower on one side, where a sentry with binoculars watched their approach then spoke into a communication device.

"They know who we are," Xian said.

"Aye," Rory said. "They've been on the lookout since my CB conversation with Siobhan a week ago."

While they drew closer, more armed men appeared along the top of the high concrete walls of the enclosure.

"This is becoming repetitive," Rory commented.

"Calm, Rory," Xian said. "You can't jeopardise this or you may never see your bride."

"State your name and business," the guard shouted once they'd reached hailing distance.

"Rory Campbell, and I'm here to see my wife. You ken her as Siobhan Kensington-Wallace."

The gates ground open. Rory kicked Boy to a trot and Xian followed, then the gate shut swiftly behind them. They faced a row of armed men holding British Defence Force light machine guns, GPMGs. One soldier stood out in front.

Rory pulled Boy up short.

"Och. I'm a friend," he shouted to the one who appeared to be the officer in charge.

The man stepped closer and lifted his headgear to reveal the stern, clean-shaven face of a man in his late thirties.

"Hello, Mr Campbell," he said. "I'm Captain Henderson. We've been expecting you."

"Hello." Rory's shoulder muscles tightened. "I'm here to see ma wife. May my friend, Xian, and I enter the Bunker, please?"

The communication handset clipped on Henderson's belt jumped to life and he listened to the low-volume message. "Follow me, Mr Campbell," he said.

They dismounted and led the horses, following Henderson down a concrete road with a detail falling in behind. The road angled steeply down, lit by electric lights either side. The air cooled with their descent, and Boy's uncomfortable nickers mixed with the *clip-clop* of the horses' tread echoing off the walls close beside them. The tunnel-road was the width of a large vehicle. Then it widened further into an area about the size of the whole Invercharing Compound. Vehicles filled this space with tanks parked by a far wall, also jeeps and armoured vehicles. Rory recognised some. Siobhan and her company had driven these to the compound when they came to assist with the submarine in Loch Ewe.

Henderson led them to a raised concrete platform, which he jumped up onto and turned to face them, holding his palm out in a halting gesture.

"Wait here, please, while I get Ms Kensington-Wallace," Henderson said.

He beckoned another soldier to come and stand on the platform. She did so, holding her GPMG before her. Henderson then left via a door, through which Rory glimpsed a concrete stairwell.

The armed escorts who'd shadowed Rory's and Xian's entry now positioned themselves around them. Rory smiled at the closest. The soldier blinked but didn't return the gesture. At the back of the car park were a row of bays. In one, a man tinkered underneath a jeep raised on a hoist. Mechanical whining, sharp and high pitched, and a clattering came from that direction. The door to the stairwell slammed and Henderson returned.

"We are locating Ms Kensington-Wallace now. She won't be long," he said, standing with legs apart and hands behind his back.

Minutes passed.

Shouted orders of the men by the vehicles in the work area echoed across the large parking bay.

A woman in uniform, wearing an uneasy expression, stepped from the stairwell and spoke into Henderson's ear. He frowned.

"Anything wrong?" Rory asked.

"No." Henderson was curt. He whispered to the woman, and she scurried off.

He resumed his stance. *At ease,* George would call it. But this soldier was *not*. His brow remained tight, and he blinked often.

"Where's my wife? I wish to see her now," Rory demanded.

"She'll be here soon, Mr Campbell," Henderson said.

Boy pranced behind him, the clattering of his hooves on the concrete floor stirring up the other horses. Rory and Xian turned to shush them.

"McMichael!" Henderson shouted. "Take these animals somewhere and tend to them."

A soldier stepped forward looking stunned. He slung his light machine gun over his shoulder and nudged his neighbour who did the same. They approached the horses, took the reins, then led them away. Boy's uneasy nickering travelled back to Rory as McMichael led the horses to the farthest side of this level.

"Don't worry, Campbell," Henderson said. "We have animals too."

Rory tried to suppress a niggle in his gut. Something *was* wrong. They were stalling.

"Why is it taking so long to get my wife?" Rory asked.

The door to the stairwell opened and a woman wearing a neat skirt suit strode out. Henderson and the other defence force personnel snapped to attention. The woman, who seemed to be about Siobhan's age, whispered to Henderson. Henderson indicated in Rory's direction.

The woman rested her gaze on Rory; her face held an expression like she'd stood in something unpleasant and was about to wipe it off her shoe.

"I'm Rory Campbell and I want to see my wife," he said then made to jump up onto the concrete platform.

The stomp of footsteps in unison came behind him as the soldiers sprang to action. Henderson stiffened and glared at him.

"It's been authorised," the woman said to Henderson, then to Rory, "Mr Campbell, the First Minister would like to see you. Please come with me."

All personnel surrounding Rory relaxed, so he climbed onto the platform and Xian followed.

"No. Just Campbell to go with the First Minister's secretary." Henderson placed a hand on Xian's arm. "You stay here."

Rory entered the stairwell and turned to glance at Xian who tipped his head. Rory followed the First Minister's secretary and, accompanied by Henderson, walked up three flights.

The door exiting the stairwell led to a long corridor floored with shiny smooth concrete. The lights were of a different glow and only came on as Rory's guide neared them. Axes in sealed glass-fronted boxes were attached to walls at various places, often near intersecting corridors, and long coiled hoses sat beneath signs that read *FIRE*.

Rory followed the woman, contemplating her suit. It was similar to the style Angela preferred to wear. He grunted. He'd probably bump into Angela here. Yet it appeared a large facility, he may strike it lucky and not see her. Then again…

They came to an area with many doors exiting from a waiting room. Paintings hung on the walls above couches. One was of an old building with the words *Holyrood Palace* engraved on a plaque mounted beneath. The painting opposite was of a straight-lined concrete building with many windows. The plaque under this one read, *Scottish Parliament Building*.

The secretary to the First Minister stopped at the office ahead of Rory, while Henderson positioned himself beside it, standing guard. Men and women sat or stood by desks with computers, most busy at their tasks, others stole sneaky looks at Rory. The soft collar of Rory's home-spun shirt grew hot around his neck.

The door to the First Minister's office opened and a tall man, military-looking with a closely cropped haircut and neat uniform, walked out. He stopped mid-stride and glared at Rory.

"William MacIntosh," Rory grimaced. "How's IT going?"

MacIntosh straightened his tie. "IT is going fine, Campbell. It's your brother's project that is giving me grief."

Rory lifted a shoulder and let it fall. "I'm sure he's doing his best under the circumstances. Being away from his home, an' all."

MacIntosh let out a short, derisive laugh. "That young man is wasted at home," he said, and continued his journey out of the office area without another comment.

Rory grunted at MacIntosh's back as the secretary knocked on the door.

"Come." The muffled voice coming from behind the door had a commanding tone and Rory tensed, straightening his shoulders.

"The First Minister will see you now, Mr Campbell." The First Minister's secretary opened the door.

Directly in front of him hung an enormous picture of a square tower standing high above a forest. Its sandstone solidity protruded proudly through lush green foliage. He couldn't decide if it was a painting or a very large photograph, but he knew its subject—the Wallace Monument.

The large office contained shelves full of books with a massive desk placed centre-stage. Behind it sat a woman wearing a tailored suit. She was dark-skinned and dark-haired, and when her gaze lifted from her desk's contents, dark eyes pierced him.

"May I call you Rory?" Bethany Watts asked; her hand motion inviting him to enter.

"Please do, First Minister." He edged forward and stood before her desk, which was as immaculately tidy as Murray's.

"Please sit." Bethany's gaze travelled over him.

"Ye'll have to excuse me, ma'am." Rory remained standing. "I've been on the road for a week, and I have nae been able to wash." He looked down at his buckskins and his jacket. He was unkempt. She must think him a vagabond.

Bethany finished studying him then made eye contact but said nothing.

"I am here for my wife," he said.

"Siobhan Kensington-Wallace is a vital member of this Bunker." Bethany's voice was hard. "The New Scottish Government needs her."

"Siobhan is my wife." Rory stepped up to her desk and placed his fists on it. "*I* need her."

"I may not be able to let her go." Bethany stood.

Rory exhaled heavily through his nose. "I ken she has an assistant. *She* can do her job." He leaned forward on his knuckles, narrowing his eyes. "I *will* take my wife with me when I leave."

Bethany's perfect mouth became a thin line. Small beads of sweat formed above her upper lip. Her deep brown eyes locked with his and her right eye twitched.

After a sharp knock on the door, a woman entered.

"Yes, Louise?" Bethany stepped back, her shoulders easing.

Rory continued to lean on her desk with white-knuckled fists.

"Ms Kensington-Wallace's brother-in-law—" Louise interrupted herself. "I mean, the young man from the Community who is assisting with the Time Machine, wishes to speak with Mr Campbell, ma'am."

Rory spun. *Louise* was the woman who had first whispered into Henderson's ear.

Louise flinched and stared up at Rory. "Shall I let him in, ma'am?" she asked.

"Yes," Bethany ordered from behind Rory.

Louise left for a second and returned with Murray.

"Rory!" Murray stepped to Rory and gave him a hug.

"Good to see you," Rory said over his head.

Murray disengaged from their hug and faced Bethany.

"I know where Siobhan is, ma'am," he said. "May I take my brother to her?"

"Certainly." Bethany's tone had a barely concealed edge of relief to it. "Louise, go with them."

"No, it's okay," Murray said. "Honestly, don't trouble yourself. We'll be fine, won't we, Rory?" He looked to Rory and raised his eyebrows a fraction.

"Dinnae you worry. Ma wee brother will take me to my wife." Rory smiled, facing Bethany and trying to make it sincere.

She indicated her consent with a slight nod.

Murray led Rory out the door and through long, dimly lit corridors with more shiny floors and plenty of other corridors and doors leading from them.

"How d'you do that?" Rory asked.

"They like me," Murray answered, striding ahead. "They appreciate brains."

"We do, too." Rory frowned.

"Yeah, I know you do, but the guys I grew up with just thought I was odd. Brendan was the only one who understood me." Murray grew quiet as they walked down a flight of stairs.

"Where are we going?" Rory asked, after passing yet another landing leading off to a floor. "Where's Siobhan?"

"Ah, well, I'll tell you when we get there." Murray's voice echoed in the stairwell.

"Get where?" Rory's skin prickled. "Tell me what?"

Defence force personnel in uniform were everywhere. Murray led Rory down six flights of stairs in total. The only exit from the Bunker appeared to be from this stairwell and up to that garage.

Where were they holding the horses? Rory wondered. So far in this bunker, nowhere looked suitable for animals.

"The Scottish Government Bunker is thirty floors deep, has three stairwells, two lift wells, one main entry and exit point... the garage level. There are sure to be smaller exits, but I haven't been informed of them... or discovered them myself yet." Murray strode beside him. "There are at least twenty thousand LED lights. It has solar and nuclear power sources." Murray's speech accelerated with the revelation of each fact. "They use electricity generated by the only functioning power station in Scotland. We've been there, Rory. It's the one at Torness." Murray's eyes lit up.

"Forget the guided tour," Rory said, holding his impatience in check. "Where's Siobhan?"

Murray ducked his head and continued to lead him from the stairwell to a narrow corridor. Numbered signs reading *Laboratory* were on every door leading off it. At the end, Murray unlocked a door and stepped through. Rory followed him into a bare room, neat and clean. Sterile. Rory blinked under the weird electric lighting.

"Yeah, you get used to the LED," Murray commented.

"How do you know what time it is?" Rory asked.

Murray lifted his arm to show his wristwatch.

The Time Machine stood in the centre of the room with the control desk to one side. Apart from that, the lab was empty.

"Where's Siobhan? Why d'you bring me to a lab?" The hairs on Rory's neck rose. "I thought we'd be going to her room."

Murray scrunched his mouth to the side. His pupils dilated, either from the dim light—or fear.

"What happened," Rory said through a tight jaw.

"It wasn't my fault, Rory—"

"What wasn't?" Rory grabbed Murray and tried not to shake him. "Where's Siobhan?"

"I don't know exactly," Murray said. "She went in the Time Machine and she hasn't come back yet."

Chapter Twelve

Scottish Government Bunker, 2061

Rory turned away and grasped his head, swallowing the bile rising in his throat.

"How are we going to get her back?" He slid his hands into his hair and gripped tight. His scalp burned. It was nothing compared to the heat of the desert in his soul—a dry barren wasteland without Siobhan. "I'm about to take her home and you've lost her in time forever!"

"Sunset," Murray announced.

Rory flung his hands down and reeled around to Murray who had calmed, apart from a bobbing Adam's apple.

"It's the equinox," Murray said. His sudden composure set Rory's teeth on edge.

"What does that have to do with it?" Rory asked.

"Siobhan travelled this morning at sunrise. The machine wasn't set to a year, so she'll probably go to the past—its usual default setting. She'll have a day catching up with her dad, most likely, then she'll return at sunset." Murray seemed confident. "Siobhan will know to get to the Time Machine for that."

Rory blinked. "How do we know when that is in this place that never sees the daylight?"

Murray held up his watch.

"Sunrise was 6:03 am. So sunset on the equinox will be 6:03 pm." Murray stated matter-of-factly.

Rory stared, curling his fingers into a clench, and counted to ten.

"How could you let her—" he began.

"It's 6:02, Rory—" Murray began, but a cry coming from the Time Machine interrupted him.

Siobhan appeared in the cubicle then tumbled out. Rory reached forward to grab her and staggered back with the force of Siobhan's exit. Holding Siobhan in his embrace, he sat down with a thud on the concrete floor. Dirt covered her clothes and fine particles dusted her loose hair and her face.

"Rory!" she cried, holding him tight.

"It's okay, Siobhan, you're back now." Rory glared up at Murray who stood motionless before them.

"When did you go to, Siobhan?" Murray asked, holding his hands out to help her up, then dropping them when he saw Rory's glower. "She's back, Rory. Don't be mad at me."

"It's not Murray's fault, Rory," Siobhan said. "I stepped into the machine at the wrong moment."

Siobhan's sapphire-blue eyes locked with his, then they filled with tears that spilled down her cheeks, leaving tracks in the grime.

"What happened, Siobhan?" Rory asked, easing her back from himself. "Why are you a mess? Is that ma shirt? Tell us what happened back there? Did you return to when the terrorists bombed the cities?"

She shook her head, her eyes still held his. "I went to the future."

"What?" Murray gasped. "How?"

Siobhan shrugged. "I don't know... It wasn't nice."

"You time travelled to the future without electrical power." Murray suppressed a shout. "Just like Brendan travelled to the past without a time machine." Murray's eyes darted from Siobhan to the Time Machine, to gazing at nothing. Then they opened wide. "Man," he whispered. "I'm right! The machine needs energy, but it must be on a Ley line!"

"Och, please explain," Rory asked. "You ken I'm nae scientific."

"I'm scientific and he's speaking gibberish to me," Siobhan said close to his face.

"The Ley line *is* the power-time conduit," Murray continued his whisper. "The power can be either electricity—and that's why this time travel device doesn't require as much energy as the scientists of the twentieth century thought—or the natural energies of the Earth. Like at an equinox or a solstice. When, like in Brendan's case, you don't even need a time machine."

Siobhan's eyes opened wide with comprehension, then faltered a fraction. "But why wouldn't it work when you tried here with electricity?"

"Arthur's Seat is special," Murray answered. "It's the convergence and origin of a number of Ley lines. So... maybe it rejects power from outside of it, and only works with its own natural source."

"Why did it work for us with electricity when you and I, and even Dad, went to the past," Rory asked, "but didn't need any for Brendan?"

"Invercharing sits on a single Ley line." Murray lifted a shoulder. "Maybe it uses the Earth's power at solstices and such but needs another power source the rest of the time."

Rory opened his mouth to speak just as someone pounded on the door.

"Hello? Have you found Ms Kensington-Wallace?" a female voice asked from behind the door.

"That's Louise. She can't see me like this." Siobhan stood. "No one can see me in this dirty state!" She faced the door. "Louise, I'm fine," Siobhan said in her usual authoritative voice, so different from the husky, scared tones of her immediate return. "I'll see you later, okay?"

"We need to get you to your room without being seen," Murray said to her.

"You've said something similar to me already today, Murray," Siobhan replied.

Rory rose from the floor and stood close to her.

"So good to see you, husband. You look great." She kissed his lips, and he slid his arms around her waist and returned it.

"Ah, we'd better get her cleaned up soon," Murray suggested. "Rory?"

Rory released his mouth from her intense kiss. "Aye," he said, not taking his eyes from hers.

"I can't go out covered in debris." Siobhan let go of him and brushed the dust out of her hair with her fingers then wiped the dirt off her face. "We just don't get this dirty in the Bunker."

"Here." Rory removed his jacket and handed it to her.

"Thanks." A shy half-smile emerged on her lips as she put his jacket over her shoulders. "Oh!" She looked down at her cargo pants and patted the dust off them.

"Siobhan?" Louise called through the door again.

"No one must find out you have time-travelled," Rory said in quiet but firm tones, eyeing first Siobhan then Murray. They both nodded.

"I'm fine, Louise." Siobhan tried the door.

"Here," Murray whispered. "I locked it." He slid his gaze from Siobhan to Rory, then unlocked and opened the door.

"I've been with Murray," Siobhan said.

Louise stood in the doorway frowning. "All day?"

"Yes, it's been fascinating," Siobhan said. "But my husband is here now," she said through a grin, "and we'll have some dinner."

Siobhan gave an affectionate look to Rory, then brushed past Louise, who squinted at his jacket draped over Siobhan's shoulders. Siobhan led them up five flights of stairs. Rory followed her every step. Siobhan's hips swayed beneath his oversized jacket and her long honey-blonde hair flowed down her shoulders and back.

Not in its usual French roll?

Rory stared at Siobhan's hair all the way to her quarters. His questions about her dishevelled state would have to wait. The long, pale corridor narrowed to smaller hallways, one of which Siobhan led them along to a row of white doors opposite a kitchen area where Xian leaned against a bench. Henderson stood nearby with his GPMG hung over his shoulder, his thumb tucked in its strap. The aroma of warming food, possibly chicken, hit Rory's nostrils. Seconds later his stomach growled, accentuating the pain of its emptiness.

"Henderson!" Siobhan yelled. "Why on Earth are you guarding Xian?" Siobhan, dwarfed by Rory's jacket, put her hand on her hip. "You may go."

Henderson snapped to attention. "First Minister's orders, Ms Kensington-Wallace."

"My name is Mrs Campbell, and you will leave right now." Siobhan held his stare.

Henderson's vision flitted from Siobhan to Rory to Xian, then he hesitated.

"I've been armed all this time and I haven't drawn my sword." Xian pointed to the handle of his Katana. "I won't attack anyone."

"Please, Iain, be sensible." Siobhan's tone softened a wee bit. "These men, one of whom is my husband, are not dangerous. You are dismissed. Thank you."

Henderson trudged out, his military stance slumping a fraction.

"Sensible lad," Rory watched the soldier walk away.

"Food," Xian said.

"Aye," Rory responded then turned to Siobhan. "Have you eaten today?"

Siobhan shook her head. "I need a shower more than food. But you eat."

She walked down the short corridor to a room and Rory followed her in. It had a bed and a wardrobe but was otherwise bare apart from boxes stacked by a desk. Siobhan stood in front of a dresser, her face beaming. He pulled her close and kissed her, savouring the warmth of her lips. She tasted of dust.

"Be packed and ready to go at a moment's notice," he whispered when he'd lifted his mouth from hers.

She blinked. "Okay." Her voice was soft velvet.

Oh man, he wanted to take her to bed right here and now. But Murray and Xian waited in the kitchen, and he was sure the Government monitored every inch of this place. Maybe he was just being paranoid.

"You eat. I'll shower. Then we'll talk." She slid out of his embrace and walked through the door. He followed her as far as the kitchen. Their guard was back.

"Henderson!" she said.

"Ms K—Mrs Campbell, it's the First Minister's orders, ma'am." Henderson swallowed.

"Well, you're not eating our dinner," Murray said, serving casserole onto four plates lined up on the bench.

Siobhan walked the other way along the corridor.

"Here, Rory." Xian nudged him with a plate of food. "Eat."

Rory tore his vision from Siobhan's retreating back.

He sat down at the table. The chicken had an odd taste about it. *Chemical preservatives*, Xian had said. Siobhan returned before they'd finished their second helpings. She wore a clean skirt and blouse, and a towel wrapped round her wet hair. The perfume of flowers filled the kitchen area.

"Henderson, make yourself useful and find some clean clothes for these men who have travelled all the way from the Highlands," Siobhan ordered. "They'll need them once they've showered."

Murray chewed his lips, repressing a grin while Henderson stomped off once more.

"Love the way she does that," Rory said, his chest heating.

Other parts were heating too.

A shower was definitely on the agenda, along with removing his wife from this place as soon as he was able.

Chapter Thirteen

Scottish Government Bunker, 2061

Next to Rory at the kitchen table, Siobhan was eating her dinner at last. Murray washed the dirty dishes and cooking utensils while Xian wiped them dry. Murray's voice drifted over to Rory as he directed the older man to the cupboards in which the utensils belonged.

Siobhan's cheeks glowed fresh, and she'd tucked her hair in its usual roll at the back of her head, exposing the soft line of her neck. Rory suppressed a groan. How he'd love to take his time loosening that hair. But they had to get out of here, and she was coming with them.

"We'll go soon," he whispered into her ear. The perfume that was unmistakably her, filled his nostrils—filled his mind. "We'll get some sleep first, Aye?"

Siobhan's chewing stopped, then she blinked.

"Rory, there's not much privacy here," she whispered back.

He raised his eyebrows. Murray's directions to Xian filled the kitchen space.

"There's something I need to do," her whispering continued.

"Aye, lass, there's something *we* need to do." He curled a brow.

Siobhan squeezed her mouth, suppressing a smile.

"What?" he asked.

"We've already done that today... several times," she said, then a grin burst through.

"What!" Rory sat straighter. "When—?"

Siobhan's finger at his mouth stopped him short. Murray and Xian paused in their post meal task. The clatter of dishes and clanking of cooking pots soon resumed.

She leaned in closer to Rory, her deep-blue eyes like midnight in the dim LED.

"There are some things I must research in our archives before we leave," she said. "It's vital information."

Rory held back all the questions he could ask her about the future. None would pass his lips while they were in this place.

The click of heels on the concrete floor rang along the corridor and Siobhan spun in her chair.

"Hi, Louise," Siobhan said, then placed her unfinished plate of chicken casserole on the table.

"I just wanted you to know the First Minister is on her way." Louise looked straight at Siobhan, avoiding Rory's stare, her mouth skewed to the side.

Bethany marched in their direction with two armed soldiers either side of her. Dark hair, dark suit, and a dark expression. Louise sidled to stand beside Siobhan at the kitchen table. Siobhan stood and Rory followed her lead.

"Siobhan," Bethany spoke to Siobhan, passing her vision over Rory. "I hope your guests will be comfortable. Louise has arranged rooms nearby for their use."

"Thank you, First Minister," Siobhan said. "I was hoping to show my husband around. Is that okay with you?"

"Yes, but only in the general access areas." Bethany clipped her reply and straightened her shoulders.

"Certainly." Siobhan sounded defensive. "I mainly wanted to show him our extensive archives."

"Oh, very good," Bethany said, her rigid posture seemed to relax a wee bit.

"Must an armed guard escort us?" Siobhan asked. She slipped her hand into Rory's, glancing at Henderson for a second. "We're entirely safe, I assure you."

Bethany's stare lingered on their clasped hands.

"You know I am here in friendship," Rory said. "I just want to be with my wife, First Minister. I'm nae going to start a revolution. In fact, I want the opposite. I, and my people, are *for* Scotland, not against her."

Bethany flicked her head and brushed away an imaginary hair from her perfectly neat hairdo. "Well, maybe you and I can have some discussion while you are here, Mr Campbell?"

"I'd like that, First Minister. Very much." Rory forced a smile, endeavouring to make the diplomatic expression touch his eyes.

Bethany turned to leave.

"Henderson can go then?" Siobhan asked Bethany's back.

The First Minister of Scotland nodded to Henderson standing at attention by the kitchen bench, watching the post meal tidy-up. He narrowed his gaze at Xian then strode out behind Bethany and the others. Louise's mouth drew in at one corner as she bobbed her head to Siobhan and followed the First Minister and her guard.

"Man, she needs to get laid or something," Xian said.

"I think the *something's* more likely," Rory said under his breath.

"Hmm." Siobhan's brow crinkled in the middle. "She's being a bit heavy-handed."

"A *bit*?" Rory said.

"Where are the children?" Xian asked, as though the thought had just occurred to him. "I haven't seen any." He fiddled with the tea towel.

"With their parents," Siobhan replied. She scraped the remains of her unfinished meal into the bin then slipped the plate into the sink. "This is the singles' quarters."

"Where do they get to run around?" Xian looked past the kitchen.

"In their play area," Siobhan answered.

"There aren't many kids." Murray stopped wiping the benches with a wet cloth and scowled at Siobhan's dirty plate in the sink. "At least, I've never seen more than a small group of children at a time. It's like they don't believe in them."

"Let's go," Siobhan said, and clasped Rory's hand then tugged him out of the kitchen.

"Can I come?" Murray asked from the sink.

"Of course," Siobhan said over her shoulder.

"Where're we going?" Xian followed them along the corridor.

"You'll love this place." Murray stepped in behind them. "Full o' stuff from every decade going right back to the 1800s, in an orderly fashion. And things, not so organised, from every time else. Plus, the stuff they rescued from libraries and museums. There's even a mummy."

Siobhan marched them to a main corridor and led them to two silver shiny doors where a guard stood. Siobhan pushed a button and smiled at Rory as the double doors slid apart to reveal a small room. Rory took a step back.

"You've never seen a lift before?" Siobhan's expression was a mixture of disbelief and amusement.

Rory shook his head.

"Wow," Xian said behind him.

"Come in." She pulled Rory into the box-like place, and Xian and Murray followed.

"What happens now?" he asked.

The doors closed with a clunk then Siobhan pressed one of the many buttons on the wall beside the door.

The floor moved. No, the whole box moved. Then Rory's feet and head gave him the sensation of falling. He grabbed the rail.

"It's okay, Rory," Siobhan said. "We're going down." Siobhan stepped close to him, put her arms around his waist, and pressed her body against his.

"You've never been in a lift?" Xian asked. "I have, as a very young child. It's fun, yeah?"

"No." Rory's stomach moved up inside him.

"We're here," Murray said. "Almost at the bottom of the Bunker." His eyes were wide, and he bounced when the lift came to a halt. "They've got very early model computers too."

The doors slid open.

"We're going this way," Siobhan said, releasing her hold on Rory.

He hurried out. Siobhan walked out of the lift, crooking a finger at Murray.

"I need your research skills," she said.

"What are we—?" Murray began.

A finger over Siobhan's lips silenced everyone.

They followed her down a short passage. To the left was an entry and a sign stating *Archives* sat above the double doorway. Rory glanced in. Sections headed *1900s, 1910s* and so on, flowed down the long narrow corridor. Siobhan led them to their right, to an atrium that opened to an enormous area with high ceilings. Bookshelves lined the walls, and ladders reached to the very top of them. More rows of tall, double-sided bookshelves filled the rest of this room except for where glass cases held objects.

"See? I told ya." Murray pointed to a large case as they marched past. "A mummy."

"Come on, Murray," Siobhan called then whispered, "we're going to the Geological History area."

Siobhan walked them through a few rooms identical to the first one, then turned down a brief corridor to an area with computers on desks, bookshelves, rock samples in glass-topped display cabinets, and a large table with a stack of paper in the centre.

"Rocks?" Xian asked. "We're looking at dirt?"

Siobhan strode to the table where a thick wad of smooth, shiny paper sat next to some pencils, and sat down to write. Murray sat by a computer and turned it on.

"What are we looking for, Siobhan?" Murray twisted in his chair to face her.

Siobhan glared at him and waved the pencil in her hand, then pointed for them to read what she'd written, again placing a finger against her lips.

Rory leaned over her shoulder and read.

Sorry, guys, especially Murray, but we can't use the computer. They may check the search history and wonder what we're up to. So, it's the good old-fashioned way. Please look for anything on large volcanic eruptions that have affected the weather and climate adversely.

Murray stood up from the computer chair and moaned, then strolled over to the table and read—then groaned. Xian frowned, biting his lower lip, then walked to the nearest bookshelf and started looking at the titles on the spines of the books.

Something tugged at Rory's mind. A flash of a dimmed sky flitted through his thoughts. He took the pencil from Siobhan.

What happens in the future? he wrote. *A volcanic eruption? Is that why you came back a mess?*

Siobhan picked up another pencil from the holder on the table and wrote:

Yes and no. Things happen because of a volcanic explosion, but I won't discuss it here. When we get home, we'll talk. But I need to gather all the information I can while we have access to this library.

Siobhan had written *when we get home*. Warmth swelled within Rory and the corner of his mouth tightened. Man, he wanted her home, but standing here staring at those beautiful eyes wouldn't get them there. He tossed the pencil on the table and wandered to the bookshelves. He ran fingers down the smooth spines of the volumes on a few rows until he came to the same place where Xian now stood reading a book. Xian pointed his chin at the shelf at waist-height. Rory leaned down and read the titles.

Aye, the volcano shelf.

Chapter Fourteen

Scottish Government Bunker, 2061

Rory's eyes were dry and gritty, and the night had passed with each of them presenting information to Siobhan, but she was not pleased with any of it. His back ached and the air was stale—not a fresh breeze had stirred, and there was a dull continual hum.

"What are you look—?" Rory began.

Siobhan interrupted Rory with a violent shake of her head.

Rory put down the textbook he'd shown her and scribbled a big question mark in the middle of the piece of paper on the large table.

Siobhan expelled a loud sigh and reached for the corner of the page, then wrote. Rory and the others bent down to read.

Volcanic eruption—northern hemisphere covered in ash—poor sunlight—harvests fail.

She grabbed the eraser and scrubbed out her writing.

Rory did a double take. He'd seen this. His most recent vision—a walk through scraggly crops. He found it hard to inhale, and not just because of the recycled air.

So, it was a true vision.

"Ahh—" Murray held up a finger. "Dendrochronology."

"Shh!" Rory chorused with Siobhan.

Murray spread his hands. "What?" he asked. "They're not gonna know—"

"Shh!" Siobhan hissed, then pointed to the shelves of books.

Murray thrust his index finger at the nearest computer.

She glared a *no*.

Murray wrote next to the large question mark on the sheet of paper:

Do you want to know or not? I could spend hours looking up what I'm thinking might be the answer, or I could search it on the Government's extensive database on that computer and have your answer in seconds.

Siobhan's shoulders sank a little, then she gave the slightest nod.

"Yes!" Murray hissed, then ran over to the computer and clicked the keyboard.

Rory left the table to stand behind Murray and peered over his shoulder. Siobhan and Xian joined him. Murray's fingers flew across the keys, the unfamiliar clicking jarring to Rory's ears. Pictures of trees cut through to expose their growth rings flicked on the screen. Murray turned to Siobhan, pointed at the screen then stepped away from the computer desk, offering her the chair. She grabbed a piece of paper from the table and, returning to the computer, wrote for at least twenty minutes. Rory wandered over to the table and thumbed through each piece of thin manufactured paper, which was nothing like the chunky pieces they made at the community. He removed any sheets on which they'd written, and the ones underneath that had impressions left from writing on the pages above and, after tearing them into tiny pieces, dropped them into the nearest bin.

Rory folded his arms in front of him. So, a volcano had caused a disaster in the future.

Cold, like the deep, dark water of Loch Ness, collected in his gut. He needed more details. How could they plan for this? Everyone should be informed to prepare for such an event, but telling the Scottish Government was out. No way was he going to let them know the Time Machine had worked.

Siobhan scooted her chair back and stood, turning both hands in a thumbs-up sign.

She pointed to Murray, then the computer and mouthed, *Delete the search history*.

Rory stepped over to Siobhan, slipped his arm around her waist and pulled her to himself.

"You understand we can't speak of it while we are here." Siobhan's whisper was as quiet as a moor at midnight. "If we're overheard, it may be misconstrued, and I'd never be able to explain myself fully without... exposing *you know what*." She mouthed her last words.

"We can go now, aye?" he asked just as quietly.

She touched her warm cheek against his, it was as soft as thistledown. "Yes, but we must leave on good terms," she whispered into his ear. "And have a conversation with Bethany promising we'll speak to all the various groups and Communities in Scotland, encouraging them to co-operate with the Scottish Government. We'll be ambassadors for peace and communication. Please be on your best behaviour and don't antagonise the woman like you did on your arrival."

Rory pulled back; his forehead tight in a frown. "How do you ken what my meeting with Bethany was like?" he asked.

"You told me." Her mouth clamped shut, unsuccessfully preventing a grin.

He blinked.

Och, I have to find out what I did with her in the future.

They walked in silence back through the archives and into the lift. This time, Rory's feet pressed into the floor of the lift, and his head and arms dragged down. He clutched the rail. Siobhan took his other hand, her lips curving at the corners.

"It's sweet," she said, her eyes twinkling.

"What is?" Rory asked. The doors slid open, and Rory's stomach wasn't sure whether to go up or down.

"Big strong man, scared of tiny lift."

"I'm not afraid."

Siobhan stayed by his side when he flew out of the lift, then they walked to her room. The aroma of fried bacon wafted down the hall toward them.

"Breakfast?" Xian yawned. "What time is it?"

"Time to eat and go," Rory said quietly as they approached the kitchen.

"Oh, good morning." Louise stood at the cooker, bacon sizzling, and eggs popping in the fat. "You must have enjoyed your tour of the archives. I was getting worried."

"It was fascinating,' Xian said. "We got lost among all that knowledge."

"Is it too early to meet with the First Minister?" Rory asked.

"No, I can book an appointment soon," Siobhan said. She took the plates of fried breakfast Louise was handing to her. "Thank you, Louise." She placed them on the table, indicating for Rory and Xian to sit and eat.

"She's free this morning. Or she'll make herself free," Louise said as she dished up the rest of the bacon and eggs then placed more into the hot pan. "It's not every day she gets to speak with one of the important leaders in Scotland."

Rory sat at the table and swallowed. Louise was talking about *him*. He would be at his best today and politely ask for permission to leave with Siobhan. It worked with Lloyd, surely it would work on Bethany-stuck-up-Watts.

"Rory?" Angela's voice, accompanied by her brisk footsteps, came from behind him. She stopped and hovered by the table.

Rory stabbed the fried egg on his plate. The runny yolk oozed out its yellow and spread through his breakfast. He stood.

"Angela, lovely to see you. How are you?" Rory offered her a kiss on the cheek.

"What are you doing here?" Angela turned her face away.

His lips met air.

"I'm here to collect my wife and return home with her." Rory stepped back and crossed his arms over his chest.

"You'll not be taking the Time Machine. I know that in some deluded way you believe you have a right to it." Angela's hand flew to her hip. "They won't let you."

"Who said anything about the Time Machine?" Murray said from where he sat at the table.

Louise had placed a fresh plate of fried eggs and bacon in front of Murray, and beside him Xian sat motionless.

"It doesn't work anyway," Rory said low and firm. "So what use is it here?"

"If it's not working, why take it back?" Angela said. Her bright red hair had a glow of its own under the LED.

"Because it belongs to us, not the Government." Rory leaned into his sister, clenching his fists tucked under his armpits.

"Have you got it to work?" Angela asked Murray.

Murray coughed around bacon, then swallowed. "No," he said and stared at his plate.

Angela's eyes narrowed. "They'll no' let Murray go." There was victory in her voice.

Rory squinted.

"Ah, I don't want to leave, Rory. Sorry." Murray made a tight smile. "Computers and all that. Is that okay?" he asked.

"For the moment," Rory answered.

"It's not up to you. You're not the boss around here." Angela's hand on her hip curled into a fist.

"I'm well aware of that, sister," Rory said. "I even have to ask permission to take my wife home."

And that still smarts.

"Isn't it a nice surprise to see your brother, Angela?" Siobhan asked.

Siobhan, always the diplomat.

Angela's head twitched. It could have been an acknowledgement. Rory accepted it as such.

"Well, I'll be on my way then," Angela said. "Plenty to do and learn here where true government takes place." Angela flicked her hair over her shoulder, then spun and walked along the corridor, her brisk tread not slowing until she turned into the stairwell and was gone.

Chapter Fifteen

Scottish Government Bunker, 2061

B reakfast was over and Siobhan leaned against the kitchen bench.
"Xian, find out where the horses are and see if they're okay." Rory stepped closer to his friend then whispered, "Get 'em ready to leave, aye?"

Xian gave a short nod.

Siobhan warmed at the closeness between Rory and his crew. On their journey to Loch Ewe and back they were faithful and loyal, and seemed like they'd do anything for him. And not just for their community, because here was Xian, in a potentially hostile situation, helping Rory bring her home.

"We'd better get to the First Minister," Siobhan said. "She doesn't like tardiness."

Siobhan took Rory's hand. Dark shadows sat beneath his eyes. He'd journeyed a week to be here, yet he was determined they'd leave today, if they could. Siobhan would do everything possible to make sure it happened.

***

Bethany's secretary was at her desk and Iain Henderson stood by the door to the First Minister's office. Iain nodded to Siobhan as she approached then kept his gaze on Rory beside her. Iain was a good man and his sticking to orders the previous evening hadn't surprised Siobhan, just irritated.

"Iain, the First Minister is expecting us," she said.

Siobhan smoothed her cargo pants and Iain opened the door.

Bethany sat in the high-backed desk chair that always dwarfed her. She was writing vigorously on the paper on her desk. The dark-rimmed spectacles resting on the tip of her nose made her appear the intelligent woman she was.

"Good morning, First Minister." Siobhan walked in with Rory a pace behind.

Bethany lifted her attention from her paperwork. "I hear you've spent the night in our archives," she said.

"Aye," Rory said, then moved to stand beside Siobhan, taking her hand in his. "What you dinnae have in there is nae worth the knowing, I expect."

"Did you find what you were looking for?" Bethany leaned back into her chair and directed her piercing gaze at Siobhan.

"We weren't looking for anything in particular," Siobhan said. "Our guests found it enthralling, and we lost track of time."

Bethany stood and walked to the front of her desk. "What can I do for you?" she asked.

"First Minister," Rory said in calm tones, "I wish to leave today and take my wife with me."

Moisture from Rory's hand pressed onto Siobhan's.

Bethany looked from Rory to Siobhan, her expression hard. Despite growing up with the woman, Siobhan found her just as hard to read.

Please, say yes, Bethany. What would her new husband would do if Bethany said no?

Siobhan's pulse thudding in her head drowned out the strained silence in the office. Siobhan stared at the mini saltire flag badge in the lapel of Bethany's neatly pressed suit.

"I don't like unpleasantness. I try to avoid it at all costs," Bethany broke the silence. "Mr Campbell rightly pointed out that no one is indispensable, and you have trained Louise well, Siobhan." Bethany paused, so Siobhan dared to look her in the eye. "With reluctance, I'm giving permission."

"Thank you, First Minister." Siobhan stood taller, the tension easing in her neck. Rory gave a brief squeeze to her hand clasped in his. "Rory and I will do the Government proud as we liaise with the groups out there. We'll report back to you regularly. We shall go as soon as I'm packed—"

Bethany held up her hand. "As most of your possessions belong to the Scottish Government," Bethany said, "you can take what you can carry, nothing more." She gestured to Rory. "Mr Campbell, your brother and the Time Machine, despite its non-functioning status, will remain here."

Rory's hand tightened around hers. Siobhan glanced up at him; the muscles in his jaw tensed, then Rory made a sharp nod.

"Well, I'd better pack. Goodbye, Bethany." Siobhan stepped forward and gave Bethany a hug, which she returned with coolness. Siobhan left the room with Rory, a dull ache within her at the confirmation of a lifelong friend's withdrawal of affection.

***

"And those bags there," Siobhan told Rory, pointing to the blue bags by her dresser.

"It's what *you* can carry, not what every man travelling with you plus the horses can carry." Rory had tucked a bag under each arm and held one in each hand.

"Rory, they're my things. My father's things. Not the Scottish Government's. They're all I have left of him." She stifled a choke.

Rory returned the bags to the floor, then put his arms around her.

"I ken this is a considerable move for you, Siobhan," he said. "I cannae tell you how much it means to me that you will leave everything for me." He spoke into her hair, his warmth surrounding her, chasing away the niggle of doubt threatening to creep in. "I'm humbled"—he swallowed— "you feel this way about me. That you trust me with yourself and your future. I promise I'll keep you safe and you'll no' regret it."

Rory's deep voice rumbled through his warm chest. The choke eased, coinciding with her welling feelings for Rory. She clung to him; her arms wrapped around his solid waist.

How much of the future should she tell him? Could she speak of her death? He'd probably insist she stay safe in the Bunker with its superior medical care. But Rory could never live here, he would not survive. Where would that leave them? Not living a married life, that's for sure. A shudder ran through her at the recollection of a broken Rory weeping into her neck. She wouldn't do it to Rory—couldn't let him get like that. If she told him she'd died in the future she went to, he'd try to fix it. But who can fix death?

He need not know at all. He would have enough on his mind with a famine and a civil war to prevent.

She'd snuck away during the night, feigning the need for the ladies' room. The medical section of the archives wasn't far from the public toilets. She'd found an obstetrics book published in 2011 and had written down all she could about placenta previa.

She would go to the Bunker when she was pregnant with their second child. That was her plan—and it would work.

"You all right, Siobhan?" Rory loosened his hold on her. "Can you finish packing now?"

"Yes," she dropped her arms from around him, and he began collecting the bags and tucking them under his arms again.

Murray came to her door. "Can I help?" he asked.

Rory pointed to bags, which Murray picked up.

"You've got a pack horse with you, yeah?" Murray asked.

"Yes, we have," Xian said from the door. He had a disgusted look on his face.

Rory's brow creased at Xian's expression. "Where are the horses?" he asked.

"They kept them in the garage," Xian replied. "They've no right to complain about the manure on their concrete."

"We've got to get out o' here." Rory glanced down at her. "No offence, Siobhan, but this is no place to be." He leaned closer and kissed her forehead. "Come, let me take you to where it's really livin'. Where everywhere you look is full o' beauty, wildness, and wisdom. Where the wind blows through you and your soul comes alive. Where ye can be truly free, *mo chroí.*" He tilted his head, and she followed him out.

Wild and free with little technology—living it rough. Such a change from the comforts of the Bunker. The niggle of doubt threatened again as she followed Rory's broad back.

No, she could do it. Would do it. She'd do anything to be with this man.

Siobhan said farewell to everyone she passed. Louise stood at the stairwell, her eyes red. She flung her arms around Siobhan.

"Keep in touch, Siobhan." She sniffed. "I'll miss you."

"Me too," Siobhan said into their hug. "I'll CB you as much as I can. Don't forget me."

"I won't. Bethany wasn't going to let you go, but meeting Rory made her realise how strongly he feels about you. Then she saw you together, and she knew it was mutual. Well, only a fool would try to keep that sort of love apart." Louise gave a nervous laugh before releasing Siobhan from her hug. "That's what she said, anyway."

Through the stairwell, soldiers stood nearby with their weapons in their hands. They followed them to the maintenance garages. Siobhan tried to gain eye contact with the men and women in uniform, but each one averted their eyes.

"We are being farewelled in the same manner we were greeted," Rory said over his shoulder.

"That's ridiculous." *They don't trust my husband?* There was *so* much work to do on the Government's relationship with the Communities.

Henderson stood by the horses. Boy whinnied and snorted when Rory approached. Rory placed Siobhan's bags on the ground, avoiding the horse droppings, and patted his stallion who soon settled at the music of Rory's deep rumblings in Gaelic. Siobhan released a warm sigh at the special relationship Rory had with his animal. She'd have to become accustomed to horses. The largest animals the Bunker husbanded were sheep. Standing next to Boy were a packhorse and two saddled horses.

"Oh," she said.

"*Oh?*" Rory turned to her. "That's your horse, Siobhan." He indicated to the smaller of the two.

Siobhan's armpits were on their way to being as damp as Rory's palms had been in Bethany's office.

"You'll be fine, lass," Rory said. "It's a long way home. You'll be an expert by the time we get there."

"Are you sure about that?" she asked. "It may not be far enough."

Rory chuckled, and Xian smiled as they both loaded most of her things onto the packhorse, and the rest on the horse she would ride.

"Well, brother," Rory said to Murray. "Dinnae ken when I'll see you again. You be careful, aye? And say goodbye to that loving sister of ours." He pulled Murray toward him and enveloped him in a hug.

Murray said goodbye then turned away from Rory, his eyes moist.

"Come here, little brother, give your sister-in-law a kiss goodbye," Siobhan said, and drew Murray into a hug. He seemed so young, yet what a sensible lad he was. "Keep it a secret," she whispered into his ear.

"You know it's safe with me." His voice was even lower. "One day you'll tell me about it, yeah? And what will happen."

"Yes, keep close to the meteorologists and geologists," she whispered back.

"My next best friends," Murray said. "I'll keep you posted."

"Are we going?" Xian asked. He spoke with impatience, something Siobhan had never heard from this gentle Chinese man.

"Aye, I'd hate to keep all these armed soldiers waiting," Rory said, then waved Siobhan to her horse and boosted her into the saddle. He handed her the reins. "Remember what to do?"

"Yes, but..." Siobhan cringed.

"Och, give 'em back," he said, indicating the reins. "I'll lead until you're a bit more confident."

He tossed the reins over the horse's head and held on to them while he mounted Boy. Siobhan on her horse trailed behind Rory, and the packhorse followed Xian. They walked their mounts up the ramp to daylight, shadowed all the way by the soldiers. The gate rumbled open, and they rode out.

Siobhan took one last look at the up-ground compound of the Scottish Government Bunker. The next time she planned to see it, she'd be pregnant and asking for assistance.

Chapter Sixteen

Scottish Government Bunker, 2061

Clanking cutlery and the hum of mealtime echoed out of the mess hall where Bethany's staff were having their lunch. She strode down the corridor to the lifts, clutching a file, relying on the hubbub of meal-time conversation to cover her exit. Once inside the lift, she pressed the button to the level that held the Bunker's detainment cells, hugged the file to her chest... and sighed.

She and Siobhan had grown up together. Not *besties,* as other girls in the Bunker had been, but being part of the children of the *elite* and growing up in this place forged friendships that may never have happened if the world hadn't changed.

Siobhan had changed. It had been subtle at first, then she never denied it. Siobhan's obsession with drone footage, her eagerness to go with the team to deal with the nuclear threat at Loch Ewe, and now her insistence on being the one to liaise with the Communities, all displayed her bias toward those *up top*. Antony saw it too.

He was correct and Siobhan had aligned herself with that stunning young man, Rory Campbell, and married him, all in the name of friendship.

It was a political choreography designed to unite Government and Community—or so it seemed.

Siobhan's sympathies for Community life reflected her own rebellion, Antony had said.

They should watch her. She was an ignorant spy unintentionally providing the intelligence while she slept with the enemy, he had also said.

So why do I feel like a Judas?

Antony was right. She hadn't believed him at first, but during their conversations in confidence he'd produced compelling arguments that had caused her to doubt Siobhan and the intentions of people who lived the Community way of life. Antony was intelligent, but a little damaged—in an appealing sort of way.

She would've stuck to her refusal to let Siobhan go, but Antony had been insistent. It offered an opportunity to monitor things *up-top* so much closer than a drone.

The lift opened, the young guard saluted then she strode past him to Antony's cell. Weights and a bench-press ran along the far wall next to his desk. An open notebook and Aristotle's *Politics: A Treatise on Government* lay on the desk and a pile of books sat on the floor.

Antony was waiting for her—he always was.

He leaned forward on his bunk, dark eyes wide and unblinking, his cheek's angry scar from the bite he'd received from his bandit accomplice at Loch Ewe, was fading to pink.

She sat on the stool opposite the bars and settled the file on her lap.

"Are the bugs in place?" he asked.

Not even a *hello?*

"Yes, Grasby is amazing," she replied. "He can make the tiniest things from all that old tech."

Antony flicked a finger at the contents of her lap.

"What have you got for me?" he asked. "What did the self-appointed *clan chief* get up to while he was here?"

***

A camouflage vehicle followed them through the suburbs of Edinburgh. Rory rode in silence with Xian beside him and Siobhan riding stiff-saddled behind them both. The locals didn't pester them like they had on their way into Edinburgh. Perhaps it was the covered jeep tailing them that deterred trouble. It was an escort of the rear-guard kind—or a surety they did exit Edinburgh. Either way, Rory didn't lose sight of the vehicle until they were well on the road and close to the Kincardine Bridge.

"Okay," Xian said once they were clear of houses and other company. "I don't expect you to tell me everything, Rory. I trust you implicitly and I decided a long time ago, that unless it caused imminent danger, I would let you do your thing, and I would do what you required of me." He paused, twisted in the saddle to glance around at Siobhan. "I'm sure you are definitely in on this too, Mrs Campbell. Usually"—he turned back to face Rory— "I'd let it go. But you've been talking major disaster with your researching volcanic explosions, and, man, like, I need to know."

The horses' rhythmic treads on the rubble of a road turning to dirt was the sole sound for a while. Ahead, the tree-covered hills were rising; behind these were the grey-brown of the Highlands, now capped in white—and home. Siobhan had implied the volcanic eruption would threaten it all.

And he'd had a vision of it.

The means of obtaining a look into the future was closed knowledge. Xian had never been privy to the existence of a time machine. Angela had let it slip over breakfast, but Xian hadn't commented—yet.

"He doesn't know, does he?" Siobhan asked from behind him.

Rory shook his head. "Och, no. Very few do."

"I think it's about time your friend did," she said. "He's a valuable part of your team, and we'll need all the help we can get."

Xian looked back at Siobhan then again to Rory. "Well?" he asked.

"Dinnae look at me, Xian." Rory lifted his chin in Siobhan's direction. "She has nae even told me the full story yet."

"In the near future," Siobhan began, "Mount Vesuvius will erupt—"

"Wait. Pompeii Mount Vesuvius?" Xian asked. "That one?"

Rory turned in his saddle, then pulled the reins of Siobhan's horse until she was up close and between himself and Xian. She clutched the pommel of the saddle at the horse's sudden trot.

"Continue, lass." Rory raised his eyebrows.

Siobhan steadied herself in the saddle. "Yes, the very same," she said. "For years, volcanologists have been expecting it to erupt again and on the same scale as the time it wiped out Pompeii. In a few years, it will spew so much volcanic ash into the atmosphere that it will block the sun's light to a degree that will cause the sky to darken, and crops to fail. There will be—"

"What?" Xian interrupted again, his brow in a knot, and his intense stare boring into Siobhan. "Where did you get this information from?"

"…a famine," Siobhan continued without answering Xian, emphasising the word to describe the nature of the future disaster. "A similar situation occurred during the Dark Ages, 536 AD, actually. A volcano, or possibly several, erupted, and it affected most of Europe. Their histories describe it as *a long winter*, or *failure of bread*. Either way, it was bad, and it will happen again and affect us up here in Scotland."

Xian's mouth had remained open after his previous questions.

Rory swallowed. Wasn't a world-wide stock market crash, which changed things forever, enough? Or periodic nuclear explosions?

Apparently not.

"So, you were covered in ash?" Rory turned to her.

She looked awkward. "No, that was… something else."

Rory's throat dried while many possibilities ran through his mind, all of them *bad*.

"I'll tell you later," Siobhan said.

"Ye had better," Rory said, his neck muscles twinging with their tightness. "My imagination's workin' overtime here."

"I got back okay, Rory." Siobhan reached over and placed her hand on his arm. "That's all that matters."

He glanced at her small hand on his forearm then covered it with his own, the warmth of both seeping into his skin. She was with him now, and he would never be without her again.

Ever.

"Got back from where?" Xian's deep brown eyes turned on Rory.

The man had a right to know. The trust on which they based their friendship was in jeopardy if he didn't tell Xian. Rory sighed.

"We, at the Invercharing Community, developed a time machine," he said. "It works—most of the time. My father used it. I've used it twice. Yesterday, Siobhan accidentally travelled to the future and back."

The telling of this secret somehow gave him a sense of release. Xian was now one less significant person in his life from whom he'd have to hide the truth.

Xian double blinked then stared ahead, silent.

"When the Government came to assist us with the submarine and the nuclear issue, they took it back with them," Rory continued. "Against my wishes. That's why Murray went. He kens how to use the thing." Rory stopped talking. Xian was too quiet. "You okay, Xian?"

Xian rocked with the movement of his horse's gait, staring ahead, and began to nod.

"Yes, Rory Campbell, and for some strange reason I believe you," Xian replied. "When I consider it, it explains some weird things about you that never made sense until now."

"Who are those men?" Siobhan pointed off to the left where riders on horseback stood on a hill beside the road, their observation of them obvious.

Xian squinted. Rory rummaged in his saddlebag for his binoculars.

"Bandits," Xian said. "But I think they're friendly."

"You mean Micah McNair?" Siobhan asked.

Rory halted his rummaging. "How do you ken about him?" he asked.

Siobhan grimaced, her eyes flicking back and forth. "You told me about him." Her voice wavered.

"In the future?" Rory narrowed his eyes.

Siobhan nodded.

"So, we'll be friends with bandits?" Xian asked. "This may be a good thing."

"*We'll* be related to Micah McNair," Siobhan said, looking sideways at Rory.

"Cèilidh," Rory whispered, and Siobhan gave a slight nod.

The riders picked their way down the hill then cantered along the road to them. Micah's face was full of that smug smile.

"Greetings, friends." Micah pulled up in front of Rory and his gaze landed on Siobhan. "And hello to you, Mrs Campbell."

"Micah, nice to meet you," Siobhan replied.

Rory slid his glance from Micah to Siobhan. She didn't need to be *that* civil to the guy.

"Why're you here?" Rory's question came through a rough voice.

"Now, be nice," Micah said, tilting his head to the side with an exaggerated hurt expression on his face. "I'm gonna save your arse, again." The smug smile returned.

Irritation twirled its finger in the back of Rory's mind and came out in his tone.

"How?" he asked.

"I'm gonna get you over the bridge," Micah said. "Maybe without even paying a tax."

Something else bothered Rory, not just Micah's self-assurance.

"You've been waiting for us?" he asked.

"Aye, and you didn't stay for long," Micah replied. "Holiday accommodations not to your liking, Rory? Or just in a hurry to get your wee wifey home, hey?" Micah's eyebrows wiggled.

"What do you want?" Rory said firmly, ignoring Micah's insinuation.

"Look, man, I just wanna help," Micah said. His horse moved its head, jingling its tack. "Make it easier for us all to get home." He looked at Siobhan and widened his eyes for a second while tilting his chin in her direction.

Micah seemed to be hinting that his father seeing Siobhan could be a danger for her. Cold flashed through Rory at the implications. She was in her forties, but still a beauty. It was true Micah was a way of getting over the Kincardine Bridge and slipping through Lloyd's trawl-net without it catching Siobhan. If that's what Micah was implying.

"Okay," Rory said. He would just have to trust Micah.

"Okay?" Micah's brows lifted for only a moment. "Good." He spun his horse and cantered ahead.

Chapter Seventeen

The Kingdom of Fife

Micah rode ahead of Rory, his long, blond dreadlocks were bound loosely behind his head. With the half dozen bandits who travelled with him, Micah led the way to the Kincardine Bridge. Lloyd's men were on this side of the bridge by a shed where people handed over taxes of cash, livestock, non-perishable foods, and objects that could be useful items in exchange for passage over the bridge.

Rory reached behind him and touched the stock of his handgun tucked in his belt, firm beneath his fingertips and reassuringly present. He nudged Boy on, following Micah's group, and joined the queue that shuffled forward. Rory scanned the line of travellers and once again, apart from Lloyd's guards, he was among the only ones overtly armed. Rory glanced at Siobhan who sat silent on her horse watching everything.

"Which way did you come when you left us to return to the Bunker?" he asked.

"We crossed this bridge," she replied. "It's the only way you can get a tank over the Forth. But we never encountered this."

Rory raised his eyebrows, pointing at the rickety structure. "You took a tank over that?"

Lloyd must have heard in advance and cleared it of his men and toll booths, not wanting the Government to discover his enterprise.

Micah dismounted to talk to one of the guards. Their conversation was heated, with Micah pointing his finger in the older man's face. The guard never flinched. Micah raised his voice, his face darkening. Bright spots appeared on the older guard's cheeks, and he straightened his stance.

"Why do we need Micah's assistance?" Siobhan asked.

"His father is in control of all of Fife, at least, and more," Rory said. "Nobody, and I mean, no body, gets across the bridge without his permission." Rory adjusted his seat, his saddle and stirrup leather creaking. "We met him on the way down."

"You could call it that," Xian said.

Siobhan cocked an eyebrow at Rory.

"Och, he gave us some accommodation which we didn't require, or ask for," he said.

"He imprisoned you?" Siobhan's expression was one of alarm.

"Aye, detained overnight." Rory fiddled with the reins. "He was a wee bit curious about us."

"About you, Rory," Xian threw over his shoulder then returned to study Micah locked in conversation with the solid-looking guard.

"Who is his father?" Siobhan asked.

"You may have heard of him," Rory said. "Derrick Lloyd is an important guy around here."

Siobhan's face had gone pale and her hands grasping the pommel of her saddle blanched white. Cool ran its fingers down Rory's spine. His woman had been to the future, and her pallor coincided with the mention of *that* man's name.

"Siobh—" Rory began.

"Okay!" Micah's raised voice rang back to Rory. Micah was now nose-to-nose with the older guard.

"Mr Lloyd wishes to see you and your companions immediately on your return, Micah." The guard's voice, raised even louder, travelled down the queue.

Micah spun away from the man and stomped toward Rory, the bandit leader's nostrils flaring. Rory leaned forward in the saddle to angle closer for Micah's report.

"Rory, I did all I could, but we've got to see my dad," he whispered. "Sorry, man, no way round it. Your woman's from the Government, aye? You could make him feel important and say they want to hold talks with him, or somethin'. He'd like that. And she'll be safe. He can't take her once he knows she's Government. She's too important, ken?"

Rory's neck heated. He glanced aside to Siobhan; her face was as tight as her grip on the pommel. It would cause more trouble to try and avoid this meeting.

"It's on your head." Rory pointed his index finger in Micah's face. "You get us out of there if you ever want to see my sister."

"Okay, man!" Micah raised his hands in surrender and turned, stomping back to his horse, his bun of dreadlocks bobbing behind him.

Micah mounted and kicked his horse on; his band followed. Rory nudged Boy in behind them and Siobhan's gelding dragged along. Xian manoeuvred his horse and the packhorse while those waiting to cross parted to allow them through. Once over the bridge, Micah led them down the road toward the old holiday park.

Siobhan sat silently on her horse, sweat beading on her forehead.

"It will be okay, Siobhan. We'll suggest a parley between Lloyd and the Scottish Government," Rory said over his pounding heart and the niggle developing in his guts. "He may be a megalomaniac, but he is an important man around here. The Government will want to have some dealings with him."

Siobhan grimaced. "It's just that in the future—" Siobhan stopped speaking as Micah was cantering his horse toward them.

"What do you know about my dad?" Micah asked Rory as he pulled his horse beside him and turned to ride with them.

"I know I don't like him," Rory said. "I'm not very fond of people who think they can own other people." Rory pressed his mouth tight.

Micah lifted his gaze from Rory's mouth. "He's a self-educated, self-made man, you ken? He grew up on the streets of Glasgow—a druggie's kid," Micah said. "He was an entrepreneur who recognised an opportunity when the stock market began its fall. Most of the looted goods from Fife's shops and warehouses, and even Edinburgh's and its surrounds, ended up in his store houses. He started with one in Fife, near Kirkcaldy, and now he's got 'em all over the place."

"You must be proud." Rory let the sarcasm drip.

"What I'm sayin' is, he's influential," Micah said. "He's got stores and stores o' stuff. And his farmlands are productive and fertile. Be on his good side, Rory. You've got an *in* with me. You never ken when you're gonna need him, aye?" Micah's eager face was almost in Rory's.

The guy was trying to make a bad situation good. An optimist. The world always needed those. Or maybe Micah was really keen for Cèilidh.

Rory glanced at Siobhan who'd remained silent.

He turned back to Micah. "I get where you're coming from. It is an *in*," he whispered. "But I want to be able to leave here."

Micah nudged his horse to the entrance of the old holiday park. Rory turned to Siobhan. Her gaze remained on Micah trotting his horse ahead, her eyes narrowing a fraction.

"This is our first opportunity to put a good word in for the Government with a local leader." Rory smiled at Siobhan, attempting to ease her discomfort.

Siobhan's expression remained tight.

"What?"

She shook her head, her mouth tense. They walked the horses beside the holiday huts occupied by scantily dressed young women and men.

Someone cat-called. "He's back," a woman said.

Rory avoided their stares.

"What was that?" Siobhan sat stiffly beside him.

"Nothing, Siobhan," Rory said. She blinked and a line appeared between her brows. "Do ye trust me?" he asked.

She lifted her chin. "Yes."

"Good," he said.

They rode to the office where he and Xian had previously met Lloyd.

They dismounted, and Micah led them into the prefabricated building, along the corridor and into the main room with its walls covered in posters. Lloyd sat in the high-backed chesterfield chair with an open book in his lap.

"You're just in time for tea," Lloyd said. He held out his wrinkled hand and pointed to the chairs nearest him. "Please, sit."

Chapter Eighteen

Derrick Lloyd's Office

Rory sat with the others in the tapestry-covered chairs arranged in a semi-circle in front of Lloyd. He surveyed the room and their grey-haired host, who had positioned Rory so he couldn't easily monitor the one and only exit directly behind him. Lloyd's guards had allowed them to keep their weapons. They had Micah to thank for that. Guards, with holstered handguns, stood on either side of the row of chairs. Rory looked aside at Siobhan who sat stiffly in the chair beside him, her vision darting around the room. Xian sat on the chair at the end.

"Thank you for bringing my guests here, son." Lloyd's mop of thick snowy-grey hair bobbed as he spoke to Micah.

Micah's smile stretched his suntanned cheeks and as he looked at his father, his eyes glowed with fondness.

A door to the side of them opened and a woman carrying a large tray set it on the coffee table in front of Lloyd. A matching china tea set, cups on saucers, a dish of jam and another of whipped cream, and a pile of scones on a gold-rimmed plate, were the contents of the tray.

"High Tea," Lloyd announced.

The side door opened again, and Rory's gaze slid up from the tray of food as Maxwell stepped into the room. Lloyd's older son surveyed the guests, his eyes narrowing when they landed on Micah sitting next to Rory. Micah stiffened then twisted to look at the posters on the wall.

"Introduce us, Micah," Lloyd asked then leaned forward in his chair. He fixed his rheumy eyes on Siobhan and a half-smile emerged.

Dinnae you ogle my wife, mister.

"I have met Mr Campbell and Mr Law," Lloyd said.

Micah stood and, with a gesture, indicated Siobhan. "This is Siobhan Campbell, Rory's wife. He's just brought her from the Government Bunker in Edinburgh."

Lloyd's right eyebrow curled. "The Bunker?" He stood and stepped around the laden coffee table to hold out a hand to Siobhan. "Pleasure to meet you, Mrs Campbell."

Siobhan stood and, towering over him, shook his hand. Her facial expression remained fixed, and she didn't reply.

"Siobhan is an important person in the Government, Father," Micah continued.

"Hmm. Is that so? Why are they letting you wander around Scotland, then?" Lloyd directed his question up to Siobhan.

Still she didn't answer. Alarm bells rang in Rory's head. This was not like her.

"My wife is a qualified scientist," he said. He wouldn't mention anything *nuclear*. "At present," Rory continued, "with myself, Siobhan is on a diplomatic mission."

Siobhan flinched beside him. "Yes, Mr Lloyd," she said, "we are, in actuality, on a fact-finding mission, hoping to initiate talks with all parties interested in the restoration of a democratic government in a united Scotland." Siobhan spoke stiffly at first, but then her speech resumed its usual authoritative tone.

The tension eased in Rory's shoulders.

"*Diplomatic mission. Holding talks.* I like the sound of this." Lloyd pushed up his sleeves, revealing his faded tattoos. "Is there a possibility of the noted leaders *outside* of the Government Bunker holding talks with the Government... *inside* the Government Bunker?"

"That is possible," Siobhan replied. "Most likely at a later stage, once we have provided the First Minister with the contact information of all concerned sectors of the population."

Siobhan had loosened up a wee bit, but her back was still stiff.

"I'd love to see the set-up down there," Lloyd said. He had returned to the coffee table and poured tea while he spoke. "I imagine, it being a bunker, that the storage facilities are massive."

Siobhan remained silent. Lloyd's eyes flashed up to hers.

"I hear there is still a substantial defence force," he said as he handed a cup of tea to Siobhan. "Sugar and milk if you wish it." He stood straighter.

Siobhan took the cup and saucer from Lloyd, which tinkled with a slight rattle, then sat down and sipped.

"You understand for security reasons I'm not permitted to say anything—about either of those subjects," Siobhan said then sipped once more.

"Scone?" Lloyd asked. "Oh, how rude of me. Micah, pour our other guests some tea."

Micah served tea to Rory then Xian and Maxwell, asking if they wanted milk and sugar as he did so. Micah offered the scones, jam, and cream, his dreadlock bun bobbing with his enthusiasm. Rory suppressed a smile. He accepted a scone, cut it in two, spread jam and dolloped a spoonful of the fluffy cream on both halves. Rory bit into the sweetened whipped cream, its sugariness strong and unfamiliar to him.

"You must have been a child, Mrs Campbell, when the Crash occurred." Lloyd spooned two sugars into his teacup and, with eyes intent on Siobhan, sat back down on his chesterfield, his silver spoon clinking against the china cup as he stirred.

Siobhan nodded, her mouth around a scone piled high with cream.

"I heard the Government called experts in their fields, and their families, underground when it was obvious the stock market wasn't recovering and things were... chaotic, shall we say," Lloyd said.

He declined a scone from Micah then paused, cup between saucer and his mouth, and waited for an answer from Siobhan.

"That is correct," Siobhan said. "It was the Scottish Government's plan to return to normal as soon as possible and have the personnel and resources on-hand to do so."

"And your parents?" Lloyd raised his brows in encouragement.

Siobhan took another bite of the cream-drowned scone and chewed slowly.

"No, only my father, who has since passed away," Siobhan finally said after licking the cream off her top lip.

"My condolences, Mrs Campbell," Lloyd said. "He was an intelligent and well-educated man?"

"Yes," Siobhan replied.

"I am a well-educated, self-taught man. I have always read widely." Lloyd placed his cup back on its saucer. "One of my priorities, once heedless destruction had diminished resources, was to rescue the written word, especially once power sources were questionable and technology-based data retrieval became obsolete. I don't believe in knowledge just for its own sake." Lloyd's eyes locked on Siobhan. When she didn't reply he continued, "Knowledge without putting the pieces in place and deriving some wisdom from it, is useless. One needs to develop a philosophy by which to operate." Lloyd sat further back in his chair. "As a businessman I deal with peoples' wants and needs. I supply the goods, in whatever form, and receive payment for them." He crossed his legs at the knee. "Now, paper money isn't much use to anyone—at present. One day, currency will return. In the interim, I trade goods in a barter system."

Siobhan remained straight backed beside Rory. He let out a silent sigh as Lloyd continued the lesson in economics and trade.

"By bartering I obtain more of the goods people demand and require," Lloyd went on. "Or I gain a labour force for my sowings and harvesting, building larger barns, etc." Lloyd uncrossed his legs and leaned forward in his chair. "I have influence. The Scottish Government would do well to remember that."

"I would like to see your facilities, Mr Lloyd." Siobhan broke the intensity of Lloyd's stare. "They seem rather extensive. May we have a tour?"

Lloyd straightened his shoulders and replaced his cup and saucer on the tray.

"I'd be delighted, Mrs Campbell," Lloyd replied. "Your husband has viewed some of this compound, but I'd be pleased to show you more." The small man's red-rimmed eyes were alight.

Rory blinked. Surely Lloyd wouldn't be a stupid Hezekiah? That ancient king of Israel who showed his enemies all his treasure and then wondered why they invaded his country? Or was it a case of *I'll show you mine if you show me yours*? Either way, the longer they stayed in this man's company, the harder it would be to get out of it.

Lloyd clasped his hands together. "I have other storehouses in Fife if you—"

"Sorry, Mr Lloyd," Rory interrupted. "We'll only be able to have a brief tour of this one. We must be on our way up north. It's a long way, you ken?"

Lloyd stared at his teacup on the low table before him, his breath whistling out through his teeth. The man tapped his foot rapidly while his clasped hands sunk into his lap. Rory slid his gaze around the room once more. The guards seemed alert but unperturbed.

"My father and I," Maxwell spoke at last, "would be honoured to hold discussions with the Scottish Government anytime they invite us, Mrs Campbell."

"That's wonderful!" Siobhan sounded exuberant. It was a little unsettling. "And I do apologise, our tour will have to be at another time, for Rory is right, and we must go."

Lloyd's gaze remained set on his teacup.

"Father," Micah stood, tension edging his tone. "I'll see my friends out and give them a mini-tour."

Lloyd fixed on the coffee table's contents for a second longer, then he rose from his chesterfield, his features locked in an amicable expression.

"Goodbye, Mrs Campbell," he said to Siobhan. "It's been most enlightening." He shook Siobhan's hand.

Rory reached out and took Lloyd's hand in a shake. Xian did the same. Micah stepped forward and embraced Lloyd in a hug, which his father returned. Behind Rory, Maxwell took in a sharp breath.

"Father?" Micah dipped his head toward Lloyd's men who'd remained during the High Tea.

Lloyd gave a nod to the men, and they stood back. Micah led Rory and the others out to their horses via the cabins where they stored their goods. Here rows and rows of cabins sat side by side. The steps creaked as they walked into one of the weather-beaten structures made of a thin metal and a plastic that had disintegrated in places around the windows and doors. Inside of this one, stacked tubs and boxes filled the empty shell and a musty aroma pervaded the air. The contents varied from dehydrated foods, such as noodles, to wind-up torches and duct-tape.

"My dad's farming lands are productive," Micah said. "He has barns where he stores his grains. Makes a mean whisky too, aye?" Micah leaned on a faded box full of tinned baked beans.

"Tinned goods last well past their expiry dates, as long as they're not blown." Siobhan pointed to a stack of boxes containing tomato soup. "Or so they say."

"Why are you showin' us all of this, Micah?" Rory crossed his arms.

Micah blinked. "I'm hurt, Rory. I thought we were friends."

"We are," Rory replied.

"Well, you helped me out," Micah said. "I'll help you."

Rory stepped in close, so close he could smell Micah's cream-tea-laden breath. "Don't be mistaken," he said. "I'm no' returnin' the favour. You have nae reported back to your dad about our stores, have ye? Man, am I glad I never let you out o' my sight at Invercharing."

"I have nae, Rory." Micah's nostrils flared.

"Rory," Siobhan's small hand rested on his arm. "Let Micah take us to our horses now. Please."

Rory made his shoulders relax and unfolded his arms. "I suppose you're coming with us."

Micah's brow flew up to his hairline. "You okay with that?"

"We're heading the same way, are we no'? Besides, your friends we met on the road may leave us alone if you do," Rory said.

"They weren't my friends." Micah stood tall. "I'll let my dad know what I'm doing, and I'll be with you soon, aye?"

Rory followed Siobhan and Xian down the creaky steps.

"So, we're good now?" Micah asked from behind Rory.

Rory turned and Micah stopped short of running into him.

"You on about my wee sister again?" Rory asked, his face was close to Micah's, whose winter-sky blue eyes peered directly at him. He had the familiar scent of a man who lived his life on a horse.

"Yeah." Micah stepped back.

"You can travel with us so I can keep an eye on you," Rory said. "Put one foot wrong and you're out. Understood?"

Micah raised his hands in surrender. "Man, you've got nothin' to worry about. She's too good for the guys in that Community. She told me they're all—"

"Oh, and you're better than them?" Rory asked.

"Cèilidh thinks so!" Micah shot back.

"Rory." Siobhan tugged at his arm.

He turned to her. *Give him a break*, she mouthed. She'd been to the future where he was family. He turned back to Micah.

"You're the leader of a bandit group." Rory put his hand up to stop Micah's protests. "That's how the guys *who aren't good enough* for Cèilidh will see it. And the rest of our Community will see it that way too. You dinnae only have me to convince."

Micah started to speak but Rory interrupted what was about to come out of the young bandit leader's mouth.

"You have a week o' travellin' with me. Put your best foot forward, aye?"

Chapter Nineteen

The Road Home

Siobhan had let her body go with the horse's gait, relaxing into it, discovering this to be more comfortable than trying to remain independent of the movement of the great beast on which she sat. Her cheek tugged, for the sedate gelding she rode would be far from a *great beast* in her husband's eyes.

It took the whole day to reach Perth. They passed gentle, green rolling hills, streaked with the grey-brown runnels carved by rainwater cascading down their sides. These alternated with fields, which ran along both sides of a bitumen road on their way through the Kingdom of Fife and along to Perthshire. Here and there, the road became dirt and rubble. The day's steady rain, assisted by the action of their horses' hooves, turned the disintegrated sections into mires.

So far, the journey was uneventful and maybe it would stay that way. The rain didn't even bother her, it was constant but soft. Siobhan adjusted her oiled skin raincoat and recalled the journey to Loch Ewe and back. Now *that* trip had been scary. She stared at Rory's back; his coat was rain-drenched and trickles of water dripped from his hat and down his back.

These would be their first nights together as man and wife, but they were no honeymoon. She gave a quiet chuckle. Nights around a campfire and sleeping under the stars were romantic, but with a group, not conducive to an audience-free love making session.

Rory turned in the saddle, smile-lines crinkling at the corners of his eyes, as if he were reading her thoughts.

"You want the reins?" he asked.

"Ah, maybe tomorrow?"

Rory grinned, his dimples pitting, then he faced forward again, riding slightly in front of her with Micah the other side of him.

"Autumn's harvest is over," Micah said as they passed brown fields with rows of straw tufts left from a grain crop.

"Aye, need to get on with plantings for the winter." Rory pointed to the cloud cover that drizzled on them. "The weather's tellin' me it'll be a hard one. Not really what we need after ruined summer harvests, thanks to being confined to barracks."

"The road is washed out up ahead," Micah said when they neared a section that was a muddy bog.

"We'll divert around it," Rory said, then led them off the road and into nearby meadow. "Had to do the same on the way down."

Siobhan listened quietly to them. She'd seen it before—men trying each other out through conversation. Micah seemed okay. They would eventually be related, so Rory must have eventually judged him as genuine, and Micah must have passed all the tests Rory would throw at him.

"Can I ask how you ken about crops and such, being a bandit and all?" Rory asked, keeping his gaze far and wide.

"I grew up in the holiday village with my mum," Micah answered. "I helped in the fields until I was twenty and still go back now and then to help with the harvests."

"Why d'you leave?"

Micah's shoulders slumped a little, and he hung his head for a second. "Let's just say Max wasn't happy with me there."

"Why?" There was an honest curiosity in Rory's question.

"He... doesn't like me." Micah's head twitched. "He thought I'd want to claim a position in ma' father's business—our father's business. Maxwell made my life hell after my mum died. I just left. I could nae be—" he covered his mouth and let out an expletive, glancing over his shoulder at Siobhan. "It was all such shite, and I could nae be bothered with it. I dinnae want any part o' that."

"So, you went banditing?" Rory asked.

"No, I went travelling," Micah replied. "Doin' odd jobs here and there, for my food and lodgings. But as I travelled further north, there were fewer jobs. I met up with some guys who'd been poachin'."

They rode for a mile or so without conversation. More meadows were brown, emptied of their crops, and they shone with the rain's moisture. Siobhan pulled the hood of her coat tighter around her against the chill on her neck.

"I'd never do what my dad's done," Micah said to Rory, who still scanned either side of the road. "I'm not the evil bastard he can be."

Rory turned a narrow stare on Micah. "I ken what you mean," Rory said. "I've had a taste of your father's meanness. He was civil to me today. Probably because of Siobhan, and him wanting to find out all he could about what was in the Bunker, an' all."

"But he's still ma dad." Micah's voice tinged with emotion, then he looked over at Siobhan. "You handled him well, Mrs Campbell. You weren't givin' anything away. He wasn't pleased, but he wants to get in the good books with the Scottish Government, so he behaved himself." He finished with a laugh and a knowing expression.

They rode into Perth and arrived at a wide green, edged by trees on the banks of the River Tay—the South Inch. Small camps dotted it here and there. Shack-like structures made of wood and others of more permanent materials, leaned against trees or remnants of old buildings, or each other. People camped in tents while other travellers were making temporary shelters to cover themselves from the rain.

Rory chose a camping place, and he and Xian strung a tarp between two trees. They settled their animals while Micah's people collected wood and clean rubbish, and when the rain eased, they lit a fire. They ate a meal of baked beans and a type of bannock, which Micah had made for them over the coals. Rory set out a bedroll under the tarp and gestured for Siobhan to sit. Gentle rain had started again, and Rory gave a tarp and some rope to Micah's crew to sling between trees on the opposite side of the fire. When the tarp was up, Micah stretched out under their shelter, leaning on his elbow.

Rory sat beside Siobhan, his face reflecting the lambent light. The fire cracked and sparks popped into the night sky. Siobhan leaned out from under the canvas tarp. The clouds patched over a twinkling sky while sparks from the fire flew heavenward to join them. Siobhan sighed.

"Aye," Rory whispered. "A place to *be*, not just exist. I dinnae ken how you could live down there for so long. Can you not feel the fresh air?" He took a deep breath in.

She followed his lead. The cool air held a scent of pine—also human body odour, and a reek of rot and sour milk, which wafted over from the nearby rubbish heap. She crinkled her nose.

"Well." Rory tilted his head in the direction of the rubbish. "Wait till we get out o' a city."

***

The warmth of Rory's arm around her waist, and his lips against her cheek, woke Siobhan. The sun's early morning glow touched the rain-soaked trees of the forest that covered Kinnoull Hill behind their camp. On the South Inch, raindrops glimmered on nearby branches to welcome a new day with prisms of fractured light.

"I'm sorry, Siobhan," Rory said. "This should be our honeymoon, but it is nae much o' one."

"You're correct there, Rory Campbell. You owe me." She returned his kiss, his stubble tickling her lips.

They packed up camp and left Perth following what remained of the A9. Rory spent the morning giving her riding lessons, and by lunchtime she took the reins with confidence.

Siobhan reflected on Rory in the future. He hadn't laughed. He'd cried his brokenness into her arms. His loss still so great and raw after three years without her. Her throat tightened. Rory had lost his parents five years ago, when his mother died of cancer and his father time travelled to the past to be with her. But Rory had time travelled to be with them less than a year ago, if Siobhan was recalling correctly, and would have seen his mother alive, but as a young woman. And witnessed his father's death.

Keeping track of those timelines could mess with your head.

So many losses in such a short time. No wonder Rory had been in such a state after she had died. He hadn't had time to work through any of those griefs when responsibility had forced him to take up his role and act on it.

She needed to help him work through his grief now so that when—if—she died, he'd cope with it better and be able to make rational decisions. Even avoid those choices that he'd believed had led him down the path of being in-debt to Lloyd.

"I'm aiming for the Community near Loch Tummel, Siobhan," Rory said, twisting in the saddle to face her. "It's in an old castle. We may get to sleep in a bed tonight. What do you think?"

Siobhan's buttocks were sore from another day in the saddle, and there was an ache in her back from a night on the ground. She nodded, the prospect of a night to themselves brought a warmth to her middle.

"You want to be at Tummel House by sundown?" Xian asked. "We'd better move."

Rory leaned over and took her reins back, then they kicked their horses to a fast trot.

"Just keep those thighs tight. Dinnae want you falling off," Rory said with a half grin.

The rest of the day passed by in a jolting blur. Thick, leafy forests, coloured with autumn's gold and red, grew closer to the narrowing path as the day wore on and the sun soon began its slide to the horizon. Cold seeped out from between the trees when dusk arrived. The drystone walls lining the road added no warmth to Siobhan's bones, while the road narrowed to a track in various shades of grey in the gathering dark.

"Not far now, Siobhan," Rory said. He got a wind-up torch from his saddlebag and lit the path a little.

Birds settling for the night filled the track with their constant chatter. Siobhan recalled this from their camping journey to Loch Ewe. It happened of a sunrise too. Or even before, when an optimistic bird sang its hope of a new day even before the sun had begun its way above the horizon. Siobhan's fingertips tingled. Now all these things would be a daily occurrence for her. No more hustle and bustle of the Bunker's occupants performing their daily duties the only sign it would be daylight *up top*, or the predetermined *lights-out* with the hum of the fans sucking air deep into the bunker to signify it was night.

As the night deepened, the birds ceased their chirps, but another sound floated toward them through the forest and along the road, gaining in volume as they travelled on.

"Is that... is that...?" she asked, cocking her head, and straining her hearing.

"Aye. It is," Rory replied.

"Bagpipes! And the music of a cèilidh." Micah laughed. "We're goin' to a party."

"But we're not invited," Siobhan said.

The music increased in intensity while they drew closer to its source, and light from the near distance flickered through the foliage.

The *clump* of hoofbeats came out of the forest's edge.

"Halt!" A young man pulled up his large horse in front of them, accompanied by two other men on horseback. "Who are you?"

His companions shouldered their rifles, only shadows in the now-dark night.

"Rory Campbell and companions seeking travellers' rights this night, my friend." Rory shone his torch near his own face. "We're from the Invercharing Community having travelled from Perth today. May we seek shelter at Tummel House Community tonight, please?"

"Rory Campbell? Caitlin Murray-Campbell's son?" the man asked.

"The one and the same," Rory replied.

"Och, come with us." The young men lowered their rifles and turned their animals, indicating they were to accompany them.

The men led them along the dimly lit road and hooves clattered behind Siobhan as Micah's companions followed. Turning a bend in the narrow road, the light that had flickered through the trees became blocks of light. The wall surrounding the castle loomed before them, dark grey in the night, the top windows of the triple-storey building peeking their brightness above it. The group passed through the gate and halted in oblongs of light streaming from the windows and doors of the lower floors. Music poured out and surrounded them with a drum beat and a jaunty bagpipe tune. They dismounted and stood around a lit brazier, their would-be hosts peering closely at each one in turn.

"This is my wife, Siobhan," Rory said and linked his arm in hers then introduced the others.

A man walked out of the large double-fronted door through the blare of music, his kilt swinging with each step. The heavy wooden door remained open, giving Siobhan a glimpse of a hall-like room, bare floorboards, and lots of people with a definite festive air.

"Mr Donaldson, sir, this is Rory Campbell," the young lookout said. "Claims he's Caitlin Murray-Campbell's son from the Invercharing Community up north, sir."

In the brazier's light, shadows flickered across the wrinkled face of the kilted man, revealing an age his gait defied. His glasses flashed in the firelight.

"Och, ye have the look of Scott Campbell about ye. There's nae denying who fathered you, young man. Welcome." Mr Donaldson extended his hand.

Rory grasped it and returned the vigorous handshake. He introduced the rest of his crew.

"Ye have come at a grand time, for our daughter is wedded today and we are celebrating this night with a cèilidh." Mr Donaldson beamed. "Ye are most welcome to join the celebrations after you have recovered from the road." He turned his gaze onto Siobhan. "Mrs Campbell, ye look a wee bitty travel worn, if I'm no' rude in saying so."

"Siobhan is tired, Mr Donaldson, and I am a poor husband, for I've dragged my wife many a mile this day when we should be on our honeymoon." Rory gave an embarrassed laugh. "She'll have to wait—"

"Honeymoon?" Mr Donaldson interrupted. "Och, no!" Mr Donaldson turned to the doorway and shouted to a kilted lad standing nearby.

"Aye, sir?" the teenager said.

"Go tell ma missus we have guests and to get the best suite ready for them," Donaldson ordered the lad.

"Sir? But the young now-Mrs Gillis and her man will be—"

"Och, no, lad," Donaldson cut him short, "not that one! The next best one, aye?"

"Aye, sir." The teenager ran back into the festivities.

"Mr Donaldson, we couldn't—" Siobhan began.

"Och, now ye could, and ye are, and a hot bath will be awaitin' you." Mr Donaldson flourished a hand then directed her in through the wide-open doors of the castle.

Chapter Twenty

Tummel House Community, Perthshire

Lush maroon carpet covered the floor of the room to which the lad led Siobhan and Rory. Siobhan placed her bags on the Turkish rug by the queen-sized bed. Fine, transparent material draped the four-poster bed—the room's main feature. Thicker curtains in a heavy material hung from each corner post. Deeper golds and dusky pinks peeked through the folds in the rich drapery faded by time and sunlight. The bedspread matched, as did the canopy above. Shiny polished antique side-tables displayed an array of ceramic figurines, and a floral two-seater couch was positioned at the end of the bed.

The echo of running water came from the bathroom off to the side. Siobhan walked into the room with fittings she guessed were from the twenty-teens. A modern bathroom in an old, still-inhabited castle. She chuckled. Square taps and hose hung over a bath deep enough for a person to sit in and still be covered by the silky water. Copious bubbles, piled high like Munros, sat on top of the bath's steaming contents.

A woman in an evening dress sparkling with sequins, swished the water in the bath.

"I'm Moira Donaldson. Welcome to our Community. I hope the bath is to your liking," she said smiling and revealing crooked brown teeth.

"Thank you, but I've taken you from your daughter's wedding," Siobhan said.

"Och, no, she's ma niece. I'm no' Mrs Donaldson senior. Ye'll soon meet her. We're mostly family here." The brown-toothed grin appeared again. "I ken ye'd be wantin' to have a wee soak, but dinnae take too lang, aye? You'll no want to miss the roast venison and the music!" She held Siobhan's shoulders and gave a gentle shake. "You and your husband come down soon."

"Thank you." Siobhan blinked as the cheery woman whisked out of the room, her dress glittering in the lantern light.

"The bath's big enough for two, aye?" Rory stepped closer, slipped his hands around Siobhan's waist, pressing his body against hers, and enveloping her in a warm hug. She drew in his scent. Horse, heather—and male body odour.

"I'm not too sure how much bathing would get done, but you really need to, Rory." She pulled a face to match her comment.

Someone pounded on the door.

"Rory!" It was Micah.

Rory's shoulders drooped and he let go of her, then traipsed to the door.

"Aye?" He flung open the door, revealing Xian and Micah, whose hand was in a knocking position at Rory's face-height.

"Oh, man, you've gotta come down. Should see the food!" Micah said, dropping his hand. "There's so much. And the music's startin' again. My guys are already there. They'll finish the venison if ye dinnae hurray."

"You okay, Xian?" Rory asked as Siobhan walked to stand beside him. "Where are the rest of you staying?"

"There's a dorm further back near the stables," Xian said. "I can keep an eye on the horses. You won't be long, will you, Rory? It's getting late and I get the feeling Donaldson wants to speak with you. Siobhan, actually." Xian slid his gaze to her.

"Oh?" Rory raised a brow.

"Yes," Xian said. "He asked me a whole lot of questions about you, Siobhan. I didn't say much, just that you're from Edinburgh and we're on our way home to the Northern Highlands. I found out that Mr Donaldson isn't the leader of this Community, his missus is," Xian finished with a slight flick of his head.

"This used to be a stately home run by the National Trust o' Scotland, ye ken?" Micah raised his brows.

"Who are these people, then?" Rory asked.

"Come doon and find oot." Micah's face loomed in front of them both.

Rory shut the door on him, then rested his hand on it while Xian and Micah's conversation receded.

"I'm having a bath. Then you will. Then we'll find out all about them," Siobhan said.

She returned to the bathroom, removed her clothes, and slipped into the water. The perfume was lilac, and the heat seeped its soothing magic into her travel-weary muscles.

"It's grand we'll be sleeping in a bed tonight," Rory said.

He stood in the open doorway, his shoulder leaning on the doorjamb and his eyes raking across the parts of her exposed above the soap bubble mountains. He unbuttoned his shirt. It slid across his muscled chest and defined abdominals and down his ropey arms. He unbuttoned his buckskins, never removing his gaze from her.

Siobhan's pulse raced and warmth spread lower—it wasn't from the bathwater.

There was a sharp knock on the door once more.

"We'll be there soon, Micah!" Rory shouted at the door.

"Ahh, Mr Campbell," an unfamiliar male voice spoke, muffled through the door. "Mistress Donaldson wishes to meet you and your wife. She's asked that you join her at the table... and soon is implied."

Rory's eyes widened, then he grabbed his buckskins to his waist and strode to the door, opening it with an apology that echoed into the bathroom.

"I thought you were our companions," Rory said. Music from the festivities below floated through the open bathroom door. "We'll be down as soon as we can."

Siobhan sank lower into the bathwater as Rory finished his conversation and returned to the bathroom. "We've been summoned," he said.

"Interesting. I've never heard of a Mrs Donaldson in a castle. Is the family linked to these lands?" Siobhan washed her raised leg, water dribbling over the sides of the tub. "Despite what you think, we in the Bunker don't know everything."

"Hmm," he said softly, "but you can forget the *we* part of that statement. You're no' going tae live there anymore."

Siobhan stood out of the bath, soap bubbles sliding down her back and legs, leaving a trail of tickling sensations. Rory ran his eyes from her head to her feet while she stood dripping on the bathmat. Without taking his eyes off her, he reached out to the towel rail and dragged a bath-towel from it.

"It's such a shame we have nae time..." He shook his head, sucking his breath between his teeth.

"Your turn." She took the towel from his hand.

He leaned forward and placed his warm lips to hers, playing gently, and stirring up emotions and desires within her. She swallowed.

"I'll get out some clean clothes from our things," she said. "We can't keep them waiting."

He stepped out of his trousers and hopped into the bathtub. "I don't really ken them. Ahh." He sank into the water, eyes closed, and leaned back.

"Scrub." She threw a ball of netted material at him.

Rory flinched and rubbed the now wet netting across his deep-ginger chest-hair, which darkened with bubbles clinging to each strand.

Siobhan tore her eyes away and headed back into the bedroom, then pulled through the clothes in her bag for a decent dress. An evening gown, which she had thrown in on a whim, lay at the bottom of a duffle bag. She raked through Rory's bag. Buckskins, shirts, underwear of a sort, and socks were the only items. Well, they hadn't expected to be attending a wedding. Then a thought came to her. Beside the bed was an internal telephone, the receiver looked like something out of the nineteen fifties room in the archives, a bone coloured—well, bone. She lifted it and an electronic purr repeated.

"Aye?" said a woman's voice. "Is this oor unexpected guests?"

"This is Siobhan Campbell," Siobhan said into the phone. "Would you help me, please?"

"What're you doin'?" Rory yelled.

The *splosh* of water escaping over the side of the bath and onto the floor, came from the bathroom. Rory stood in the doorway. Clusters of bubbles slid down his nude torso, powerless to hide his masculinity. Her mouth tugged at the corners.

"Could you send up some clothes for my husband?" she asked the woman on the internal phone. "He doesn't have a thing to wear to the wedding."

"Och, aye, of course, hen. I can do that for ye," the woman replied.

"Siobhan," Rory wrapped a towel around his waist. "I have—"

"Buckskins," Siobhan interrupted, "are not wedding attire."

"I'll be right up," the woman on the line said. "I have just the thing."

Siobhan hung up.

Rory dried himself and shaved with the razor that sat on the shelf above the sink. There was a tap on the door and Siobhan opened it to an older woman who stooped over a clothing bag.

"There ye are, hen." The woman's head held a tremor all the while she handed the bag to Siobhan. "He'll look dashing it that, will he no'?" she asked.

The clear window in the cloth bag exposed a square of tartan, a vivid blue, which was almost purple, and dark-green check.

"Wonderful, thank you," Siobhan said.

The woman left and Siobhan turned to Rory, who now stood in the bathroom doorway, a fresh shaving nick oozing on his chin. "What have you got?" he asked.

Siobhan undid the clothing bag. Inside was a full gentleman's kilt and a white shirt. She held the shirt up to Rory.

"That will fit," she said.

"Och, it's Clan Murray." Rory stepped over to smooth his hands over the finely woven wool cloth. "At least I will nae have to concern myself with clean jocks."

Chapter Twenty-One

Tummel House Community

Shaking away the fatigue of the long day's ride, Rory stepped down the broad, curved wooden staircase with Siobhan by his side. Tired lines under her eyes and all, she had dressed and made herself very presentable. Despite her weariness, she was indeed a beauty.

He sniffed deep—flowers again. Her scent swirled in his mind as surely as did the desire in his body. This elegant woman was his wife, except he hadn't made her so—yet. He recalled she had hinted that in the future he had made love to her all the day they were together. His gut clenched at this twinge of jealousy for his future self, catching him by surprise.

"Mrs Campbell!" Mr Donaldson stood at the foot of the stairs; admiration oozing from his voice. "And Mr Campbell," he said. "Och, you look grand in that kilt."

Rory tore his eyes away from Siobhan in her deep-blue dress. He pushed the image of her just-as-deep-blue eyes out of his thoughts and faced their host.

"I must thank whoever has loaned it to me," Rory said. "For giving me a chance to wear the tartan of ma mother's clan."

"Och, son, we kenned you'd wear it with pride." There was fondness in Mr Donaldson's tone. "Now you must come and meet my wife," he said, offering his arm to Siobhan. "She's the boss around here. None of us would have survived the turmoil after the stock market crash if not for her."

Mr Donaldson led them past the entrance to the large room from which the music of drums, piano-accordion, fiddle and bagpipes blared. Inside, couples with linked arms spun around and around each other. Rory paused to watch as Micah swung a young woman off her feet, his dreads flying out behind him. The men in his crew danced and spun with other women in the room.

"Aye, your companions have dined and are enjoying themselves at our cèilidh," Mr Donaldson said. "But you must come and eat. We have kept some venison back for you both."

The gold rims of the old man's spectacles glinted in the light of the candles that rested in the holders along the wall of the corridor. He led them to a room as large as the one in which the cèilidh was taking place. Long trestle tables lined the walls, covered in white tablecloths and sprigs of purple heather sat around yet more candles as a centre-piece.

Most of the tables were empty, the guests now participating in the cèilidh. An older woman, grey hair piled on top of her head and wearing a neatly tailored dress with a tartan sash over her shoulder, fixed her gaze on them as they followed Mr Donaldson to where she sat at the top table. The woman's eyes raked Siobhan from head to foot, then Rory, her gaze settling on his face. He could have been an item in one of the glass cases in the Bunker's archives. Her stern expression gave way to a smile as they approached.

"My dear, may I present Mr and Mrs Campbell of the Invercharing Community." Donaldson ushered them toward the trestle table where his wife sat.

"Welcome," she said. "Please come sit beside me and eat." Mrs Donaldson waved in a come-here gesture.

"Thank you for allowing us to join the wedding celebrations." Rory held Siobhan's cool hand, allowing her to go in front of him and sit next to Mrs Donaldson, then he made to sit beside Siobhan.

"No, no, you come the other side of me, Mr Campbell," Mrs Donaldson said. "I want a close look at you both."

Rory sat to her right. A young man placed a platter of hot roast venison and vegetables in front of them. Oat cakes and cheese were set next to the centre-piece, and a decanter of whisky and glasses were beside them. An older woman set clean plates before Rory and Siobhan. A serving woman poured gravy over the meat Rory had placed on his own plate. A strong gamey scent of venison wafted into Rory's nostrils.

Rory's stomach hurt with hunger and his palate moistened to receive the forkful of venison dripping in gravy. It had been a while since Rory had had roasted venison. Their time of confinement in the compound, waiting out the nuclear fallout cloud, had offered little variety in the food department, and jerky was the nearest thing to meat he'd had in a while. Succulent, gamey meat melted on his tongue; there was a hint of port in the gravy.

"Eat all you wish." Mrs Donaldson's expression was one of warm and genuine friendliness. "Tell me where ye lived in Edinburgh, Mrs Campbell," Mrs Donaldson asked as she spooned generous helpings of roasted parsnip and potatoes onto their plates.

"I lived in the Government Bunker, Mrs Donaldson," Siobhan answered. "But I am eager to find out how this Community came to be. Wasn't this once a stately home run by the National Trust of Scotland?" Siobhan held her fork loosely.

"Aye, that's true," Mrs Donaldson began. "When vandals began raiding the stately homes, we barricaded ourselves in and defended this grand old place." Her emphatic nod set her topknot bobbing. "The other staff who worked here brought their families, and those who belonged to our mock army also joined us with their families."

"Staff?" Siobhan had watched Mrs Donaldson throughout her explanation, her food untouched. "Your family didn't own this estate?" she asked.

"No, we did nae," Mrs Donaldson replied. "I was the manager and worked for the National Trust o' Scotland. I was determined the opportunistic rabble, who were making the most of a dark time in our history, would not destroy this beautiful castle that had been a significant part of Scotland's past. No, this estate had survived the Jacobite rebellion, and it would endure an economic crisis if we had anything to do with it."

"And it did, my dear," Mr Donaldson said.

"You had a mock army?" Rory asked, cutting a slice of cheese then placing it on an oatcake.

"Aye, it was part of the day out in the grounds, ye see?" Mrs Donaldson answered. "We'd have mock battles. The men were all kitted out in kilts and full Highland regalia. They'd march to the pipes and drum. Och, it was a grand sight."

"Aye, a grand sight," Mr Donaldson said. He poured whisky into each glass and handed one to Siobhan. "Single malt from the Highlands." He winked at Rory and handed him a glass filled with a generous dram.

"They were a real army when push came tae shove," Mrs Donaldson continued. "We had armaments, alright. And we defended this place with all we were worth. It's oor castle the noo," Mrs Donaldson leaned forward, squinting in the candlelight. "And nae body's goin' tae tak it frae us, ken?"

"Ma wife runs a tight ship. Or should I say castle?" Mr Donaldson said. "We have our chores, and everyone must attend to their assigned tasks to ensure the Community runs smoothly. There are nae favourites. We, all o' us, work hard to provide food, care for the animals, keep the buildings maintained, our members clothed, and the army trained and supplied to defend us—for, unfortunately, that is still required."

Siobhan stared at the glass Donaldson handed her. Her face was pale.

Just as pale as on the way to Derrick Lloyd's place.

"Are ye okay, lass?" Mrs Donaldson asked Siobhan. "Ye are looking a wee bitty peely-wally."

"We've travelled a long way these past two days," Rory said, standing and stepping away from the table.

"I must admit, I feel a little lightheaded." Siobhan let go of her glass and blinked over her untouched meal.

"Ye must eat something, Mrs Campbell," Mr Donaldson said.

"It's lovely," Siobhan said. "But I don't think I could."

Rory stepped behind Mrs Donaldson's chair and reached for Siobhan. "Perhaps I'd better get my wife upstairs," he said.

"Aye, do," Mrs Donaldson said.

"Come, Siobhan." Rory placed his hand under her elbow and helped her to stand.

Siobhan was getting paler by the moment. Rory assisted her out of the grand hall, and they crept to the staircase.

"You okay?" Rory asked Siobhan, his shoulders tensing.

Siobhan answered with a slight nod. Her eyes were half closed and the muscles around her neck and collarbones, clearly seen in the low-cut evening dress, stood out with each breath. Halfway up the stairs all her weight leaned into his hand supporting her, and her head sagged.

"Siobhan!" Rory scooped her up in his arms and raced up the staircase to their room.

"Are ye all right, Mrs Campbell?" The woman who'd run the bath, Moira, stood on the staircase. "Och, let me help ye," she said and followed him into the bedroom.

He placed Siobhan on the large bed.

"Loosen her clothing." Moira rolled Siobhan and made to unzip her dress.

"Oh, I'm okay," Siobhan mumbled.

"You sure, Siobhan?" Rory asked. "You just passed oot!" Rory rubbed the back of his neck.

"Her colour is improving," Moira said.

"I'm fine now, Moira. Thank you," Siobhan said.

"Och, okay, I'll leave ye," Moira said. "I'll tell Mrs Donaldson you are all right the noo." Moira left, closing the door behind her.

"Siobhan? What's wrong?" he asked. "Are they someone to worry about in the future? You seemed pale for a while back there. Ye have nae eaten a thing. I'll get them to send something up." He stood still, waiting for her to answer.

A knock came at the door and Moira burst in carrying a tray full of food.

"Mrs Donaldson insists Mrs Campbell has some food when she's feeling up to it." Moira placed the tray on the coffee table at the foot of the bed. "A good night's sleep is what ye require, young lady," she said to Siobhan, then she turned to Rory. "You let your wife have an undisturbed night, so she recovers, aye?"

"Aye," he answered.

Rory's forehead tightened. He followed Moira to the door, shut it behind her and paced back to Siobhan. She lay with her eyes closed, barely stirring. Her cheeks were pale, but a shade of pink had reappeared on her lips. She put her hand to her forehead, and her breathing seemed much easier.

"What's goin' on, lass?" he asked, pushing down a tempest of concern. He needed to focus.

"I don't know. I just came over all funny. Lightheaded." She indicated with her chin to the tray on the coffee table. "I couldn't face food."

"You must eat," he said.

"No." She shook her head. "I'd bring it up."

"Just no' feeling well? Not bad people in the future?" he asked.

She nodded and her cleavage rose with a deep breath. "I think Moira's right," she said. "I need sleep."

Rory pursed his lips. Her colour *was* returning.

"Dinnae scare me like that." He kissed her cheek. It was cool and salty. "Sleep then. I love you. Get better, aye?"

She didn't answer. The rise and fall of her chest steadied and slowed with her slumber.

"Don't be sick," Rory whispered. "We need to get home, and soon."

Chapter Twenty-Two

Tummel House Community

Faint tapping brought Rory out from sleep and the smell of leftover food going off wafted up from the tray of scraps of last evening's meal. Siobhan had slept and Rory had eaten the lot but had fallen asleep late. The music thumping through the floor had continued to the wee hours. Rory rolled over and reached out for Siobhan, but the bed was empty. He got up. Tapping came from the door but retching came from the bathroom.

"Siobhan?" Rory hurried to the bathroom. Siobhan wore a dressing gown and was kneeling over the toilet, gagging into the bowl.

"You're being sick?" he asked. "But you haven't eaten?"

Siobhan sat back, gasping and holding her hair away from her face. "Tell me about it."

The tapping grew louder.

"You'll be okay?" he asked.

"Yes." She let go of her hair. "They've been knocking for a while."

Rory walked to the door.

"Rory!" Xian hissed through the door.

"Aye." Rory opened it. "What's wrong?"

"Your presence is wanted at the breakfast table," Xian said.

"We're being summoned again?"

"Yes," Xian whispered. "Man, the missus seems to rule with an iron fist. You'd better get down there. She keeps asking me questions I'd rather you answered."

Rory glanced at the bathroom. It was empty and Siobhan had moved to the bed and now sat on its edge.

"You go, Rory," she said and pulled the dressing gown closer around her.

"I'll see you down there shortly, okay?" Xian said.

Rory's forehead tightened. He shut the door, strode to the bed, and knelt in front of Siobhan. Her colour had returned to her pale beauty, not the *pale-unwell* of last evening. She seemed herself again, apart from dark circles under her eyes.

"You look better," he said. "Ah... breakfast?"

"No, I'll get ready to leave. Be back as soon as you can." She leaned in close. "Just take me home, please," she asked.

"Aye, lass," he said then caressed her cheek; it was cool. "Are you up to a day on the road?"

"Yes," she said. "I feel better now I've got rid of whatever bothered my tummy."

Rory dressed and left her then met Xian in the passage downstairs. Breakfast was in the same hall as last evening's wedding feast where people of all ages sat along the tables still arranged from the wedding breakfast. A baby in a highchair cried as its mother wiped its face. A young child ran past Rory out of the hall, followed by two others who grabbed a ball and a bat that leaned against the wall beside the door. A fire roared in the fireplace at the top end of the room. The aroma of fried bacon, porridge and coffee, which had wafted into Rory's face while he walked the corridor with Xian, now hit him full-on and his mouth watered.

Mrs Donaldson sat in the same place as the previous evening and beckoned to him. "Come, sit next to me."

Mr Donaldson sat to her left, peering over his spectacles at Rory. "How is your wee wifey this morning?" he asked.

"Siobhan is feeling a bit better, thank you, and anxious to be going home." Rory sat on the seat beside Mrs Donaldson.

A youth placed a plate of bacon and bannocks before Rory. "Coffee, sir?"

"Och, please," he replied. "Have nae had coffee for a wee while, ken."

The lad poured the coffee and Rory took a sip of the scalding bitterness.

"When you say home, you mean the Invercharing Community, don't you?" Mrs Donaldson asked.

"Aye," Rory answered.

"But your wife said she is from the Government Bunker," Mrs Donaldson said.

"That is true, but we are now married, so I'm taking her home." Rory forked a mouthful of succulent bacon.

"So, the Scottish Government is coming out of its bunker?" Mrs Donaldson asked, her gaze following his hands while he continued eating. "About time." There was a touch of derision in Mrs Donaldson's tone.

"So it is," Mr Donaldson said and pushed a butter dish across to Rory.

"Siobhan and I are to spread the word," Rory said, "for any who would be interested in holding conversations with the Government as they endeavour to lead once more."

"So, there will be elections?" Mrs Donaldson asked.

"Och, there's a First Minister. Bethany Watts." Rory bit into his bannock.

"And how was she elected?" Mrs Donaldson asked.

"Those who live in the Bunker voted her in," Rory said.

Mrs Donaldson pulled her tartan shawl tighter around herself then straightened in her chair while Mr Donaldson stirred his tea with lips pursed.

"So, if the Scottish Government is to govern once more, will we get a chance to have representatives and vote in whomever *we* wish to represent us?" Mrs Donaldson asked. "Or is it to be a government elected by the chosen few?"

Good points, Mrs.

"And will we—nae, *when* will we be taxed?" she asked.

Rory finished his bacon, its saltiness lingering on his tongue. Siobhan should be here. She had the answers to the questions Mrs Donaldson asked.

"And will we be allowed to keep oor army"—she leaned into him— "until law and order is truly established? They'll no' take my army."

"This is true," Mr Donaldson said and lifted his gaze from his hot drink to set it on Rory.

"These are the sort o' subjects you need to talk about with the Government," Rory replied. "I take it you would be interested in such discussions."

"Ye are right there, laddie." Mrs Donaldson glanced at her husband. "We're in. You just name the time and place."

"Siobhan will be pleased to hear it," Rory said. "We'll get back to you once we're home and have reported to the Government."

"Ye must stay until your new wife is feeling better," Mrs Donaldson said. "At least till she's had some breakfast."

Rory thanked Mrs Donaldson, sculled his coffee, shoved the last morsel of bannock into his mouth, and rose from the table. At the far end of the breakfast hall, Xian and Micah stepped away from their own table and walked out of the hall. Rory left and ran up the stairs two at a time, then pushed open the door to their room. Siobhan was dressed and packing her saddle bags, her hair neatly in a French roll.

"Ready when you are." Siobhan's face glowed her healthy natural colour and her eyes sparkled.

"Ahh... ye are okay, then?" Rory's hand rested on the doorknob. "The Donaldsons insist we dinnae leave until you have eaten." He chewed his lip. "Ye up to that?"

"Yes, I think I am now," Siobhan said. "It's truly passed, whatever it was. And a good night's sleep on a comfy mattress has helped immensely."

Rory grabbed the packed bags and walked down the stairs with Siobhan.

"I'll not be long," Siobhan said then headed for the breakfast hall.

Rory turned to the back door that led to the stables where Micah and Xian readied the horses.

"One for the road, young Campbell?" Mr Donaldson said. He followed Rory, a hipflask in his hand. "Ye must understand, my wife and I have worked hard to have this life." He stepped beside Rory as they headed for the stables. "It could have been a disaster. We may have been overwhelmed at first by the troubles, but we hung in there and have a good life, as ye can well see. Almost normal."

Rory took the still proffered flask and had a sip. Warmth slid down his throat and heated his middle, mirroring the respect he had for this man, his wife, and their Community.

"I ken what you're saying," Rory said. "My parents sacrificed all to forge the Community where I live, and many come for safety and normality in this"— he sighed— "corrupted world." He took another pull of *uisge beatha*. "I ken where your wife's coming from, honestly, I do. You dinnae need to explain or apologise."

"My woman's a hard one," Mr Donaldson said. "But once you've won her over, she's on your side for life."

***

They rode hard for the next two days, and by the middle of the third day the heaviness of fatigue dragged on Siobhan's limbs. Rory pushed the horses, alternating a fast walk with a trot throughout the days of light rain interspersed with watery sunshine. Densely forested mountains blanketed in misty rain lay either side, increasing in height and severity as the days wore on. By late afternoon, Siobhan's lower back twinged, followed by a dull ache that didn't go away.

Rory ordered a halt.

"Come over here, lass," he said. "You look miserable."

Siobhan leaned forward and lifted her leg over the saddle. Her inner thigh muscles spasmed and her leg stuck on the horse's rump. Rory jumped off Boy, his feet landing lightly and his face holding an ill-concealed grin.

"Don't you laugh at me, Rory Campbell," she said. "You were born in a saddle. I was not."

He stepped around behind her and brought his hands to her waist, surrounding her in his strong grip.

"Just ease yoursel' off slowly," he said. "I've got you."

She landed on the ground and staggered, her legs and feet—no—the whole lower half of her body, were not obeying her. Rory walked her to Boy. The tall stallion nickered at her approach, and she patted his long black forehead and muzzle while the feeling returned to her legs. Then Rory helped her into the saddle and mounted behind her. Xian took her horse's reins and led it with the packhorse.

Wet mist dampened Siobhan's cheeks and trickled down her face. A heaviness collected inside her, and emotions weighed on her as her mind scrambled for a justifiable reason to be so churned up.

Must be PMT, she thought. Although she was usually unaffected by it, unlike the other women she'd lived with in the Bunker. Then her shoulders trembled, and she couldn't stop it. She ached, and she was all mixed up inside, and she wanted to be home, *now*, with Rory, in a place that was *theirs*.

Xian glanced at her then nudged the horses ahead to walk with Micah and his men. The thumb of Rory's left hand rubbed the reins.

"Are you no' happy, Siobhan?" he asked. "I'm sorry I laughed at you."

The *clip-clop* of Boy's tread filled the air for a short distance.

"You mad at me?" he asked. "You want to go home?"

"Yes," she said through a tight throat.

"I'll turn around now, then."

"Turn around, why?" She sniffed tears away.

"The Bunker—" he began.

"Is not my home," she said. "You know that."

"Why are you so upset?" he asked. "The ride too much for you? I dinnae have a vehicle. Och well, I do but nae fuel—"

"Rory, I'm fine. I'm just a little emotional. I'm sorry." She sniffed again.

He put his arm around her waist, slipping into her coat and holding her tight to him. "Well then, we'll be home soon. Hang in there." His large hand under her coat heated most of her waist.

"You think I'm a wimp," she said.

"What?"

"You think I'm weak," she said. Warm, wet tears blended with the cool mist coating her cheeks. "A soft, pampered..."

He held her tighter. "Ssh," he said into her ear. "That's the last thing I think you are." He snorted. "You can whip those soldiers in the Bunker into line. You can stand up to Bethany-stuck-up-I'm-the-Queen-of-the-Castle-Watts." He shook his head. "Weak is something you are not."

They rode on in silence, except for the birds chirping in the thick forest beside the road to Inverness.

"I love you, Siobhan," he said. "You're strong and brave. You're stepping out into the unknown and I'm amazed that you are but, boy, I'm thankful too. In all honesty, you're married to a man you barely ken. You're going to live with a Community of people who you also dinnae ken. You're leaving all the comforts of the world you grew up in and you're having a camping trip to get to your new life. A camping trip in the wilds of the A9."

They both laughed then. She leaned into him; the body heat rising from his open collar warmed her neck and her heart warmed with her love for him.

"We don't know each other in-depth, but we know enough to start, yes?" she said resting her hand on his tucked into her coat.

"Aye," he said softly.

"I knew from the journey to Loch Ewe, and then dealing with the nuclear problem on that submarine," Siobhan said, "that you are the man I want to be with. No matter how much time together that may be."

His chest rose behind her as he took a breath to speak. "We have nae had a chance to talk fully about your journey to the future. How did you manage to avoid yourself?" he asked.

Siobhan sat straighter. "Ahh, I—*me*—in the future, was busy."

"All day? What with?"

"Our children," she said.

"Och—"

Yelling came from the forest to their left and bandits emerged from the tree line. Ahead, Micah and his men spun back with Xian to join her and Rory, making a tight group to ward off the approaching, and possibly unfriendly, bandits.

"Och, no!" Rory shouted over Siobhan's head at Micah. "I thought you'd warned these bandits off, McNair!"

Micah's face was a storm. He pulled his handgun out, raised it in the air and fired a shot. The man leading the charge of the bandits turned to the sound and pulled on his reins and ordered his people to cease. They stopped yelling, except for one woman whose focus was on Rory. She maintained her charge, her massive shoulders moving forward with the motion of the horse, her stocky thighs urging it on.

Rory slipped his arm out from Siobhan's coat and jolted her forward, pressing her face into Boy's rough mane. Rory's large hand, firm in the centre of her back, held her down.

"Deet!" the head bandit yelled. "Deet!" he screamed as the cropped-haired woman continued to charge at Rory. In the corner of Siobhan's vision, Rory held his handgun and aimed at the woman rushing toward them.

"Stop, ye stupid woman, afore ye get killed!" The leader galloped his horse to join her. "Stop!" he yelled, almost at her horse's rear.

This caught her attention, and she slid her gaze from Rory to her leader who shook his head, then she left off her charge, easing her horse away from Siobhan and Rory. Boy pranced and skittered, hooves clattering on the road. Rory pulled him up, preventing his flight. Siobhan lifted her head as Deet rode past; she glared at Rory with pure hate emanating from her deep brown eyes. Siobhan shivered.

"Jock! The deal was you left us alone. Okay?" Micah shouted at their leader who'd stopped his horse near Rory and Siobhan.

"Aye, I ken. Did nae see it was you first off, aye?" Jock glowered at Deet.

"Get lost," Micah yelled. "Take ya savage woman with ye, yeah?"

"Okay." Jock's reply was sullen. The woman had returned and pulled her horse up close to him. "Deet's still sore from where ya friend stabbed her. Where're ye headed?" He pointed to the direction they would go. "Back the ways? North?"

Rory breathed hard behind Siobhan as Micah turned to face him. There was a silent question between them. Rory would want to know if they could trust them, and Micah seemed to know this particular group of bandits. Micah's nod was barely visible.

"Yeah," Micah said.

Jock looked Siobhan up and down, like a man used to making an assessment of a person from the briefest of encounters. So did the woman named Deet whose lip curled in a snarl.

"Ye best no' take the rest of the A9 to Inverness. Bad yun's ahead. Ye'd better aim for campin' on Culloden tha night. Safer that way, ken."

"Thank ye for the advice," Micah said then rummaged in his saddlebags, lifted out some tinned foods, and handed them to Jock.

"We're being followed," Rory said and nudged Boy closer to Jock's horse. "Maybe you can distract them for us."

Siobhan swivelled in the saddle to look Rory in the eye. "Followed?" she asked. "By whom?"

"Your friends from the Bunker," he growled.

"How do you know?" Siobhan's shoulders bristled. "It could be anybody."

Rory dipped into his pocket, pulled out a small object and held it up between his thumb and forefinger. It was a round disc with electronic circuitry and wires. The disc had been battered, and the wires hung loosely from it.

"Where did you get that?" Cold clamped the back of her neck. It was a technology she was sure that bandits, and even some communities, wouldn't possess.

"I stood on it," Rory said. "It was lying on the floor of our room at Tummel House." He clasped his fist around the tiny device. "And I'm sure *they* would nae have anything like this."

"It may have fallen out of my bag when I dug deep for my evening gown." Siobhan's face tightened as she screwed it in disbelief. "That's a listening device, if I'm not mistaken," she said. A sinking feeling accompanied the revelation. "We're being spied on?"

"They need to stay close to hear anything. Been doing that since leavin' the Bunker," Rory said. "Dinnae look so bothered, Siobhan. If they planned to harm us, they would've by now."

"Don't they trust us—me?" she asked.

"Och, Siobhan, it's me they dinnae like," Rory said. "And that Bethany Watts is nosey."

"It's not Bethany." Her words came out through a quiet growl. "I'd bet all I own on Antony being behind this. He's been whispering into Bethany's ear."

A line furrowed vertically above Rory's nose. "I thought he was locked away," he said.

"He is. Bethany visits often," Siobhan replied. "He seems to have an influence on her."

Rory's jaw muscles tightened, then he crushed the electronic circuitry in his hand.

"Hold them up as much as ye can, if you would nae mind," Rory said to the bandits.

Deet's mouth broadened in a grin.

"We need them alive to question," Rory directed this statement at Deet.

Deet shrugged and turned her horse toward the forest and the group melted back into the tree cover.

Chapter Twenty-Three

Culloden Moor

Mists gathered as the day drew on. They reached Culloden Moor at sunset, having diverted from the remains of the A9 and journeyed overland toward the moor. Siobhan had remained sitting in front of Rory in the saddle. His arms had been tensed around her all the journey, and his hands unusually white-knuckled on the reins. He continually looked around as they rode, watching for any other travellers or bandits who'd be a threat to them. Siobhan was used to this with Rory, but he seemed to be extra vigilant.

They slowed their horses to a walk to pass through the dense forest, their breath fogging their faces as they emerged from the wall of trees to a broad mist-shrouded moor. The cold clamped around Siobhan and she shivered, the only sense of warmth coming through her jacket where she contacted with Rory.

"Dinnae be afraid, Siobhan," Rory said. "The ghosts of those who died here have sensed the love and respect of those who pilgrimage to this place, and they're settled in their rest now."

Vapour swirled in a slight breeze, as if the very ghosts Rory spoke of were waving to her. Apart from their horses' tread the place was silent.

"There's a crofter's cottage, of a sorts, to our left." Micah pointed his chin in that direction. "A bothy now. We still have travellers' rights, and it might be available."

They arrived at a small stone dwelling with a thatched roof. Light shone through the windows and the murmurings of conversation reached them.

"I'll go speak to them," Micah said.

A man emerged from the bothy and chatted to Micah, frowning at first in the lamplight that spilled out from the doorway. Rory nudged Boy closer. The smell of something cooking, probably a stew, wafted toward Siobhan. Her stomach churned, and she swallowed, fighting down the bile.

Micah returned. "They say the place is full but they're happy if we set up outside next to the hut for shelter." He shrugged. "It will provide some protection from the cold."

The odour of cooking meat blew into Siobhan's nostrils. Her stomach lifted and she put her hand to her mouth.

"Xian, you okay setting up?" Rory asked. "I think I need to show Siobhan around a bit."

Rory jumped down and eased her off Boy. Siobhan went to the packhorse and got another coat from her kit. Micah spoke to Rory in low tones, then Rory stepped over to her.

"You've probably never been to Culloden, have you?" Rory's tone was tight. "Let's stretch our legs."

They strode in silence, the churn in Siobhan's stomach easing as they left the cooking odours behind them. Her legs were tight at first, but the further they walked, the more they eased. She wasn't a horsewoman, but she really *had* to get used to *all* of this. Rory held her upper arm and walked stiffly beside her, looking straight ahead, and his mouth was a thin line.

They wandered the still, flat grassland mixed with low growing heather, the mist parting and swirling around them. A strong outdoor scent surrounded her, with the smell of the woods near the moor's edge and, closer, damp heather and grass. Nocturnal insects chirped their mournful night song as Rory led her by granite rocks spaced randomly apart. The moorland evoked a reverence; it was a sacred place. Rory got out his wind-up torch and pointed with its light.

"Grave markers," Rory said.

Siobhan tucked a stray hair behind her ear. Her teachers in the Bunker had taught this era of Scottish history. It was a massacre, and if she recalled correctly, the gravestones marked clans. Too many had died to leave individual memorials. The Duke of Cumberland had led the British forces and those Scots on the side of King George II against Bonnie Prince Charlie and the Scots who supported his claim to the crown. From the Duke of Cumberland's exploits on this very moor, this son of a king had earned the nickname he deserved—the Butcher.

They reached a large round cairn, the height of two men at least. Rory shone his torchlight on it. Inscribed on the large flat stone at its base were the words:

The battle of Culloden was fought on this moor 16th April 1746.

Simply written, but the end of an era, as the Highland clearances followed. Siobhan halted, taking a deep breath to wave away the nausea that had surged within her. The history of this eerie moor reminded her of the battle occurring when she'd left future-Rory. It would be history repeating itself. Rory had seemed sure the Scottish Government would destroy the Invercharing Community and everyone in it—himself, their children, Murray and all whom she would hold dear. And if Antony had his way, the Government would treat all other Communities in the same manner.

"What's wrong, Siobhan?" he asked. "Have you got something to tell me?"

Rory kept a firm grip on her arm and now steered her to face him as they stood by the tall, round cairn. The dim moonlight filtered through the mist, illuminating Rory's face. His brow creased in the middle and his jaw was tight.

"In the future, Rory, there's a civil war," she said. "You command an Alliance of Communities, bandits, and... others. It's not good."

"What?" Rory forced out the word then loosened his grip on her arm. "How?"

"I didn't get the whole story, but Lloyd is not good news." She placed her hand on his arm and stared into his eyes. "Don't get involved with him," she said firmly. "He'll hold you... us, over a barrel when the famine hits. And Antony becomes First Minister."

"No!" Rory shouted into the night. "Are you sure?"

"It's what you and Murray told me," she answered.

Rory let go of her, and, rubbing his mouth and chin, he turned his back to her. He placed his hands on the cairn and leaned into it. His shoulders rose and fell, and he seemed deep in thought for a few moments. The silence of this sacred place of historic memorial pressed upon Siobhan. She closed her eyes, willing the future to never hold a place of remembrance with their names engraved on a cairn.

Rory spun back to face her.

"That's not what I meant about something to tell me." His mouth was a thin line in the moonlight. "Do you truly want me for your husband?"

"Yes." Siobhan did a double take. "What are you asking me—?"

"Are ye pregnant?" he interrupted.

"W—what? No, my period's a bit late but—why?"

Rory shuffled his shoulders a little, then swallowed and said, "Micah, who grew up around women, says you look like you have morning sickness, which does nae always happen just of a morning, ken?"

Siobhan stood immobile, her mouth dropping open. She recounted all she was feeling—the intense emotions and crying over nothing, the tiredness, the nausea, and the fact she had just admitted to Rory—her period was late.

"Ooh! I just may be," she said. A flutter hit her belly—not nausea—followed by a calm understanding.

"You *just may be*?" Rory rasped. "When we have nae even had sex yet?"

She slid her gaze back to Rory's face. His eyes were wide with hurt and sharp ice hit her chest.

"Rory! You're the father. You and I, in the future, certainly had sex." She clenched her hands by her sides. "Don't you trust me?" she whispered hoarsely.

Rory blinked and jutted his jaw. "But how could you be... already?"

"I don't know." She lifted her shoulders a fraction. "It must have accelerated somehow when I travelled back. Rory"—she made him look into her eyes— "*you're* the father. There is no one else. Are you accusing me of being unfaithful? Do you really think I'd—?" Her throat closed, choking on his implied accusation.

He stood back from her, dragging the air through his nostrils, like a raging wind in the otherwise silent night.

"I won't plead for you to believe me, Rory Campbell," she said. "The other day at Lloyd's, as we passed those prostitutes who wolf-whistled at you, you asked if I trusted you. I assumed you were asking if I trusted that you had been faithful to me."

"Aye." His deep voice filled the night.

"Yes," she repeated to him, then said, "well, you need to believe *me* when I say that you are the only man I have had a sexual encounter with in at least the past two years, so if I *am* pregnant, it is *you* who has fathered this child."

Rory's nostrils flared. Then he hung his head, shoulders drooping.

"Och, I'm just trying to understand." He lifted his head and looked her in the eye. "I hate myself for havin' asked you. But it must be the only explanation. The time travel...'n havin' morning sickness and that within a couple of days o'... you know?" He tilted his head to the side and in the moonlight his dimples showed faintly.

"Having fantastic sex with you, Rory Campbell," she said.

The ice was melting.

Time travel makes life so confusing. But she'd waited so long and wouldn't wait any longer for Rory—in *this* time.

"It was fant—?" he began.

She interrupted him and, moving closer, lifted her lips to his. He received them and she kissed his mouth harder, slipping her hands up around his muscled neck and through the soft hair at the base of his skull.

Rory tugged her to himself, holding her hard against him. He moaned and released her, ripping off her coat, then his. He threw them on the ground behind her then eased her down onto the makeshift bed, the thick coats retaining their body heat warmed her naked back.

Rory flung off his trousers. She unzipped hers and he helped her slide them down to her boots, where they snagged. He dragged her boots from her feet, his face broadening with a grin and Siobhan's stomach danced with her laughter. He lay on top of her—lean, warm and firm, and kissed her quickly. Lifting his head back, he stared into her face, his eyes dark and earnest in the moonlight. Then his soft, moist lips encompassed hers and journeyed to her neck, stirring sensations that flew across her skin and burrowed deep inside her. His strong arms held her tighter as she ran her fingers along the length of his bare back, taught muscles rippled beneath her fingertips and a shudder ran through him.

She curled her legs around him, and drew him in.

Chapter Twenty-Four

Culloden Moor

Siobhan walked back to the camp with Rory, his arm tight around her waist—keeping her close to his side. Micah's band had secured the tarps to the trees beside the bothy, and their belongings were now strewn underneath the makeshift tents. A campfire burned a healthy glow against the bothy's sandstone wall.

"There's jerky and I'll prepare bannocks," Micah said, rustling in a saddlebag and bringing out a cast-iron pan.

A woodpile sat next to the bothy, and Xian rolled some logs over for seating around the campfire. Micah handed out jerky and soon hot bannocks followed. After they'd eaten, Micah's men bid them all goodnight and went to their bedrolls while Xian remained sitting on a log by the fire with Micah.

"You've eaten tonight," Rory said and moved his log-stool nearer to Siobhan. He put his arm around her, the firelight glinting in his eyes. "That's good. Got your appetite back."

"Micah's bannocks are first class," she said and lifted her mug of tea in salute. "You should've been a chef, Micah."

"Thank you, Mrs Campbell. It means the world to me that you like my cooking." A genuine smile lit Micah's face as he sat on a log opposite them.

"Please, call me Siobhan," she said.

"Don't make it easier for him to suck up to you, Siobhan," Rory said, his lips next to her cheek. "He's trying everything he can to get into my good-books, ye ken."

"Isn't he already?" she asked.

Rory's mouth drew in at one side.

"Well?" Micah asked.

"He's after ma wee sister," Rory said, ignoring Micah. "You know that?"

"Yes, I know that, Rory." Siobhan raised her eyebrows. She *had* been to the future where Micah and Cèilidh were married.

"I think I'll go sleep. All this food needs digesting," she said to Rory.

She mouthed *talk* and flicked her gaze across to Micah and back, then made herself comfortable in her bedroll under the tarp. The conversation from the fire-circle drifted over. Micah sat opposite Rory, his face side-on to Siobhan.

"Tell me about your mother," Micah asked Rory. "There's lots of stories about her, but what was she really like?"

From the other side of the fire, Rory's face was half-lit by the flames now dying down to embers. "Really?" Rory asked. "You really want tae know?"

"Man, your parents were legends," Micah said. "Of course, I wanna know."

Rory gazed into the fire, his eyes softening. "My mother loved me. Loved all of us. I wasn't as close to her as I would have liked, but my parents were busy with running the Community. She was smart, brave and sensible with lots of ideas and skills. Instead of being consumed by the difficulties, she thought of the good things to work on. Not just the practical things but the beautiful things, such as art and music. She made me, and my brothers and sisters, learn an instrument, ken? Some of us were better than others. I'd rather ride ma horse than play a tin whistle." He snorted a laugh.

"You miss her, man," Micah said.

Rory lifted his head, eyes glistening in the firelight.

"I get it. I miss my mum too," Micah said and looked at the ground. "She was the only one who really loved me, no matter what. She loved me because I was hers. Not because I was good at cooking, or horse riding. Or sneaking things from the stores." Micah chuckled, then his expression turned sober. "Unconditional love, that's what they call it, and she did it."

"What about your father, the King of Fife?" Rory asked.

Micah stared at the flames for some moments, the lines around his eyes grew deeper.

"He likes me, but... unconditional love"—Micah shook his head, his dreads falling over his shoulders— "he knows nothin' about. I'd do anything to make him love me like that." Micah spoke the last words so softly Siobhan could barely hear them.

Siobhan's chest tightened a little and her eyes prickled as she thought about how her father had loved her always. She snuggled deeper into her bedroll.

"Your dad, man, he was *awesome*." Micah broke the brief silence. "We came across him once, when we were out poachin', a long time ago."

Rory grasped his mug, and Xian remained quietly listening to Rory and Micah's conversation.

"We thought we were goners when he caught us," Micah continued. "He was a giant. I thought *I* was tall, but..." Micah mimicked someone taller standing in front of himself. "He looked mean, but he took pity on us. We must've seemed hungry, ken? Well, we were."

Coals popped and sparks flew into the night sky.

"You must miss him too," Micah said and looked over at Rory for a second, then his gaze returned to the flames. "I would, if I had a man like him for a father."

Rory's shoulders lowered a fraction. "I do," he said. "He wasn't just my father. He was my best friend." Rory's voice caught a little. "He taught me how to ride. Gave me Boy. Taught me to survive in the wild. How to handle a firearm. How to hunt. How to... kill. How to defend mysel' and no' kill a man. How to tell right from wrong. Whether a person is lying or no'." Rory's hands tensed around his mug, his knuckles white. "He showed me what loving a woman can mean and how much a man must love her, to claim he truly does."

He glanced at Siobhan then. Tears welled in his lower lids, threatening to spill.

Siobhan's throat constricted, then she let out a quiet, slow sigh. Rory was opening up at last.

"Yeah," Micah said. "He was a great man." Micah's dreads fell across his face.

Rory took a deep breath in and fiddled with the mug, having now loosened his grip on it.

"There's going to be a famine," he said into the flames.

Siobhan grasped the covers of her bedroll. Why had he chosen *that* topic to change the course of the conversation?

Xian leaned forward, until now hidden from Siobhan's view by Rory's form, revealing his expression reflecting her own thoughts.

Surely Rory wouldn't disclose the existence of the Time Machine to Micah?

"What?" Micah's face scrunched as he lifted his head. He pulled his hair behind him and, slipping a leather thong off his wrist, he tied his dreadlocks back. "How'd ye ken that?"

"I have visions." Rory looked over to Micah. "They've come true."

"Wow! Man, like really?"

"Aye," Rory said.

"That's awesome. What are they of?" Micha asked.

"I knew when the Government convoy was coming to our Community."

"Like, you saw it?" Micah leaned his elbows on his knees, threatening to topple into the campfire.

Rory nodded.

"Wow," Micah said. "Ye ken that odd lot who are led by that old professor, Webster? His woman, Dierdra, would love to ken all this. She reads fortunes."

"Oh, aye." Rory frowned.

"She read mine once. Said my woman would belong to an important family." Micah stared straight at Rory.

Rory scratched his upper lip then continued. "Anyway, we need to prepare for this famine. We need—"

"What causes it?" Micah interrupted.

"A volcanic eruption." Rory's eyes glinted and in the firelight his hair blazed ginger.

"What!" Micah turned to Xian. "You're not actin' surprised. Ye ken all this?"

Xian nodded.

"We've gotta tell my dad—"

"No, we don't." Rory held his up hand. "Your father has enough goods stored. He'll be okay."

"He needs to store more. You said it would be a famine," Micah said.

"What will you tell him?" Rory asked. "That Rory-the-seer predicts a sky full o' volcanic ash? Think he's goin' tae believe you? You'll just make me oot tae be a fool."

"But—" Micah began.

"Dinnae." Rory's tone was firm with a hint of violence, then his shoulders relaxed. "You'll abide by what I'm askin' if you want tae see my sister."

"You black-mailin' me to silence?" Micah asked.

"Aye," Rory's answer was firm.

"You afraid you'll look stupid?" Micah asked.

Rory's face hardened for a second.

"Man, ye are," Micah said then let out a soft laugh. "Okay, your secret's safe with me. But people need to prepare."

"And they will," Rory said.

"When's this gonna happen?"

"Not sure of a date," Rory answered. "Visions dinnae come with a calendar. I just ken it will be soon and we must plant more, grow more, increase our livestock and store more food and let the other Communities know to increase their yields and store all they can."

"My men can help," Micah said. "After all, it's gonna be my family too. Isn't it?"

The corner of Rory's mouth curled upwards. "Aye, I suppose."

"Wha hoo!" Micah's face beamed true happiness.

Rory glanced over to Siobhan. His expression was thoughtful. Her mouth tightened. It seemed he'd made his decision about this man based on her knowledge of the future. Only time would tell if *that* future was the one now awaiting them.

Chapter Twenty-Five

Invercharing Community, 2061

A grating, with a final metallic screech, accompanied the opening of the huge gate to the Invercharing Community Compound, and home. Kendra stood in the centre of the forecourt with her hands on her hips; her long, thick, dark plait hung over her front.

"Took the long way around, did you, boss?" Kendra squinted against the midmorning sun.

"Och, the horses were almost as tired as we were. I could nae push them." Rory slid his leg over Boy and landed to help Siobhan down from the saddle.

If he were to be truthful, Siobhan's nausea had prevented anything faster than a walk. The worst of their travel hazards were behind them, and the only one champing at the bit to get home had been Micah—who now jumped off his horse, threw the reins to one of his crew, and ran inside.

"What did I miss?" Rory said over his shoulder to Kendra while he unloaded Siobhan's bags from the packhorse.

"A baby," Kendra said then picked up a bag in each hand.

"How did you—? Oh, Callum and Mandy! What did they have?" Rory asked.

"A boy, brother," Callum shouted from the entranceway of the main building and strode toward him. They met in a bear hug.

"Well done," Rory said into his twin's ear. "Can't wait to meet him."

"Is Mandy well?" Siobhan asked from behind them.

"She's braw. Welcome home, Siobhan." Callum embraced her. "We're so glad you're here at last," he said.

"Aye, we all are," Kendra said. "Never seen such a moping—"

"That's enough," Rory interrupted, heat burning his cheeks. "I did nae miss this abuse, that's for certain."

He picked up the bags and indicated with a tilt of his head toward the main door. "Come, Siobhan, we can settle you in. Then I—we—must meet with the Chief Council."

A tired smile barely lifted the corner of Siobhan's mouth. He'd get used to the *we* soon enough and he needed her brains at this meeting.

"I'll call the Council together, then?" George said from the doorway.

"George. Thank you."

"Wonderful to have you here, Siobhan," George said as Rory walked past. "And not just for Rory's sake."

***

After he and Siobhan had eaten some tea and sourdough bread in their quarters, Rory took Siobhan to the room of the farmhouse used for Chief Council sessions. Dr Farquhar sat at the top of the makeshift long table, his jowls hanging below his chin. Rory recalled that his mother had said he was a doctor of the old-school type, from the days when a doctor's word was law and people regarded them like gods. Dr Farquhar had learned that it wouldn't be so on this Council, and he'd been a vital resource in the formative years of the Community. He was an elderly man, but retirement was an unknown in the Community.

Aunty Bec, who sat next to Dr Farquhar, was a testament to that. Both she and Uncle Brendan were now in their late seventies and still as active as they could manage. George Stobbart sat beside them, straight-backed and broad-shouldered in his mid-sixties. Mr Grant, who'd also joined the Community in its early days, sat opposite him.

"Angela would be present if the allure of *real government* hadn't magnetised her to the Government Bunker," Rory said to those gathered.

Uncle Brendan cocked a brow. Rory clenched his jaw and a twinge of muscle spasm shot up to his temple.

"Sorry I'm late," Christine said as she snuck in the door.

Her blonde hair hung in a ponytail over her plain home-spun top and wisps of hair had come out of its tie. She would've had a busy morning attending to the unwell of the Community.

"Thank you, everyone, for leaving your duties and meeting at such short notice," Rory began. "I'm hoping you will be happy with Siobhan's presence here with us at this Council meeting."

Heads nodded around the table, but not all the faces held an amicable expression. Rory's forehead tightened.

"What has the Government been up to, son?" Dr Farquhar asked, his jowls wobbling with each word.

"The Scottish Government is serious about meeting with leaders of the various groups of us out here." Rory remained standing behind the chair assigned to him. "They want to be effective again."

"Would that be other Communities, or any others who dinnae live underground?" Mr Grant asked.

"It means anyone willing to pull together to build Scotland once more, Mr Grant," Siobhan said.

"Hmph," Mr Grant replied. "What will they want from us? Will they lord it over us, or can we ever be equals?" His hands resting on the table clutched tight to a pencil and paper. "What if we don't want to change our way of running this Community?"

"What about our resources?" Dr Farquhar asked, leaning on the table. "They may take our fighting men and women for their own defence force."

"These are all points for discussion and negotiation, gentlemen." Siobhan pushed a stray hair behind her ear. "No one will make you do anything. You won't lose your autonomy."

Siobhan's face was pale and dark circles showed under her eyes. Rory pulled her chair out and indicated for her to sit. Maybe he should've insisted they rest and then meet later on in the day. But they had so little time to prepare for such a significant event.

Rory rolled his shoulders and remained standing behind his chair. Dr Farquhar and Mr Grant stared at Siobhan, their scowls identical.

"Tell us about the Bunker, Rory," Uncle Brendan, sitting to Rory's left, asked, leaning forward, his eyes bright with curiosity.

"I must admit it was an eye-opener," Rory said. "What they have in that Bunker... We spent some time in the archives. Full o' history. But we can speak of this at another time. The most pressing thing has to do with just that. Time."

Christine stopped fidgeting, George sat straighter and Mr Farquhar's jowls shook a wee bit more.

"The Time Machine worked." Rory placed his hand on the back of his chair.

"No!" Uncle Brendan jolted in his seat. "Murray got it to work?"

"He did, but the Government does nae ken it," Rory said.

"How did you keep it from them, Rory?" Aunty Bec asked.

Rory glanced down at Siobhan, who gave a slight nod.

"Murray and Siobhan were the only ones with the machine when Siobhan got caught in it and ended up in the future." Rory spread his gaze along to every face, capturing each startled and surprised expression. Dr Farquhar gasped, then glowered at Siobhan.

"It normally goes to the past, doesn't it?" George asked. "What did you see, Siobhan?"

Siobhan described the volcanic eruption and ensuing famine due to crop failure. Rory had primed her to omit the fact of civil war until he'd learned and understood all she could recall. When she'd finished, George blinked, and the rest of the Chief Council were silent. The ticking of the wall clock thundered through the room.

Uncle Brendan stirred. "A dark age once more," he said.

"Yes, but we are pre-warned," Siobhan stated.

"And we must prepare," Rory said. "I'll get those in charge of planting the harvests to gather more seeds, increase our sowing, therefore our crop yields—"

"When will this be?" Dr Farquhar interrupted.

"Within the next five years," Siobhan said.

"And we need to store our produce effectively, so it lasts," Uncle Brendan said, his mind was as busy as ever.

"How long will this famine go on?" Christine asked.

"We're nae sure." Rory looked along the table at her, throwing all the conviction he could into his voice. "But it happens."

"We must inform our fellow Communities." Aunty Bec jiggled in her seat.

"This seems a great undertaking," Dr Farquhar said. "Someone must oversee this project." He looked at Rory.

"But he runs the Militia," George said.

"There are others who can do that," Dr Farquhar retorted. "This serious matter calls for sensible leadership."

Mr Grant stood. He'd remained quiet, his expression gaining in severity by the moment.

"Friends," he sighed. "I fear I dinnae have the energy for all o' this. More of our Community members must help direct and manage this important undertaking. I ken this is not a good time as, according to our time-traveller"— he dipped his head in Siobhan's direction— "the world will be in crisis once more. But I believe this Council needs more people of vitality, especially now it's required for this new problem. One which I cannae deny is a great threat. I ken the young ones are busy, but their strength and vision are vital, now more than ever." He looked at his hands clasped in front of him. "Dr Farquhar and I have discussed this." He turned to Dr Farquhar. "Reg, I hope ye dinnae mind if I say this. We were planning to retire from the Chief Council soon. But I think we must do it now and make way for those who will fight this challenge, as, if the future remains as Mrs Campbell saw, it will be soon upon us."

"Why don't you hold an election?" Siobhan asked, startling Rory out of the numbness creeping through him, about to engulf him. How could these men abandon them now? Abandon *him* now?

All heads turned to Siobhan.

"You base the Community System on democracy, don't you?" she asked. "Well, why not see who would be interested in governing, particularly at this crucial time, and have a ballot? Then you'll not just second people to a position, but have those who are willing and, like Mr Grant and Dr Farquhar say, have the *energy* to do what is required for the survival of this Community."

Rory dragged his thumb along his upper lip and embarrassed smiles emerged on one or two faces.

"We have never held elections, young lady. Not because we don't believe in democracy." An outright amused grin spread Dr Farquhar's jowls wide. "A change in personnel has not been required until now."

Rory caught Siobhan's wide-eyed gaze.

"I believe this is an excellent suggestion," Uncle Brendan said. "Thank you, Siobhan. Who's with us on this idea?"

A chorus of *ayes* erupted from the Chief Council.

They planned the elections and the meeting soon ended, and Rory stepped from the Chief Council meeting room into the passage, swerving to avoid knocking into Kendra.

"Your bandit friend," Kendra said and leaned in closer to Rory. "You know, the one who's after your wee sister?"

"What about him?" Rory asked.

"He's found some guys," Kendra spoke low into his ear. "And is, well, *questioning them*, is the way I'll put it."

Chapter Twenty-Six

Invercharing Community, 2061

Rory stifled a groan and followed Kendra outside to the large sheds. Siobhan kept close while Kendra led them to the barn where they used to house the Time Machine.

"I'm not sure if you'd want to see this, Siobhan," Kendra said as she rested her hand on the large latch of the barn's door.

"Now you have me intrigued, Kendra," Siobhan replied. "It will be informative, I'm sure."

Kendra's right eye squinted. "Informative is not the way I'd put it." She opened the door.

They stepped in to groans echoing off the far wall of this shed. Two chairs were at the end on the earthen floor, facing away from the door. A man sat on each, their hands tied behind them, heads drooping. They both wore civilian clothes of factory-made quality. Micah's hand swung down and slapped the face of the man on the right. The man's head snapped to the side and blood sprayed from his mouth. He groaned. Micah's men stood stony faced behind him. Micah raised his hand high, ready to hit him again.

"What are you doing, Micah?" Rory shouted and stormed in. "We don't treat people like that here!"

One man sat with his head bowed, motionless. He could've been unconscious. Blood streamed from the nose of the one who'd received the slap, and his eyes were swelling.

Micah pulled his hand back to his side and clenched it into a fist. "They were spying on you."

"It was obvious they were followin' us." Rory stood nose-to-nose with Micah. Winter-blue eyes stared back in defiance. "Did you find oot why before you slapped them into oblivion?"

"Aye, the Government does nae trust ye," Micah said.

"Also obvious!" Rory yelled into Micah's face.

"Man, they bugged you. They were listenin'. *To everything*," Micah said. "But I've destroyed the recordings."

"Did you listen to them?" Rory asked.

"No." Micah stared directly at Rory.

"They're gone?" Rory asked.

"Yeah." Micah stared back.

"Thanks." Rory softened his tone a fraction then stepped back.

"Do you no' value your privacy?" Micah asked. "What sort of government spies on its people?"

"Any sort, you naïve fool!" Rory ground his teeth. "Kendra will help your guys take these men to the detainment rooms." To Kendra he said, "Get them cleaned up and tended to by Cèilidh, or Christine if it's required."

Kendra and one of Micah's crew began to untie the men.

"Keep it quiet," Rory ordered.

He ran his gaze up and down Micah. His knuckles were raw and covered with blood, beads of sweat sat on his forehead, and the metallic scent of blood filled the area. Micah had tied his dreads back—he'd meant business.

"Let Cèilidh know it was Micah, if she asks," he said to Kendra. "She should know what she's getting herself into."

"Man, I did this for you," Micah said, his shoulders heaving. "And your woman. You guys could be in danger. Hell, this whole Community could." Pleading sat behind his words.

"You're trying too hard to get my approval," Rory said through the bile in his throat.

He caught Siobhan's arm and tugged her to walk out of the barn. She'd remained silent with a shocked expression filling her features. He needed to distance himself from this treatment of Government people. His veins boiled.

He spun and faced Micah. "They're our allies, for heaven's sake!"

Micah flinched.

"Siobhan may know these men, but neither of them is recognisable in their current state," Rory spat at him.

"Och, you're such a hard-arse." Micah burst out. "Everyone kens how tough you are! I mean *everyone*. All the bandits are shit-scared of you, even the ones who spent three months here."

"Being tough doesn't mean you disregard the rights of others, even if they're violating yours." Rory speared a finger at him, willing himself to remain where he stood and so prevent more violence. "Never do this sort o' thing again, Micah. There's a time and a place for physical persuasion. But it's not here, and not now. And never to the Government's people."

***

"You call it the training shed," Siobhan said through deep breaths. "But it's really the torture chamber."

Siobhan's home-spun shirt clung to her back with sweat. They'd been home for two weeks and every day Rory had ensured she spent the afternoons on the mats learning martial art skills under Kendra's instruction, while he performed his militia duties. Today Kendra taught her wrestling skills.

"Again," Kendra said.

Kendra lay on the mat and wriggled her fingers in a come-here gesture. When Siobhan was within arm's reach, Kendra grabbed her collar and twisted, her arm now tightening across Siobhan's neck on the right, threatening to cut off the blood supply to her brain on that side.

"Before I strangle a pregnant woman—which I'm told isn't a good idea—what're you goin' to do?" Kendra asked.

"Grab your thumb and…" she said then finished her answer by demonstrating it and getting out of Kendra's grasp.

Siobhan's mouth lifted at the side. Kendra changed the grip to her advantage and pulled Siobhan's arm out to a stretch.

"You're exposed now," Kendra said. "And you've lost any upper-hand you'd gained." Kendra briefly let go. "Don't smile too soon." She placed her arm around Siobhan's and held it in a lock, tucking it tight into her shoulder as she squatted on all fours beside her.

Siobhan swung her legs over and grabbed at Kendra's back, slipping her left foot down to her legs, hooking her heel around Kendra's thigh and pulling her over, and slipping her right leg beneath Kendra as she did. Sweat cooled Siobhan's brow as she pushed with all her might and flipped Kendra over, ending on top of her and swiftly changing the lock into one around Kendra's neck.

Kendra *tapped* her submission. "Well done. You're a natural."

"Thanks," Siobhan's mouth stretched. "Can't wait to do some kicks and punches."

"I don't think that's a good idea," Rory said from the edge of the mat. "Not until the baby's born, aye?"

"How long have you been there?" Siobhan asked Rory, then knelt and bowed to Kendra who returned it.

Siobhan strode to Rory, his smile erupting as she approached.

"How'd you learn to be so good at grappling?" he asked.

"Grappling? Ah, I don't know. I never was interested in the judo they taught in the Bunker... But I'm loving this." She slipped her arms around his waist as he looked intently into her eyes. "And yes, I won't attempt anything that would harm our baby."

"You seem to know what to do instinctively." His grin broadened.

"What time will you be finished today?" She kissed him quickly.

"We will be working late tonight," he said. "The Council want you and I to start deciding on the ballots and finding out who does and doesn't want to be nominated for election."

Siobhan let out a quiet sigh. That would mean another late night falling into bed exhausted. It had happened almost every night since their return, and she was fast learning that life in a Community was hard graft.

***

Rory leaned against the wall inside the main hall filled with members of the Community placing their votes. They were to vote for their preferred nine out of those who had agreed to nomination for a place on the Chief Council. Those with the most votes would be in.

"Secret ballot like the Greeks did it," Xian said then shoved the folded ballot card into the slot at the top of the wooden ballot box.

"I'm sure they wouldn't have wasted so much paper," Kendra said. "Glad I'm not on paper recycling duty."

"What do you think, Rory?" Xian asked. "Who, apart from you, will they elect?"

Rory shook his head. "I never bet on anything, Xian."

"You'll be there, boss," Kendra said. "Haven't you been listening to what people are saying?"

"I've heard a few whispers that my wife should nae have been allowed a vote, being a recent addition to the Community." He lifted an eyebrow. "And a grumble from Micah's camp."

"It raised some questions," Xian said. "When *do* new arrivals become eligible for a vote?"

Rory grunted. "When he's married to ma sister and not before."

***

"We have counted and recounted the votes," Uncle Brendan said as he stood on the raised platform in the main hall where the whole Invercharing Community gathered.

Rory stood in the crowd, surrounded by murmured comments and speculations. His guts danced—not a jig but a jerk. He was nervous, he'd own that.

Siobhan slipped her arm in his, tugging on him. She'd snuck in through the back of the hall, having spent time with Mandy and their nephew. The tightness in Rory's shoulders eased with her presence beside him. He put his arm around her slim waist and tucked her to his side. He'd only seen her for a wee bit today and, in fact, they had spent little time together at all since their return. Catching up with George and the militia, and planning their strategies for food collection and storage, plus all the incidentals for this ballot, had taken up most of Rory's time.

"George Stobbart." Uncle Brendan began the announcement of the successful candidates. "Christine Maynard. Rebecca Hamilton," Uncle Brendan laughed. "Brendan Hamilton. Oh, that's me." Clapping erupted around Rory, and giggles rose from someone nearby.

Xian leaned into Rory's shoulder. "I'm surprised he hasn't announced your name yet." He glanced across Rory to Siobhan. "Or yours, Mrs Campbell," he said.

Rory stared straight ahead.

What if they don't elect me?

He chewed the inside of his cheek. He desired to serve the Invercharing Community and make sure they would be safe from the future Siobhan had described, especially the civil war. Though he would only mention that to the Chief Council if all his efforts to prepare for a famine failed. He'd serve his people even if he wasn't on the Council.

"Callum Campbell," Uncle Brendan called from the platform.

A shout broke from the members of the militia who stood along the back wall. Callum grinned and flicked a querying glance at him. Rory shrugged.

"Mary McKenzie," Uncle Brendan continued, "Michael Moore." Rory joined in the applause for the election of the head teacher and the Community's artisan skilled in weaving.

"Not looking good, man," Xian said under his breath.

"Xian Law." More cheers came from the militia members.

"What!" Xian's jaw dropped. "I said I'd be okay if they elected me, but I didn't think…"

Rory's chest vibrated with chuckles for his friend. Or maybe it was nerves. Siobhan was frowning again, and her eyes held a question. He swallowed down the pain in the back of his throat that had risen from his stomach.

"Now, ladies and gentlemen," Uncle Brendan said when the cheering died down. "We have one more member to announce and we have saved this until last. We have been overwhelmed by your votes." Uncle Brendan stood straighter and cast his gaze around the gathered Community. "As you know, the ballot was for nine members to sit on the Chief Council and every single one of you voted for this man—Rory Campbell."

Siobhan kissed him on the cheek and Xian slapped him on the back. Rory let out the breath he'd held for so long as those present clapped and cheered. His task might be easier now. He fought down his rapid heart rate and tucked Siobhan closer into his side as his thoughts swirled.

He could do this. He *had* to. There was no question. He would never be the great leader either of his parents were, but he'd do his best. He could work with those newly appointed, and it would be a good team.

Rory loosened his grip on Siobhan's waist and made his way outside holding her hand tight as they shuffled through the cheering crowd. They grabbed their coats as guys from the militia thumped him on the back and older members of the Community shook his hand.

"I need some air," he said to Siobhan walking beside him, eyes bright and with a proud smile filling her face.

They strode out the narrow far gate leading to a winding track that snaked its way up the hill behind the compound. The crunch of footsteps on the stony track came behind them.

"Nice afternoon for a walk," Xian said.

"Och, he's going to his place of contemplation." George's deep tones rumbled.

The wind picked up as the track took them higher. The cool of a late autumn day was refreshing and a warning. Winter was near, and after that, a season to sow and reap as much as possible. Their boots ground on the old metal road as they reached the rise next to a natural platform that looked back over their glen. They stopped in the lee that sheltered them from the wind.

"Congratulations, Rory." George was the first to speak. "But for those of us who know you, there was no doubt."

"I congratulate the others also," Rory said.

He cast his vision over the green narrow valley before them. The ground was a deep brown where the crops had been harvested and most fields laid to rest over winter, except the few growing turnips and other stock feed. Sheep and goats nibbled on the steep-sided bens that lined their narrow, secluded glen. Highland cattle strolled lazily beside the wide burn that ran through it, their long shaggy coats blown by the wind. A militia outpost further along kept an eye out for poachers and unfriendly bandits who hoped to sneak-steal their livestock.

Rory sucked in the mountain air and pulled Siobhan close. She shivered against him.

"You're still acclimatising to the outdoor life, aye?" he said into her hair.

The coming winter would be her first *up top* here in the real weather since her childhood. She snuggled into his side.

"Do you understand what I mean now, Rory?" Xian spoke to his left. "You're their *leader*."

"Aye," George said, the breeze ruffling his greying hair. "Every person of voting age put you as one of their nine. And from what Brendan tells me, most marked you their number-one preference. Their first choice."

"I shall endeavour to not disappoint." Rory braced himself against the stiffening breeze. "I'll serve them with all my energy while I work as a member of the Chief Council."

"We all know you're dedicated, Rory." Siobhan's soft voice reached his ear.

"You're more than that to them," Xian said. "More than just a part of the Chief Council." Xian turned to George. "Isn't he?"

George nodded but kept silent.

"What're you guys saying?" Rory rubbed his cheek, his stubble flicking beneath his fingers.

Xian had hinted at this before, on their journey to Edinburgh. Were they meaning he should be the head of this Community like some clan chief of old? Or like Mrs Donaldson?

His friends remained quiet while he made eye contact with them. George looked at him from over his glasses and Xian crossed his arms, his mouth curling upward on one side.

"Something to think about, Ruairidh," George said.

"Why d'you say ma name the Gaelic way?" he asked George.

"It means red king," Xian said, and George gave a silent, enigmatic grin.

Why had his parents named him so? Did they believe he was destined for the heavy responsibility of ruling?

Och, no. No way was he up to bein' a *king*. A sole ruler. He'd need all the support from those dear to him just to keep right on the Chief Council. But he wouldn't voice these thoughts to his friends. He glanced at Siobhan, his turmoil easing with her presence there.

A gust of wind brushed his face and ran its cool fingers through his hair, and something tugged at his soul.

Was it destiny?

Siobhan had been there and seen his future-self. She hadn't told him all but held back. He'd sensed it, but not pushed.

But maybe now he should.

Chapter Twenty-Seven

Invercharing Community, 2061

Xian and George walked down the hill, their backs disappearing from Rory's view.

"Come, I'll show you something," Rory said then took Siobhan's hand and led her upward.

They continued on the path that wound through green grass blown flat by the wind. Rory led Siobhan along the wide ridge-back of the ben. She buttoned her coat, pulling her collar tight against the brisk wind. The track ended in a large granite rock face and Rory turned her to the view facing north. Rory shoved his hands in his pockets and indicated ahead with a flick of his chin to deep, blue lochs nestled in between high grey mountains.

"I've climbed most of these peaks, and I ken every track and place of shelter." Rory ran his vision over the vista before them while he spoke. "I've known it in the blinding glare of a summer sky shining off the lochs. Ken which tumble of stones and boulders to rest on beside the water."

He'd tell Siobhan the grazing lands of each herd of deer, the nesting ground of the capercaillie and grouse, and the high pines that held the nests of the osprey, if she asked. Rory blinked back the moisture gathering in his eyes and swallowed the choke in his throat. To say he loved this land would use words that fell so far short of what he truly felt.

"It's beautiful." She sighed beside him.

"Aye." He joined her sigh with one of his own then lifted his face into the wind and braced himself for thoughts of what was to come. "And a responsibility," he said.

He rested his chin on Siobhan's head while she continued to regard the view.

"You need to tell me more of the future," he said. "We've begun our preparations for storing food, but you mentioned civil war. I'd hate for anything to tear this beauty apart, and I'm more concerned for my people." He straightened up, searching to make eye contact with her.

Siobhan swallowed. "Like I said, you'll be the commander of the Alliance. Lloyd was part of it in that future and he threatened to enslave the youth if we didn't fight his way. He had it over us because we owed him."

"I'm no' surprised he's trouble." Rory shook his head. "In the future you went to, we needed his supplies. If all goes well these next growing seasons, we won't. I don't like him. Too self-interested. One to keep an eye on."

"Yes, for sure," Siobhan agreed.

"You said the Alliance fights the Government. Why?" he asked. "We're on the same side, are we no'?"

"Not in that future." She slipped her arms around his waist and squeezed tight. "Rory, don't fall out with the Government."

"I dinnae intend to." Rory faced the mountains before him. "An Alliance of Communities in the future makes sense, being of one mind and lifestyle philosophy. But *command* them?"

A heaviness returned to his shoulders. Would Xian and George push for him to be the sole leader?

He knew the future, from Siobhan, and what they must do to ensure survival when the famine hit. People looked to him to lead... They saw something in him.

Rory bowed his head.

"What's wrong?" Siobhan looked up at him.

He shrugged. "What people expect of me."

"They're right, Rory. You're the man for the job, in this time and this place, you're the one to get them through it."

He released a long slow breath.

"In the future, you begged me to change things when I returned," Siobhan said, "so *that* future wouldn't happen."

"Did I? I dinnae like the thought o' changing history." His neck prickled. "The last time I travelled I avoided seein' ma parents, stuck to the mission of meeting your father, and determined not to change anything. The first time I went back, I was trying to prevent a change in the future, our present, because my father took a time journey without permission, you ken?" His throat tightened; he forced his words through it. "Look what that did. Dad died..." His voice broke.

"Rory?" Siobhan said gently into his ear.

"Och, I failed him." Tears mingled with his words, and he was unable to hold them back. "When we stormed the slavers' holding-house, I led the way and provided cover. I wore my SAPI vest and had a more powerful firearm than Dad, or Alistair. I did nae keep Dad safe. He got shot. Four times in the gut. He bled out..." Rory's shoulders shook.

Siobhan's arms tightened around him, shushing him.

"You're not responsible, Rory." Her hands cupped his cheeks and lifted his head until he looked her in the eye. "The men who took your mother and sister are. You did all possible." She brushed his tears away. "Unfortunately, there is often collateral damage. You're a soldier, you know that. I'm so sorry it was your father, a brave and wonderful man by the sounds of it. Just like you, my love."

Rory's breath came haltingly. George had trained him for the prospect of deaths in a clash, but his own father's death was still hard to come to terms with, even though, as a soldier, his father would have been prepared for it.

"He'd be proud of you," Siobhan said, interrupting his thoughts. "And pleased that you will get us through what lies ahead."

Rory wiped the rest of his tears off his face with the heel of his hand. "Aye. I hope he forgives me."

"Rory, he'd say there's nothing to forgive," Siobhan said. "You helped save your mother. If you hadn't, there wouldn't be this present, would there?"

He was unable to speak; his throat so tight he'd lost his voice.

"You must step up now, Rory," she continued, "and be the leader they meant you to be." Her tone was eager, desperate.

Siobhan's words echoed in his mind.

He must.

He wouldn't back away from what they all must face. How could he stand before the one who requires an account of the actions of everyone in this life if he did? No, he wouldn't disappoint and fail those who looked to him to pull them through. He'd not let his parents down, either. They'd spent *their* lives building and defending this Community.

This was *his* task for *his* time.

He would protect those he'd pledged to lead, even if it meant fighting to secure peace.

Rory wrapped his arms around Siobhan, and resting his face in her hair, he prayed for wisdom.

PART TWO

Autumn's brown heather carpets the mountainside.

Early snow dusts the granite-grey peaks.

In the dark grey sky sit angry clouds whipped by the wind.

A stag steps from a copse of pine, halts and tips pointed tines over his back. Nose high, he sniffs the glen. A sharp honk of warning, and his does scatter.

The Saltire flutters behind a tank traversing the green and orange-brown carpet of heather, crunching the grey rock in its path, leaving two churned strips of dark.

Armed Government soldiers flank it on either side.

Thudding fills Ruairidh's ears.

A yell comes from his core, ascends via his racing heart, and works its way out through adrenaline-forced lungs.

"For land and love!"

His brothers join their rage-filled cries to his.

Callum, Xian, Kendra—all close by his side.

The strong, brave militia from Invercharing, and many others, are at his back.

On this, hinges all.

Home and hearth, they used to say.

Home—Siobhan and their sons.

But in the place in his soul that is home, in her stead...

A void.

Chapter Twenty-Eight

Invercharing Community, 2063

Sweat dampened Rory's brow. The wisps of hair that escaped his ponytail stuck to his face. The heat tempted him to remove his shirt, which clung to his back, but the memory of the sunburn was enough to squash that idea. He was thankful for the two good summers of bountiful harvests since they'd started storing food. Rory leaned against the cart that they loaded with oats. It had been another long summer's day and Rory expected everyone available to assist in the harvest. Siobhan had come early in the morning and helped for as long as she could before young Jake became hungry and fractious in the hot sun.

"We'll fill the new storage bins this year, with any luck," Uncle Brendan said, his grey hair tucked under his broad-brimmed hat. He tossed the sheaf of oats into the cart.

"We'd better. More mouths to feed since Cèilidh and Micah are wed, and his men have joined us," Rory said. "Not to mention the bairns those two make."

"Hmm, very fertile sister you have there," Uncle Brendan said. Droplets of sweat trickled down his cheeks, which were a similar colour to his red shirt. "Twins do run in your family." His face broke into a grin then he turned back to the harvest.

Rory glanced at the nearby sentry post where Callum was speaking to the militia on duty. The bandits of the opportunistic kind had been active lately, the Community's extra sowings producing plentiful crops had intrigued them. All the Communities had increased their sowings and yields at Rory's insistence. Some questioned, but Rory explained the logical prudence of such a program and avoided any mention of darkened skies filled with volcanic ash.

A cry came from the young woman in the field where Uncle Brendan had headed. She waved her arms at Rory, then removed her hat and threw it in the air, her face tight with concern. Rory ran to her, crunching over the short stalks left by the harvest, and sped along the row of stubble where the woman stood. Someone lay on the ground at her feet, face down—a male form wearing a red shirt.

"Uncle Brendan?" Rory's feet pounded on the loose earth in time with his pulse. "Get Christine!" Rory shouted to the militia at the sentry post. "Guys, help me here!"

He ran to Uncle Brendan and rolled him over. He was pale, bluish even, with no hint of the ruddiness of his exertions of a few moments earlier.

Rory shook him. He didn't respond. Rory thumped his chest. His eyes stayed open, staring, dirt caking his forehead and nose, and he was motionless. Footsteps crunched the straw stubble nearby.

"What's happened?" It was Callum. "Uncle Brendan!" Callum fell on his knees beside him and pressed his fingers on his neck. "I cannae find a pulse."

Rory laced his fingers and placed his hands in the centre of Uncle Brendan's chest. He pressed thirty times then stopped.

"Check for a pulse!" he ordered Callum.

Callum placed his fingers on Uncle Brendan's neck again then shook his head.

Rory did another set of thirty. Sweat fell off his brow in large drops and spattered on his hands clasped on Uncle Brendan's chest. "We'll keep doing it till we get something," he said.

Foot tread thumped toward them. "Christine's comin'." It was Kendra.

Rory continued his external compressions. A snap beneath his clasped hands vibrated up his arm and sent a sickening to his stomach.

"What was that?" Callum bore his alarmed stare into him.

Rory swallowed and kept pressing down, willing Uncle Brendan's heart to start.

"He just dropped," the young woman who'd harvested next to Uncle Brendan, explained.

The thud of pounding hooves echoed toward them. Rory glanced up from his compressions, his torso drenched with sweat and his mouth dry. Christine jumped from a horse, holding her medical bag, and ran toward them. He stopped his compressions and Callum felt for a pulse.

Christine knelt beside Uncle Brendan, and with an old stethoscope listened for a heartbeat. Her brows drew tight, and her lips squeezed together.

"Keep going," she said.

"Did you hear anything?" Rory asked.

Christine shook her head then turned at the approach of another horse. Rory followed her gaze and continued pressing on Uncle Brendan. It was Aunty Bec. She dismounted and left her horse with Christine's and Kendra's. She ran, hair flying and thin arms pumping as she trod the uneven ground.

"Brendan!" Her breathless wail halted Rory.

Aunty Bec knelt, her old knees hitting the ground hard, and Rory sat back on his haunches to give her space. She rested her head on Uncle Brendan's chest and moaned, then sat back, her cheeks wet with tears.

Rory placed his hands on Uncle Brendan to continue compressions.

"No." Aunty Bec put her thin bony fingers over his. "Leave it. He's gone," she said. "No use subjecting him to the violence of resuscitation. Let him be." She bowed her head and tears wet Uncle Brendan's shirt, mixing with the dirt from the field.

Rory took his hands away. The others stood around in silence, watching Aunty Bec cry. Sheep bleated, eager to be let into the field to eat the remaining stalks. The wind blew in Rory's face and whisked Aunty Bec's hair across hers. Rory shuffled closer and put an arm on her shoulder.

"I'm sorry, Aunty," he murmured into her hair then kissed her forehead as her wail began.

***

The Community gathered in the main hall, much like they had two years earlier. This time, though, it wouldn't be Brendan Hamilton reading out the results of the votes. His position on the Chief Council required filling and although his death had shocked the Community, they could waste no time and an immediate replacement was necessary.

Siobhan jiggled Jake on her hip. His chubby fingers played with the shiny metallic buttons of her blouse. With eyes as blue as his father's, his gaze flicked up to her then darted around the room, taking it all in, his blond curls bobbing with each twist of his head. Maybe he would be quiet long enough for her to stay and hear the results.

It was the same procedure as the previous election. Anyone willing was up for a vote. She hadn't wanted to govern, as such, in the past. Well, not in the Bunker. But with the future she'd encountered, it was crucial that people who knew, and were capable, were the ones on the team. It would be wonderful to work beside Rory on the Chief Council. She would see more of him that way and experience the part of him she admired the most.

She swallowed at the churning within her—it was a mixture of emotions.

She could be a valuable member of the team and, if she was voted in, it would signify the Community had accepted her at last.

She'd married one of their men and left everything! For heaven's sake, wasn't she one of them now? Couldn't she have a chance to use her skills? What more did she have to prove?

She jiggled Jake more vigorously. He made baby noises and his practice words jolted in his throat in time with her movements.

She'd worked like a Trojan with Rory right up to delivering Jake, doing all she could in establishing the increased food production and storage, plus acquiring supplies from the black market, no less. It hadn't ceased to amaze her what was obtainable through such channels.

She wouldn't expect to gain a place on the Council because she was Rory's wife.

But surely her dedication to them...

Rory walked through the door at the front of the hall along with the other members of the Chief Council. George Stobbart stood at the centre of the raised platform holding a piece of paper. Rory scanned the crowd, found her, then his gaze lingered on their son.

"Martin Moffatt," George announced, "has been successful in obtaining a seat on the Council." Applause rose from those assembled.

Rory's second cousin, the old physicist, had won the place. A sigh rose from within her. She continued jiggling Jake and he whimpered, his baby words the start of a cry. It took her mind off the tightness in her throat.

People turned their heads in her direction, attracted by Jake's unsettled noises. Siobhan dropped her gaze to the floor. Mandy and Cèilidh had stayed in the nursery area with their children, not as interested as she was in the outcome of the Chief Council by-election.

Some support from Rory would have been nice.

Helpful, even.

Siobhan's eyelids quivered and she tried to stop them narrowing. She'd expected him to have encouraged them to at least consider her. But he'd made no attempt to promote her. Nor to reassure his people she was for them, not against, and that she was a wholehearted Community member now. In heart and soul.

She squeezed her mouth tight, preventing a grimace.

Jake cried and Siobhan raised her head at the same time Rory looked her way.

I'm going home, she mouthed. He nodded and turned to speak to George.

Siobhan put on a smile and walked through the crowd who all seemed happy with the outcome. Martin was a decent man. And clever—no—*brilliant*. He'd been here from the start and a key intelligence in devising the Time Machine.

Not an outsider, like herself.

Heavy foot-tread came behind her, hastening as she reached their front door. It was Rory, and he followed her in.

"Well, that was a good result." Rory lifted Jake from her arms. "Hello, wee man," he said and kissed their baby. He put his free arm around her and placed his mouth to hers for a kiss. She didn't return it.

He stepped back from her. "You're disappointed."

Siobhan shrugged out of his one-armed embrace and walked into the living room.

Rory followed, carrying Jake. "It was democratic—"

"Did I have a chance?" she interrupted, turning to face Rory full-on.

Rory blinked. "The people chose."

"Do you know the votes?"

"Siobhan." Rory's tone was someplace between commiseration and reproach. "Martin is a good man. His scientific knowledge will be invaluable."

"And I'm *not* scientific?" Her forefinger pressed into her sternum.

"Siobhan—" he began.

"How many votes did I get?" She strode into the kitchen and stood before the sink, fighting to keep her hands by her sides.

Rory huffed and placed Jake on the floor with his toys. "If you are askin' me how close you got, well, not very." Rory's expression was candid.

Siobhan spun and faced out the window. A horse drawing a dray of baled hay made its way past, the *clip-clop* of its hooves and its unique animal scent wafting through the open window. On the floor, their son giggled as he played with a toy, a wooden dray.

"They stick with what they know," Rory said and stepped into the kitchen behind her. "They haven't really got to know you yet."

"They still see me as Government, don't they? Because of that, I can't be trusted." She spun back to face him. "Even after almost two years."

"No. Siobhan." He took a breath to stifle his annoyance—as was his habit. "You have been a hard-worker in all of this. Ye dinnae have to be *on* the Council. You're a great organiser. Hell, we need those. We don't know how you find the rare equipment from the black market, like the suture material—and the important stuff too, like those fresh 9mms. At a good price. You're quite the negotiator."

Siobhan didn't reply. He didn't get it. They still hadn't accepted her.

"You never even suggested me," she said. The hurt came out in her voice.

"I cannae." Rory rubbed the back of his neck. "That would seem like I'm pushin' my own agenda." His hand fell to his side.

"You could have mentioned me."

Rory stood like a wall before her, stony faced and silent.

"You never tried." Her words slipped between gritted teeth. "That hurts the most, husband."

Rory's nostrils flared, and a word escaped as he spun and stalked to the door.
She let him go. She didn't need to understand Gaelic.
His tone was cursing in anybody's language.

Chapter Twenty-Nine

Invercharing Community, 2063

Jake was asleep at last. Siobhan slipped his bedroom door closed with a quiet click. The boy adored his father and fussed when Rory wasn't home at bedtime. Since the words they'd had after the election, it had occurred more often. Siobhan snorted.

Words.

That was their first full-blown argument, but it had been brewing for a while.

It was so difficult—being married.

Siobhan rested her forehead on the bedroom door and twirled her wedding ring around her finger. Things had altered. The closeness of being newly married had gradually given way to a business-like relationship. The organisation and logistics for growing and storing food had occupied Rory's time and taken most of his energy. Not to mention his continued oversight of the militia.

When she wasn't negotiating with black marketeers and ensuring accurate records of all the items stored, she spent her energy on their young son. Her soul warmed with her love for her boy. Jake was a precious treasure. More so, because all the medical texts had stated that, at her age, there was a high possibility that she was near menopause. Yet she had conceived Jake the first time she and Rory had made love—in the future. A tingle passed through her body at the recollection.

Siobhan stood taller and fiddled with the embroidered name-plaque Rory's sister Kelly had made for little Jake.

In their first year of marriage, they'd visited the nearest Communities and discussed with them the pros and cons of coming under the New Scottish Government's banner. Rory took her to the Glencoe Community to visit his youngest sister, Kelly, and her husband, Alistair, who were both now in their fifties. Kelly had travelled to the past the same time Rory had made his first time travel trip. His youngest sister was older than him. *Hmm.*

It had taken Rory from his responsibilities for the few weeks they were away. On their return, Siobhan had heard quiet comments regarding Rory's neglect of the important things at home. She'd sensed disapproval in the reserved conversations of the older members of the Community. She'd stifled her initial defensive reactions, but the sting was still there.

The tour was a success at first, as the Communities were open to discussion, but with reservations, for they all wished to maintain their autonomy. Siobhan didn't blame them. The Government had promised protection and co-operation, but their recent actions—talk of re-instituting taxes, delineating boundaries in preparation for elections, and murmurings of enlistment to the Scottish Defence Force—revealed an innate self-interest, signifying to those who ran the Communities that the New Scottish Government's needs would always come first. Hesitation on the Communities' part had led to a cooling of discussions.

With the strengthening of the relationship with the New Scottish Government placed on hold, Rory's entire focus was on surviving the famine that lay ahead.

The front door opened and clicked shut behind Rory as he leaned his rifle next to the door jamb. He stepped to her with a tired smile and a crease making its way to permanency on his brow.

"Go sit on the couch," she said. "I'll get you some tea while I check if your dinner is still warm."

"I'd like that," he said. His soft voice and blue eyes were close to her face, melting away the simmer her musings had just stirred.

Rory dropped onto the couch while she put the pot of water over the hotplate on the solid fuel stove and examined his meal keeping warm on the warm-side of the stove. Perhaps it was still edible. She and Jake had eaten dinner two hours ago.

Rory rested his head in his hands, then passed his fingers through his long hair, catching his grey streak. She came behind him and massaged his neck and shoulders; they were hard as concrete.

She made a pot of tea and carried it to the coffee table with two mugs. Siobhan poured the tea and passed him the strongest mug. He drank and soon placed the mug on the table. Their home was now quiet, the passing bustle of those coming home from the late autumn harvests had ceased with sunset. She placed Rory's meal and cutlery next to the mugs. Rory stared at the dried stew, making no attempt to pick up the fork. He hadn't spoken a word since plonking himself on the couch.

"What's up, Rory?" Siobhan asked then adjusted the blue cushion beside him and eased herself back.

"The Council believes, and so do I, that we should get the Time Machine back." Rory's mouth pulled to the side. "The Government still have nae got it to work, after all this time." He leaned closer to her. "Or so they think." He raised his brow and looked into her eyes. "And it's about time ma wee brother came here to be with us. It's over two years now and that's long enough to be away from home. They cannae have the Time Machine any longer, Siobhan. What if they accidentally make it work, like you did? Then they'd be all out to change the past. I just know it. How could anyone stop that financial crash?"

He picked up his mug and sipped his tea again, staring ahead.

"Where would you begin, anyway?" Rory's cynicism hung in the room. "Stop them printing extra bank notes after the 2008 Crash? Or before that, stop the greedy banks from issuing loans to anyone, making possible the dream of owning your own home at the expense of the reality of *not* being able to afford it? Or the connectedness of that modern world. How would you change that? When one country's economy was so tied into another's, when one failed, they all fell like dominoes?" He sighed. "May as well return to the beginning of time and try to change human nature." He looked at her from over the rim of his mug. "Yes, they taught us history, too."

Siobhan took another sip of her tea, pushing down the annoyance swirling in her chest. The quiet was loud.

"What's wrong, Siobhan?"

"Nothing," she answered briskly, fighting at the swirl, which now included irritation at her inability to hide what she was feeling.

"Och, there is." Rory thudded his mug on the table. "You've been on quiet-fume since I got home."

"I'm fine, thank you." She didn't stifle the peeve in her tone. "Your son settled, eventually."

"I'm sorry I'm home late again." He placed a large warm hand over hers, which scrunched the handful of skirt she held.

"I only get to see you if we happen to be working at the same storage barn." The swirl pushed the words out. "Your son can go for days without getting more than you sitting by his cot watching him sleep because you're home so late. He'll grow up not knowing who you are."

"He kens me!" Rory said.

"No." She let the reprimand stay in her tone. "I mean, really *know* who you are."

"I'm sorry, lass, but things are ramping up. That volcano's sure to blow soon and we have to be ready."

"Yes, and your son, who is growing up in this world, needs to know what being a man is all about," Siobhan said. "And I want him to learn it from you."

Rory's narrow gaze rested on her. "Is that all that's bothering you?"

Siobhan swallowed through a tight throat. She stood and walked to the sink with her dirty mug, blinking back tears.

"Are you no' happy, Siobhan?" Disappointment laced Rory's tone. "Do you wish to go back to the Bunker?"

"No." She spun from the sink. "I want to be here with you. *With* you." Her breathing stuttered.

"But you are."

"Rory, you must make us a priority," she said. He opened his mouth to reply, but she didn't let him. "Yes, you're the leader. You have a team, and you must allocate the work evenly. Your brother manages to have time with Mandy and their children." Her tone rose a pitch. "Let others do more, Rory. We need you…" Her voice cracked.

"Siobhan. Lass. I'm sorry." Rory stood. "But you ken what the—"

"Yes, I do *ken* what the world's about to experience!" she yelled. "I've seen the results of it. I've been there! And we are doing all this so we can have a life. But, Rory, we want—I want—that life to be with you. And not just in snippets." She snapped her fingers in the air beside her.

Rory straightened. His shoulders rose as he inhaled. "Och, Siobhan, I'm sorry. I'll do my best to balance it out a wee bit better."

"Rory Campbell, it's not all down to you. There are people willing and able. You don't have to do everything yourself."

Rory rubbed his neck and worked his jaw. "Och, you dinnae ken all that needs to be done out there." His nostrils flared.

"Probably not, because they won't trust me! Well," she lowered her voice, "your close friends do. The general Community don't want me in a leadership role."

Rory's glare landed on her for a second before he stormed past the coffee table, his knees bumping into it. The unused cutlery clattered off the table as he strode to the door. Siobhan flinched.

"Where are you going?" she asked.

"I need some air." His gruff reply was barely audible over the slam of the door.

***

Rory cursed under his breath. Slamming that door would wake up wee Jake but the suffocating emotions had started again. He strode outside, then allowed himself to stomp his way to the front of the compound.

The sentry at the heavy iron gate gave him a respectful nod. He returned a curt one and walked beside the fence and up the east side where he stood, hands on hips and gulped in the chilled night air. He lifted his face to the night sky and let it out.

They said you couldn't please everyone.

Well, *they* knew what they were talking about.

"How can I be a leader *and* a husband and father?" he whispered to the Highland night.

There were only so many hours in a day. Only so much one man could do in a lifetime.

What if that lifetime is in a period of history when dire events are about to happen, and that man knows it because his wife has been to the future?

"How many history books have the answer to that one!" he spoke a little louder this time. He glanced at the tower. The sentries were too far away; they wouldn't hear him.

The sky was a deep midnight blue, like Siobhan's eyes in dimmed lighting.

Man, I love her.

And he'd failed her. His chest tore at the thought. His ache became heated; his fists curled and the tightness in his shoulders reached his temples.

To his right, the dogs barked, and yells echoed through the cool air. They came from the sentry post further down near the entrance to their glen where the fields of crops and stock were guarded.

Rory ran to the gate. "What is it?" he called to the lookout.

"Looks like a group of bandits, sir." The guard on watch held the battered pair of night vision glasses to his eyes. "Attacking the sentries up front. They've let the animals loose, Mr Campbell, sir."

Damn.

Chapter Thirty

Invercharing Community, 2063

The babbling chatter of toddlers and an escalating cry of a baby blared behind Siobhan as she walked out of the Community's nursery area where she'd left Jake. It was good for him to socialise with the other young children while she performed her role of coordinating the recording and storage of food and supplies. Jake loved his cousins. Micah and Cèilidh were prolific with their sets of twins, and Callum and Mandy had recently had their third child.

Jake had a brother in the future—her baby. The pregnancy that would kill her. She briefly closed her eyes on her grimace.

What a way to think of it!

If she didn't alter this present, that's how their personal history would pan out. Of all the things she'd informed Rory of regarding her trip to that future, her death was the one detail she hadn't mentioned.

And would never.

Her proposed course of action *would* work. No need to give Rory more anxiety. And if it didn't work? Well, the future was the future and some things you couldn't change. She swallowed past a thick throat. She would set the plan in motion once she became pregnant again.

Again. Well, you have to have sex to get pregnant.

That hadn't happened that often lately. In fact, since their argument last month, not at all. It was tense sleeping next to Rory, wondering if he would make the first move, or if she should. Life was so tiring, lately he'd often fallen asleep soon after lying down.

Kendra strode toward Siobhan along the long corridor coming from the stables, her bow over her shoulder and the usual quiver of arrows at her belt.

"Siobhan!" Her eyebrows almost met in the middle with her scowl. "Where's Rory?" she asked.

"There's a Chief Council meeting," Siobhan replied. "Why?"

"Bandit trouble. I'm getting some militia together, but I want him, Callum, and Xian to know what's goin' on." Kendra spun on her heel and faced the direction of the Chief Council meeting room. "I can't wait till they're finished their bletherin'." She looked at her. "Siobhan, could you tell him for me, please? I need to get the guys and get going."

"I'll let him know," Siobhan replied and made her way past the tall, lady militia member.

"We'll be up near the lookout on Bheinn Fionn," Kendra said. "They're that close!"

Siobhan nodded to Kendra's back.

Micah would go with them, most probably. He'd settled well into Community life, and they had accepted him more readily. They'd trust a bandit over a Government representative. She stomped most of the way to the meeting room, gritting her teeth against the hurt once more.

The door was open when Siobhan approached, so she quietened her step and paused right before it.

"Taxes?" Martin's voice floated out of the open door. "In what form?"

"Och, well, we have nae money, so goods," Rory answered.

"They'll be taxing us of our young and able soon." It was Callum's voice. "For their defence force."

"What else did Angela say?" Christine asked.

"That our close ties would ensure a strong alliance," Rory replied.

The room was quiet except for the shuffling of papers, which came from the same direction as Rory's voice.

"What about retaining our independence?" Mary McKenzie, the head teacher, sounded defensive.

Someone continued to shuffle papers on the table top.

"If we join with them, what resources will they give us in return for these taxes they demand?" Callum's deep tones rumbled.

A *crack*, like a pencil slamming on a table top, echoed out the door. Siobhan took a step back.

"They've only ever shown that the Government comes first," Mary McKenzie, the probable slammer of the pencil, continued. "They'll take from us, call us allies and the next thing we ken, we'll be swallowed up in them. They'll monitor oor way of life, our self-sufficiency, our egalitarian governing—"

"They already have," Christine interrupted the older woman.

"What do you mean?" Mary asked. "When?"

"Christine!" Rory spoke at last, his voice holding an edge.

"Tell us, Rory Campbell," Martin said.

"Och." Resignation filled Rory's tone. "When I brought Siobhan back, they'd bugged her gear and followed us." A chair creaked. "Micah dealt with it. The men—recovered—and we sent them back to the Government with a *please explain*."

"Did they?" Bec asked.

No sound came from the room.

Rory must have shaken his head, for the Government had yet to respond to that one, and it was nearly two years ago.

Well, the Community did beat up their men.

Siobhan grimaced, aware she was eavesdropping but her feet stayed in place, nor could she move forward and make her presence known.

"Rory," George spoke. "You know the Government better than anyone. What do you think? Should we align ourselves with them?"

"We should." Rory's reply was quick. "Because we need them," Rory continued. "We require their resources for what will eventuate. Having said that, I truly believe we'll lose our autonomy. That's the price we'll pay. The Community System, much to my deep regret, will never be the same if we do."

"Bottom line, brother," Callum asked. "If we didn't have to, would you?"

"No," Rory said, and for a few moments no one spoke; no papers shuffled. "We'll become a Government outpost. And, because of our ties to the Government—through my marriage to Siobhan—it would be difficult to resist them."

Cold clenched Siobhan's shoulders.

Rory was proclaiming to all that deep down, he wasn't happy with their connection to the New Scottish Government. The connection he'd made because of *her*.

Her throat burned. She blinked and clamped her hand over her mouth, stifling a gasp that threatened to give away her position just outside the door. A band ran around her chest and pressed in, tighter and tighter. She turned with care and trod with a light step away and along the corridor.

Once back on the main walkway, she scurried through the compound, avoiding others busy with their assigned tasks. She never eased her pace and ran the last short distance to their rooms. She flung open the door, slammed it behind her and then exhaled. She leaned against the door, her legs wobbling and her arms trembling.

"He's betrayed me!" she shouted into their hallway. "My own husband had discredited the Government to his Chief Council." She continued into the stillness of their accommodation. "Virtually stated the New Scottish Government is tyrannical and only wants to have power over *us*." Her voice had risen. "That, only from necessity, would he even consider joining, and the cost would be significant. Why has he never shared *this*?" she vented as she strode to the kitchen.

Siobhan grabbed a clean glass from the cupboard and filled it with water from the tap.

"Why tell his inner thoughts to the Chief Council before sharing them with *me*?" she asked after taking a sip from the glass shaking in her hand. "I could refute and correct and advise. Speak for the Government. Speak *to* the Government on the Community's behalf." She took another sip; the clear Scottish water went down the wrong way and she choked.

"But, no," she said once her throat had cleared. "No one wants *my* input."

Bile rose. She clunked the half-full glass into the sink and leaned against the bench, breathing in deeply until the nauseating hurt passed and the shaking settled.

Siobhan strode to the bedroom, dragged her few clothes from the wardrobe and stuffed them into her duffle bag.

Fumes, white and hot, began to rise deep within her.

Rory had walked away often enough. *It's my turn now!*

She ran into Jake's room, found another bag suitable for strapping on a saddle, and shoved it full of clothes and baby things she'd need for her little boy.

She would not leave without him.

Chapter Thirty-One

Invercharing Community, 2063

Siobhan snuck the long way around to the stables, avoiding most people. The percussive clang of the smithy's mallet rang out from his forge and reverberated across the yard between the stables and the other animal shelters. He pounded out horseshoes, his attention focused on his task. Horses thundered out of the stable and Siobhan tucked herself against a wall and hid behind a post.

Damn. Rory and the other militia members on the Chief Council must have found out about the bandits without her passing on Kendra's message.

"Micah," Rory shouted, and Siobhan's heart hammered at her husband's voice. "Ask someone to let Siobhan know where I've gone. We'll meet you and your men there, okay?"

Boy cantered past with Rory astride, his rifle hanging over his shoulder and magazines of ammunition protruding from the top of his saddlebags. Xian followed close, his Katana in its sheath strung across his back, as always.

Siobhan stepped from behind the post. Micah, now alone in the deserted yard, marched across to the stables, his hand shielding his eyes from the afternoon sunlight.

"Siobhan," he said then stopped dead. "I guess you heard... What're you doing?"

Siobhan didn't answer.

"Why the bags?" Micah asked then strode forward, his loose dreads hung over his shoulders, and his suntanned forehead was a mass of crinkles. "Where're you goin'?"

Siobhan stood. Decision time. She required an ally and Micah always seemed keen to please.

"I need your help, Micah," Siobhan said then walked the few paces across the empty yard to where the ex-bandit stood.

"Oh, no, no, no." He held up his hands, palms outward. "I know you guys aren't happy, but don't get me involved."

"Please, take me to the Bunker," she asked.

"No, ma'am." Micah's dreads vibrated with the tremor of his head shake. "I'll no' do that to a man who has given me a chance."

"Escort me to the Bunker and I will ensure your father gets a private interview with the First Minister." Her old authoritative tone returned.

The trembling dreads ceased their motion. Micah's ribcage rose and fell.

"Okay. You be ready in five. I've gotta organise my men for this bandit chase Rory's on." His glare bore into her. "What about your son?"

"Jake's coming too," she said.

"You're gonna kill him," Micah said. "Ya ken that?"

"I can take care of my child," she said.

Micah's dreads vibrated again. "No, ma'am, I mean Rory."

"You will be my escort, not my counsellor!" Siobhan ground out the words, as the white heat flashed again within her.

"Okay, okay. Five minutes, back here," he said, pointing to the ground at his feet with his index finger.

"If you tell anyone—" she began.

"No, ma'am. I wouldn't dare."

"Take these while I get Jake," Siobhan said, thrusting the duffle bags at Micah then strode to the building that housed the nursery.

Taking deep breaths, trusting it would assist a calm appearance, she stepped to the nursery, paused before entering and smoothed down her jumper and cargo pants. Jake was inside, bashing a toy xylophone, its tuneless metallic clang resounding with every thump of the mallet her baby held. A smile filled his face and pure delight oozed from him.

"Just getting Jake," she said to the women on duty. She picked up her little boy and dressed him in his jacket then grabbed his bag. "Say bye-bye."

Jake waved at the women as she whisked him out the door.

Micah waited with two saddled horses, one loaded with her duffle bags.

"The guards will wonder what's goin' on if you ride outta here all kitted up." Micah raised his brows briefly.

"Oh." Siobhan chewed her lower lip.

"You go out the back. I'll ride out the front." Micah tilted his head down, his dreads now secured in a tie. "The guards'll think I'm taking supplies to Rory, or somethin'," he whispered. "I'll meet you round by the hills at the rear of the compound, and we'll cut across and down. Long way around, but if you want out, that's the way, yeah?"

She lifted her chin in assent then grabbed her jacket from her saddlebags and put it on. Micah mounted and left trailing her loaded horse.

Siobhan informed the single guard at the small back gate of the compound that she was taking a stroll up the hill behind the glen. Siobhan rested Jake on her hip, and he looked around at the trees and sky. He was so bright. Her eyes pricked with forming tears. Whatever had gone wrong with her and Rory, at least she'd have this beautiful blond, curly-haired boy. Her throat tightened for, apart from hair colour, he was so much like his father.

Siobhan climbed the steep incline and puffed; her arms were tight from holding Jake, and her leg muscles burned. The cool breeze brought moisture with it. She turned for the last glance at the narrow glen, home to the Invercharing Community. White mist crept over the hills and hugged the surrounding mountains. She pulled up Jake's hood and clutched him tighter and continued along the lower edge of the hill then followed an overgrown track that circuited the very edge of the Community's boundary. Micah sat waiting on his horse by a copse of rowan nestled in a dip between the hills.

Micah slipped off his mount and led her horse forward. He held Jake while she mounted, then passed him up to her.

"You know we'll be camping tonight?" he asked then remounted and nudged his horse to a walk ahead of hers. "I don't see any bedroll or cooking gear in your stuff."

Siobhan's shoulders drooped. In her feverish desire to leave, she hadn't suitably prepared for their journey.

"Just as well I grabbed some things, hey?"

"Thank you, Micah," she said to Micah's back.

Relief rippled over her, and she brushed away tears that threatened.

"Not a lot, mind you," Micah said. "You made me hurry."

The late afternoon wore on and the autumn mists thickened as the evening neared. Siobhan wrapped her coat around Jake who was sitting in front of her in the saddle, and he was soon lulled to a rocking sleep. That wonderful little-boy scent of his wafted up amongst the heat escaping from the coat tucked around him. She held him close and placed a kiss on his curly head, her soul welling with her love for him.

Micah took them on a path that hugged the mountain on the farther side. There were more trees here, as the sides of the mountains were not as steep, and the wind lessened. At times the route seemed circuitous, but every clump of trees and gorse looked the same, and the mist shrouded the hillside in an obscuring cloak.

"We gotta find a place to camp soon, with the night drawing in, and all," Micah said over his shoulder while he rode ahead of her on the narrow track.

Yes, she'd picked the wrong time of the year to be travelling, with autumn here and winter just around the corner. Then a thought struck her.

"What will Cèilidh say?"

"She'll think I'm off sortin' bandits with Rory."

Siobhan sunk in her saddle. "How long before you're missed?"

"That depends on how long your man's away dealin' with the bandits I'm helping him with, ken?" Micah replied.

They came to a copse of gorse and rode through a narrowing of growth. They brushed past the prickly branches of the natural entrance. It opened up to a clearing hedged by gorse bushes the height of a man. Micah halted his horse and jumped down to the grassy space.

"We'll make camp here. There's plenty of shelter." He stood with his hands set on his hips. "Did you think of a tent?"

"No." *Again.* She groaned to herself at her lack of preparation.

"I've got a tarp we can string up somewhere," Micah said. "We'll get soaked by the mist without it, ken?"

Soon Micah had a warm fire blazing. It burned down to coals then he cooked bannocks over them. Jake had woken when they'd dismounted and cried when he saw the unfamiliar surroundings but now settled after some food. Siobhan wrapped him in all her clothing for warmth and padding from the hard ground. He slept on her coat, bundled under the tarp.

The mist thinned for a gap and the full moon stared down at Siobhan. She grimaced at the connection between romance and a full moon. At present, she and Rory were barely a sliver of a crescent moon. She ground her teeth on her grimace. Her mother had died when she was young, and her father had never remarried. A married relationship wasn't on-hand for her to observe until she lived in the Bunker.

Siobhan sighed. Aunty Rajna compared marriage to the moon. Siobhan scraped at her memory to recall Aunty's words. *Just as the moon waxes and wanes, so does the intimacy of married love. It isn't always a full moon,* she said. Siobhan let a smile tweak at the corner of her mouth for a second as she heard Aunty's voice in her head. *Life changes shape like the moon and our love does with it. It is what it is at any given point. Crescent or new or full. It is still the moon, is it not?*

If Siobhan kept on her current path, their moon would wane into nothingness.

But if she stayed...

Micah held a long stick wrapped with bannock dough over the coals. "You want this last bannock, Siobhan?"

He glanced at the tight gap in the gorse through which they'd made their way.

"Yes, please." Siobhan took the offered toasted bannock dough. Her stomach had settled, and her earlier adrenaline-fueled trembles and wooziness had eased the further away they rode from the compound. With her stomach almost full, she anticipated sleeping well after her emotionally and physically exhausting day.

Micah looked up and stared at the gap in the gorse again. The thump of a horse's hooves vibrated under her.

"Someone's coming!" she whispered.

A flare of alarm ran through her and she glanced at her toddler sleeping soundly in a bundle of clothes. Were there bandits out this way? Surely Micah had contacts, and they'd be okay?

"Sorry, Siobhan," Micah said, his gaze remained on the break in the gorse hedge.

Siobhan spun and faced the entrance to their secluded campsite, and stared at the gap.

Then Rory rode in.

Chapter Thirty-Two

The Gorse Covered Mountainside

Siobhan stood taller, her nails digging into her palms. Rory slipped off Boy while Micah, without a word, grabbed Boy's reins and led the stallion out of the gorse enclosure.

Siobhan fixed her feet to the ground, and a tremble shook her entire body as Rory strode unflinchingly toward her. He had dark circles under his eyes, his face was grimy, and his jaw set. He stopped two paces away, glanced at Jake sleeping bundled in her coat, then bore his stare into her.

"I won't beg, Siobhan," he said speaking low, firm and determined.

Sweat moistened her palms while she willed herself to calmness.

"What do you want?" Firm tones again from her husband. "Would you go? Leave me and take our son with you?"

Heat flushed through her body, and she acknowledged it for what it was. Anger at Rory for letting her down. And at herself for irrationally grabbing Jake and running—determined to leave the Community behind but aching at the thought of being without Rory.

"I want you to make Jake and myself a priority."

"But you are!" His heated words flew out.

"It doesn't seem like it." Her voice strangled as she blinked back the tears.

Rory's mouth tensed and he looked away, gulping. "Do you realise the pressure you put me under making demands like this?" he asked.

"*Demands?* They're not demands," she said. "They're what I expected from a husband." Her voice broke, so she dragged in air. "I know there's a lot about to happen, but we need to see you."

He turned back to her, a question in his eyes.

"*I* need you, Rory," she said, answering that question.

"And I you, Siobhan." His expression remained hard. "I can't do it without you."

"Can't do what, Rory? Because you seem not to need us at all."

"All of it," he said and waved his hands around him. "Lead. Be a father. Love you. Live this life." Rory's voice broke.

Siobhan pushed aside the hurt that the emotion in his voice had conjured. "I need something else from you," she said.

He tilted his head.

"I need you to not undermine my efforts at Community-Government co-operation," she said.

"What?"

"Will you trust the Government for my sake, as well as the future's," she asked, "and not bad-mouth the New Scottish Government to the whole Chief Council?"

"What, you heard—?"

"Yes," she interrupted, "and that was the last straw."

"Och!" Rory rubbed the back of his neck.

Night birds called, and an owl hooted in the distance. Rory dropped his hand to his side and took a step toward her.

"I ken you're disappointed in me, Siobhan." His voice strained with each word. "I dinnae really ken what you were expecting when you married me."

Siobhan didn't reply. Tears pricked her eyes while emotions, far too intense for her to feel individually, bubbled up and choked her throat so barely a breath came out.

"The perfect man, or woman for that matter, is boring," he said and gave a tiny shake to his head. "You're not faultless."

"Neither are you." She broke her resolve to keep silent.

"You kenned full well I was nae!" he yelled.

She flinched at Rory's loud response. He stepped closer, closing the space between them. His warmth radiated from him and reached her face.

"I'm just a man," he said. "Not your knight in shining armor, even though I do ride a horse." He attempted a smile.

She couldn't muster one.

"When you get close to someone and let your guard down," he continued, "you find out things you don't like. That's inevitable. But you choose to love them anyway, Siobhan. When you open up your heart, you risk them not accepting what you truly are." He moved even closer so there was nothing between them. "I'm afraid of a few things at the moment and you're the only one I'll admit that to." His hands held her arms in a gentle grip. "My greatest fear is losing you."

Rory put his arms around her, pulling her to him; his body heat pressed the full length of her front. "I've never been afraid to come to you, my wife, naked in body and soul. When I love you ...I am *me*. No one else sees me like that—only you... my woman. All I can be is me." He paused for a heartbeat, his eyes searching hers. "I have promised to love you no matter what I see. And I will. I'm yours for all time, Siobhan. Whatever time may bring us."

Rory's words, first heard in the future, echoed within her.

His breath moved the loose strands of hair on her cheek, tickling her face with a soft touch.

"*Gra mo chroí*," Rory said, "please don't take from me everything—everyone—who holds my heart—my life—together."

His voice was small, as if he knew he'd just contradicted his opening determination to not beg. He remained still, not moving the rest of the way to her; the inches between their lips seemed like light years.

Can I live without this man? This incredible man who has just bared his soul?

No.

She had to love Rory despite his choices, despite their circumstances or any disappointment in him she might feel, or any possible hints of neglect.

She should have known, for she married a leader, and she would have to share him with his people.

Rory's gaze hadn't faltered.

"We have to work on this," she said, and lifted her hand to his face, pressing her fingers to his cheek and stroking his lips with her thumb. "It can't stay like this."

His expression softened at last. "It won't."

He tilted his cheek into her palm and Siobhan kissed him, his eyes closing and his lips holding her caress.

A crack thundered from behind them, far to the south. A ripple of vibration ran beneath them, skimming the earth as it flowed over and under the ground on which they stood. The echo of that crack reverberated through the night air. Knocked right through her, through her body, and Rory's pressed to hers. Its loud boom sent screeching birds out from their night perches. The horses, including Boy on the other side of the gorse, shrieked. The light pounding of the hooves of deer awakened by the din echoed along the hillside beside them.

Jake woke with a startled cry and Siobhan slipped from Rory's embrace to bundle Jake in her arms. She held their toddler close, shushing and rocking away his whimpers as Rory came to her side and put his arms around them both.

Rory held her like a vice, and she locked her gaze with his.

"Och, lass. Let me take you home now. It's started."

Chapter Thirty-Three

The Gorse Covered Mountainside

"Daddy," Jake cried.

Siobhan climbed onto the mare, and Rory lifted Jake into her arms.

"Ssh, sweetheart, we're going home now." Siobhan placed Jake in front of her, still wrapped in her clothes, then tucked him into her coat.

Rory helped Micah pack up and load the other horses, then Micah led the way back out of their sheltered campsite. Rory rode behind Siobhan until they left the gorse and could ride two abreast, then Rory pulled Boy in beside her.

"He's so faithful to you, Rory," Siobhan said. "Micah would do anything for you."

Rory gave a curt nod and glared at Micah's back, and his jaw clenched.

"It was my fault, Rory. I made him," she said to the side of his face.

Rory jolted in the saddle. "You must have given him some incentive."

"I promised an interview for his father with Bethany Watts." Siobhan chewed the inside of her cheek.

"Really?" Rory's whisper was hoarse. "After knowing what trouble that man will be in the future?"

"It required a bribe," she said and fiddled with the reins. "He's loyal to you."

The rocking of the horse's gait had lulled Jake to sleep. His head leaned heavily against her, his soft curly hair right beneath her chin. Her breath hitched and warm tears flowed down her face unstoppable.

"Siobhan, *mo chroí*, what's goin' on?" Rory leaned over from his saddle and placed an arm on her shoulder. "The last time you were like this... all emotional, you were pregnant with Jake."

The horses' hooves clopped on the path. She sniffed her nose clear and wiped the wet from her face with the heel of her hand.

"*Are* you pregnant?" Rory asked.

Siobhan blinked. *Am I?* She sat straighter and sniffed, forcing calm into her voice while ice danced in her stomach.

"Maybe," she replied.

"I'll take you to the medical centre when we return," Rory said. "It's never too late in the day for Aunty Bec. She'll understand."

***

Once they unloaded the horses, Siobhan followed Rory to the medical centre after sending a message to Bec. Siobhan cuddled Jake; her baby's eyes were half closed, and his head lolled against her. They by-passed the hall which hummed with people gathering.

"Discussing the boom they heard, no doubt," Rory said as they slipped through the compound's buildings unnoticed.

Xian strode along the corridor toward them, sharing his stare between her and Rory.

"The place shook," Xian said, "and the buildings weren't the only things rattled. The people are meeting in the hall."

Rory glanced at Siobhan. "I need to do something first, Xian," he said. "The Chief Council knows what to say. They can reassure people until I arrive."

"Okay," Xian continued along the corridor.

Siobhan cradled Jake and gave Rory a half smile. "I'll put Jake to bed first."

"No. I want you to see Aunty Bec now," Rory said. "The Chief Council and everyone else can wait for her too."

Rory pushed open the doors to the medical centre and ushered her in. Bec walked in a moment later, her dressing gown tied tight around her, and her hair pulled back in a loose bun. The puffiness of sleep surrounded her eyes, and she looked all of her seventy-odd years.

Bec peered first at Rory, then at Siobhan. "Rory will put your toddler to bed while we have a chat," she said.

Bec turned to Rory after he took Jake from Siobhan's arms, and they held a brief whispered conversation.

"On you go, son," Bec spoke louder to Rory. "Siobhan will be along soon."

Rory gave her a silent nod and left.

"You're the only person he'll take orders from without question," Siobhan said while she and Bec stared at Rory's back disappearing along the passage.

A soft laugh escaped the older woman's lips. "He's known me all his life. I attended his twin birth. I'd like to think he considers me a mother figure, even though *no one* could replace that wonderful woman." Bec looked into Siobhan's eyes. "Such a shame you never met Caitlin. She would approve of you. You're exactly what he needs."

The pricking behind Siobhan's eyes gave way to streams of tears moistening her face.

"Come, sit down, Siobhan," Bec said.

Siobhan stepped closer to a trolley.

"No, dear. Come with me." Bec guided her to a room off to one side where a two-seater couch, with barely stuffed cushions and low arms, sat against the wall. Bec sat and handed Siobhan a hankie, and Siobhan wiped her nose on the fresh cloth.

"You've had an eventful day," Bec said from the other end of the couch.

Siobhan snorted a laugh. "Understatement."

"Care to tell me about it?" Bec asked.

Siobhan dragged in a faltering breath, all pretense of control escaping her. "I'm not very good at this." Tears slicked her face as she stifled chokes.

"Not good at what, dear?"

"This married thing. It's really hard," Siobhan replied.

"Uh, huh," Bec said.

"It's all supposed to work out, yes?" Siobhan began, "You meet the guy. He's absolutely gorgeous and wonderful and everything you've ever dreamed of. Literally. And more, 'cos he can travel through time and is an awesome fighter and everybody looks to him to see them through the mess." Siobhan dragged air through a clogged throat.

"I sense there's a 'but' coming," Bec said.

"But"—Siobhan waved the hankie around— "Oh, a whole lot of stuff…"

Bec shuffled closer and placed her hand on Siobhan's. Bec's hand was cool and thin, and the veins stood out like a blue delta on its back.

"Were you expecting instant success? No issues? No struggles? The perfect man?" Bec asked.

"No." Siobhan sighed. "I just thought it would be different. Not easy, far from it, considering we're from opposite—no, *opposing*—worlds." Siobhan paused, regaining control over her breathing and her emotions. "I thought he'd realise. Oh, I don't know. No one's perfect but…"

"You thought you'd found what they call your *soulmate*," Bec said.

"Yes, that's it!"

"You believed you would meet that special someone, and everything would work out?" Bec added.

"Yes."

"That's not who your soulmate is, Siobhan."

"No?" Siobhan's brow tightened. "Who is it, then?"

"A soulmate is the person who stays with you for a lifetime, for as long as that may be," Bec began. "One who is there during the great times; by your side during the hum-drum boring bits of life; and with you, walking beside you, pulling you through, when the hard times come. Learning about you, and themselves, while it's all happening. And loving you even more when it's done. No matter what has to be done to get there."

Siobhan sniffed. She'd told Rory they had to work on it so at least she was on the right track. The tightness in her chest returned and her emotions exploded. She threw the hankie over her face and let the sobs come.

"Rory whispered you might be pregnant, Siobhan," Bec said when her crying eased.

Siobhan nodded behind the hankie. "I'm late."

If she was, then it would be time to initiate her plan. Siobhan dropped the sodden cloth from her eyes to see Bec had tears in hers.

"I'm sorry, Bec. All this talk of soulmates and you lost yours this summer. I'm so stupid—"

"No, dear." Bec's words were thick as she held Siobhan's hand. "Not stupid, only human."

Bec was so easy to talk to. No wonder she was the person Rory had always gone to about the important issues in life since his parents had passed. Bec listened with eyes full of compassion, and the wisdom seventy-and-more years of life often gave a person.

Then it all came out. Those things Siobhan would never tell Rory, but at last she could say to someone.

"Bec, when I travelled to the future," Siobhan said, "I was dead."

Bec's head twitched a little. "Pardon?"

"When I went forward in time and found out about the famine after the volcanic eruption, the one that occurred tonight." Siobhan swallowed at the memory. "Well, I had died having a baby."

Bec pulled back, eyes wide and blinking often. "How?" She took her hand away from Siobhan's. "What was it that we didn't save you, girl?" Bec's questions came fast, her hands trembling in her lap.

"I had placenta previa," Siobhan said, "according to Murray."

"What did Rory-of-the-future say about it?" Bec asked.

"He told me I had to make sure I didn't die." Siobhan stifled a sob at the memory.

"Rory asked you to alter the past?" Bec's eyebrows shot into her hairline. "That's not like him."

"He was a broken man after I'd died," Siobhan said.

"I bet he was," Bec replied.

"Future Rory felt he'd made some mistakes," Siobhan explained, "and blamed himself for the tight spot the Communities will be in. But a volcano and a famine couldn't be his fault. Stocking supplies, as we are, will hopefully avoid the pressure future-Rory felt to make the decisions he did."

Bec clasped her hands and looked beyond Siobhan. "Placenta previa. Yes, that is something we may not have been able to handle." She spoke more to herself and pursed her lips so the wrinkles radiated out from them like the sun's rays. Then she looked Siobhan in the eye. "Why did I attempt to manage that?" she asked. "We should have sent you off to the Bunker. They'd have the equipment to deal with an obstetric emergency, safely perform a caesarean and deliver you a wee bit early. And they'd have the equipment to deal with a pre-term neonate." Bec bore an unblinking stare into Siobhan.

"You weren't there, Bec," Siobhan said in a small voice.

"Why not?" Bec asked. "Where was I?"

Siobhan swallowed, trying with all her might to calm the expression on her own face.

Bec tilted her head slowly, understanding dawning on her features. "Oh. I die before you have this baby," she said then turned away, nodding to herself and sighing. "So, I'll be with my soulmate soon."

"Oh, Bec, I'm sorry—" Siobhan began.

"We have to get you to the Bunker the moment we confirm you have problems," Bec interrupted.

"Rory doesn't know," Siobhan said.

"Doesn't know what, dear?" Bec asked. "Oh, you've not told him you... in that future?"

"No," Siobhan replied. "And I never will. So, promise me, Bec, that you won't. Patient confidentiality, please."

Bec raised her eyebrows only slightly. "Very well," she said. "I think I understand why you're not telling Rory. He would never allow changes to history. It would have been a dire future for him to ask you to change things now."

"It was. You haven't heard the half of it." Siobhan's shoulders sank a little. "Rory hasn't divulged to the Chief Council everything I saw, and I don't think he will unless he needs to."

"So, there are more problems than a volcano causing a famine?" Bec asked.

"Yes." Siobhan opened her mouth to speak further but Bec put up a staying hand.

"I don't need to know. If what you say is true, I'll be out of it." Her grave expression turned into one of conviction. "I have every confidence in your man, Rory. He'll know how to handle it."

"Yes, he will." Siobhan spoke with the certainty she had of *her man's* ability to deal with the coming crisis. "But I must be there for him. Help me please, Bec."

"Yes. If you are pregnant, I'll tell Christine of our plans if you have any complications," Bec said. "I won't mention specifics, just *complications*. So, if it is this pregnancy in which you… well, we'll have you at the Bunker before the third trimester when this obstetric complication becomes serious. Okay?"

"Thanks." Siobhan rested against the couch.

"Now." Bec stood up. "Let's examine you and see what we're up against."

Chapter Thirty-Four

Invercharing Community, 2063

Dimmed skies had started two months ago, after the resounding blast that signified the eruption. Rory raised his face to the breeze blowing off Bheinn Fionn and gazed at the granite spine jutting through the grass-covered mountainside and leading off to the distance. He pointed to the elongated, fluffy clouds that skimmed along the grey rock.

"Those clouds are like the longboats of the Vikings," he whispered to Siobhan.

They stood together, along with the whole Invercharing Community, at the cemetery on the back hill, for the burial of Rebecca Hamilton. He dropped his gaze to the freshly filled grave at his feet.

"Maybe Bec's soul will rise up to that longboat and sail away to meet your Uncle Brendan," Siobhan suggested.

Rory looked above the Viking boat cloud, to the thick ash-cloak covering their dome of sky, deepening the grey hue of the familiar clouds. The wind blew his loose hair across his face, leaving strands stuck to his tears. Siobhan's cool, small hand slipped into his.

"The generation that established the Invercharing Community are steadily leaving this world," he placed his other hand loosely over Siobhan's. "Leaving ours to deal with the concerns of this life." A wisp of jealousy gusted through Rory's thoughts. "They are now free."

Siobhan tightened her grip on him. Rory's moments of panic at her attempt to leave a couple of months ago had subsided and he put her uncharacteristic behaviour of that night down to her pregnancy hormones. They had promised each other they would 'work at it'. He looked at her upturned face. The corners of his mouth pulled, fighting with the flatness of grief.

"What?" Siobhan frowned.

"One out. One in." He shrugged.

"Yes, it usually goes that way." She turned away, tugging him after her and they descended the steep hill. The icy wind chilled Rory's cheeks.

"Winter's here." Rory drew Siobhan to his side, and they hiked down the hill with the other mourners. "We must make sure we have a grand Christmas this year, a special celebration despite those who'll be missing." He summoned thoughts of winter festivities to chase away the ache.

Christine and Kendra walked ahead of them, their arms wrapped around each other. At the base of the hill, just before entering the compound's fence, Christine turned to Rory and Siobhan.

"Siobhan," she said. "I've been thinking over yesterday's ante-natal exam." Christine looked from Siobhan to Rory, then her lips tweaked half a grimace. "I'll need to speak with you both at your earliest convenience."

"Earliest convenience?" Rory's heart staggered a wee bit. "This is soundin' official. What's going on?"

Too many things had gone wrong recently.

"I... I just need to talk to you both," Christine said, rubbing at her ear then turned back to Kendra. They both walked to the compound's back building.

"It's okay," Siobhan said to Rory, tugging him forward. "We can see her after the wake." She smiled but it was a hesitant one.

"You know about this?" he asked.

She faced ahead and resumed walking.

He stopped and planted his feet. "Tell me."

Siobhan's stride continued and stretched the arm of her hand held in his. She turned. "Not here, Rory."

He pulled Siobhan along in silence all the way to their quarters. "Okay," he said when he'd closed the door.

"I'm not sure," Siobhan looked away.

"You are. Dinnae lie to me." He leaned down to catch her gaze focused on the floor. "It's something you found out in the future, isn't it?"

"I'm not lying about anything"—she lifted her head— "so, I would appreciate you never accusing me of that." Her eyes had a fire in them, and a hint of worry. "Murray told me I had trouble with this pregnancy," she finally said. "Christine's probably just about to inform us."

"What sort o' trouble?" he asked, a churn forming deep in his guts.

She shrugged.

"We'll go see Christine now." He opened the door.

"Now?" Siobhan hesitated. "But people are gathering for the wake."

"It's something serious and I want tae know."

"What makes you think it's serious?" she asked.

"You do." He stood with the door half open. Her pupils were wide, and her hand trembled ever-so-slightly. "I ken you," he said. "Something's wrong and I need to know what."

Siobhan hung her head and sighed. "I'll let Christine confirm it." She looked up at him then. "I could be wrong."

"How?" He almost snapped, but held it in check. "You've been to the future. Ye ken things."

"But we've changed it," she said. "We're doing things we hadn't done in the past of that future I went to."

"Aye, you're right. How much have we changed?" he asked.

"Hopefully enough." Her mouth pulled to the side.

Heavy footsteps trod toward them along the corridor.

"Rory?" It was George.

"Aye?" Rory tore his eyes away from Siobhan, who looked relieved at the interruption.

"We've been invited to Christmas at the Bunker," George said.

***

Scottish Government Bunker, Edinburgh

The lift doors opened onto the floor where the cells were situated. Bethany strode out and acknowledged the guard standing to attention.

"Ensure we are not disturbed, please," she said, extending her hand to the guard at the inner door to the single cell area, which held the one and only high-profile prisoner. "That will be all, thank you."

The young man handed her the keys, flicked a knowing look across to the prisoner, and left the room. Bethany shut the door behind him and locked the separate cell area.

"Good news, I hope?" Antony said from his desk. "Many acceptances to our little *soiree* at Christmas?"

She opened the door to his cell and stepped in. Weights and a bench-press ran along the far wall next to his desk, which was covered in papers. *Mein Kampf* lay open next to Churchill's *Memoirs of the Second World War*.

"On the whole, the invitation to spend Christmas with the New Scottish Government has been well received," she replied. "Please don't be flippant, Antony. We have important things to discuss, such as the darkening skies after the earth tremor, which our scientists have now confirmed coincided with Vesuvius erupting."

"Wow!" Antony's eyebrows lifted into his closely cropped hairline.

"They have positive intel from our friends in Southern Italy—what's left of it." She took a slow pace closer. "You know the delegates will stay for a day or two? Some of them will have come a long way."

"Hmm, that turncoat, Siobhan no-longer Kensington-Wallace, and her wild-boy of a husband will have almost a week's travel to get here," Antony said, rising from his desk. "I suppose you'll have to suffer them for a while."

Bethany curled a brow, ignoring the obvious hatred behind Antony's words.

"Other Community leaders have accepted," Bethany reported. "There are the relatives of Mr Campbell who live in the Glencoe Community and a weird old woman who runs a Community in a castle, which used to belong to the National Trust of Scotland, of all things."

"Oh aye, near Loch Tummel," Antony scoffed. "I've heard they turned the mock army into a real one."

"Don't knock it. We may need them."

"What about the bandit leader MacIntosh spoke to on the side while he was at Invercharing? I can't recall his name."

"Micah McNair?" Bethany offered. "He's now married to Mr Campbell's younger sister."

"Really?" Antony's eyes narrowed. "I wonder if he's shared that piece of his past with his wife."

Antony stood a breath away from Bethany.

Prison was good for him, improved his focus, and, due to his good behaviour, he'd been given permission for walks in the upper compound.

"Derrick Lloyd, the self-proclaimed King of Fife, has accepted," she said, her gaze slipping to the close-fitting prison shirt he wore.

"Now it's my turn to say 'don't mock'," Antony said, his own eyes searching her blouse. "An alliance with such a powerful man would be an advantage to the New Scottish Government. A capitalist entrepreneur is more like it. Bring back the good old days, hey?" The spicy scent of aftershave from the 1980s, purloined from the stores, no doubt, wafted across Bethany's face while Antony spoke, his hands gesticulating with every word. "Not the self-sufficient, self-governed, organised, militia-loving Communities—"

Bethany rolled her eyes and interrupted, "Yes, I know you hate them."

"Then you also know we don't need people like that," Antony said. "They won't co-operate with us, Beth. They live an existence that doesn't require a central government. For us to survive, they must be disbanded. And can you see the Campbell boy doing that?"

"Siobhan claims he's loyal to us," Bethany began. "He told me himself that Communities are all for Scotland and he strikes me as the kind of man who would fight for—"

"Whatever benefits his own agenda!" Antony finished.

Bethany shook her head wordlessly. Antony's deep brown eyes locked with hers, his expression changing from serious to smouldering intensity, sending her pulse up a notch.

"Enough of that." His voice was softer, and he pulled her to himself.

"We should plan our approach for the Christmas conference, Antony."

"Later," he said.

All thoughts of strategy flew from her mind, chased away by the ministrations of Antony's mouth, tongue, hands and ... the rest of him.

Chapter Thirty-Five

Invercharing Community, 2063

"What!" Rory closed his mouth on the expletive that would follow. A child cried in the far corner of the medical centre, and forceps clanged in a metal tray as Cèilidh tended to the dressing of a youth who'd injured himself while chopping wood.

"No," Rory shook his head, stifling the word so it was a low mumble, along with the desire to hold Siobhan and never let go.

Christine got up from the couch in the quiet area of the medical centre and shut the door, creating privacy, of a sort.

"Before she passed, Dr Bec told me if there was any complication with Siobhan's pregnancy, she was to go straight to the Bunker where they could deal with it safely," Christine said in authoritative tones. "Rory, you can't deny your wife—"

"Och! I'm not. I just dinnae like it, that's all!" His nostrils flared. "It's just that Siobhan will be in the Bunker for the next six months, instead of being here. I'll miss ma wee boy, too for I cannae stay there with you, Siobhan."

He slid his arms around Siobhan's waist, not caring they were in the busy medical centre and patients and medics alike could look through the windows into the quiet corner if they wished.

"I know, Rory, but I must go." Siobhan's voice was soft in his ear, but her tone held something else. Was it fear?

"You'll be okay, Siobhan," he asked. "They'll know what placenta-whatever is, will they no'?"

"Aye," Christine answered for Siobhan. "I've already contacted their medical staff. They're happy—no insisting—she comes as soon as you can."

"No' on a horse, lass." He let go of Siobhan's waist and stood back. "We'll take a wagon. It will still be over a week on a rattly thing, but we'll drive slow, aye? And Jake will cope better with it, too."

Siobhan's shoulders eased their tension, so did her expression.

If only I felt as relieved as Siobhan.

"Well, at least it coincides with the Christmas celebrations," Christine said, her voice overflowing with enthusiasm. "You'll be a wee bit early, Rory, but you may as well stay for them."

"Aye." He tilted his head. "Cannae be away for long. I'll have to return. Just hope the weather holds. Those bandits are getting more eager and reckless. The abnormally darker skies are stirring them up."

***

Fife

Siobhan half lay, half sat in the rear of the wagon and shuffled her feet, stretching her legs out on the thin mattress covering the bottom of the wagon and wriggling her cold, numb toes. The seat in the front next to Rory was hard and backache had set in again, despite the thick cushion she'd brought. All the way from Invercharing, Jake had alternated between sitting beside his father while watching the road pass by, and chatting about everything, or playing with his toys next to her in the tray of the wagon.

"You wait there, Siobhan," Rory said. A halo of misted breath floated around Rory's face in the semi-darkness. "I'll see if there's anywhere nearby—"

"But my dad will put us up!" Micah said, pulling his mount's reins and settling the animal's impatient nickers. "Come on, man. He won't try anything. We're all expected at the Bunker tomorrow."

Rory faced Siobhan, his crinkled brow exposed his inner fight with resignation, then he looked back to Micah.

Siobhan poked her head out through the canvas awning that kept out some of the Scottish winter. Night was already here. Winter's days were not only short but even darker and colder with the ashen screen continually covering the sun from the volcano's eruption which had spread its cloud over the northern hemisphere. They couldn't get to the Bunker soon enough, as far as Siobhan was concerned. There would be efficient heating there.

"Your wifey and yoor wee boy deserve a decent place to stay tonight, Rory," Micah continued his reasoning. "I give you my word, we'll be okay."

Rory turned to her in the back of the wagon. "What do you think, Siobhan?"

"Jake's chestier," she said. "Getting him out of the cold air would help. And I need a soft, warm place to rest. I'd rather not turn up at the Bunker looking haggard and forlorn."

Rory's cheek muscles tensed, then he let out a misty breath once more. "Verra well."

"Good!" Micah had barely let the word out when he kicked his horse to a canter.

Cèilidh had remained at home in Invercharing with their children. Siobhan shrugged, trying to shake away the slight resentment. Cèilidh's pregnancies, despite being twins, had gone without a hitch.

Rory drove the wagon as it rattled down the road to the old holiday park, while the figure of Micah on his horse moved away into the night. Light dotted the darkness ahead to her left, and soon the forms of the old holiday cabins loomed closer. Rory drove the horses onto the track that led to the central area of the village. Light spilled from the cabins and the shadows of the occupants crossed the narrow verandas.

Men milled around the main building where Siobhan and Rory had first met Lloyd. Memories of a scone piled high with cream tweaked the corner of Siobhan's mouth. The men carried boxes and bags over to the parked wagons where Micah's horse stood, its nose in a feed trough and its tail swishing. Rory drove the horses in that direction. Micah came running beside the wagon.

"Ma dad's chuffed." Micah's eyes sparkled in the lantern light. "He says he'd be delighted to accommodate you and your family for the night and travel with you in convoy to the Scottish Government Bunker to celebrate Christmas."

"I'm sure he would," Rory said, hiding none of his derision. He pulled the horses to a stop in front of the stable area. "We'll be in once I've unhitched and tended to ma' animals."

"Och, no." Micah sounded offended.

He called into the stable area, then a young lad came running out, bobbing his head to acknowledge Micah's orders to tend to the horses. Micah helped unload the bags while Siobhan stepped down from the wagon with care.

"I need to bathe and bed my boy after some food, Micah." Siobhan lifted Jake from the wagon. The night air hit her boy's chest and he coughed and grizzled.

"Oh, aye," Micah said. "I've got the cook onto that already, Siobhan. Uncle Micah will make sure wee Jaykie's got a comfy bed for the night." He nuzzled his face into Jake's and planted a kiss on her toddler's cheek. Jake cried fully. "Och, no. *Wheesht*, lad," Micah said.

Micah carried their bags and led them inside the main building. Siobhan rested Jake on her hip and shushed him, and Rory walked behind with a duffle bag in each hand. They followed Micah to a room, which had an en suite, a double bed, and a cot in the corner.

"This is all very civilised," Siobhan took Jake's coat and shoes off and sat him in the cot while Micah and Rory placed their bags on the bed.

"Of course, it is." Micah stood taller. "Mavis will bring the wean's dinner in soon. But you must dine with my father and me this evening." Micah beamed.

"Thank you, Micah." Rory seemed genuine.

"Don't take long." Micah shut the door behind him.

Siobhan turned and faced Rory. His expression was tight.

"What?" she asked.

"I don't like it." Rory's right eye narrowed. "If we go in convoy with Lloyd, it will seem like we're aligned with him." He looked at her then. "And we definitely are not."

***

The chill soon left Rory's bones with the warmth of the heated room seeping into him. Jake settled down after Siobhan fed him the stew Mavis had brought and was soon asleep in the cot. Micah led them down the passage to the room where Lloyd had first entertained them. Now, a long, solid wood table stood in the centre of the room, surrounded by chairs that had lighter wood marquetry inlays on their backs. It was set for five. The cutlery shone silver and the crockery, a fine bone china, had gold edging on each plate.

"Somebody wishes to impress," Rory whispered into Siobhan's ear as they entered.

"Let him," she whispered back. "A nice meal in a classy setting would be a great change."

"Dinnae be fooled. There's nothin' classy about this man." A side door opened, and Rory cut his whisper short.

Lloyd entered followed by his son and heir, Maxwell. "Good evening and welcome, friends," Lloyd said, holding his hands high and with a superior smile filling his face. "I hear congratulations are in order on account of you both expecting your second child. I trust all is well with you, Mrs Campbell."

The cunning bastard knows things are no.

Rory controlled an exhalation, attempting to settle the tension between his shoulder blades. He'd have to bear the charade of friendship. His wife and his boy needed a good meal and a comfortable bed. It was a price Rory would pay, but his senses were on high alert.

"Maxwell, son." Lloyd straightened to look Mr Lloyd junior in the eye. "Show our guests where they are to be seated. Dinner is ready."

"Thank you for accommodating us at such short notice, Mr Lloyd," Siobhan said. She had switched on her peace-keeping mode.

"We are very grateful." Rory joined the diplomacy. "It's been a long journey."

"My pleasure," Lloyd said. His expression seemed amicable.

Lloyd sat at the head of the table while Maxwell directed them to sit, with Micah next to Siobhan and Rory opposite them, and Maxwell sat at the far end of the table. Lloyd had once again seated Rory with his back to the main exit.

"So, Micah," Lloyd said unfolding a linen napkin and placing it in his lap. "Your friends, colleagues, whatever you seem to call them—"

"My bandit associates, father?" Micah supplied the term then shook out the napkin that sat at his place setting.

"Aye, son," Lloyd said.

"Och, they're sending representatives to the Bunker, if that's what you're askin'." Micah placed the napkin in his lap.

"And you'll both be attending on behalf of the Communities, Mr and Mrs Campbell?" Lloyd asked.

Mavis brought a tureen of soup to the table.

"We're representing Invercharing," Rory said. "Other Communities are sendin' their own delegates."

Mavis lifted the lid from the tureen and the aroma of seasoned potatoes wafted into Rory's face. Steam billowed up while she served the soup. His stomach grumbled—it had been a long time since their light snack on the road.

"Oh, wonderful," Lloyd said. "I look forward to meeting the other Community leaders."

The man tried hard, but he gave away his roots with his excitement. *Streetwise Glasgow*, Dad would've called the accent sneaking through.

"You haven't come across any other Communities, Mr Lloyd?" Siobhan asked. "I imagine your network has quite a reach."

"Only the one up near Arbroath." Lloyd spooned the soup into his mouth and soon finished his bowl. "They have supplied our main course. Ever had smokies?" He directed his question to Siobhan, who shook her head.

Mavis cleared the table and soon returned with a hot platter of brown fish. A smoky aroma surrounded her while she served a portion onto each plate. Two teenage girls followed closely behind her and served out the vegetables.

"What do you think the Government is up to, Father?" Micah asked.

Lloyd placed a forkful of smoked fish into his mouth and chewed.

"Micah, the Government isn't up to anything," Siobhan interjected. "Only meeting the leaders of the people and offering hospitality." Her irritation came through with her tone. "Pardon my rudeness, Mr Lloyd, but I'm certain the New Scottish Government only has goodwill and conversation in mind for this Christmas meeting."

"*New Scottish Government*," Lloyd said. "Aye, I heard they'd already named themselves." Hoary brows lifted above steel-grey eyes.

"Well, no," Siobhan replied, "but that's what we're aiming for."

"I hope so, as I would like to be consulted," Lloyd said. His fork remained immobile, a chunk of smokies dangling from its tines.

"And you will. As you are attending, your voice will be heard," Siobhan said with conviction, but a sliver of defensiveness slid through.

"I expect more than just a voice, Mrs Campbell," Lloyd said. "I am an influential figure in these parts. A significant force. A successful businessman who trades throughout the country. No matter whose side you're on, you cannot deny it."

"I don't, Mr Lloyd," Siobhan replied. "And we will be so pleased to hear what you have to say on restoring a government for the people and, indeed, rebuilding Scotland to her former glory."

"We?" Lloyd asked.

"The Government." Siobhan's cheeks pinked under Lloyd's stare.

"It won't be easy," Micah said around a mouthful of dinner.

"No, son, it won't," Lloyd slid his glance sideways at his younger son. "You are correct. Here's hoping it will not involve conflict. Although conflict is, at times, inevitable." Lloyd spoke through the clinking of cutlery on the gold-rimmed plates and the muffled voices of women in the kitchen. "It has been a necessity in the past."

The salty smokiness of fish melted like butter on Rory's tongue—along with the last dregs of respect he could muster for this man who was their host.

"How so, Mr Lloyd?" Rory kept his tone level, his desire to understand this man restraining the hate in his voice.

"Read your history, Mr Campbell," Lloyd replied. "For it records war as beneficial to developing civilisations. It forces societies to be organised, manage their resources—including people."

Siobhan's knife thunked on the table.

"Think of the technological advances we owed to those two World Wars," Lloyd continued, now looking up from his meal. "Medical advances such as penicillin! Means of detection—RADAR. You may have come across that yourself, young Campbell, on your journey in that submarine."

Rory swallowed his mouthful of creamy mashed potato, all enjoyment gone.

"Aye, news travels," Lloyd said without pausing for a response from Rory. He continued looking at Siobhan and he said, "Computers, now they were a big innovation."

The fork's handle dug into Rory's palm while his mind took one step ahead of Lloyd's conversation. Part of him wished it to stop. The other part needed to know for sure where it was headed.

"We need a good war to develop our world again." Lloyd paused in his dissertation and placed a forkful of dinner in his mouth.

"What about the lives that are sacrificed in gaining that knowledge and development?" Rory said, trying not to speak through clenched teeth.

Lloyd didn't flinch at the tone Rory had thrown at him. "Collateral," he said. "Sorting out the rabble from the genius. We want stronger, smarter, and improved versions of humans to run the new world that will emerge."

Siobhan's fork clattered on her plate. "Are you speaking of eugenics, Mr Lloyd?"

"Ah yes, you are on my wavelength, Mrs Campbell. A pure race of Celtic-Scots origin. I'd like that." Lloyd sat back in his chair and gazed ahead, thoughtfully. "The Celts—they understood what war and sacrifice were about. They were the thinkers of their day."

Siobhan stood. "I'd better check on our baby." She walked to the end of the table where she paused and briefly met Rory's eye. Her hands trembled. "Actually, I'm exhausted," she said. "Thank you for a delicious dinner," she said to Lloyd. "I must get to bed now. Goodnight."

Maxwell stood and closed the door behind her. Rory returned his gaze to the Nazi-cum-Celt-lover at the head of the table. Lloyd's rheumy stare was focused on the remains of his mashed potato, his eating utensils standing upright in his white-knuckled grip.

Rory searched for an equal reason to leave but it would risk the ire of their host, despite Micah's presence. Instead, he gritted his teeth and settled in for what he expected would be a dessert of further revelations.

Chapter Thirty-Six

Scottish Government Bunker

Winter made its presence known to Siobhan's toes, despite the thick-soled rabbit-skin boots she wore. Their day had started early in the cold predawn. It was now late afternoon and the sun had set two hours ago. Rory drove the wagon on the road that wound to the back of Arthur's Seat. The high concrete wall surrounding the entry to the Scottish Government Bunker glowed grey in the dim moonlight. Siobhan let out a slow sigh, attempting to relieve the quivering in her belly, not sure if it was only the baby's movement causing the fluttering. They approached the high metal doors. They opened and let their cart rattle in. Micah and his closest men rode their horses behind their wagon. Jock and Deet had joined them soon after crossing the Kincardine Bridge.

Lloyd and his entourage had travelled close with them all day. Rory drove the wagon and sat in a stony silence. When the rocking of the wagon had lulled Jake to sleep, Siobhan took a turn seated next to Rory.

"You have to admit, being on Lloyd's bad side at this juncture, wouldn't be beneficial," she said and rubbed Rory's back. "You'll need to hide your dislike of the man."

The previous evening after dinner, Rory had come to bed fuming and asked for a neck and shoulder rub. His teeth-gritting had made his muscles feel like concrete.

"Ye are being a wee bit generous with the term *dislike*, Siobhan."

He drove the wagon down the steep driveway to the garage level. The clang of the horseshoes echoed off the concrete walls and woke Jake who now cried as Siobhan gathered him in her arms. Rory parked the cart right before the loading platform.

The door from the stairwell flew open, Murray ran out, and jumped down to them. Rory leaped from the wagon, grabbed his brother in a hug and held hard. Murray disengaged himself from Rory and kissed Siobhan on the cheek, then took Jake who stopped crying to stare wide-eyed at Murray.

"Hello, little man. I'm your Uncle Murray." He jiggled Jake. "You look like a blond Rory. Only prettier."

Siobhan let herself laugh, drawing on the glow of her fondness for Murray, which settled some of her internal jitters.

"It's a pity you'll grow up to be ugly like your daddy," Murray said.

"Och, that's enough cheek. I've only just arrived!" Rory shouted from the rear of the wagon where he was unloading their bags.

Jake examined every feature on his uncle's face while a soldier directed Rory and Lloyd's men to the section prepared for the horses.

"Wow, Rory must feel like he's had his arm cut off. He didn't bring Boy." Murray grinned at his nephew and blinked a few times. "Come on, Siobhan, I'll take you in. Rory will find his way around," Murray said over his shoulder. He tucked Jake onto his hip, then led the way into the main stairwell. "There're people here who've been waiting for you two." Murray led them down the corridor to the accommodation area.

"Who in particular?" Siobhan asked, stepping into the corridor where her room used to be.

"Siobhan!"

Siobhan spun at Louise's shout and her old friend enveloped her in a hug. She swallowed hard on the lump in her throat.

"You all must prepare and dress in your best," Louise said and let go of Siobhan, a slight blush high on her cheeks. "We're having a special dinner tonight. It's Midwinter's Eve." Louise's face shone in the LED and her eyes sparkled. "You look great, Siobhan. I couldn't believe it when they said you *had* to come for medical reasons."

Siobhan put her index finger to her lips and looked behind her. Louise lowered her voice. "Sorry."

Rory had caught up carrying a bag in each hand and one tucked under an arm. Lloyd strode behind him, Maxwell and one of his guards carrying his luggage.

"You'll be in rooms down this way, Mr Lloyd." Henderson, who had appeared from the corridor that ran off to the right, halted Lloyd and Maxwell.

"Dinner is at seven followed by socialising in the main room," Louise said.

Louise looked back to Siobhan and held her arms with quivering hands. "We've decorated it for Christmas. A tree like we used to have when we were children. And an open fire! They've rigged a pipe to vent out the smoke!"

***

Hot water ran in rivulets down Siobhan's back, the soothing heat melting away the chill in her leg muscles, aches in her lower back, and numb cold in her toes. The bathroom attached to the double room had a shelf above the sink chock-full of shampoos, body lotions and *l'eau de toilettes*. Siobhan stepped from the shower recess into the steamy room and took the lid off every bottle and sniffed each one.

"Will they provide a babysitter?" Rory called through the crack in the door.

Jake was already asleep in an old travel cot Rory had set up and crammed next to the bed. "I don't think we should wake him," he said. "He's sleeping with a full belly after that mush you gave him." He pushed the door further open and eyed her.

She stood nude in front of the mirror, her skin streaked red from the water's heat. Rory stepped behind her and trailed his fingertips down each arm, soft and slow as he sought the reflection of her eyes in the misted mirror. Her skin tingled and the hairs on her arms rose. His head tilted and his lips traced her neck with a soft warmth, sending pleasant shivers throughout her body. She gasped, relishing his closeness. It had been an arduous week, and his caresses were tempting. She leaned back against him, his solidity reassuring and his presence a comfort. He would leave after Christmas. She wasn't sure how she'd manage without him here.

His hands roamed to her breasts, which were firming with her pregnancy, and he cupped them.

"Hmm." His breath brushed her nape. He moved one hand further down and rested it below her navel where a bump had formed. His thumb rubbed the mound with tenderness. He raised his face to engage with her vision in the mirror, now clear of condensation. His soft smile set the crinkles beside his eyes.

A knock came at the door.

Rory's lips halted at her earlobe, and he gave a sharp grunt.

"Mrs Campbell?" a female voice asked through the door. "It's Dr Liz Longford. May I speak with you? I thought I should check you over after your long journey and get some baselines."

Siobhan turned in Rory's embrace and gave him a quick kiss. "Tell her I'll be right there."

***

Siobhan's blue evening gown was tight across her belly, but on this occasion she didn't mind. Let those in the Bunker know how fruitful living with a healthy man from *up top* could be. The obstetric examination hadn't taken long but Dr Liz reported her mother's medical history. Siobhan blinked back moisture and recollections while digesting the news of the reason her own mother had died in childbirth—a haemorrhage due to placenta previa. Her father had never revealed that to her.

The tables filled with guests arriving at the reception dinner. The members of the Bunker in charge of decorations had decked out the largest hall for Christmas. The walls were festooned with swags of pine branches, dusted in white to imitate snow. These covered paintings of past monarchs and ministers, which were removed from Holyrood House and the New Parliament Building years ago. A large pine tree stood in a corner, covered in stylish decorations with similar dustings of fake snow and plenty of ribbons in Royal Stewart tartan. Piles of presents sat at its base, all wrapped in tartan paper. Central on the nearest wall, sat a cast-iron fireplace and flue, as promised, with wood set ready to light.

A long table covered in a white cloth ran down the centre of the room. Siobhan estimated it would seat one hundred. Centre pieces of candles surrounded by baubles and pinecones alternated with bowls and platters of festive foods.

They must have depleted the archives and stores. The Government was out to impress. A wave of heat flushed through Siobhan. It wouldn't impress those Communities who were struggling at present. Their food reserves were already being rationed. Had the guys here not done their mathematics when the sunlight started failing?

Kelly called to her from across the room. She was also dressed in an evening gown. Her boyish figure had stayed slim after all these years of hard work, and Rory maintained she remained an awesome fighter. Alistair stood beside her. He was tall, thin and greying, and his face kept the gentle expression Siobhan remembered from their first visit to the Glencoe Community.

Siobhan waited for Kelly to reach her and embraced her older, but younger, sister-in-law. Siobhan's trip to Glencoe in the early months of their marriage, to meet Kelly and Alistair, had cemented an instant bond with these two hardy and generous souls. Siobhan sensed in Kelly's character traits that she believed Caitlin would have exhibited—compassion and pragmatism.

After greeting Alistair, Rory ushered Siobhan to the place-settings assigned for them.

"*Hello,*" came from along the table and caught Siobhan and Rory's attention.

Rory waved back to Mrs Donaldson, who was wearing her tailored dress crossed over with a wide tartan sash, and nodded to Mr Donaldson who was in his kilt of the same tartan. Siobhan smiled at them both while the chatter of the guests around the table quietened.

Bethany sat at the very head of the dinner table and all eyes were now on her. She rose and commenced her welcome speech.

"Thank you to all for agreeing to come in a spirit of co-operation and camaraderie and limiting personal weapons—" she began but was interrupted by a side door flying open.

Angela strode in wearing a clinging, green evening dress, which contrasted well with her red hair. She knew how to dress to invite attention, for every male-head in the room lingered on her entrance.

"I beg your pardon, First Minister," Angela said then took her place halfway along the table.

"It's embarrassing that Angela's related to us," Rory whispered over his shoulder to Siobhan as he sat facing Bethany. "Always wanting people to notice her."

"Ssh," Siobhan said when he opened his mouth to say more.

Bethany continued her speech. "We must all reconsider the use of our own resources in light of—well a lack of light."

Bethany paused and allowed for a moment of appreciation of her humour. Soft chuckles came from the seated guests.

"You are welcome to tour the Bunker, under the supervision of one of our designated guides." Bethany slid a brief glance in Angela's direction. "But now, as we believe in preserving the traditions of the past, please eat and drink and enjoy our pre-Christmas festivities on this Midwinter's Eve." She raised her glass, and the diners stood.

"*Slànte mhor*," Bethany toasted.

"*Slànte mhor*," the guests of the New Scottish Government responded and lifted their drinks to the toast.

"Where's Lloyd?" Rory whispered to Siobhan once they'd sat down.

Siobhan scanned the room. Leaders from the other Communities sat forward of Rory, including the Donaldsons, and Maxwell Lloyd sat near the top of the table beside Angela. Further down near their end of the table, and on either side of Kelly, Alistair and Murray, were Micah and delegates from the bandit groups. High-ranking members of the Government and the surviving members of the Brains Trust sat strategically in between.

But no Lloyd.

Siobhan returned her gaze to Rory. His eyes were slits and his nostrils flared. A door opened and behind them someone entered the hall.

"Psst, Rory," Murray hissed.

Rory turned in the direction he indicated. Siobhan twisted slightly in her chair to view the door. Hidden among the hustle and bustle of those serving the first course, Lloyd slipped in and made his way to the empty seat in between Maxwell and Angela.

After dinner, they cleared the room of the dining table and chairs, and a quartet performed while people mingled. Siobhan's feet ached and travel weariness echoed in her muscles. The comfortable couches lining the walls looked so inviting. She sat on an overstuffed green cloth sofa and was soon joined by Rory, then Alistair, while Kelly stood watching the musicians.

"You know, it's strange," Alistair said, his Canadian accent still holding strong. "Whenever I see you, Rory"—he leaned forward on the sofa and rested his elbows on his thighs— "you're almost the same as... back then."

"I'm barely four years older, ken," Rory whispered.

"It might have been yesterday for you," Alistair said. "But I'll never forget what happened all those years ago for me when... We couldn't have done it without you. You know that, right?"

Rory took a sharp breath.

"Sorry, Rory, I know it hurts," Alistair said. "But I also know, for some strange reason, you blame yourself for how it all went down."

Rory stared at his fingers entwined in front of him.

"I know this isn't a good time or place, but I've wanted to tell you this for so long." Alistair placed his hand on Rory's shoulder. "We wouldn't have pulled it off if you weren't there. We would've all died. I'm convinced of that. I'm so sorry that..." Alistair's voice broke.

Rory lifted his head and looked at him.

Alistair swallowed then continued. "Man, I miss your dad. I thought he hated me but, looking back, he was trying me out, testing me, but preparing me too. And I know you miss him." Alistair spoke so low Siobhan could only just hear him. "If you hadn't been there, Rory. The future wouldn't be *this*." He lifted his other hand for a brief moment. "Caitlin Murray-Campbell would not have survived. Hell, you wouldn't *be*. I would never have known the love of your sister, and more importantly for this time we live in, the Community System may not have been as well-devised and founded as it was." He leaned closer to Rory. "You're a hero and you have nothing, and I mean *nothing*, to feel guilty about. If Scott was still alive, he'd be so proud of the man you are—just as I am."

Rory bowed his head, hiding his ache and the emotion it would show. His shoulders trembled.

Alistair's whispered words came across to Siobhan. "And because the Communities are so well founded, we'll be able to hold our own when the Government tries to negotiate away our autonomy."

Siobhan swallowed and placed her hand on Rory's arm; his ropey muscles knotted tight beneath her fingers. Rory needed to hear his brother-in-law absolve him of any blame over his father's death, that was for certain. But Alistair exhibited the same reservations as Rory regarding the intentions of the New Scottish Government. Siobhan's neck muscles tensed. Somehow, a collaboration between Government and Communities *had* to work. Or the civil war she experienced in the future would occur.

Chapter Thirty-Seven

Scottish Government Bunker. Winter Solstice, 2063

"Meetings *all* day." Murray sat on their bed, bouncing Jake on his knee. Jake squealed until Murray put him down on the floor, where he ran around in the confined space. "Yep, he's like you, Rory," Murray said. "Can't keep still. Have you taught him how to ride yet? Dad had you on a horse by now, or so I'm told."

"How 'bout you take him to the child-minding place, Murray?" Rory asked, forcing a grin at him. He'd be happier if Murray minded Jake himself, but Murray had responsibilities now that he was part of the science team in the Bunker. Rory suppressed another shiver, they kept coming in this place of no natural light and stale air.

"What?" Rory answered Siobhan's sapphire-blue eyes staring sternly at him. He recalled the first time he saw them in LED—deep, vast pools.

"Be patient," she said. "You'll be out of here after Christmas. Just think of me still in the place *where daylight never dwells,* as you like to call it." She slipped her arms around his waist and placed a kiss on his lips.

"It's dark all day today, anyway." Murray chased Jake and caught his hand. "Well, almost. It's the Winter Solstice. Sun won't rise till 08:42 a.m. and sets as early as 3:40 p.m."

"Thank you, Mr Numbers," Rory said to Murray, then looked back to Siobhan. "You keep away from the you-know-what today, okay?"

"Definitely." Siobhan's eyes widened. "I never want to get caught in that again."

***

Rory sat beside Siobhan at the front of the room, Micah was next to them and the Donaldsons were nearby. Bethany-stuck-up-Watts did her usual ingratiating welcome, and the *this is what the New Scottish Government is all about* speech. She touched on the country re-establishing itself, reorganising, restructuring, and stated taxation would be required for infrastructure repair and development. Rory grimaced. Invercharing were tied into that one already.

The next speaker was a defence force officer who hinted at conscription to a united security force. Rory sensed Mrs Donaldson's posture stiffening even from where he sat in front of her. He had squirmed at the prospect of his own youngsters leaving the Community to defend the Government. Looking around on this visit, he'd noticed there weren't many young people, or children, in the Bunker.

He could see some good in conscription. The militia might learn a thing or two—or teach the Government something new. There would be provisos, of course. Limited contracts and availability of troops should the Communities require them.

Rory rolled his shoulders. A morning of inactivity was uncomfortable. He stretched his neck and did a secret scan of the room. Lloyd was absent again.

The session broke for morning tea and Rory left Siobhan speaking to Deet, while he headed over to the coffee machine where Maxwell was dispensing a hot drink.

"Good morning," Rory said to Maxwell, who grunted a reply. "Your father hasn't made it this morning. Is he okay?"

"Aye," Maxwell replied. Hot water sloshed over his hand from the urn's spout, and he flinched. "Ahh!"

"Better put some cold water on it," Rory said. "Go to the Gents."

Maxwell dropped the cup on the table and made a sharp exit out of the refreshment area.

The afternoon talks were on power supplies and getting the much-needed maintenance attended to on the wind and hydroelectricity units, and determining the feasibility of repairing abandoned facilities throughout Scotland. It required an inventory of the available and viable resources. They didn't mention nuclear power plants.

Rory stood by the coffee machine during a late afternoon tea break. Coffee was the only good thing about this place. The Donaldsons approached him, Mrs Donaldson's face was eye-piercingly stern.

"Mrs Donaldson, how have you found the discussions?" Rory braced himself for the response.

"You ken how I feel about their defence force ideas." She dropped her voice. "It's our young people they want as they only have ageing soldiers. I'm sure ye hae noted that, Rory."

"Hmm," Rory replied then took a sip of his coffee. His enjoyment of the dark brown liquid might dispel his discomfort regarding that issue, even if it was only for a moment.

"This government," Mrs Donaldson continued in a low voice, "is yet tae fully convince me they'll treat us as friends and not just a resource to exploit."

"They'll soon be scrounging for our fuel," Mr Donaldson observed. "Did ye see those tanks? How on earth do they run them?"

"Aye, that will be next," Mrs Donaldson concurred as Micah approached.

Mr Donaldson poured his wife a coffee. "Don't you think so, son?" Mr Donaldson peered through his glasses at Micah.

"Aye, sir," Micah answered in a brisk manner. A fine sheen of sweat covered his brow, and he scratched the back of his neck and stared directly at Rory. "You got a minute?" he asked him.

Rory kept hold of his coffee while following Micah to a quieter area with comfortable sofas.

"They're gonna be speakin' on fuels and stuff soon and I know Dad would be interested in that, but I can't find him," Micah said.

"Why you tellin' me?" Rory asked. "What's it to me if your father isn't making the most of his time in the Government Bunker?"

"It's just that—" Micah closed his mouth on that sentence. "Okay, Rory. Maxwell will ken where he is." He stomped off, his dreads bobbing in their bun.

Rory walked toward the entry to the meeting hall, but a sharp tap on his back stopped him short. He turned. Murray stood frowning, his lips disappearing in a scrunch and air coming loudly through his nose.

"What?" Rory asked. Alarm bells rang in his head, deafening all other thoughts.

"Need you to come with me right now," Murray said then spun.

Rory trailed Murray without speaking. He hurried from the central meeting area and out to the stairwell. They ran down four flights of stairs and turned off at the level where, if Rory remembered correctly, they housed the Time Machine.

Cold shot up from his guts and filled every part of him.

"What are ye about to show me, Murray?" he asked, stifling the yell welling up.

"Quiet!" Murray's reply was sharp.

Murray led him down the corridor to the lab that was home to the machine. The door stood open.

Rory stepped through. A pod lay crumpled on the floor of the Time Machine. Dirty footprints led away from it and faded as they progressed out the doorway.

Rory blinked, his skin crawling. "Who?"

"I don't know, but I locked this door. Someone's forced it." Murray pointed to the broken door handle. "And used it. They've returned. See these footprints?" He indicated to the floor. "They must've used the energy of the Solstice. That means they went this morning and have been gone all day. Sunset was half an hour ago."

"Och, no!" Rory yelled, his guts churning with the icy sensations gathering in them. "That bastard, Derrick Lloyd. That's why Maxwell was so jittery this morning over coffee."

The man's name hung in the silence between them.

"Is there any way of finding out where he went?" he asked. "Future or past?"

Murray shrugged. "There was no year set on the console. Just like when Siobhan travelled to the future."

Rory closed his eyes and swallowed. If it was the future, he would now have even more power. He'd have learned what he could hold over Rory, and how to go about it.

Rory's breath came haltingly. "How did he know?" Rory asked, fighting the numbness threatening. "Who told him?"

"Rory?" Murray's question filled the lab.

"We're all sworn to secrecy," Rory said and opened his eyes. "Even Cèilidh. I made her promise before she married Micah."

Murray's wide eyed stare bore into him. His wee brother, like everyone else, looked to him for the answer. Sometimes this being a leader was—

"Angela's giving guided tours," Murray said. "She betrayed us once before."

Murray's accusation seemed reasonable… but Angela would gain nothing from it. And she only operated if she benefitted.

"No," Rory said with certainty. "Revealing the Time Machine to Lloyd would be regarded as a betrayal of the government she's worked so hard at ingratiating herself with."

Rory unclenched his fists, stifling the heat welling from deep within.

"I knew it!" he ground out. "This machine is more open to abuse here in this Bunker than anywhere!"

"Siobhan's been there too, Rory," Murray said, bringing him out of his introspection. "She's told you what the future holds. We're prepared. We're better than that arsehole, Lloyd."

Murray's simple faith in *good will always triumph*, as naïve as Rory was beginning to think that was, was all he had to hold on to.

Chapter Thirty-Eight

Scottish Government Bunker. Spring Equinox, 2064

"They will give me another four weeks and then they'll perform a caesarean section. The placenta hasn't moved up at all. Over," Siobhan said into the CB radio handset in one of the few private side rooms of the Bunker's communication centre.

I'll be there, Siobhan. Over. Rory voice came through the handset.

"You'd better be."

Siobhan rested her forehead on her hand, with her elbow on the desk where the radio sat. It had been three long months of a growing belly and a fractious almost-two-year-old.

"I'll get Jake next time," she said. "He's at nursery. He loves it and I don't wish to disturb him. Over."

I'll be there as soon as I can after the Fuel Summit Lloyd has insisted on holding at his palace in Fife. Over.

"It's not a palace, Rory." She laughed into the handpiece. "It's a restored stately home. Over."

Aye, well, Martin kens it, Rory said. *Lloyd kidnapped and held him there at the start of the Crash. He'll tell you that story one day. Needless to say, he'll no' come with me. Only Xian and I will be attending. And I might bring Kendra too. Never know when you'll need muscle. Over.*

Siobhan's mouth tugged to the side. "I love you, Rory, and I miss you so much. Over." Hot tears slid from her eyes and trickled past the upturned corners of her mouth.

Damned hormones!

Och, heart o' my own heart, I cannae say how much I'm missing you and long to be with you. I have tae go. Love you. Over and out. Rory's end cut off.

Siobhan scooted the chair out from beneath her, stood and, pressing her hand into the small of her back, walked out of the communication centre. The waddle had started, and she was glad Rory couldn't see how ungainly she looked. Dr Liz and Aunty Rajna had both graciously said a pregnant woman was a beautiful thing.

Did. Not. Feel. Like. It.

***

Bethany dismissed the guard and closed the door that led to Antony's cell area. The door to his cell was open and his desk was its usual untidy array of open books and scattered papers. The stack of books standing beside it rose higher with each visit. Antony sat on the edge of his cot, brows drawn and his features dark. She'd come prepared mentally, and physically, for an afternoon of sex, but as he raised his head with the scar on his cheek glowing a dark purple, Bethany's switch from lover to First Minister was rapid.

"Talk to me." She crossed her arms, tucking the elderly packet of condoms into her blazer pocket.

"I need to know what he's up to." Antony looked at her from underneath his brows.

Bethany squinted. "I'm assuming you refer to the capitalist entrepreneur whom you hold in such high regard."

"Yes. Why his place?" Antony asked.

"Derrick Lloyd wants to impress *us*."

"There's more," Antony clasped his hands in front of himself. "A fuel summit," he sneered. "He's got some stashed away somewhere, that's what."

Bethany snorted and Antony glared at her, his scar looking angrier.

"We require more than just a *stash*." She sat on the cot beside him. "We need a viable, continuous supply, and Lloyd mentioned rapeseed oil. He has very fertile lands in Fife. We sent drones over them. He has planted his fields with what we assume is rapeseed, and he has many large barns. Most have storage vats. We suspect he's producing it in vast quantities. Now that the Government is re-establishing itself, we need to use all our vehicles, especially in security and defence. We can convert them to use this fuel. Whatever we all come up with, it will have to be ongoing. It appears Lloyd can do it."

And he needs to do it soon.

"Are they all going?" Antony asked. "Will the king-of-the-compound and his side-kick wifey be there?" Derision filled Antony's expression, bordering on hate.

Bethany straightened her shoulders, stood and stepped away from the bed, preparing for his reaction. She couldn't evade this next revelation any longer.

"Mr Campbell has been invited. Siobhan won't be attending."

"So, she's being the good *wee wifey* and remaining in the camp like an obedient woman?" he said through a snarl. "All her grand intentions to fix the world have come to nothing. She's still unable to change those Community hippies."

"I don't think that's her fault. I believe she's had difficulty gaining everyone's trust because of her origins with us." Bethany surprised herself with her defence of Siobhan. Louise had let slip a confidence she was sure Siobhan would never have wanted her to be privy to. "Anyway, she's not in 'the camp'."

Antony leaned back on his cot. "Where is she?"

"Here."

Antony flew to stand and towered over her. "Why?"

"Siobhan is pregnant, but it's complicated." She wouldn't flinch as Antony stretched to his full height.

"How long has she been here?"

"What does that matter?" Bethany crossed her arms.

"Why haven't you told me?" he demanded.

Why *had* she not informed him? Was she jealous? Protecting Siobhan?

Yes, to both. Siobhan was a beauty, brilliant, and a former lover of Antony's, but now vulnerable.

"Siobhan needs our medical supervision and is in our care for the best outcome for her and her baby." Bethany stared Antony down, trusting the good sense of the situation would stir up some humanity in the man.

It was times like this she questioned her attraction to him. *Damaged but desirable.*

"How do you know Derrick Lloyd?" she asked.

Antony blinked, his posture slowly relaxing at the change of subject. "I don't."

"He enquired about you while he was here at Christmas," she said. "I thought your incarceration was almost secret, but he knew."

"Campbell told him. He would've relished delivering that news."

"Why?" Bethany tilted her head. "If you don't know him."

"If Lloyd has this vegetable-oil fuel to offer…" Antony shrugged off her line of questioning. "Beth, you've got to get a hold of it all. And I mean *all*."

"Yes, I'm completely aware of that." She used her official First Minister tones on Antony. "It may be vital."

"No. If he doesn't agree to your terms, it's your duty to *second* it for the New Scottish Government." Antony grabbed her by the upper arms. "Confiscate it, if you must."

Bethany gasped at the suddenness of his grip. "Very well."

"And I want to see her."

"Who?" Bethany's gut clenched, anticipating the answer.

"Siobhan."

"No." She used her First Minister tones once more.

Never.

Chapter Thirty-Nine

Tummel House Community, Perthshire

"Thank you, Mrs Donaldson, for putting us up for the night." Sitting next to the matriarch of the Tummel House Community, Rory sipped on his second coffee. They ate in the medium sized room off the main kitchen. The hall where Rory had dined on his previous visit to Tummel House Community was empty of people, with chairs and tables stacked neatly against the walls. Bare floorboards were all Rory glimpsed on his way to the breakfast room.

Women placed platters of breakfast fare on the table in front of him and men swished past in kilts. Younger men and women passed outside the windows, headed for the gardens with hoes and baskets in hand. A group of men followed carrying firearms and traps.

Beside him, Kendra forked up crispy fried bacon and Xian buttered hot crumpets.

"We may join you at that cockroach's place later in the week," Mrs Donaldson said.

She glanced over at Xian as he took a bite of his buttery crumpet, then leaned past Rory and picked a freshly toasted one off the serving plate.

"Now, dear, be a wee bit kinder." Mr Donaldson looked over the top of his spectacles at her.

"The man is an insect," she said. "He should have died already." The butter melted to nothing as soon as Mrs Donaldson spread it on the hot crumpet.

"He's a survivor, dear," Mr Donaldson said.

"Aye, at the expense of others." She peered up from her breakfast and pierced Rory with her gaze. "You be careful. That man has his own agenda and he'll stick to it. I dinnae fear for ma army but something's afoot."

"I ken, ma'am." Rory finished his coffee. "I intend on findin' out soon enough."

"If ye need us"—Mrs Donaldson placed a bony hand on his forearm, her eyes narrowing— "my army is yours, son." She gave a curt nod, her top knot wobbling in unison with her head movement.

Rory swallowed the lump in his throat. "Thank you, Mrs Donaldson. I appreciate your support and your offer. I have my people, and my man, Micah, is already there with his men."

"You just remember, Rory." Mrs Donaldson's hand remained on his arm. "Ye can call on us."

"Aye," he said, "we carry a portable CB."

***

Scottish Government Bunker, Edinburgh

Siobhan's trainers squeaked with every step. It should have been irritating, but she found it reassuring. Almost like a pedometer.

"Walking is good exercise," she repeated to herself. She kept up her stamina with a daily exercise routine. "It helps the backache at least." She grimaced. "In theory." She placed her hand on the small of her back and pressed. "Most days."

Siobhan found herself at the stairwell and took the way downstairs to the garages. The rumble of engines, and shouts of commands rose through this natural acoustic funnel. Personnel who would attend Lloyd's fuel summit were loading the vehicles.

Siobhan stepped heavily down the stairs. It seemed ironic that they would drive internal-combustion-engine-powered vehicles—the highest consumers of fuels—to this summit, but the electric cars could only do short journeys before their batteries required recharging. Even if the many recharge points that once dotted around Britain still existed, the national grid didn't. The batteries of the Government's cars were charged by their power supply from the nuclear power station, which was guarded and maintained by government personnel.

Yes, fuels and energies were a vital issue and an important aspect of restoring Scotland's infrastructure.

She strolled through the door to the garage floor then out onto the empty loading platform. The jeeps taking the First Minister and her security team were parked in front of it.

"Jake's in the nursery." Murray stepped beside her.

"Thanks, Uncle Murray. He loves you." Siobhan grinned up at him.

Murray returned it with one of his own.

Thank heavens for Murray. Without Rory, he was her sanity. And it had been a relief to tell someone else of her time in the future, knowing with certainty Murray would keep it secret.

"Wonder what's up." Murray lifted his chin in the direction of the activity. "They're not giving much away." He nudged closer. "One of the team focusing on energy supplies let slip our fuel storage holds next to nothing."

"Almost out of fuel?" Siobhan asked, lowering her voice. "They're using a fair amount just getting to this summit."

"They've researched how to convert our vehicles to function with a vegetable-oil-based fuel," Murray said. "The engineers and mechanics are ready to go on a conversion."

"Vegetable oil?" She gasped. "When we visited Lloyd's old holiday park in Fife, reluctantly I might add, I noticed rapeseed growing in the fields. You can make canola oil out of that."

Murray gave a slow nod. "I wish I knew what he did when he went you-know-where in the you-know-what." Murray flicked his eyes beside him to the personnel nearby.

"Thing is, Murray," she said, "we're just guessing it was him."

"Oh, it was," Murray replied. "Rory said he'd seen him walking to his room later that evening and he was 'more than his usual cagey self', to quote your husband."

Siobhan screwed her mouth to the side. "I suppose so, but we don't know *when* he travelled to. We're just assuming it was forward, because it was when I went." She whispered her last words.

Bethany and her entourage strode through the doorway to the garages and stood on the loading platform beside them. The First Minister wore a crisply pressed suit in brown and grey camouflage, her hair pulled back tight and revealing an almost-as-tight expression.

"Good luck, Bethany," Siobhan said.

Bethany returned Siobhan's well-wishes with her First Minister smile and walked across to her vehicle.

Henderson walked past and acknowledged Siobhan. Soon all summit participants were in the vehicles and the air filled with fumes as engines revved and the convoy drove up the concrete ramp to the outside world. Siobhan stepped through the doorway and back into the stairwell, coughing with the irritating fumes tickling the back of her throat. Murray followed. Her throat tightened again, this time with the thought of these people seeing her husband before she could.

"You okay, Siobhan?" The warmth of his hand seeped into her shoulder.

She gave a brief shrug in reply, unable to speak.

"You'll see him soon," Murray said.

Tears trickled down her cheeks. She pulled the hanky out of her track suit pants and dabbed at her face.

"Ah, sorry," Murray said, and he placed his arm around her, slow and hesitant.

"It's okay. Stupid hormones! I'm full of them." She blew her nose and returned her hanky to the pocket of the only comfortable pants she could fit into.

"What ya goin' to do today?" Murray asked, obviously grasping for a distraction.

"Walk," she replied.

"But you've done that," he said.

"Yes." Her shoulders sagged and she paced forward. "And I'll keep doing it until Jake has finished his day in the nursery. My very pregnant brain isn't coping with study, reading, or thinking of any kind."

"You know where I go when I'm like that?" Murray asked.

Siobhan stopped, placed her hand on her hip, and stared up at Murray. "When are you ever too hormonal to think?"

"I mean when I want a break from books and screens?" He raised his eyebrows.

"Okay, do tell," she said.

"Hydroponics." He stepped back and grinned.

Siobhan's brow tightened. "Hydroponics? Can't recall having ever been there. Where is it?"

Murray beamed. "Follow me."

He walked to the stairwell and took one flight down, then took a left and went to the rear of this corridor where there was another stairwell, which Siobhan hadn't seen for many years.

"Oh, I recognise where you're taking me," she said. "I haven't been here since my primary school days."

Siobhan followed Murray and went up this flight of stairs, which served the opposite side of the Bunker. They arrived at another stairwell that opened to a short concourse where crates of vegetables lay on pallets awaiting collection and transport to the kitchens.

Murray gripped the handle of the double doors, his grin spreading. "Voilà." He opened the door.

Siobhan stepped through an exceptionally fine mesh screen covering the immediate entrance to a huge, long hall. Green foliage and natural light greeted Siobhan, warmth bathed her, and moisture tickled her face. Large skylights directed daylight into the massive hall. This light was supplemented by rows of daylight bulbs directed downward to the growing plant life.

Murray led her between the first two aisles. She walked by tomato plants tied up to poles. The plants sat in wide, white tubes, which ran the length of the great hall. The music of trickling water permeated the air. It came from the tubes in which the plants grew, and the pipes connected to each row of crops, and lining the walls. Tubes of cabbages, green beans, and lettuce arranged in rows, ran along to her right. A larger space with wider cylinders grew onion, carrot, and potato plants. Espaliered fruit trees lined the far walls, bathed in sunlight directed by especially angled skylight shafts and mirrors.

An insect buzzed past Siobhan's face and travelled to the nearby line of flowering plants. Siobhan peered closer. Tiny bodies, in various shades of yellow and black, hovered around the plants. They danced in and out of the flowers, their hum growing louder with her approach.

"Hope you're not allergic to bee stings." Murray stood close to a flurry of buzzing creatures. "I could watch them for hours. You know the world nearly lost most of the bee species? The reduction in human activity seems to have increased the populations. Or so the drone watchers say." He laughed. "Pardon the pun." He then stood back. The furry buzzing creatures moved away from that plant, legs laden with pollen, and started work on the next one. "There are hives against the far wall. A guy tends to them," Murray said. "He's not allergic."

Murray waved to a man in overalls who was holding a narrow, soft brush and stood at the other end of a line of tomatoes brushing the yellow flowers. "Hi, Bob," he called.

Bob returned the wave, barely lifting his attention from his task.

"The bees don't get everywhere," Murray explained.

"This is your secret place?"

"Yep," he said. "Bet you wish you'd found this when you lived here."

"I was too busy viewing the drone footage," Siobhan replied.

Siobhan glanced down the aisle at Bob. A child's laugh echoed up to the ceiling then an adult female voice *shushed*. Bob looked away from his task of pollinating the tomato plants. Murray stopped walking and Siobhan held her breath. The giggle happened again.

"So, you're not the only one who comes here?" Siobhan eyed Murray, who stood stock still, straining to hear more.

Bob had left his post and walked in the direction of the noise. The giggle followed by another *shush,* occurred once more.

"Kids?" Siobhan suggested. "A school outing?"

Murray's light brows drew together. "Not whenever I've been here during the day."

"Oi!" Bob yelled.

Murray ran toward his friend and Siobhan followed at a walk, catching up to Murray when he stopped by a row in the furthest corner of the hydroponics hall. In among tall corn, camp chairs lay sprawled and upturned, and behind them, sitting on top of piled bedrolls, were a woman and four children. One child looked at Siobhan and ran to her.

"Aunty Vonn!" The little girl's voice was so familiar.

"Michaela! Come here," Cèilidh yelled at her daughter.

"Cèilidh?" Murray had passed Bob and stopped in front of his sister. "What're you guys doin' here?"

Cèilidh scowled, ignoring her brother and again called her daughter back, her voice echoing in the high ceiling.

Michaela ran to Siobhan and threw herself onto her legs, then grasped her tight.

"Why're you hiding?" Murray asked, his gaze followed his sister's pursuit of his niece.

Cèilidh reached Siobhan and grabbed her two-and-a-half-year-old by the arms and tried to peel her away from Siobhan, continuing her severe frown at her daughter.

"Are you okay?" Siobhan asked Cèilidh then helped her ease Michaela's arms from around her legs. "Is everything all right... between you and—?"

"Aye, all's fine," Cèilidh answered, not making eye contact with Siobhan.

She marched her daughter back to the campsite.

"Uncle Murray!" Aiden, their oldest nephew, approached his uncle with a beaming face. "We camping," he said in his little boy-voice.

"Shush!" Cèilidh said, stress lacing her command.

"What's going on?" Murray put his hand on Cèilidh's shoulder and turned her to face him. She kept her head bowed, her eyes on her children and shushed any noises they made.

"I'll leave ye to sort this," Bob said and walked back in the direction of his tomato plants.

"Cèilidh," Siobhan encouraged. "Tell us why you are at the Bunker and hiding from us, your family."

Cèilidh raised her head, her eyes pooled with tears. "We must talk. But not here..." She glanced at her children.

"Please watch the children while Cèilidh and I have a chat," Siobhan asked Murray.

He picked up one of the babies crawling into the corn just as her twin headed in the same direction.

Siobhan took her sister-in-law by the hand and led her to the row of runner beans. The children's delighted laughter lifted to the skylights as they played with their uncle.

Cèilidh faced Siobhan. "I'm sorry, but I think the man I married is not on our side," she said then closed her eyes and tears squeezed out.

The skin on the back of Siobhan's neck crawled. "Has it to do with this summit?" she asked.

Cèilidh nodded. Childish shouts continued from the far corner of the huge hall, accompanied by babies' protests.

"You need to tell me more," Siobhan said, placing her hands on Cèilidh's shoulders.

Cèilidh shook her head, mute.

"Please," Siobhan pleaded.

"He's my husband," Cèilidh sniffed.

"Mine is there too!" Cold trickled down Siobhan's spine. "What's going to happen?"

"Nothing bad." Cèilidh's expression was unconvincing. "Micah says it'll be okay."

Siobhan dug her fingers into Cèilidh.

"I'm not into politics," Cèilidh said. "And you understand more than me."

"What?" Siobhan could barely hear over the thundering pulse in her ears.

"I don't know what he means," Cèilidh said. "Micah whispered *coo* last time he spoke to his men in our kitchen, ken?"

"Coo?" Siobhan asked.

Cèilidh nodded.

Siobhan gasped. The crawling on the back of her neck turned into electric shocks. Cèilidh meant *coup*.

"Will it happen at Lloyd's?" Siobhan asked.

Cèilidh cringed as she nodded again.

"Murray!" Siobhan spun. "We need to get to the CB room."

Chapter Forty

Fife

An enormous expanse of sky domed above Bethany and, unlike the few times she had walked the inner perimeter of the Bunker's entry-compound, it wasn't blue but a washed-out dirty-grey, with a thick line of dullness just above the horizon. The convoy drove out of Edinburgh and soon the views were of green rolling hills covered in trees weighed down with foliage, lying behind grassed meadows. Ploughed furrows, deep and brown, lined up straight and even, scored fields with linear rows made with precision and care. Men walked behind horses pulling ploughs while others followed throwing seeds in freshly dug furrows. It was all so picturesque, like a painting or an old sepia photograph of times passed, only in colour.

It was the colours that overwhelmed Bethany. She sighed and blinked, and the tears slid down her face as she imagined how it would appear if the sun's full light shone.

Why had she never ventured out before?

It was glorious, wonderful, majestic, incredible, magnificent...

"Are you all right, First Minister?" Henderson's deep voice came from the front passenger seat.

Bethany gave a quiet sniff. "Yes, of course, Iain," she said. "I was observing the state of the countryside. Spring sowings, I think they call it."

"Aye, ma'am."

An hour later they were in Fife. It was flatter, still with softer hills here and there, but fewer drystone walls, and the sea was nearby. Bethany opened the window a fraction letting in the sea breeze. Saltiness assailed her senses. And her memory. Summer holidays, beaches, and the wind blowing sea spray into her face. She was young again, and her parents were still alive. Long before—

"First Minister," Henderson said, breaking her reverie once more.

He pointed to a stone building, stately in appearance with many tall windows, surrounded by a solid fence, situated beside the road ahead. It was neat and tidy, and flanked by fields of deep brown with a hint of green—the shoots of crops just emerging.

"Mr Lloyd's headquarters, ma'am."

The lead vehicle approached the driveway to this property where two guards holding submachine guns stood to attention. One held up his hand in a halting gesture. The driver stopped and wound down the window. The guard looked in and waved the car on then did the same to Bethany's vehicle. Guards stood at sentry points along the perimeter fence. The driveway curved around the side of the stately home and ended at the front entrance where men in uniform stood guard, all having a military look about them.

Bethany's driver stopped their vehicle next to the entrance, which was a double door set with panes of leadlight glass sitting at the top of stone steps. Derrick Lloyd descended before walking to her vehicle's door and opening it. He looked older and more stooped, but those grey eyes were as sharp as they had been at Christmas, perhaps even more so. His son, Maxwell, followed him, dressed in a suit and tie, looking like a model in a magazine, designer-label-style.

"Welcome, First Minister," Lloyd said then took her hand and grinned.

He escorted her from the car to the front reception room, with Henderson following a pace behind. Thick carpets in a rich, deep red covered the floors, and a chandelier hung from the ceiling, the electric light glowing softly with illuminated halos surrounding each light bulb. Bethany craned her neck, noting the ornate cornices.

"From the Victorian Era, First Minister." Lloyd's voice travelled up to her.

"It's beautiful," she said.

Bethany let her gaze come back to the pink and white marble fireplace above which hung an enormous mirror, edged in gold filigree scrolling. An ornate clock sat on the fireplace's wide mantelpiece, domed in glass to showcase its exposed inner workings and a pendulum in perpetual motion, with more gold filigree lacing its less functional parts.

"How?" Bethany stifled her tone. She would not show any amazement.

"I'm a collector," Lloyd replied. "I've been doing so for years." Lloyd hid none of his smugness.

"When people have barely survived?" she asked.

"I'm a businessman, First Minister," Lloyd said. "I trade in the goods people require. As you are aware, money has not been a currency for many years now, and bartering can take on many forms." His smile revealed two front teeth eroded by dental caries. "Please, take a seat, First Minister." Lloyd indicated the two long, red velvet studded couches beside them.

Bethany sat on the couch to her right while Henderson stood behind it. Lloyd seated himself opposite and Maxwell stood beside him.

"Maxwell, pour the First Minister a drink." Lloyd pointed to the whisky decanter tray on the Georgian wine-table beside the couch. "Scotch?" he asked Bethany.

"Oh, no I—" she began.

"Please, don't refuse a twenty-one-year-old single malt from the Clyde Valley," he chided.

Bethany took the glass from Maxwell and sipped. It burned the back of her throat and threatened to set her nose on fire. She swallowed and tried to stifle a choke, without success.

Lloyd laughed a quiet, self-assured laugh. "You don't have scotch in the Bunker?"

"I rarely drink," she said, her voice still husky. "I prefer to keep a clear head, especially when negotiations are on the agenda."

"Aye, truly we must start, for the day will get away from us and you'll soon be leaving," Lloyd said. "I'm sorry you decided against staying. Perhaps if you had known how I could accommodate you and your entourage, you may have wished to stay longer. It's not too late. I have everything you would require."

"Thank you, but they will need me back at the Government Bunker." She sipped once more, and a creaminess now tempered the burn in her throat.

Lloyd leaned forward, his arms resting on his knees, cupping the whisky glass he held. "I believe in getting straight to the issue, Miss Watts. I have rapeseed oil, which you can purchase for a reasonable price."

"The Government has a fleet of vehicles that require an ongoing supply." She took another sip. "If we convert our vehicles to use the oil, you must guarantee it."

"You will convert *all* your vehicles?" Lloyd asked.

"Most likely."

"Even the tanks and other military vehicles?"

Bethany nodded. They would be first, but *he* didn't need to know that.

"If I agree, you will pay in gold bullion," Lloyd said.

"Pardon?" Bethany's brow pulled tight, and she stifled a choke unrelated to the whisky.

"You heard me."

"I—we assumed you would barter for it." Bethany sat forward on the couch.

"I am willing to take it in silver, platinum or copper." Lloyd took a casual sip of the amber liquid.

"Precious metals aren't currency at present," Bethany said.

"That's true." The clock on the mantel piece chimed through Lloyd's answer. "But if you and the New Scottish Government are successful, and the country gets back on its feet once more, commerce will recommence, and currency-based trade will soon replace bartering. History shows that precious metals have always been the standard for a currency-based economy. I wish to be at the forefront."

"I cannot make any promises. Goodness!" Bethany couldn't keep the incredulity from her voice. "You're asking a lot."

"Come now, Miss Watts. You're not implying that the New Scottish Government doesn't have vaults full of the stuff and a mint press ready to make it into coin?" Lloyd sat back on the couch. "A barrel of oil is roughly two hundred litres," the businessman continued.

"Are you certain that, under the current circumstances"—Bethany squinted an eye—"with the darkened skies affecting crop growth, you will be able to maintain it?"

The drones had shown large storage vats here at this property, and a building they were certain held an oil-press, plus three others in Fife belonging to Mr Lloyd.

"I'm not a soothsayer, Miss Watts," Lloyd said. "I don't suffer from the delusion that I can predict the future, but I will say that the dimmed heavens won't last forever... At least, I hope they won't."

The ticking of the clock on the mantel piece was the only sound in the quiet room. Lloyd and his son stared at her without flinching.

"I also wish to have a place in the New Scottish Government," Lloyd said. He didn't blink, still resting his forearms on his thighs.

Bethany drew a calming breath. They'd anticipated this. Antony had warned her a man such as Lloyd wouldn't be content to sit on the side lines when the world verged toward normal, and trade recommenced. Bethany willed herself to composure. This man's ambitious nature had shown itself in her conversations with him at Christmas. As to serving his country as a member of the New Scottish Government—his own self would be the only person benefitting.

"Mr Lloyd, that isn't for me to decide," she finally replied. "There will be elections. You need to put yourself, and what you represent, to the people."

"Now, young lady, you know that will take a long time to happen." Lloyd's tone was stern, then his eyes narrowed. "I'm an old man. I want in *now*, not in two years' time when your people finally get their shite together. I won't have much time of my own left to enjoy the benefits." Lloyd's lips were a thin line.

Bethany blinked.

"Michael, you can leave," Lloyd ordered.

Lloyd hadn't removed his stare from her. The man who stood by the door, dressed in the dark uniform of Lloyd's security, turned to leave. For the first time, Bethany noted the firearm strapped to this security man's thigh.

"So can your man, Miss Watts," Lloyd said.

"No, sir." Henderson's firm voice came from behind her.

"I wish to discuss something of national importance with the First Minister." Lloyd directed his announcement over Bethany's head to Henderson. His raised voice sent a chill down Bethany's spine. He took a slow breath and focused on her. "First Minister, we need privacy for what I will reveal to you."

Lloyd's grey eyes were like two steel daggers boring into her.

She didn't move. Neither did Henderson.

"Major McLellan is aware of what I'm about to tell you. He wouldn't wish anyone but you to possess this information. He"— Lloyd flicked his gaze up to Henderson— "must leave now."

So, Antony knew.

The alarm that had commenced in Bethany's mind receded a little. He'd lied about knowing Lloyd. He'd never done so before. It must be crucial for him to deny her this information. Well, she would find out what Lloyd wished to tell her.

"You may leave," she said to Henderson without glancing behind.

The pad of his footsteps on the soft carpet trailed out the door, which then closed and the sole sound for a time was the echo of the clock's quarter-hour chime. It competed with the pulse thudding in Bethany's head.

Maxwell remained standing statuesque behind his father.

"I know about the Time Machine and that its mechanism has been a mystery to you," Lloyd said then placed his empty glass on the table and leaned back into the couch. The thudding in Bethany's head became a tumult. "I'm a learned man, Miss Watts," Lloyd continued. "I did not attend university, but I have spent most of my very long adult life acquiring knowledge."

Bethany blinked, trying to steady herself, not answering.

"The Community representative," Lloyd continued, "Murray Campbell, has known for a time how to operate the machine."

"Yes, but it hasn't worked since we brought it to the Bunker," Bethany said, "and we suspect—"

"Oh, it *has* worked," Lloyd interrupted.

Bethany frowned. "How?"

"It doesn't require electricity." Lloyd's rheumy eyes narrowed with his smugness. "It's not a time machine, it's actually a portal."

Bethany sat up, her brow cooling with sweat.

"I see this is quite a revelation for you, Miss Watts." Lloyd smirked. "I've travelled in it."

Bethany gasped. "How? When?"

"While enjoying your hospitality at Christmas," Lloyd said, "your head technician, MacIntosh, gave me a free ride."

"How did he—?"

"Questions, questions." Lloyd clasped his hands in front of him. "For a First Minister, you don't know much, do you?"

Bethany took a breath while a storm in her ribcage commenced its accompaniment to the tumult in her mind.

"I'm sorry, First Minister," Lloyd said. "I've been a patient man, but even I can run in short supply. You see, in the future, I am important. And your lover, Antony—" he paused here. "Aye, little has escaped me. McLellan will be First Minister and well, when I looked for you, you were nowhere to be found."

Bethany's hands were trembling.

"So, I decided we should not mess with fate. In fact, we should assist it as much as possible." Lloyd's expression filled with greed. "I was delighted to discover like-minded people residing in the Government Bunker. Surprised at the rank of some. And with a little help from my son—" He twisted his mouth and gave a slight shake of his head. "No, I must give Micah more credit, for he revealed the Time Machine to me." His eyes lifted from his clasped hands. "Micah interrogated your spies who followed the Campbells home and listened to their recordings before destroying them. Micah's mother taught him thievery; I like to think I taught him espionage." His smile, full of pride, encompassed his face.

Bethany found the air was difficult to drag into her lungs.

"Michael!" Lloyd snapped his fingers at the door.

Bethany flinched in her seat. A thud came from behind the door. It opened and revealed Henderson's legs laying outstretched on the rich red carpet. Lloyd's henchman strode to her, grabbed her by the wrists, dragged her out of the room then along the corridor. Her scotch glass thudded to the floor and lay ignored on the carpet at Henderson's feet. Drawn along by Michael, she passed the open doors of rooms that led off this hallway. Bethany glanced through heavy curtains and out the windows of the large ornately decorated rooms. Men in dark uniforms, all armed with submachine guns, guarded each window and the fence outside, and double guards were at the front and back of the driveway. Her government personnel were nowhere.

"Aye, it is secure, Miss Watts," Lloyd said as he and Maxwell strolled behind her.

Bethany lost a shoe as Michael dragged her past the last window. A guard by a room down the hallway opened the door and Michael thrust her in.

"I trust the accommodations are to your liking, Miss Watts," Lloyd said, his face full of resolve as he shut the door on her.

Chapter Forty-One

Scottish Government Bunker

Siobhan ran as well as possible with the weight of her pregnant belly protruding forward and an ache niggling her back. She'd reached the double doors of the hydroponic hall, holding her belly and splinting it with her arms for support, when Murray caught up with her.

"Bill MacIntosh hid them," he said.

Siobhan leaned on the concourse rail just before the doors to the stairwell.

Traitor! Who else is behind this coup?

"Lloyd wants rid of Bethany," she said. "He's got her on his turf in a vulnerable place with a limited security detail. The man has an army." Her throat tightened. Her childhood friend's life may be in danger. Then cold flashed through her body, leaving her skin moist with sweat. Rory would soon be there... "We must avoid MacIntosh. The communications room is near where the tech guys hang out. Damn."

"I know a back way," Murray said then took her hand and hurried through to the stairwell and down one flight, marched her across to the stair that belonged to the main section of the Bunker, but veered left to a side door.

"How do you know all this?" Siobhan's words came through each breath.

"I don't sleep well," Murray threw over his shoulder, picking up his pace. "An active mind, and all that."

Murray led her to a narrower staircase then continued on. Siobhan let go of his hand, allowing him to run ahead. She stopped at the third flight of stairs, her breath coming hard.

All this pregnancy weight is making me slow.

Murray had opened the door to that floor a crack and stood listening. He turned and placed a finger to his lips as voices coinciding with shadows passed, then beckoned her to come with him. They stepped into the dim corridor where open doors lay ahead to their left, and Murray sidled beside each one to determine if anyone was in them. When he discovered each was clear, Murray waved her forward.

They turned left down the corridor that held the room with the CB radios. A shadow loomed in a doorway. Murray pushed her back into an empty office and peered out its door. Voices receded along the hall, then Murray led her out.

"You're good at this cloak and dagger stuff, Murray," Siobhan whispered.

"Yes, but not good enough."

Siobhan spun to a familiar voice.

Antony stood behind them.

"What are you doing out of prison?" Murray stepped in front of Siobhan.

"Out of my way, kid." Antony pushed Murray aside and grasped Siobhan's upper arm with force. "Do something with him, would you?" He spoke to the shadowed figure behind him, indicating to Murray.

Bill MacIntosh stepped forward and grabbed Murray, placing him in a headlock, and dragged him along. Antony pushed Siobhan ahead of himself and turned them back the way they had come.

"You know I'm not happy with you, Murray." MacIntosh spoke to Murray tucked tightly under his arm. "You're the smartest of the lot of them, but you're still dumb. How long did you think you could keep the real workings of the Time Machine from us? Thankfully, our bugs worked, and our spies have good memories despite being beaten half to death. As head of IT, I have certain privileges, and being the only one to debrief the techy guys who followed Siobhan home was one of them." He chuckled softly. "And I only report to those I wish to."

Antony stopped at a small, empty room to their right. "In here'll do." He pushed Siobhan in and planted her hard on the chair in front of the desk.

A pulling pain shot into Siobhan's pelvis. "Ow!"

"Oh? Sorry, *little mother*. Did that hurt?" Sarcasm laced Antony's words. "Bet it didn't hurt as much as this." He thrust his index finger at his own cheek where a purple scar glowed angrily.

MacIntosh manoeuvered to the other chair tucked behind the desk, easing his lock on Murray to get by the desk. Murray wriggled his way loose from MacIntosh's hold and thrust with fingers sharp into MacIntosh's side. Bill grunted, then bent forward. Murray lifted his elbow high and descended onto Bill's back, landing with the force of his full weight pointed between the man's shoulder blades, forcing MacIntosh's body down. MacIntosh's head caught on the edge of the desk. Murray jumped, knees-first, onto MacIntosh's back and continued the downward action. Bill's neck cracked and the sickening bone crunch filled the room. MacIntosh's floppy body slumped to the floor. Murray spun to face Antony, red faced and puffing from his exertion.

"What!" Antony yelled, releasing his grip on Siobhan and stepping to Murray.

Murray looked directly at Siobhan, with an expression like he was trying to tell her something just as Antony punched his mouth. Murray fell backward against the office wall, his head slamming hard into the plaster, then slid to the floor, his hands tucked awkwardly behind him.

Antony spun back to her. "Don't you move!"

Siobhan flinched with the suddenness of Antony's order.

"You bloody Campbells are nothing but trouble!" he shouted. "It just can't happen soon enough!"

Siobhan breathed in deep, drawing on her courage and ignoring the intermittent tightness in her belly.

"It works on a Ley line," Antony said. "Lloyd told me. But you know that. You've known it all along." Antony bent down and sneered into her face. The acrid scent of male perspiration sweated out under stress wafted into her nostrils. "I can't wait till it's all over and that *boy* of yours is well and truly out of it." He stood and straightened his shoulders, doing that shuffle he always did when on the defensive. "My only regret will be Beth—" He tugged at his ear. "Collateral damage. It's to be expected," he said, snapping himself back.

A wave of tightness started at the top of Siobhan's protruding belly and made its way down, pushing into the insides of her pelvis. She took a deep breath and let it out slowly. The pain stayed so she took another.

"What're you doing?" Antony stood back. "Oh, no. You won't fool me and use *that* as an excuse. Beth told me you're not due for another month yet."

Siobhan focused on Murray whose nose was bleeding, and his eyelids fluttered. He was regaining consciousness. She'd do anything to take her mind off the pain and the sirens screeching in her brain.

Antony stood before her, staring, nostrils flaring. Foot tread echoed along the hall outside, and Antony turned to the noise. The pain in Siobhan's pelvis and back receded to a tightness. Murray opened his eyes and moved his hand from behind his back.

He held a handgun—MacIntosh's handgun.

The clipped footsteps drew nearer, and Antony strode to the door. So far, he hadn't produced a weapon. Both his hands were empty. Siobhan had noted earlier he had no handgun tucked into his belt at the front, and now she viewed his back. None there either.

Siobhan pushed herself off the chair. Antony still had his back to her, pushing the door to. She trusted the thud of the closing door, plus Antony's attention on the footsteps outside, to mask her movements. She landed hard on her knees before Murray and caught the gun he thrust into her hands.

"Safety's off," Murray whispered.

"What!" Antony's growl came from behind her as Siobhan made to stand. Antony leaped toward her from the door and grabbed the gun in her hands. "Give me that!"

Siobhan held tight to the stock of the pistol as Antony's massive hand surrounded her own. He landed on her, forcing her flat on her back. With one hand he pushed her shoulder down. With the other, he held her hands grasping the handgun and shoved it away and out to her right.

Antony's torso pressed on her abdomen, pushing her very pregnant uterus onto her major blood vessels. A light-headedness came over her. She pulled her right leg up and shoved on his thigh, trying to lift his weight off her. She blinked and focused on her hand still holding the gun, determined he wouldn't remove it from her.

Antony grunted with his efforts. She pushed his thigh with her foot again. Spots came before her eyes. She slid her foot right up to Antony's groin and put all her fading energy into thrusting him away with the point of her heel. Her vision cleared as his astonished face came into view, the force on her hands disappearing.

Siobhan twisted the gun and aimed.

A loud crack rang in her ears.

The side of his face, once emblazoned with that angry scar, disappeared, taking an eye with it. She pushed him off herself. The other eye, full of shock, stared at her. She rose from the floor onto all fours, her head clearing further with better blood flow. Still her tightening uterus pushed pain into her back.

"Murray?" She steadied her breathing while the pain reached a crescendo and then receded.

"I'm okay." He sounded dopey and nasal. "Are you?"

"Ah, I will be," she said. Her head cleared and so did the pain. "Where did you learn those moves?"

"Dad," Murray answered. "He insisted we all know how to fight and handle firearms, even the nerd." He smiled beneath his bloodied nose. "You go CB Rory." He kicked Antony's limp arm off his feet. "I'll be there soon."

Siobhan turned to the thoughts flashing through her mind. She recalled self-defence lessons with Rory. He'd stressed that most women weren't stronger than the average man, not even Kendra, he'd said with a laugh. But a supple, fit woman could out-manoeuvre a man any day.

Well, husband, you were right.

She shifted her knees to get up off the floor—pain pushing low in her pelvis.

"No. Wait, please," she begged her body. "I've got to get to the CB."

"You sure you're okay?" Murray asked again as she handed him the gun.

"Keep an eye on them, just in case..." she said.

"Yeah, well, I think you have the hair trigger to thank for Antony being out of action." Murray took the pistol and switched the safety back on. "Your grappling skills were pretty cool, too."

Chapter Forty-Two

Scottish Government Bunker

Siobhan glanced at her watch. It was 7 p.m. Wherever Rory, Kendra and Xian were on their journey to Lloyd's in Fife, they would be camped for the night. The hall in the communications area was quiet; the personnel monitoring the radios would be at their evening meal.

Who could she trust? Who else was involved in this treachery?

Siobhan halted at the doorway of the room next to the short-wave radios. A technician turned from the screen where tech staff viewed drone footage, and removed the sound excluding headphones from his ears.

"Mrs Campbell?"

Alec MacAllister was one of the younger members of the Bunker's population. An honest young lad.

Please don't destroy my trust in the goodness of human nature.

Tightness pressed inside her pelvis. She bent forward and rested her hands on the back of the nearest chair.

"Are you okay, Mrs Campbell?" Alec asked then stood to face her.

Siobhan breathed through the tightness. "I need to contact my husband."

"The CB room's next door but can I get you some help?" Alec asked.

"No, I'm fine." The tightness receded, and she straightened. "Do you love your country?"

"Pardon?" The young man's stare intensified.

"Do you love Scotland and believe in the New Scottish Government?" she asked more firmly.

"Aye, ma'am." Alec blinked and stood to attention.

"Then you can help me," she said. "You're viewing drone footage?"

"Today's views of Kirkcaldy, ma'am."

"Show me."

"I should get clearance for you—"

"Alec, this is of national importance," she interrupted, "and I know what to look for!"

"...We only have daylight footage," he said. "None of our drones have a functioning night vision camera anymore."

Alec brought up a view of a substantial, well-established stately home in the middle of fields with early crops, long sheds, and storage vats. He zoomed the vision in. From a distance, there were dark dots by the solid stone fence that surrounded the house. Close up, these dots were armed men, wearing the familiar garb of Lloyd's personnel.

His army.

"This is Mr Lloyd's property where the First Minister is attending the fuel summit. He has quite a lot of security," Alec noted. "The issue at present, ma'am, is that the talks have taken longer than expected and the First Minister's convoy will have to return to the Bunker in the dark. And they haven't yet contacted us by CB."

"That's the thing, Alec. I don't think she'll be travelling home tonight," Siobhan said.

"No? They were planning to," Alec said. "Mr Lloyd's hospitality was declined."

Siobhan shook her head. "Please show me the most recent footage you have."

"Aye, ma'am. I haven't yet examined it myself." Alec went to the appropriate section. The sunset footage showed dim figures collecting near one of the larger sheds, they stood in guard formation.

"Was that shed guarded previously?" Siobhan asked then pulled up a chair and sat next to Alec, ignoring the tension starting in her abdomen.

"No, ma'am. I'll rewind." Alec rewound and played the scene.

Lloyd's dark uniformed men held Scottish Government personnel at gunpoint and herded them into the large shed where they now stood guard.

"Oh, no." Alec's voice held his disbelief and shock.

"I didn't see the First Minister. Where's Bethany?" Her question came out choked as it mixed with the last of the tightening in her abdomen, bordering on pain.

Alec adjusted the view and zoomed in close on the people being forced into the shed. No Bethany but Alistair was there, and Micah.

But Micah was pointing a gun at government personnel.

A cold chill ran down her spine, kicking off another tightening which increased in pressure, and her back ached.

"I must CB Rory," she said through an expelled breath.

"Mrs Campbell, ma'am, if you don't mind me saying so," Alec pleaded, "you're all sweaty and I think what you really need to do is go the medical centre, ma'am."

"Get me to a CB."

Alec hurried to the next room and turned on the nearest CB. Siobhan followed and sat beside him. She turned the dial to the frequency Rory used.

Alec hovered. "Mrs Campbell, ma'am. I'm going tae alert my superior. We'll need to send support for our detained security but with our low supply of petrol... Ah, and I'll get Dr Longford, okay?"

Siobhan nodded as another contraction started.

Oh, slow down, please, she mind-yelled at her body.

Rory should go and help. It made sense. He was closer and could muster aid. He'd stayed at the Tummel House Community on his way down and they had an army.

But I need you, Rory.

Another contraction started, forcing a cry between her lips. She breathed through it.

The pain tailed off and annoyance took over. Rory would choose to help. He'd go to Lloyd's first. He'd not make *her* a priority.

She blew out a long sigh. "Breaker. Breaker. Rory," she said into the handset.

Her man was needed elsewhere. For important things in a crucial time. He was a leader, she reminded herself.

Siobhan repeated her mantra.

"I married a man who leads a people, and I must share him with them."

And determine to love him, no matter what decision he makes.

"Mrs Campbell, ma'am?" Alec's strangled voice filtered through her resolve. She ignored him.

"Rory. Come in. Over." Desperation echoed through her words.

Siobhan! Rory's voice came loudly through the handset. *What's wrong?*

Chapter Forty-Three

Perth

Rory removed Boy's saddle and brushed him down. His horse gave gentle nickers, showing his appreciation for his master's care.

"Aye, pal," Rory whispered into the dark horse's ear. "You deserve it," he said in the language of the Highlands.

It had been a long day of solid riding. They'd be in Edinburgh soon and he'd be with Siobhan and Jake, but only after the diversion of this summit. Rory grimaced at the thought of another meeting with Lloyd.

"Hot tea in a wee bit, boss," Kendra said from the campfire while Xian arrived with an armful of wood. They'd set up camp, stringing tarps among the trees on the lower reaches of Kinnoull Hill.

Beside Rory's saddle, which was placed ready to be his pillow for the night, the CB sputtered into life.

Rory. Come in. Over. It was Siobhan, and his heart jolted at her tone.

He grabbed the handset. "Siobhan! What's wrong? Over."

Where are you? Over.

"Just outside o' Perth," he said. "Why? Over."

You must hurry to Kirkcaldy. Lloyd has detained our soldiers, and we can't see Bethany. Over.

"How do you ken this?"

Drone footage from late this afternoon. Rory, Micah is there. Over.

"I ken he's waiting for us and spending some time with his family," Rory said. "He took Cèilidh and the kids down early to see their grandfather. Over."

Siobhan spoke, but a wave of static passed through her words, obliterating them. Then it cleared.

...said something's up. A coup. I fear for Bethany's life. Over. Siobhan's voice was breathy through the handset.

"Surely they'd no' assassinate a First Minister? Over."

But it *was* Lloyd they were dealing with. The man *had* time travelled and probably seen the future. Cold clenched Rory's guts. Siobhan hadn't responded.

"Siobhan?"

Static, then *Ahh*. The line was still open. Siobhan must be clasping the handset tight, for in the background, voices raised, and their tones held alarm.

"What's going on?" Rory said, but he wouldn't be heard.

Damn.

"What's happening, boss?" Kendra asked.

Rory glanced at Kendra.

"Turn it up, Rory." Xian touched the volume dial. "We might catch something."

Mrs Campbell, we'll take you to the medical centre now. Alec, notify Dr Longford.

Orders continued in the background and Siobhan's gasp was loud, her mouth close to the handset. Then it went silent.

"Will somebody tell me what's happening! Over," Rory yelled into the handset now free to receive.

Ah, Mr Campbell, sir, this is Alec MacAllister. Um, your wife is in labour and they're taking her to Dr Longford. Over.

"But it's too soon to be in labour. Och, she's there to have a caesarean, is she no'? Not to do the usual," Rory shouted into the handset.

Mr Campbell? It was a different voice. *We'll inform you of any updates after Dr Longford examines your wife. Over.*

"Is she okay? Over."

We're still assessing that, sir. Over.

"But tell me—Och!" Rory shoved the handset back in the CB's bag and stood. "I'm going now." He picked up his saddle and threw it over Boy's back.

Kendra poured the boiled water for the tea over the fire and started packing while Xian loaded the horses.

"You're fortunate that it's a full moon tonight, Rory," Xian said, saddling his own horse. "But we still won't reach there until nearly morning."

"Aye." He rolled up his bedroll and tied it to the saddle. "I'll carry the CB. They'll need tae let me know." He jumped onto Boy, jerking the reins. His tired stallion flicked his head in protest. "You dinnae have tae come."

"Aye, we do, Rory." Kendra pulled herself up into the saddle.

They rode for two hours with the moon lighting their path.

"We'll cut through between Loch Leven and the Lomond Hills—"

The CB sitting in the bag over Rory's shoulder jumped to life.

Rory. It was Siobhan.

"Siobhan, you okay? Baby okay? Over." The handset shook in his grasp.

They've put me on a drip to stop the contractions. They're holding it off for as long as possible. We're both okay. Where are you?

"On my way to you. Over."

Rory, I'll be fine. Help the First Min.... Static overtook the rest of her sentence.

"What?" Rory clasped the handset closer to his face.

Alistair is there. Defence guys are coming but... White noise whooshed through Siobhan's words. *Little fuel... not make it... You know Lloyd. It may end up a blood bath. Over.*

Rory rubbed his thumb between his brows, still holding the CB handset, his insides tearing. He should be with Siobhan, his woman, the mother of his children. But Scotland needed him. Realisation blew its calming breeze over him.

Siobhan was giving him permission.

"I'll ask Mrs Donaldson to send her army. We'll need her back up. Siobhan, I'll come to you as fast as I can. Hold out till I'm there, please. Over."

Yes. Good luck. Do your thing, Rory. I love you... Static resumed and blocked her sentence.

"Siobhan?"

The CB was silent.

Rory moved the Hz to the Tummel House Community's dial.

Chapter Forty-Four

Perth to Fife

"It'll take them a day, boss," Kendra said from her horse that tossed its head, chewing its bit. "For the Tummel army to arrive."

"We can check things out before they do," Xian answered for Rory.

Rory nudged Boy to a canter, his stallion snorting his displeasure. They'd walked their horses all day and now forced a hard overnight ride. But they had to do it.

They passed through a wide valley, the silent Lomond hills to their left and the still, quiet waters of Loch Leven on their right. The night's orb continually dimmed with an ashen haze, reflected on the glassy surface of the loch. Farmhouses lay dotted ahead. Fields sown with crops were the landscape here, every inch planted and utilised.

Lloyd's lands.

Far ahead lay the Firth of Forth, with a glistening sheen on its rippling surface in the early predawn.

"We must push harder," Rory said. "Get there before daylight. We need some cover."

He kicked Boy, urging his tired horse harder, pushing himself with the pounding urgency from within. The sooner he dealt with whatever he found at Lloyd's, the sooner he could get to Edinburgh and Siobhan.

It wasn't long before the large mansion belonging to the lands they'd crossed came into view. Rory pulled Boy up, the horse panting hard, foaming at the bit. Xian and Kendra's horses fared no better.

"We're exposed here. We must hide the horses somewhere then creep closer." Rory pointed to the copse nearby. "There."

He headed to the trees, Xian and Kendra following, walking their panting horses to the shelter of the small wood. A burn ran through it, and they let the horses drink. They did the same and refilled their water bottles from the burn, then Rory led them further into the wood where they tied their mounts.

"Load up with your gear," he ordered.

"Aye, boss."

"There's no cover in those fields." Xian peered through the foliage.

"Take everything." Rory shoved his ammunition clips from his saddlebags into his jacket pockets.

Kendra had her bow and arrows, plus the rifle she was growing attached to. Xian had his Katana, and he also emptied his bags of bullets for his handpiece.

Rory checked he had a full magazine in his Glock and gave himself a mental pat on the back for always keeping his long-range rifle clean and ready. He looped the strap of the portable CB over his shoulder, volume turned low. They crept along the old road that led up to the outbuildings, keeping to the cover of the low drystone walls and natural dips in the land.

"The sheds are the obvious place to hold a number of hostages," Rory whispered once they drew nearer.

They lay on the ground and crawled into an overgrown hedgerow, which provided excellent cover. Rory looked through the sight of his rifle while Kendra used the high-powered lenses.

"Not many guards back here," Kendra commented.

"I'll get a little closer," Xian said, "and see what's around the side."

"I could pick them off from here." Rory held a guard in his crosshairs.

"No, Rory." Xian was firm. "We have no idea. Let me look first."

Rory lifted his eyes from his telescopic sight and turned to Xian. A stern expression greeted him.

"Aye," he said with reluctance. "Okay."

Xian crept away and Rory resumed his observations through his rifle's sight. "I wish I'd got more from Siobhan before…"

"Well, she was pre-occupied." Kendra's hand tightened on his shoulder. "She'll be okay, Rory," she said in a quiet voice.

Rory's heart softened. It was unusual for Kendra to be so… demonstrative. Her concern touched him for only a moment. They had work to do, and he needed to focus. A guard wandered behind the shed and urinated against the rear wall. Another followed and joined his companion.

"I'm surprised," Kendra said. "I thought his men would be more disciplined."

"Maybe they're stretched with the visitors becoming detainees." Rory continued looking through his sight. "All that's required is to let whoever's in there know we're here."

"We should wait for Tummel House Army," Kendra said in his ear. "We can't do this with only us three."

"Lloyd will have confiscated the Government Defence guys' weapons. We just need to provide them with some so they can join in when we make a move on their guards."

The branches of the wild rose and privet jolted. Kendra went for her firearm.

"You're almost invisible!" she said to Xian as he returned, relaxing her grip on her rifle.

"There's only a handful out front," Xian said, ignoring Kendra's comment. "That will change once it's daylight. I heard people inside. I think one of them was that Henderson guy who stalked me when we stayed the night in the Bunker."

None spoke for a moment. In the trees and along the hedgerows, birds stirred, their early morning calls breaking the silence.

"Where would you keep your armoury in a place like this?" Rory asked them both.

"Locked away," Kendra answered.

"Inside the house?" Rory speculated.

"No. Not all of it." Xian's mouth pulled to the side. "But in a close, lockable outbuilding."

Rory nodded. "Find it. Raid it. Arm the Government guys."

"How?" Kendra asked.

"Look closely at that shed they're guardin'." Rory indicated with a tilt of his head.

Kendra put the high-powered binoculars to her eyes. "Oh, I get it. Although the spaces between the slats of those windows are a wee bitty small."

"A handgun isn't a large item. Even a bigger piece could be pushed through." Rory turned to Xian. "You lead the way. We'll cover you while you find where they store the guns. I'll come over while Kendra covers us, and we'll get the weapons to the Government guys."

"We're not waiting for Tummel House?" Kendra asked.

"No time."

Chapter Forty-Five

Lloyd's Mansion Kingdom of Fife

Beams of daylight poked through the heavy curtain and landed on the Persian rug. The four-poster bed and antique furniture would have impressed Bethany if she wasn't being held against her will. She perched on the edge of the bed and wrapped the cashmere throw rug tighter around herself. Sleep had eluded her, and cold shakiness had settled in her middle. Even the dawn chorus outside, evidence that the world would go on without her, couldn't melt the ice collecting inside.

As civilised as Lloyd appeared, the glimpse into his soul last evening had convinced her that her life's value held little meaning for him.

This was a takeover. A polite one so far, apart from when they roughed her up leading her to this room—but a takeover no less.

The door opened and Maxwell stood there.

"You're expected at breakfast," he said and strode away, leaving the door open.

Bethany slid off the bed and walked to the door, then peered to her left. Maxwell strutted along the hallway. The aroma of fried bacon and coffee wafted through the corridor and hit her nose, so she followed. At the far end of this corridor, Maxwell stood at a door to the left and directed her in.

Lloyd sat at the head of a table in a bay window.

"Come, Miss Watts, have a seat." Lloyd gestured to the chair opposite.

Bethany stepped over and sat in the carver chair while Maxwell remained at the doorway.

"I trust you slept well," Lloyd asked.

"No," she replied.

A tight smile crossed Lloyd's face. "Please, enjoy our fare."

He indicated to the silver-plated serving dishes on the table before her. The bacon was tempting. She served herself some and a spoon full of the scrambled eggs, which were a bright yellow, not the pale of powdered egg. The salty bacon and creamy egg warmed her mouth and slid down her throat, sending the cold into a dark corner.

"I want you to give up the First Minister-ship," Lloyd said then scooped egg into his mouth with the nonchalance of the psychopath he was.

"The Scottish people elected me—"

"What?" A short scoff escaped Lloyd. "The residents of the Government Bunker?"

"And"—she continued, ignoring his derision and the cold rising once more— "*They* will decide if I'm to be removed."

Lloyd stared across the table at her, his head trembling to contain his smirk. Bethany turned away to the view provided by the bay window; she couldn't stand to look at Lloyd's face.

Outside, a guard dropped to the ground. Rory Campbell pulled his hand from the guard's mouth and his knife out of the man's back. *What!* Bethany willed her expression to calmness and returned her gaze to Lloyd. He forked baked beans with gusto, the noises of his own breakfast consumption masking any coming from the yard.

Lloyd poured himself coffee and Bethany returned to observe the activity in the yard. The door to the closest outhouse was open and the Chinese man who usually accompanied Campbell, came out of it—carrying handguns. Both he and Campbell disappeared around the corner.

"I won't capitulate, Mr Lloyd," she spoke in a loud voice. "What shall you do now?"

Lloyd's forkful of scrambled egg stopped mid-ascent to his lips. He returned it to his plate and gave her his full attention.

"You have guts. I see why they voted you in," he said. "Pity you don't have the right people on your side."

Antony is on my side. He must be. But Antony didn't have any power, imprisoned as he was.

"Don't think McLellan will be any help to you," Lloyd said. "He and I... let me put it this way: we work together quite well." Lloyd raised his eyebrows.

The shivers started, accompanied by a sense of danger similar to what she felt whenever she was with Antony. But it wasn't the exciting, sexually stimulating sense of danger. Her attraction to the damaged and intriguing man had led her here. To where Antony's deception was revealed. He'd been playing chess. Not chess where you are careful with your queen, but the chess in which to achieve your objective—keeping the king safe—you would sacrifice her to gain it. Bethany's heartbeat rocked her chest, coinciding with another understanding.

Capitulation or decapitation were her only choices here.

And it would be soon.

The pop of distant gunfire came from behind the house. Lloyd's head flicked up from his toast and Maxwell sped out of the room.

"What have you done?" Lloyd's accusing stare bore into her.

Bethany blinked. The gunfire increased, then the window high above her cracked and glass rained down. Bethany gasped and ducked sideways, lying flat, face-down on the carpet. Lloyd rose and shoved past the breakfast table; cutlery clattered, and crockery rattled.

"What's happening?" he shouted out the door of the breakfast room.

"I'm trying to find out, Father," Maxwell yelled down the corridor.

"Someone's forced the armoury and we can't reach it to see what they've taken," another voice from the hallway said. "Someone's taking shots and they're knocking off anyone who gets near."

"What's the noise from the back building?" Lloyd yelled.

Bethany crept to the window, avoiding shards of glass. Bodies lay near the open door to what must have been the arms store to which Maxwell referred. A young woman, vicious looking, ran in and came out with an armful of guns and a bag over her shoulder. She must be with Campbell, for she wasn't in the uniform of Lloyd's people.

A man with a dreadlock hairstyle ran into the room. "It's Rory Campbell, Father," he said.

It was the bandit-turned-community man.

Lloyd followed him out.

So, I won't be the only one double-crossed today.

Chapter Forty-Six

Lloyd's Mansion Kingdom of Fife

Rory rested his rifle on the barrel beside an outhouse, a small shed that provided the best view. Through his sight, guards in dark uniform darted toward the shed where they held the now-armed Government Defence Force Personnel. Rory took down two more of Lloyd's men as a clamour erupted, echoing in the iron-sheeting shed. Bullets pinged and maximum noise concentrated at the locked doors.

A group of bandits stood behind Lloyd's soldiers who'd made their way close to the now-broken door. Rory focused through his rifle's sight. Deet came into view, a shotgun chocked into her meaty shoulder. Rory lifted his eye away from his rifle's sight and examined the scene. Jock's bandit group spread in a loose formation behind and around her. Jock was the closest.

So, ae they part of it too?

Returning to his sight, he aimed for Deet who was now clearly in his crosshairs. Her shoulder kicked then one of Lloyd's men dropped.

Rory took his eye from the sight and his finger off the trigger.

"What!" Xian said next to him.

Jock and his group fired at the guards who'd aimed their weapons at the open door of the makeshift prison. Bodies dropped to the ground.

In the silence that followed, the bandits lowered their weapons and government personnel exited the shed. The mixed group now huddled in discussion.

Rory glanced at Xian who followed, leaving Kendra to cover them.

Rory lowered his rifle as he walked to the crowd. "You're going tae have to tell me what's happening here—"

"Mr Campbell, sir," Henderson said. He wore a black eye and an ugly bump to his forehead. "They have the First Minister in the house."

"And we're on yoor side, Campbell." Jock turned to him, his shotgun held in a relaxed grip. "That turncoat brother-in-law of yours is in tha' big hoose with his faither."

Rory's legs lost their ability to operate mid-stride.

Betrayed? Numbness held him.

"No, surely he's helpin' out," Rory said.

"We're going in." Henderson strode off, heading for the main house. Rory kicked himself into action and fell in behind with Xian and the other Government personnel.

"They're heavily armed inside," Jock explained to Henderson as he walked beside Rory.

They reached the back doorway as gunfire cracked from the far side of the stately home. Bullets whizzed past, and the newly formed team spread out, took cover and returned fire. Rory ducked behind a nearby shed close to the backdoor. Xian leaned on the wall next to him.

"I'll go in while they're distracting 'em." Rory indicated with his chin to the unguarded back door. "Cover me, Xian." He gave the CB to Xian, then slung his rifle over his shoulder and took out his Glock. Xian nodded, a grim expression on his face.

Rory waited for a lull in the gunfire, then sprinted to the door, shouldering it open. Muffled gunfire rattled through the walls of the mansion. The aroma of coffee and fried bacon brushed past Rory's nose. Footsteps trod ahead of him; angry voices travelled down the hallway. Figures stepped from the end of the hall and aimed his way. Rory ducked left into the nearest room. Bullets whizzed past and thunked into the walls in the direction from which he'd come. The room was bookshelf-lined, a large desk sat centre stage, and overstuffed high-backed chairs dotted the space.

The hiss of whispered voices came along the corridor. Rory took a pace out, fired rapidly down the hall, then ducked back into the library. Two dull thuds on the carpet told him he'd neutralised that threat.

Rory stepped out of the library with care, thick-piled carpet masking his footfall. Floorboards creaked in the room to his left. Rory kicked the door open. Micah's dreads swirled as he spun, handgun raised, gripped in both hands, aimed and ready. Rory jumped back as Micah's bullet cracked into a crystal vase displayed on an antique sideboard to his right and opposite to the doorway where Micah stood. Glass shattered and sprayed.

"Micah. It's me. Your brother." Rory wiped the sweat from his brow. His heart rate kicked up another level and his mouth dried. Adrenaline surged while he leaned on the wall beside the door to the room where Micah stood.

Along the hall a clock chimed. Rory strained for any noise of movement in the room.

"Micah, think of your family." Rory wiped his hands on his buckskins for a better grip on his Glock. "What about Cèilidh and your children?"

"My family's here, man. Always has been." Micah's voice was right behind the door. He spoke deep and flat.

Rory blinked. Nausea rose from his stomach, but he bit it back.

"Micah, why?" His words were forced out through a thick throat. "We took you in. We love you. You're part of us. How—"

"You're not my brother," Micah interrupted. "You're not my dad." Emotion broke around the periphery of Micah's voice. "You never really got me, man. And every time I did something for you, you always questioned my motives."

"What?" Rory strained to get the word out. He stared at Micah's crazed reflection in the fragments of broken glass lying opposite him on the carpet before the damaged sideboard. Micah moved toward the doorway.

"Those Government spies—" Micah began.

"You beat them half to death—"

"When I led you to your wife who ran off on you," Micah said.

"You helped her in the first place," Rory countered. "Look, this has nothin' to do with taking the First Minister. What are you planning to do with Bethany Watts? Let her go."

"You knew. Rory. But you never let me in." Micah's tone seeped accusation. "You knew my dad would be important to our future, but you've hated him all along."

Micah's voice came closer. A floorboard creaked. Loud bangs of gunfire came from the front door. Wood splintered, and glass shattered. Men yelled.

Rory stepped through the doorway beside him, his Glock held low. He spun into Micah's face and whacked Micah's hands holding his gun, shoving them up and against the doorjamb. A crack rang out, stinging Rory's hearing. Behind him, the painting above the shattered sideboard crashed onto the antique below. At the same time, Rory pressed his Glock into Micah's knee and squeezed the trigger. Micah screamed his shock, his piece thudding on the carpet. Wide, winter-blue eyes pleaded into Rory's face before Micah lowered to the floor, grabbing his destroyed knee.

Rory snatched Micah's handgun off the carpet as Bethany sprang up from her crouch behind a heavy sofa.

"Lloyd has a safe room," Bethany said. "Micah was taking me there."

"First Minister, this way." Henderson spoke behind Rory. Those entering through the destroyed Victorian front doorway followed closely behind him. "We'll guard you in a vehicle while we find Lloyd."

Bethany took a step along the hall to make her way out, then paused and turned back to Rory.

"Mr Campbell. Thank you for what you've done here." She bowed her head a touch. "You've saved my life. I've been so wrong about you. I was misinformed and have made wrong judgements." She looked him in the eye. "For that, I apologise."

"You're welcome, ma'am." It was all Rory could think of saying. Too many emotions fought for supremacy. Urgency and desperation won.

"Henderson, can I leave you with this traitor?" Rory pointed to Micah whose groans grew louder. "He needs medical attention."

Henderson crunched through broken glass and shattered timber to step closer to Rory. His forehead crinkled where it wasn't covered in a deepening bruise.

"What are you planning, Mr Campbell?" he asked. "We haven't secured this situation yet."

"The Tummel House Community's army will be here soon. They'll assist you." Rory turned and hurried to the back door.

"But sir," Henderson yelled behind him. "We could use your team's help."

"My team will be here," Rory shouted back. "But *I* have to get to the Bunker *now*."

Chapter Forty-Seven

Lloyd's Mansion Kingdom of Fife

Rory Campbell ran out the door.

"Are you okay, ma'am?" Henderson's voice registered in Bethany's ear. She shook her gaze off Mr Campbell—a remarkable young man.

"Yes, Henderson. I think I've fared better than you."

Henderson's green left eye peered out from a swollen, purple lid. "Let's get you to the vehicle, First Minister, and we'll search for the safe room."

"He'd know where it is." The man who always accompanied Mr Campbell pointed to Micah McNair, who lay groaning and dripping blood onto the carpet.

"Aye, a good idea, Xian," Henderson said then stepped to McNair. "Show us where the safe room is," he commanded.

Micah stared up at him from his supine position on the floor with a look of incredulity. "You're jokin', right?" Micah let out a gasp. "Fix ma leg first. Then I might tell ya."

Henderson's foot flicked out and jolted the calf below the knee in question.

McNair screamed.

"Iain!" Bethany glared at Henderson. "Where's our medic?" She looked around at the other personnel; one acknowledged and ran out the door. "Help me get him on the couch." She leaned down and grasped hold of McNair's arm.

Xian and Henderson took over the manoeuvring of McNair and placed the injured man on the length of the couch. A few minutes later a woman with a medical kit entered the parlour and opened her kit beside McNair.

"Ma'am, we need to secure you in a vehicle," Henderson said. "We'll see to this." He turned to Xian. "Please take the First Minister to our lead vehicle, it's just outside."

Xian nodded and led her through the smashed Victorian doorway and down the stone steps. Black-clad figures gathered farther along the road that led to Kirkcaldy, and more on the road which the Government convoy had taken coming from the Kincardine Bridge.

No gunfire disturbed the grounds of the stately home, only the hum of conversations interspersed with shouted orders. Her government security detail moved among and communicated with some ragged-looking individuals.

"Bandits," Xian said beside her. "On our side." He halted in his walk to the vehicle, listening.

"What can you hear—?" she began to ask.

Xian placed a finger to his lips, then jogged to the rear of the mansion. A thundering vibrated through the ground, and shouts came from that direction. Bethany ran to stand next to Xian where, in between the two large sheds at the back of the mansion, they had a long view of the fields.

Horses bearing riders rode over the nearest field, four abreast. Row upon row. A sea of riders, all bearing arms, that looked to be anything from a rifle to an old flintlock musket—from what she could tell. And every rider wore a kilt; each one a plaid in the softer colours of the hunting tartans.

"It's the Tummel House Army." Xian sounded composed. He looked it too, apart from the tense way he held his shoulders.

Bethany walked with Xian, joining the others awaiting the approaching force. Her security team and the bandits by the sheds gave a cheer as the mounted soldiers arrived and an older man, who she recalled was Mr Donaldson, rode forward. A younger man, his spitting image, rode beside him. Donaldson scanned the crowd and smiled when his gaze rested on Xian and Bethany.

"Thank you for coming so promptly, Mr Donaldson," Bethany said. "We have Lloyd somewhere in the house in a safe room. His men have scattered to the far fields at the front with more gathering further along the road."

"I think they've come from their posts guarding the Kincardine Bridge," Xian offered. "They're regrouping, so we'd better move and position ourselves."

"Aye." Donaldson dismounted, his kilt swishing in Bethany's face as he did so. "But we have Bessie on her way doon and ye'll want to make good use of her."

"Bessie?" Bethany raised her brows.

"An 1814 six-pound cannon in perfect working order, with plenty o' balls and oor home-made black powder. She's travelling on a dray so she's a wee bitty delayed in gettin' here. Have tae move a bit slower, aye?" He pressed his hands into his back and stretched tall. "Where's this safe room, then? Have ye got into that yet?" He unshouldered an ancient-looking shotgun.

"We're still finding its location," Bethany said then led the way to the front entrance while the army behind her dismounted.

Horses whinnied, tack jangled and the murmurings of men in serious tones fell behind. When they reached the smashed front door of the Victorian mansion, Henderson stepped out.

"Beth—First Minister, why are you not in the vehicle?" Henderson asked, his one clear eye looking in Donaldson's direction.

Donaldson bustled up the stairs and brushed past Iain. He moved with a slight stiffness to his legs, probably from a long ride on a horse, but he was agile all the same.

"Have ye found oot where this safe room is, laddie?" Donaldson asked.

"Aye sir," Iain replied. "It's where the old cellar used to be, but we can't get in—"

"I was always under the impression that is the general idea, is it no'?" Donaldson said.

"It's a solid door with a keypad—" Henderson began.

"It was the cellar, ye say?" Donaldson asked.

Henderson blinked, one-eyed and silent. Bethany suppressed a grin as the competence and experience of Donaldson came to the fore.

"If we hold our position, and keep those dark devils who are crowdin' doon that road frae coming any closer, once Bessie arrives, we can blast a way in frae the ootside, ken?" Donaldson turned his stare to Bethany, awaiting her answer and permission.

"Let's try negotiation first," she replied, then to Henderson. "Can we hear him through the door? Are we sure he's in there?"

"Aye, First Minister," Henderson said. "We think his son Maxwell is in there too."

Henderson spun and indicated for an armed guard to accompany them, then led the way through the stately home, past the breakfast room and to the Victorian kitchen. Bethany marched with the others to the functional and much less ornate section of the house. Two fireplaces, one snugly fitted with a cast-iron stove, sat side by side along one wall of the kitchen, and a sturdy wooden table filled most of the floor space. A door further back led to a narrow and utilitarian stone stair, down which Henderson led Bethany, Xian, Donaldson and the guard.

"This must abutt the outer wall at the far side o' this mansion, aye?" Donaldson's voice amplified off the cold stone walls.

Cool mustiness brushed Bethany's face as the light from the doorway above receded and ahead Henderson turned on a torch. They came to an abrupt halt at the bottom of half a dozen stairs and the armed guard held his weapon ready. A solid metal door with a keypad beside shone in the light of Henderson's torch.

"Lloyd!" Donaldson shouted. "Answer us, man, if ye value yer life!"

Laughter, derisive in tone, came through the muffled layers of metal and reinforcing materials.

"Mr Lloyd, be a man and open this door." Bethany raised her voice. "Face the consequences of your failed coup and we'll deal appropriately with you. Otherwise, we will break in, one way or another."

Gunfire peppered the air outside, the noise funnelling down the narrow stairwell.

"I'll go see what's happening." Xian ran up the steps.

"Lloyd, who's in there with you?" Henderson shouted at the door.

Gunfire continued to echo from above. The stairwell was quiet apart from the breaths of the three men standing with Bethany. Her upper lip cooled with a thin layer of sweat.

"Mr Lloyd, save yourself and surrender," Bethany yelled. "Where is your son? Don't you care about Maxwell?"

"Och, the man's too reticent," Donaldson said. "Once oor Bessie's here we'll try again. Lad, you guard this door till we set up oor cannon," he ordered the guard. Donaldson faced Bethany. "The man's committed treason, has he not? Dinnae be soft on him. Any delay he kens may be to his advantage. Like the noo'." He thrust a thumb in the direction of the upstairs and outside. "His men have regrouped. We cannae be too compassionate. It's him or us ye ken, lass. I mean, First Minister." Donaldson dipped his head in a brief bow.

Behind him, the door flew open, and Bethany's ears rang with the clamour of repeated gunfire in the restricted space.

Chapter Forty-Eight

Scottish Government Bunker

Siobhan's heart beating against her ribcage increased its rate yet another notch. They'd warned her the salbutamol drip would cause tachycardia. And the tremor in her hands. She lay back and breathed away the panic it mimicked. Murray sat beside her bed in the medical centre, his nose packed with gauze and a rich purple developing around his eyes.

"Jake's with Cèilidh and the kids in my room, yes?" Her speech was rapid.

"Aye, Siobhan." Murray sounded like he had a heavy cold. "That's the seventh time you've asked me."

"Have we heard from Rory since last night?" The scratching sound of toenails against crisp sheets accompanied Siobhan's jiggling feet.

Murray shook his head, then grimaced.

Siobhan slipped out of the covers.

"What're you doing?" Murray leaned forward in his chair.

"I can't stand this." She sat on the edge of the bed and put on her slippers. "I'm going to the communication room."

Dr Liz walked into the room. "Siobhan, please go back to bed... Oh!"

Siobhan looked up at the alarm in Dr Liz's voice.

"Medic, get the monitor!" Dr Liz ordered, her eyes focusing on Siobhan's groin. "How long have you been haemorrhaging?"

Siobhan stood and looked down, registering the extra warmth in that area. And the blood stains seeping wider.

"Prep theatre!" Dr Liz blurred in Siobhan's vision.

Spots formed in Siobhan's vision. Then, overcome by a light-headedness, she sank.

"Mummy's gone, darling girl." Her father's arms surrounded her, warm and strong. He rested his chin on her forehead, his three-day growth prickling her skin.

"What about the baby, Daddy?"

"He's gone with Mummy, sweetheart." He sighed.

"Didn't they want to be with us?"

"Siobhan. Siobhan!" Dr Liz spoke close by her face. "Stay with me, Siobhan."

Murray mumbled beside her.

"It's not that simple." The doctor's voice angled in Murray's direction. "It's not just Siobhan bleeding, but the foetus could be too. We have to perform a caesarean section as speedily as possible."

Murray mumbled once more; his voice strangled with apprehension.

"Yes, do that," Dr Liz answered him.

***

White foam streaked Boy's black withers. Rory rode him hard after leaving Kirkcaldy. The Kincardine Bridge was in sight but devoid of the usual guards at the entry points. In the late morning light, the dust rose along the bridge that traversed the River Forth as the crowds hurried across without being accosted for a toll. Clearly, Lloyd had deployed those men to his stately home. Rory yelled at the travellers to move out of his way. People encumbered by the caged animals, bags of grain and other objects regarded as suitable taxes, parted before him and he trotted Boy across. Thoughts of apology or thanks passed through his mind, but they ricocheted off his blinding determination to get to the Bunker, which competed with a heated swirl in his throat and a numbness at Micah's treachery.

A betrayal of Community, friendship, and family.

And of brotherhood.

Rory searched his memory in vain for the tell tale signs of Micah's impending desertion. Of double allegiances and loyalties divided. Of secret meetings and covert messages.

Micah had always been so eager, desperate even, to please him. Had he not acknowledged the guy enough? Had he not given Micah the approval he so obviously desired?

Maybe not.

But in the end, the man's need for his father's admiration had won over all other ties. Even those to his own wife and children.

Rory gripped the reins tighter. Had he been naïve to think a one-time bandit could change?

How blind I've been.

Now Rory's throat ached.

Micah was a brother.

But no more.

He nudged Boy on, thrusting aside all thoughts and hurts associated with Micah.

Tummel House Army would have arrived at Kirkcaldy with reinforcements. Rory's shoulders eased. The hasty alliance between Community, Government and bandits would need the muscle of Donaldson's army.

He reached the other side of the Kincardine Bridge and the portable CB over his shoulder jumped to life.

Rory. It was Murray.

A fist clutched Rory inside and held firm to his guts.

"Aye, Murray. Over." His voice came out hard.

Rory kicked Boy to a canter, holding the handset close to his mouth.

They're operating on Siobhan. Over.

"What? Now? Why?" *Forget the overs!*

She's bleeding. That means the baby might be too. Over.

"But she said she was okay," Rory rasped. "They'd stopped the contractions."

They're trying to save them both. Murray's voice strained at the edges and trembled as it came through the handset.

"I'll be there as soon as I can," Rory yelled. "Keep me posted. Over."

Aye. I will. Out. The radio died.

Rory dug his heels into Boy's flanks and rode low over his neck, urging his stallion on with his whole body, pushing down the fist that gripped and twisted his insides like a drowning man grasping at a rope.

Chapter Forty-Nine

Lloyd's Mansion Kingdom of Fife

Bethany's flight up the narrow steps was a blur as her temples pounded with her pulse. Her upper arm burned where Henderson retained his tight grip after dragging her up the stone stairs. The cracking of automatic gunfire repeated behind them while they retreated and collapsed on the wooden floorboards of the kitchen.

Donaldson flew out of the stairwell, his grey hair sticking up wildly and his expression grim.

"That wee *haggersnash* has retreated, but not afore snuffing the life oot of that young lad. My condolences at losing one of yer men, ma'am," he said.

Bethany stared at the stairwell, willing her thundering ears to recover.

"I'll get more men to guard these stairs," Henderson said. "No one will reach the top of them. Security will use their grenades to blow them if that door opens a crack without warning or signs of surrender."

Henderson marched her to the front door. Outside, bullets had riddled the vehicle in which he'd previously insisted Bethany seek shelter. They withdrew to the main lounge room and Bethany scurried behind a substantial antique couch while the gun battle continued to rage outside. After Henderson had organised the guard at the entrance to the cellar, he returned and posted an armed defence force member who squatted beside Bethany, her weapon at the ready. They hunkered down behind the couch for the rest of the morning, with Henderson returning on occasions to check on her and report on his and Donaldson's joint handling of the situation.

The room grew stuffy as the hours dragged, and Bethany's foot cramped as she remained in a squat behind the solid couch. Her mouth dried but going to the kitchen for a glass of water wasn't a safe option. Heavy footsteps stomped down the corridor leading to her room of safety. Donaldson entered; the reek of cordite hovered around him, and Bethany pinched her nose against the sharpness. Henderson followed close behind.

"Bessie's arrived!" Donaldson said. "My men are occupying those black devils of Lloyds while we drag her round the side and set her up to pound the cellar wall." He looked pointedly at Bethany. "Do I have your permission, ma'am?"

Bethany clutched the collar of her blouse at her throat. She'd never been involved in allowing—ordering—the demise of another human. But Lloyd had revealed his greed and his ambitions. He'd intended to take her life, displaying a total disregard for the leadership position she held.

Her neck dampened with sweat, soaking her collar.

"Yes," she replied.

Donaldson left the room. She gazed at the carpet looming lush-red before her.

"First Minister… Bethany." Henderson knelt beside her and placed his hand on her arm. "You have no choice," he said. "He would have killed you."

She swallowed.

"He would have taken the first-ministership for himself. Who knows what he would have done next? You're not only saving yourself; you're saving Scotland." Henderson rose and followed Donaldson.

Twenty minutes later, one of Donaldson's kilted men entered.

"Ma'am. Mr Donaldson wishes ye to remove yoursel' from the hoose. We are completing Bessie's set-up. It'll no' be safe when we start pounding the wall o' the hoose with the cannon, ma'am." He dipped a bow and waited expectantly for her to move.

Bethany stirred from the shelter of the solid furniture and, glancing sideways at her defence force minder, accompanied the young man. Gunfire battered the front of the mansion, answered instantly with retorts from the Tummel House Army's firearms, plus those of Government personnel and bandit allies. Bethany followed the soldier's lead and clambered out the bay window of the breakfast room.

A group of Tummel House Army personnel gathered around a cannon on wheels, directing its muzzle at the rear wall outside the cellar. Heavy horse pulled an empty cart away, and a neat pile of cannon balls sat nearby. A kilted soldier was carrying a wide, cylindrical leather case to the cannon and the artillery crew.

Henderson approached Bethany. "It's best we get you away from this, First Minister." He gently grasped her elbow and steered her to the outer sheds.

Bethany strode into the larger shed and turned to the nearest window where she could see the Tummel House soldiers in charge of Bessie. Donaldson had called this cannon *light artillery*. The soldier who had been carrying the leather case now opened it to remove a small package wrapped in material and he loaded this into the cannon's mouth. A cannon ball and a coil of rope followed. The soldier standing at the other end lit a large taper and the soldiers all stood back.

A *whoosh* and a *bang* echoed up and around, followed instantly by a thunderous clap reverberating off the house and through the shed. It rocked Bethany. She stood staring out the bare window, rubbing her ears, unable to take her eyes off the scene before her. The crew manning the cannon set about immediately preparing for the next firing.

Rubble from the building crunched and clattered to the ground. After less than a minute of flurried activity surrounding the cannon, another boom ensued. Bethany covered her ears, aching tinnitus predominant in her head.

Two more *booms*, then shouts, all dulled by her hands over her ears. Someone tapped her shoulder.

"First Minister." Henderson turned her to face him, and she lowered her hands. "The end wall has collapsed. They're checking for survivors."

More shouting came from the yards outside. Men milled around the pile of rubble and debris at the base of the rear wall. Jagged sections of brick framed an internal view of the chimneys of the Victorian kitchen.

Xian ran to Bethany. "They're retreating, First Minister. Lloyd's men know it's over," he said.

Donaldson strode toward her, his brow creased, but his shoulders sat wide and proud.

"Pursue them," Bethany ordered Donaldson. "They must be brought to justice."

"Aye, ma'am." He saluted, then called over one of his men and gave orders.

Moments later, mounted men tore past her, led by Donaldson's son. Kilts flew, exposing bare legs as the men waved their guns, their voices roaring a Highland battle cry. Bethany shrank back into the shed, curbing the bolt of fear at the deep male voices saturated with battle-lust. A sense of pity for Lloyd's men flashed through her.

A government security member ran to where she stood with Henderson.

"Ma'am, sir." He gulped for air. "We've confirmed there's only one body. It's that of an old man."

Chapter Fifty

Edinburgh

Boy stumbled again crossing the Royal Mile of Edinburgh Old Town, the stallion's hooves clattering on the street. Buildings, centuries old, passed by Rory in a blur. He had avoided this part of Edinburgh on previous visits, but it was the quickest way to Arthur's Seat.

Rory pushed Boy on through mountains of rubbish that lined the streets. The reek of human excrement and soured milk wafted from in between rusted car carcasses, litter and rubble lay strewn before buildings covered in graffiti. Rory snorted at the city that once boasted its place as Scotland's capital. He turned Boy down Holyrood Road, the main street after the Royal Mile, as Xian had said he should.

A group of people, mostly men, milled around on a street corner, leaning in close conversation. Their heads turned at the ring of Boy's shod hooves on the cobbled road. Firearms hung at the belts of their ragged trousers, and the stocks of rifles, bows, and the handles of long knives sat above the dull clad shoulders of the group concentrating on Rory's approach.

They stirred from their positions to bar Rory's path. He pulled Boy up at the same time taking his Glock from its home at his back and aiming at the man in front of him.

"Please move out of my way." Rory tightened his grip on his handgun.

A man on the left of the human barrier notched an arrow to the bow he'd slipped off his shoulder. There was a *click-clack* as a woman to Rory's right loaded and aimed her semi-automatic rifle. The man in the centre raised his hand, and all activity around him stilled.

"I'm trying to be polite here." Rory's brow dripped with sweat.

"Now, lads, let's just hear the man oot." The spokesman's stare stuck on Rory. "Well, why should we no' take whatever we want from ye?"

"No reason at all in this world, but I'd like to think even you have some compassion on a man who's aiming to get to his wife who's having his baby but"—Rory spoke through a shuddered breath— "with difficulty."

The man squinted at Rory and lowered his hand.

"I'll not let her die on me too." Rory's voice was as firm as his grip and aim.

"I'll have that." The man lifted his chin, indicating the long-range rifle slung over Rory's shoulder.

His father's long-range rifle.

The last piece of him.

Rory's tongue stuck to the roof of his mouth. He slowly shook his head. "No," he said with as much force as he could temper with manners.

The man tilted his head and pursed his lips. "Och, weel. Ye dinnae get tae be with yoor wifey then." He strode forward and his companions raised their weapons.

"Look, this was my father's... He died, and this is all I have left of him," Rory said.

"We all hae somebody who died on us," the man said.

The gazes of those standing before Rory bore into him. Rory mentally ran through his inventory of the valuable possessions on him, focusing on the most expendable.

"I have food."

The man paused and tucked his thumb in the rope he used for a belt. "Och, lad, we'll have that too." He and his companions remained where they stood.

Rory gritted his teeth at his next suggestion. It might just be enough.

"You can have anything else except this rifle and ma horse."

The man stepped forward, laughing. Rory altered his grip on his Glock, his finger tight to the trigger. The man stopped mid-stride and squinted up at him.

"*You'll* be dead in seconds if ye shoot me," he said.

"Aye, but so will you," Rory growled. "Decide what ye want other than ma faither's rifle."

"What's in the wee baggy slung over your other shoulder?" the man asked.

"A CB radio—"

"Och, that'll do nicely." The man wriggled his finger sat Rory, palm up, and kept them in that position.

Heat rose up Rory's neck. He lifted the CB's strap from over his shoulder and handed the portable CB in its bag to the man.

"Can I go now?" Rory ground out. Boy snorted beneath him, ears twitching.

"Och weel, that handgun you're pointin' at me is quite a nice piece, is it no'?" the man said. "It'll be mine tha' noo." His expression didn't waver.

Rory swallowed, only partially succeeding in passing thick saliva down a dry throat. He leaned over and gave up his Glock.

"That saddle ye are sittin' upon is a fine piece of workmanship," the thief said. "I'll have that too."

"What!"

"Ye heard me," the man growled.

Rory bit his tongue and dismounted. He removed the saddle, keeping his saddlebags slung over Boy's rump, and surrendered it. He jumped back on a saddle blanket soaked with horse sweat.

The man flicked his head in the direction Rory was travelling. "Go to ye wifey and bairn." A chorus of protest rose from his companions. "Och, the lad's genuine." He raised his hand along with his voice. "Look at the way he's punished that fine-lookin' animal."

His companion beside him murmured.

"Let 'im through," he shouted, then spat on the road in front of Boy, who gave a tired but irritated whinny.

Rory kicked Boy to a canter and rode through the thin gap in the line-up before him. His shoulders burned and his neck prickled, but they fired no shots, so he nudged Boy past more boarded houses and derelict shops.

Boy gave a heavy snort, and his breath came hard. Rory cantered him on the narrow road that led behind the hill and wound its way up to the solid gates that were the entry to the Bunker. The sentry on lookout at the top of the gates shouted and waved. The thick metal doors rolled open. Rory dug his heels in, and air rushed out of Boy's nostrils, his canter slowing to a tired trot. Rory steered him down the concrete driveway deep into the Bunker, barely acknowledging the defence force personnel surrounding him.

Boy's hooves echoed as he stumbled along to the loading platform where the entry to the stairwell was situated, and he panted hard as Rory slid off.

A young lad, not much older than Murray, exited the stairwell. "Mr Campbell, I'll show you to the medical centre."

Behind Rory, Boy gave a breathy-snort, then whinnied. An exhausted whinny that bordered on fear. It pierced Rory's soul.

Rory spun.

Boy collapsed, his legs folding underneath him, grazing knees and bashing his frothing mouth on the concrete. Blood dribbled from his lips.

"*Boy!*" The word wrenched from Rory's heart while he ran and grabbed the reins. He bent over his stallion, chest tightening. His lifelong friend rolled and lay down, his shiny black coat mottled in lathered sweat, his sides heaving.

"Do you have a vet?" Rory screamed. "*Please?* I must get to Siobhan. Somebody, tend to ma horse, please!" He just got the words out through a tight, dry throat.

"We'll call someone," the lad said. "Sir?"

Rory had seen it before, when riders pushed their horses too hard. He dragged his eyes away from his failing stallion.

"Where is she? Is she okay?" Rory rushed toward the young man, forcing himself to leave all thoughts and feelings for his horse in the garage, and concentrate on his wife and child. He followed the lad, picking up his pace, then ran through the door and up the stairs.

Chapter Fifty-One

Scottish Government Bunker

The sensation of crisp sheets against her skin returned to Siobhan.

"We have a blood bank here." Dr Liz's words seemed far away. "If required, we have the means to transfuse them both with compatible blood from a universal donor. Your wife is haemodynamically stable and the neonate, I mean, your son, appears to be unaffected. We acted in a suitable time-frame, Mr Campbell."

"She'll be okay then?" Rory's deep masculine voice was right next to Siobhan, and she turned to him.

A blurred head of dark-russet hair was near her. She sniffed sleepily.

Horse and heather.

Strongly horse.

And the rusty-scented ferrous of blood... and... baby?

"Siobhan, my heart," Rory said.

Turning her head a little further, her vision cleared. A gurning grizzle came from the bundle of linen he held. A tiny fist stretched up and knocked Rory's bearded chin. He blinked and smiled down at the bundle.

"Rory?" Her voice slurred.

"Aye, Siobhan. A healthy wee boy," Rory's voice was husky and cracked at the edges.

"You made it." She relaxed onto the pillow, too dopey to move any further, her legs still heavy.

She reached out her hand and stroked his cheek, bristly facial hair brushing stiffly against her fingertips. "Yours for all time, whatever time may bring us."

"Aye," he said with love in his eyes.

The lusty cry of her baby hit her ears. A healthy, hungry newborn.

"You must suckle him, Siobhan," Dr Liz said.

"Here, Siobhan." Rory leaned over her and placed the baby-scented bundle on her. "You told me his name was Connald. You ken? When you returned."

***

Heavy muscles clamped Rory in an exhaustion that weighed his thoughts as well. Siobhan dropped off to sleep after rousing and feeding the baby. Connald was a strong, braw wee mite. Rory breathed in deep, her scent and his, and then marched out of the ward of the medical centre.

Tension returned to his shoulders, plus a niggle resumed, one that he'd previously pushed aside.

Murry stood just outside the medical centre. "It's all good, yeah?"

He gave Rory a hug, his scrawny arms wrapping around him tight.

"I believe I have you to thank for Siobhan's safety," Rory said. He let go of Murray, whose eyelids were purple with fresh bruising.

"Yeah, but she's got skills," Murray said. "Should've seen her fight off—"

Rory brushed past his gushing younger brother; his fists curled, and his arms rigid beside him.

"Why are you so annoyed?" Murray leaned against the wall to let him pass. "She didn't die this time."

Rory stopped mid-stride and spun back to Murray. "What do you mean 'this time'?"

"What?" Murray's speech faltered around the word, then he cringed. "Ah, she didn't tell you?" Murray bit his lip.

"Tell me what?" Rory snapped. He took a step closer to stand over Murray.

"That in the future she travelled to, she'd died having Connald," Murray said, hunching into himself while his face contorted into an uncomfortable expression. "I probably shouldn't have said that."

"No, maybe not," Rory said.

His feet wouldn't move, and the familiar hand that had grabbed his guts while riding here, did so again. Then Siobhan's reasoning dawned on him and the heated emotions swirling in him eased their cyclonic dance.

She had protected him from living a life without her. She'd said in the future she went to he'd wanted her to change the past. Tampering with history, past or future, was something he would never have considered, nor allowed.

But he'd asked her to make sure that particular future didn't occur. For the sake of a famine. A civil war.

And her life.

Rory's leg muscles obeyed his will once more, and he marched along the corridor.

"Where're you going?" Murray started to follow.

"Ma horse," Rory threw over his shoulder as he strode to the large stairwell that led to the lower floors and the garage. He ran down the stairs, thoughts of Boy overshadowing his relief that Siobhan and wee Connald had made it. He came to the floor where the garages were situated.

"Where would they take Boy?" he shouted to Murray, who had followed behind but had not kept up with his pace.

"In the back of the garage," Murray called back. "That's where they stabled the horses when you were here before—"

"He's dying." Rory's statement echoed up the stairwell while his brother caught up.

"What?"

"I pushed him hard." Rory choked through his words. "Where would the vet be?" He opened the door to the garage floor.

Rory stepped onto the loading platform. In front of it, a man stooped over the dark form of Boy lying on his side on the cold concrete. Another man milled around, and a woman held up a bag of intravenous fluid attached to a line.

"How is he?" Rory jumped off the loading bay platform and knelt beside Boy, stroking his muzzle.

"Ah, Mr Campbell, sir." The veterinarian injected something into the IV in Boy's neck. "We'll do all we can, but I can't promise anything."

"Thank you." Rory's voice cracked, then he swallowed. "Can we move him somewhere—?"

"We'll bring the hay," the vet said. "The stable *to* the horse, Mr Campbell."

***

Siobhan woke with a start, her arms empty. She rolled to her left. Beside her bed, in a clear plastic cot, Connald slept silently. A pink, crinkled face and a button nose peeked out of a bundle tightly wrapped in a pale-yellow blanket. Siobhan pressed her hands to her lower tummy and rested back on her bed. The pain medication was wearing off and soreness gathered where they'd cut her. A bag of IV fluid hung on a pole beside her. The tubing ran through a box-shaped pump and drops slowly formed in the clear chamber in the tubing just above the pump, then fell with a bounce to the fluid level in the lower section of the chamber.

Soft murmurings of the staff wafted to her cubicle while they tidied the far end of the medical centre. It seemed the surgical theatres had been busier than ever and now the critical care section of the Bunker's hospital wing had two patients. She could tell by the looks shot in her direction it was probably Antony and MacIntosh.

Her throat tightened with rising bile.

They hadn't hesitated to injure her, and fracture Murray's nose. Antony's actions had brought him to that point, and she wasn't responsible for them. But she couldn't help regretting what Antony's choices had led him to.

Her plan had succeeded.

Her chest stuttered and silent tears slid down her cheeks, wet warmth trickling into her ears and shaky inhalations following.

She rested her gaze on her newborn, now blurred through her wet vision.

She didn't die having him. She'd changed the past as Rory in *that* future had requested, and now, if all remained well, that broken man would never be.

And her Rory was here, soon enough to hold their son before she'd come round. Showing how much they both meant to him.

Rory had reported the situation at Lloyd's was being handled by the Tummel House Army and a joint force of government, bandits and the Community crew he'd left behind. Just as well, the small force the Government sent had failed in their attempts at South Queensferry to cross the Forth by boat.

And Rory had left them all to it.

She sank heavy limbs deeper into the bed, allowing exhaustion and relief to take over.

***

Boy rested quietly. Rory had sat by him and held his head in his lap while they'd screened him and lay thin foam mattresses and blankets around and under him as best they could.

Rory let tears slide down his cheeks and into his beard. Weeping at the thought of losing Boy seemed insignificant when compared to his tears of joy that Siobhan and Connald had survived.

That was his world.

Balances. The need to be with his wife and child had outstripped the welfare of his dearest equine friend. His world could never again be the relative calm of his youth when his parents' love and protection had surrounded him. His insides heated, like a smouldering fury.

Rory slipped out from under his stallion.

"Are you going, Mr Campbell?" the veterinarian asked.

"Aye, I must see my wife and new baby."

"Oh, yes, congratulations," the vet said.

Rory acknowledged the man who seemed a vague form before him, his mind now elsewhere.

He had pushed it aside during the hours on Boy's back, then smothered the idea while he held his son and sat beside Siobhan as she awoke. But he could do it no longer, and thoughts of what he must do arose front and centre in his consciousness, lifted by the thermals of his rage.

Rory clambered onto the loading bay and stepped through the stairwell. Murray was on his way down the stairs.

"How's Siobhan?" he asked Murray when he joined him one flight up.

"Still sleeping. And Connald too. Did she really tell you his name when she returned from the future?" Bruising crept past the sticking plaster covering Murray's nose.

Rory climbed the stairs, taking two at a time and ignoring his brother's question. He reached the exit to the next floor and wrenched the door open. Rory strode along, scanning the hallway and corridor with Murray close on his heels. Lights flicked on then off, darkness filling the space in front and behind their journey. It wasn't long before he found what he was searching for. Rory marched to the glass cabinet beside the fire-hose reel, raised his elbow and smashed the glass.

"What're you doing?" Murray's voice rose a pitch.

"What are *we* doing?" Rory corrected, raising the axe so the head almost touched Murray's chin. "How do I get to it?"

"No." Murray shook his head violently, then stopped and put his hands to his temples.

Rory tightened his grip on the axe handle, knuckles whitening.

"We can't trust them." Rory swiped the axe aside and thrust his face into Murray's. "Not to misuse it. Not to keep other people from it!"

"But it saved Siobhan!" Murray said.

"Och, I know." Rory stepped back and leaned against the wall of the Bunker. Cold from the concrete wall seeped through his shirt. He gazed up at the LED. "By manipulating now to prevent… But it can't happen. Not again. Not ever. It's *not* right." He lifted his eyebrows and pierced his stare into Murray. "No one, Government, Community, or anybody, can be trusted to not meddle with time for their own purposes. Not even myself, it seems."

"But it isn't only the machine," Murray whispered. "It's Ley line involvement—"

"Do you fully understand how it works?" Rory interrupted. "I mean, this cubicle has *something* to do with it, but do you know what?"

Murray lifted his shoulders and let them fall.

"*They* don't know everything," Rory continued. "And those who think they do are probably dead by now, anyway. Or will be forced to keep quiet. I'll deal with Micah."

Rory locked gazes with Murray. The silence echoed down the deserted corridor.

"You understand what I'm meanin', don't you?" he asked. "You're always going on about the time-space continuous—"

"Space-time continuum," Murray corrected.

Rory waggled his head, acknowledging Murray, then he lifted the axe and knocked the handle against his left hand a couple of times.

"It's a different timeline." Murray swallowed. "Siobhan changed our *now* so *that* future doesn't even happen. That's why the me in that future hadn't seen her travel in his past."

Rory scrunched his forehead. "What?"

"It means we're on an alternate timeline," Murray said. "The future that Siobhan travelled to"—he flicked his fingers in a puff of smoke gesture— "won't even happen. It will be a different story now with Siobhan in it. And we're surviving a famine without Lloyd's help. If he's even around anymore." He hesitated for only a second longer. "Follow me."

Rory held the axe against his side and strode behind Murray, along corridors, down stairs for four floors, and along another short corridor to the lab. Murray took out a key and clicked the lock open, they both stepped in, and Murray locked the door behind them.

The room was its usual bare, except for the cubicle and the console.

The gusts of Murray's rapid mouth-breathing filled the quiet lab and competed with the thudding in Rory's temples.

It was too much an object of desire.

"I have to do it." Rory raised the axe and, driving all his strength and body weight into it, he let it fall.

THE END

If you enjoyed this novel, please leave a review.

Join Jenn's Community, receive regular newsletters, a free book and be the first to know dates of her new releases.

www.jennleeswriter.com

Acknowledgements

First, I wish to thank you, dear reader, for waiting so patiently for *Community Chronicles Book 4*. Thank you to those who have contacted me personally to tell me how much you enjoy this series and pester me for the next book. And give me ideas for more.

It warms this little independently published author's heart to hear you say such things.

Thank you to my editor, Abigail Nathan of Bothersome Words, for a thorough edit. I have learned much from it.

Thanks always to aspiring romance author, Mindy Graham and Co., for ongoing support and encouragement, reviewing and proof-reading.

Much appreciation to my Beta readers for taking the time to read the pre-edited version:
Author J I Rogers, Sue Jacka, Jill Williams and Ileana Noble.

The Indie-author Facebook groups in which I'm involved:
Adam Croft's Indie Author Mindset
Bryan Cohen's Amazon Ads School
Mark Dawson's Self-Publishing Show
Science Fiction Novelists Facebook group
All your comments and the topics you discuss keep me going.

Special thanks go to Lorraine McCluskey for the information regarding a sick horse. And Leanne Prosser, you mention horsey things to me so often, it all filters in somehow. Thanks.

Thanks to Fionajayde Media for the covers.

My family for their ongoing support and interest. Special thanks to our daughter Emma, who comes to the rescue on all things IT every second day.

Always thanks to my husband Frank, the example of unconditional love in my life, and who never ceases to amaze me with his support for my obsession.

Thank you, Frank, for understanding that it's something 'I have to do'.
Jenn
August 2020.

About the Author

Jenn Lees writes fantasy.

The Crossing: Arlan's Pledge Book 1, soon to be re-released as *Of Myths and Portals.* Finalist in the OZMA Book Awards for Fantasy Fiction CIBA 2021(manuscript).

Arlan's Pledge Book Two is currently a Semi-finalist in the OZMA Book Awards for Fantasy Fiction CIBA 2023 (manuscript).

An Ink & Insights Competition judge says of her writing:

'*Beautifully crafted, full of rich setting descriptions, tension that caught my attention and kept it, and characters that leapt off the page. This author is a skilled storyteller.*' (Melody Quinn)

An Australian nurse turned writer, Jenn has travelled extensively and lived on three continents.

Scotland remains her source of inspiration.

Jenn loves walking through a forest and climbing a mountain to experience the view.

Her only disappointment in life is that time travel is not possible... apparently.

Join Jenn's Community, receive regular newsletters and a free novella.
www.jennleeswriter.com

Also By

The Community Chronicles Series.
ALL AVAILABLE IN PAPERBACK, EBOOK OR LISTEN TO AUDIO IN APPLE BOOKS(AI NARRATED)

Of Myths and Portals: Arlan's Pledge Book One
DESTINY MUST CLAIM THEM

'Everything about this novel is captivating, from the world-building all the way to the enticingly romantic love story that readers feel is unfolding directly in front of them. This novel makes readers want to hold on to the world and clutch every page until the end, simply because it's that good.' InD'tale Magazine April '23

Previously released as The Crossing. Arlan's Pledge Book One.
Finalist in OZMA Book Awards for Fantasy Fiction 2022 CIBAs

And later this year:

Of Warriors and Sages: Arlan's Pledge Book Two
THE HEART-QUEST MUST WIN
Currently Semi-finalist OZMA Fantasy Book Awards 2023 CIBAs (manuscript form)

Of High Kings and Mages: Arlan's Pledge Book Three
A KING MUST DIE

MURTAIREAN: AN ASSASSIN'S TALE
A Novel in the Dál Cruinne Series
AN ASSASSIN'S TWO HITS: ONE FROM THE PAST TO HAUNT HIM. ONE TO FREE HIM

A MAGE WHO PURSUES ... AND A WARRIOR WOMAN WHO LINKS IT ALL

Leyna, a warrior-woman and high-end thief, turned her back on her title of Lady Leynarve of Monsae after her parents' murder. Bent on revenge, Leyna travels to a hit where assassins gather, intent on finding and killing the one who ruined her life.

Vygeas, a mercenary and assassin, has the gift of heightened perception, enabling him to sense his opponents' emotions and anticipate their every move. Sickened by the warmongering, Vygeas awaits execution. But he's given one final task to win his freedom... kill a mark and avoid the gallows.

Unaware of Vygeas' trade, Leyna hitches a ride with the handsome sell-sword.

Vygeas realises he has encountered the beautiful Leyna's family before... on a previous hit. While pursued by a powerful sorcerer-mage, they combine their skills to thwart his attempts to capture Leyna and destroy Vygeas.

Fighting their joint foes without, and battling their torments within, Vygeas and Leyna discover a truth that could destroy their newly forged relationship.

Will their pasts divide them, or will love be the greater force?

If you like magic and swordplay, gutsy heroines and smouldering heroes, then you'll love this action-packed fantasy.
Murtairean is the first novel in Jenn Lees' fantasy series set in the world of Dál Cruinne.

OF MYTHS AND PORTALS: ARLAN'S PLEDGE BOOK ONE

A warrior fighting his destiny
A woman desperately seeking hers
A magic portal that joins them both

Arlan, warrior son of the High King, lives in Dál Gaedhle, a world of warriors, magic and recently reawakened dragons.
He is certain to become the war chief of his clan.

Destiny seems to ignore Arlan's desire to forge his own path in life.

Adopted as a baby and orphaned as a young adult, Scottish librarian, Rhiannon, is now adrift after losing her job due to economic cuts and lives a second-rate life, feeling more out of place than ever in our world.

Destiny seems to ignore Rhiannon's dream to find her true purpose.

When Arlan bursts into her world through a portal, an awesome warrior on his war horse and brandishing weapons, he turns her existence up-side-down.

With his world on the brink of war, and Rhiannon challenging his attitudes, Arlan struggles to choose between his growing feelings for Rhiannon and his responsibilities to his people.

Rhiannon doesn't want Arlan to leave. He understands her on a level no one else ever has. But is her desire to fight beside him in his world even possible?

Destiny must claim them

(Previously published as *The Crossing: Arlan's Pledge Book One*)

www.ingramcontent.com/pod-product-compliance
Ingram Content Group UK Ltd.
Pitfield, Milton Keynes, MK11 3LW, UK
UKHW041305180426
11947UKWH00009B/691